THE MAO CASE

Qiu Xiaolong

First published in Great Britain in 2009 by Sceptre
An imprint of Hodder & Stoughton
An Hachette UK company

First published in paperback in 2009

1

A CIP catalogue record for this title is available from the British Library

B format ISBN 978 0 340 97859 7
A format export 978 0 340 97860 3

Printed and bound by Clays Ltd, St Ives plc

Hodder & Stoughton policy is to use papers that are natural, renewable
and recyclable products and made from wood grown in sustainable forests.
The logging and manufacturing processes are expected to conform to
the environmental regulations of the country of origin.

Hodder & Stoughton Ltd
338 Euston Road
London NW1 3BH

www.hodder.co.uk

For the people that suffered under Mao

ACKNOWLEDGMENTS

I am indebted to many people for their support, particularly to Patricia Mirrlees, whose warm friendship thawed the frozen moments of writing; to Yang Xianyi, whose example of moral integrity inspired the characters in the story; and to Keith Kahla, whose brilliant editorial work helped to present it in its present form.

THE MAO CASE

ONE

CHIEF INSPECTOR CHEN CAO was in no mood to speak at the political studies meeting of the Shanghai Police Bureau's Party committee.

His mood was due to the topic of the day—the urgency of building spiritual civilization in China. "Spiritual civilization" was a political catchphrase much emphasized in the Party newspapers starting in the mid-nineties. *People's Daily* had another editorial on the subject just that morning. In the same issue, however, yet another high-ranking Party official was exposed in a corruption scandal.

So where could the "spiritual civilization" come from? Surely, it wasn't something that could be pulled out of thin air like a rabbit out of a magician's hat. Still, Chen had to sit, stiff and serious, at the middle of the conference room table, nodding like a robot, while others talked.

You cannot connect nothing to nothing with broken fingernails . . .

Whether this bleak image came from a poem he had read long ago, while lying in the sun on some beach, was a detail he couldn't recall.

In spite of the Party's propaganda, materialism was sweeping over

China. It was a well-known joke that the old political slogan "Look to the future" had become an even more popular maxim, "Look to the money," for in Chinese, both "future" and "money" are pronounced as *qian*, exactly the same. But that wasn't a joke, not exactly. So where would the "spiritual civilization" come from?

"Nowadays, people look at nothing but their own feet," Party Secretary Li Guohua, the top Party boss in the bureau, spoke, gravely, his heavy eye bags trembling in the afternoon light. "We have to reemphasize the glorious tradition of our Party. We have to rebuild the Communist value system. We have to reeducate people . . ."

Were people to blame for this? Chen lit a cigarette, rubbing the ridge of his nose with his forefinger and middle finger. After all the political movements under Mao, after the Cultural Revolution, after the eventful summer of 1989, after the numerous corruption cases within the Party system—

"People care for nothing but money," Inspector Liao, the head of the homicide squad, chipped in loudly. "Let me give you an example. I went to a restaurant last week. An old Hunan restaurant that has been in business for many years, but all of a sudden, it's a Mao restaurant. There are pictures of Mao, and of his bewitching personal secretaries, posted all over the walls. The menu is full of special dishes that were supposedly favorites of Mao. And so-called Xiang Sister Waitresses, clad in *dudou*-style bodices with Mao quotations printed on them, strutted around like hookers. The restaurant is shamelessly capitalizing on Mao, who would die from shock if he were resurrected today."

"And there's the joke," Detective Jiang said, "about Mao walking into Tiananmen Square, where a shrewd businessman used him as an instant picture model for tourists, making tons of money. A crying shame—"

"Leave Mao alone," Party Secretary Li cut in angrily.

A crying shame or not, a joke at the expense of Mao remained a political taboo, Chen observed, pulling over the ashtray. Still, the joke was a vivid illustration of present-day society. Mao had turned into a profitable brand name. *Retribution or karma?* Chen mused, watching the smoke rings spiral up in the conference room, when he became aware of Li's fidgeting beside him. He had to say something.

"Economic basis and ideological superstructure." Chen managed to come out with a couple of Marxist terms he had learned in his college years, but then he checked himself. According to Marx, there is a corresponding relation between the ideological superstructure and the economic basis. What marked the present-day "socialism of Chinese characteristics" was, however, the very incongruity between the two. With the market economy totally capitalistic—and at the "primitive accumulation stage," to use another Marxist phrase—what kind of a communist superstructure or spiritual civilization could be expected?

Still, he'd better think of something fast. It was expected of him—not only as an "intellectual" having majored in English before being assigned by the state to the police bureau, but also as a chief inspector, and an emerging Party cadre.

"Come on, Chief Inspector Chen, you're not just a police officer, but a published poet too," Commissar Zhang urged. A "revolutionary of the older generation," long retired, Zhang still attended the bureau's political studies meetings, believing that the current problems were the result of insufficient political study. "Surely you have a lot to tell us about the necessity of rebuilding a spiritual civilization."

What was behind Zhang's remark, Chen could easily guess. It wasn't just an implicit criticism of his being a poet, but also of his being, in Zhang's eyes, too liberal.

"When I came in to work this morning on a crowded bus," Chen started over again, clearing his throat, "an old man with a crutch struggled aboard. He fell hard when the bus lurched to a stop. No one got up to give him a seat. A young passenger, seated, commented that it's no longer the age of Comrade Lei Feng, Mao's selfless Communist role model—"

He left his sentence unfinished again. Perhaps it was coincidental that Mao kept coming up like a returning ghost. Chen ground out his cigarette, ready to finish his sentence when his cell phone rang shrilly. Without looking at the others in room, he answered it.

3

"Hi, this is Yong," a woman's voice said, clear and crisp, "I'm calling about Ling."

Ling was Chen's girlfriend in Beijing, or to be exact, ex-girlfriend, though they hadn't exactly said so explicitly. Yong, a friend and former colleague of Ling's, had tried to help during their prolonged off-and-on relationship, which went back as early as his college years.

"Oh? What's happened to Ling?" he exclaimed, drawing surprised stares from his colleagues. He stood up in a hurry, saying to the room, "Sorry, I have to take this."

"Ling got married," Yong said.

"What?" he said, striding out into the corridor.

He really shouldn't have been astonished. Their relationship had long been on the rocks, what with the insurmountable problem of her being an HCC—a high cadre's child, her father was a top-ranking Party cadre, with his being unable to imagine himself becoming an HCC, because of her, even for her sake. The friction was intensified by his dislike of the social injustice, with the distance between Beijing and Shanghai, and by so many things between them . . .

Ling was not to blame, he had kept telling himself. Still, the news came as a shattering blow.

"He's another HCC, but also a successful businessman and a Party official. She doesn't really care for all that, you know . . ."

He listened, leaning into a corner, gazing at the opposite wall, which resembled a piece of blank paper. Somehow he felt like an audience, listening to a story about something that had happened to others.

"You should have tried harder," Yong said, in Ling's defense. "You can't expect a woman to wait forever."

"I understand."

"It may not be too late." Yong delivered her Parthian shot. "She still cares so much for you. Come to Beijing, and I'll tell you a lot of things. You've not been to Beijing for such a long time. I almost forget what you look like."

So Yong wasn't willing to give up even when Ling herself already

4

had, having married somebody else. Yong, essentially, wanted him to make a trip to Beijing for a possible "salvage mission."

How long the phone conversation in the corridor lasted, he didn't know.

When he finally went back into the conference room, the political study was coming to a close. Commissar Zhang shook his head like a rattle drum. Li gave Chen a long inquiring look. Taking a seat next to the Party secretary, Chen refrained from saying anything until the session ended.

As people began to leave, Li drew Chen aside. "Is everything all right, Comrade Chief Inspector Chen?"

"Everything is fine," Chen said, shifting back into his official role. "It's an important issue that we discussed today."

Afterward, instead of going back to his own apartment, Chen decided to pay a visit to his mother. It wasn't a night that he would enjoy making dinner for himself.

As he turned onto Jiujiang Road, however, he slowed down. It was almost six. His mother lived alone in the old neighborhood, frail in her health, and frugal in her way. He'd better buy some cooked food for the unannounced visit. There was a small eatery around the corner, he recalled. In his elementary school years, he had passed by the place many times, peeping in curiously without ever stepping in.

A little boy was rolling a rusted iron hoop on a side street, a familiar scene yet one he hadn't seen for a long time. It was as if the hoop was rolling back the memories from childhood in the gathering dusk. He was struck with a sense of déjà vu.

He had second thoughts about visiting his mother. He missed her, feeling bad for having not been able to take care of her as much as he would have liked. But an evening there could also mean another of her lectures about his continuing bachelorhood, where she quoted the Confucian statement, "*There are things that make a man unfilial, and to have no offspring is the most serious.*" It wasn't the evening for that.

Casting a quick look at the front of the eatery, which appeared scruffy, sordid, and little changed from years ago, he walked into a shabby scene inside. There was a bare bulb dangling down from the water- and smoke-stained ceiling, shedding dim light on three or four smeared, dilapidated tables. Most of the customers looked as grungy as the place, having only cheap liquor and dishes of boiled peanuts.

A waitress, a plump and short woman in her mid-fifties, handed him a dirty menu in peevish silence. Ordering a Qingdao beer, two cold dishes—dried tofu in red sauce and a thousand-year egg in soy sauce—he asked her, "Any specials here?"

"The pork intestine, lung, heart, and whatnot, all steamed with distilled rice grain. Our chef still makes his own rice wine. It's a specialty of the old Shanghai cuisine. I don't think you'll have it anywhere else."

"Great. I'll have that," he said, closing the menu. "Oh, the smoked carp head too. A small one."

She eyed him up and down in surprise—apparently, he was a big customer for this small place. He was no less surprised at himself, for still having such a good appetite this evening.

At a table near the back, one of the customers looked over his shoulder. Chen recognized him as Gang, from the old neighborhood. Gang had been a powerful leader of a Shanghai Red Guard organization in the early days of the Cultural Revolution, but he had since gone downhill, ending up as a jobless drunken loafer, muddling around the neighborhood. About the vicissitude of the legendary ex–Red Guard, Chen had heard from his mother.

Gang turned further around, clearing his throat and banging on the table dramatically. "Sages and scholars are solitary for thousands of years. Only a drunkard leaves his name behind."

That sounded like a quote from Li Bai, a Tang-dynasty poet well-known for his passion for the cup.

"Do you know who I am?" Gang went on. "The commander in chief of the Third Red Guard Headquarters in Shanghai. A loyal soldier for Mao, leading millions of Red Guards to fight for him. In the end, he threw us to a pack of wolves."

The waitress put the cold dishes and Qingdao beer on Chen's table. "The noodles and the chef's special will come shortly."

The moment she walked away, Gang rose and shambled over, grinning from ear to ear and carrying a tiny bottle of liquor called a "small firecracker" among the drunkards.

"So you are a newcomer here, young man. I would like to give you a word or two of advice. Life is short, sixty or seventy years, no point worrying away your days till your hair turns white. Heartbroken for a woman? Come on. A woman is just like that smoked fish head. Not much meat but too many bones, staring at you with ghastly eyes on a white platter. If you're not careful, you get a bone stuck in your throat. Think about Mao. Such a man, and yet he, too, was ruined by his woman—or women. He fucked his brains out in the end!"

Gang talked like a drunkard, hardly coherent with so many conversational leaps, but it was intriguing, even stunning, to Chen.

"So you had your day during the Cultural Revolution," Chen said, gesturing for Gang to share the table with him.

"Revolution's like a bitch. She seduces you, and she dumps you like a mop smeared with the shit and dirt from her ass." Gang took his seat opposite Chen, picking up a piece of dried tofu with his fingers, sucking at his empty liquor bottle. "And a bitch is like revolution too, muddling your head and heart."

"That's how you ended up here—because of both women and revolution?"

"There's nothing left—well, nothing but the cup for me. It never gives you up. When you are smashed, you dance with your own shadow, so loyal to you, so sweet, so patient, and never stepping on your toes. Life is short, like a drop of dew in the early morning. The black ravens are already circling, nearer and nearer, above your head. So cheers, I raise my cup.

"Since it's your first time here, it's for me to treat," Gang said, taking a large gulp of the beer as Chen pushed his cup to him. "I have a mind to lead you down to the road of the world."

Chen wondered at the prospect of Gang leading a cop down that road. Gang reached into his pants pocket. He came up with only a couple of pennies. He fumbled again. Still, the same pennies sat on the table. "I'm damned. This morning I changed my pants and left my wallet at home. Loan me ten yuan, young man. I'll return it to you tomorrow."

It was a trick, obviously, but Chen took a perverse delight in his company that evening and handed over two ten yuan bills.

"Auntie Yao, a bottle of Yang River Liquor, a dish of pork cheek meat, and a dozen chicken feet in hot sauce," Gang shouted toward the kitchen, waving his hand like the Red Guard Commander he had once been.

Auntie Yao—the middle-aged waitress—emerged from the kitchen, taking Gang's order and money as she examined him closely.

"You dirty rascal! Up to your old tricks again?"

There was a roar of laughter in the eatery, like in a sitcom, when she started dragging Gang forcibly back to his own table, grasping his collar, the way a hawk does with a chicken.

"Don't listen to him." She came back to Chen. "He plays the same dirty trick on every new customer here, telling the same story over and again, so that they take pity and give him money for booze. What's worse, one of the young customers fell under his curse, turning into a damned drunkard just like him."

"Thank you, Auntie Yao," Chen said. "Don't worry about me. I want to have a quiet meal here."

"Good. I don't think he'll bother you again—not until he's done with his horseshit," she said, glaring over her shoulder.

"Don't worry about me, Auntie Yao," Gang echoed from his table as she retreated into the kitchen.

Auntie Yao must have been the restaurant's only waitress, having worked there for years and knowing the regular customers well. She soon returned to Chen's table with the noodles and the chef's special.

The special came in a small rustic urn, still steaming, as if from a rural kitchen. The beef noodles looked both hot and fresh.

She sat on a stool not far from his table, as if guarding him, making sure that Chen had a quiet meal.

But he wasn't going to have one that evening.

He was just putting the chopsticks into the fragrant-smelling urn when his cell phone rang. Possibly another call from Yong, he thought, who didn't give up easily.

"Comrade Chief Inspector Chen, this is Huang Keming from Beijing."

"Oh, Minister Huang."

"We need to talk. Is it a good time for you?"

It was not, but Chen chose not to say so to the new Minister of Public Security. Nor was it really a question from Huang. Chen rose, hurrying out of the eatery, both hands covering the phone. "Yes, please go ahead, Minister Huang."

"Do you know about Shang Yunguan, a movie queen during the fifties?"

"Shang Yunguan . . . I watched one or two of her movies long ago. But they didn't leave much of an impression. She committed suicide at the beginning of the Cultural Revolution, I think."

"She did, but in the fifties and early sixties, she was very popular. When Chairman Mao came to Shanghai, he danced with her at parties arranged by the local government."

"Yes, Minister Huang?" Chen asked, wondering where this was going.

"She could have taken—or been given—something from him. There were many opportunities."

"Something from Mao?" Chen was instantly alert, though hardly able to smother the sarcasm in his voice. "What could that possibly be?"

"We don't know."

"Perhaps pictures with captions saying 'Our great leader encouraged a revolutionary artist to make a new contribution,' or 'Let hundreds of flowers bloom.' Our newspapers and magazines were full of his pictures."

9

"Shang could have left it to her daughter Qian," Huang went on without responding, "who died in an accident toward the end of the Cultural Revolution, leaving behind a daughter of her own, named Jiao. So you are going to approach Jiao."

"Why?"

"She may have it."

"Something from Mao—the Mao material, you mean?"

"Yes, you could say that."

"Did Shang, Qian, or Jiao ever show this material to anyone?"

"No. Not that we are aware of."

"Then there may not even be any such material."

"Why would you think that?"

"With someone like Shang, a popular movie actress, her home must have been thoroughly ransacked and searched by Red Guards. They never found anything, right? The Mao material—whatever it could be—wasn't something like a life-saving imperial decree like in ancient time. Even if it existed, it didn't save her; if anything, it probably only caused her trouble. How would she have been able to leave it to her daughter Qian? And how could Qian, dying in an accident, have given it to her daughter Jiao?"

"Comrade Chief Inspector Chen!" Huang obviously was not pleased with Chen's response. "We cannot afford to overlook this possibility. There are some quite suspicious things about Jiao. About a year ago, for instance, she suddenly quit her job and moved into a luxurious apartment. Where did the money come from? Now she's regularly attending parties with people from Hong Kong, Taiwan, or Western countries. What is she really up to? What's more, the host of these parties, a certain Mr. Xie, is someone who bears a deep grudge against Mao. So she could be trying to sell the Mao material for a large advance."

"An advance for a book? If she has the money already, I don't think we can do anything about it. The publisher would now have the material—the Mao material."

"Perhaps not yet, or not entirely. Something might have been arranged, out of consideration for her safety. If such a book were published while she was in China, she could get in trouble. She knows better—"

"Has she applied for a passport?"

"No, not yet. If she did anything too obvious, it wouldn't do her any good."

It sounded like a conspiracy scenario to Chen. The minister must have some reason to be concerned, but Chen had many questions.

"Why the sudden attention to this?" Chen resumed after a pause. "Shang died years ago."

"It's a long story but, in short, it's because of two books. The first one is entitled *Cloud and Rain in Shanghai*. You must have heard of it."

"No, I haven't."

"You are too busy, Chief Inspector Chen. It's a best seller about Qian, and about Shang too."

"Really? A best seller?"

"Yes. And then the other book is the memoir by Mao's personal doctor."

"That one I've heard of, but I haven't read it."

"With that book we learned our lesson the hard way. When the doctor applied for a passport so he could go to the States for health reasons, we let him go. His book was then published there. It's full of fabrications about Mao's private life. However, readers are so interested in those horrible details that they swallow them without a hiccup. The book is selling like hotcakes all over the world. In some languages, it has been reprinted ten times in one year."

Chen had heard stories about Mao's private life. In the years shortly after the Cultural Revolution, when Madam Mao was denounced as a white-bone devil, lurid details about her life as a third-rate movie actress started coming out, with some particulars having direct or indirect connection to Mao. The Beijing authorities soon put an end to the "hearsay." Since, after all, there's no separating Madam Mao from Mao.

"So these two books have led us to be concerned about the possibility that Jiao might have something left behind by Shang. Something that she could use against the interest of our Party."

"I'm still lost, Minister Huang."

"I don't think we need to go into details on the phone. You'll learn more from the case file compiled by Internal Security."

"Internal Security is already investigating?" Chen said, frowning. Internal Security was usually assigned the most sensitive political cases. "If so, why call me in?"

"They've been following Jiao for weeks, but without success. So their plan is to take tougher measures, but some leading comrades in Beijing don't think that's a good idea. Comrade Zhao, the ex-secretary of the Central Party Discipline Committee, is one of them. Indeed, we have to think about repercussions. Both Xie and Jiao are known in their circles and have connections to Western media. Besides, if we push too hard, Jiao might act rashly, out of desperation."

"What can I do?"

"You are going to approach Jiao from a different angle. Check her out, as well as the people associated with her, and more importantly, discover what was left by Shang and retrieve it—"

"Hold on. What different angle?"

"Well, whatever approach you think will work. Soft rather than tough, you know what I mean."

"No, I don't. I'm no 007, Minister Huang."

"This is an assignment you can't say no to, Comrade Chief Inspector Chen. Any slander against Mao, the founder of the Chinese Communist Party, will affect the legitimacy of our Party. This is a special task and, Comrade Zhao recommended you to me. Based on what Internal Security has learned, one possible approach would be through the parties she frequents. You can blend in, speaking your English or quoting your poetry."

"So I am to approach Jiao as anything but a cop—"

"It's in the interest of the Party."

"Comrade Zhao said that to me in another case," Chen said, realizing that it was pointless for him to argue. "But there's still no guarantee that Shang left anything behind."

"You don't have to worry about that. You go ahead in whatever manner you choose, and we trust you. I've already talked to your Party Secretary Li. He's going to retire soon, you know. When this job is accomplished, you'll advance to a position of greater responsibility."

It was an unmistakable hint, but was Chen looking forward to such a position of greater responsibility? Still, he knew he had no choice.

Minister Huang said farewell and hung up. Chen closed the phone.

When he moved back into the eatery, the noodles on the table were quite cold, the house special, greasy and gray on the surface of the urn, and the beer, stale and bubbleless. He had no appetite left.

Auntie Yao hurried over, offering to warm up the noodles, which, having soaked so long in the soup, would taste like paste anyway.

"No, thank you," he said, shaking his head as he took out his wallet. Gang came limping over to Chen again.

"Now I recognize you," Gang said. "You used to live in the neighborhood, calling me Uncle Gang. Don't you remember that?"

"You are . . . ?" Chen said, unwilling to admit he had long recognized him.

"A successful man may not have a good memory," Gang said with a fleeting gleam in his eyes. "I'll take care of the leftovers for you."

"I've not touched anything—except the fish head," Chen said.

"I trust you," Gang patted on his shoulder. "Now you're somebody."

The smoked carp head stared at the two of them with its ghastly eyes.

TWO

WHEN CHEN GOT BACK to his apartment, it was past eight.

The room was a scene of desolation, as if corresponding to his state of mind: the bed unmade, the cup on the nightstand half empty, a mildew-covered orange pit in the ashtray looking like a mole—the mole on Mao's chin.

He pressed hard on the lid of the thermos bottle. Not a single drop of water came out. Putting the kettle on the stove, he hoped that a cup of good tea might help to clear his head.

But what first came to mind was, unexpectedly, a fragmented image of Ling serving tea in a Beijing quadrangle house, her fingers breaking and strewing petals into his teacup, standing by the paper window in a white summer dress, silhouetted against the night like a flowering pear tree . . .

The news of her marriage wasn't entirely unexpected. She wasn't to blame, he told himself again; she couldn't help being the daughter of a Politburo member.

No more than he could help being a cop at heart.

He willed himself to focus on the waiting work, pressing a fist against his left cheek, as if battling a toothache. He didn't want to conduct an investigation concerning Mao, even indirectly. Mao's portrait still hung high on the gate of Tiananmen Square, and it could be a political suicide for a Party member cop to be even tangentially associated with the skeleton of Mao's private life.

Chen took out a piece of paper and was trying to scribble something down to help him think, when Party Secretary Li called.

"Minister Huang told me about your special assignment. Don't worry about your work at the bureau," Li said. "And you don't have to tell me anything about it."

"I don't know what to say, Party Secretary Li." The water began boiling and the kettle hissing. Li, at one time a mentor for Chen in bureau politics, had come to regard him as a rival. "I hardly know anything about it, not yet. It's just that I cannot refuse the assignment."

"The minister told me that you are to have access to all the available resources of the bureau. So simply tell me what you need."

"Well, first, don't tell anyone about the assignment. Instead, say I'm taking a leave for personal reasons." He added, "Detective Yu should take over the work of the Special Case Squad."

"I'll announce his temporary appointment tomorrow. I know that you trust Detective Yu. Are you going to tell him anything?"

"No, not about the assignment."

"I'll take care of everything at the bureau. Call me whenever you need anything."

"I will, Party Secretary Li."

Putting down the phone, Chen paced about the room for a minute or two before he went over to the boiling kettle, only to discover that the tea box was empty. Rummaging through the drawer, he failed to find any tea. No coffee either, which didn't matter, as the coffee maker had been broken for weeks.

He leaned back, stroking his chin. He had cut himself shaving this morning. It had been a rotten day from the beginning.

Suddenly there was a knock at the door. To his surprise, it turned out to be a special delivery package containing the Jiao files from Internal Security. He wasn't expecting to get it so quickly.

He sat down at the table with a cup of hot water, and an impressive file spread over several manila folders. Internal Security had done a comprehensive job. The file contained not only information about Jiao, but about Qian and Shang as well, covering all three generations.

Chen decided to start with Shang. He lit a cigarette and took a sip of water. The water quality was terrible, and it tasted strange without tea leaves.

Shang had come from a "good family" in the thirties. While still in college, she was named the college "queen," nicknamed a "phoenix," before being discovered by a movie director. Soon she came to prominence as a young, graceful actress. After 1949, because of her family background and her husband's political trouble, her career suffered. It was said that her career's decline also had something to do with her pre-1949 image. She was known mostly for playing upper-class ladies, elegant in their magnificent houses and stylish dresses, and those roles had practically disappeared from the movie screens of socialist China. Mao had declared that literature and art should serve workers, farmers, and soldiers through representation of them on stages and screens. Suddenly, however, her photos began to reappear in the newspapers, in articles that said Chairman Mao was encouraging Shang and her colleagues to make new, revolutionary films. She then starred in several movies, playing workers or farmers, and she won major awards for the roles. Her resurgent career was cut short by the outbreak of the Cultural Revolution. Like other well-known artists, she was subjected to mass criticism and persecution. What's more, a special team was sent by the Cultural Revolution Group of the Central Committee of the Communist Party to interrogate her. Shortly afterward, Shang committed suicide, leaving her daughter Qian alone.

A sad story, but not uncommon in those years, Chen reflected, rising and rummaging through the drawer again. This time he uncovered a tiny ginseng tea bag. How long it had been lying there, he had no idea. He tossed it into the cup, hoping it could somehow boost up his energy. He had practically skipped his dinner, thanks to the phone call from Beijing.

Sipping at the ginseng tea, he settled back down to the file and began reading the part about the second generation, Qian, the heroine of the best seller *Cloud and Rain in Shanghai*.

An orphan after Shang's death, Qian had a hard time adjusting to her drastically changed life. Shang's problem shadowed her—Qian was forcibly exposed to what the file referred to as Shang's "shameless sex saga"—and the daughter grew up to be a "shameless slut." In those years, a girl of black—politically questionable—family background was supposed to behave with extra care, but Qian abandoned herself to youthful passion. She fell in love with a young man named Tan, also of black family background. Despairing of their future in China, they made a desperate attempt to sneak into Hong Kong. They were caught and marched back to Shanghai, where Tan committed suicide. Qian survived because she was pregnant. She gave birth to a daughter, but soon after fell for a boy named Peng, about ten years younger than she, who was said to look like Tan. Peng was thrown into jail for sexual perversity. Not long afterward, toward the end of the Cultural Revolution, she died in an accident.

Chen set down the file and finished the bitter ginseng tea. It was a Cultural Revolution tragedy that involved two generations. What had happened during those years now appeared absurd, cruel, and was almost unbelievable. Understandably, the Beijing government wanted people to look ahead and not back.

Finally, Chen spread out the investigation report on Jiao, focusing on what was suspicious about her. Jiao was born after Tan's death. Qian's fatal accident had happened while Jiao was still an infant. The girl grew up in an orphanage. Like "a tramped and trodden weed" from a sentimental popular song, Jiao failed to get into a high school. Nor could she find a decent job. Unlike other girls her age, she had no friends or fun but instead was prey to the tragic memories of her family, even though others had mostly forgotten that part of the history. After two or three years struggling along, with one odd job after another, she began working as a receptionist at a private company. Then, with the publication of *Cloud and Rain in Shanghai*, Jiao suddenly quit her job, bought a luxurious apartment, and started a totally different life.

She was suspected of getting a lot of money from the book, but the publisher denied having paid any to her. Then people supposed there was a man behind her metamorphosis. Usually, a Big Buck "keeper" would show off his kept girl like a piece of valuable property, and his identity would come out in time. However, with Jiao, Internal Security had drawn a blank. In spite of their vigilant surveillance, they didn't see a single man entering her apartment or walking in her company. In yet another scenario, she had inherited a lot of money. But Shang left nothing to the family—all her valuable property had been swept away by the Red Guards in the early days of the Cultural Revolution. Internal Security checked out Jiao's bank account and found she had very little. She had bought the apartment outright—"a briefcase full of cash"—without having to apply for a mortgage.

For a young girl, she seemed to be wrapped in mysteries, but according to Internal Security, she wasn't the only suspicious one.

Xie, to whose mansion Jiao had become a regular visitor of late, was another one. Xie's grandfather had owned a large company in the thirties and had built a huge house for the family—Xie Mansion, which was then considered one of the most magnificent buildings in Shanghai. Xie's father took over the business in the forties, only to become a "black capitalist" in the fifties. Xie grew up listening to stories about the old glories, holding parties and salons while keeping the doors and windows firmly shut. Sheltered by the resplendent mansion and the family's remaining fortune, he dallied in painting instead of working a regular job. It was nothing short of a miracle that he managed to keep the house intact through the Cultural Revolution. In the mid-eighties, he began to throw parties at his home again. But most of the partygoers were more or less like him—no longer young, and impoverished in every way except in their memories of their once illustrious family. For them, the parties were their dreams coming true, albeit for only one night. Soon, a collective fashionable nostalgia took hold of the city itself, and the parties became well known. Some took great pride in going to Xie Mansion, as if it was symbolic of their social status. Taiwanese and foreigners began to join in. One Western newspaper wrote that the parties were "the last landscape of the disappearing old city."

The last landscape or not, the situation for the person hosting the parties was not idyllic after all. Without a regular job, Xie had a hard time maintaining the house and paying for the parties. His wife had divorced him and emigrated to the United States several years ago, leaving Xie alone in the empty house. He consoled himself by collecting the odds and ends left over from the thirties, like an Underwood typewriter, silver-plated dinnerware, a pair of trumpet-shaped speakers, several antique phones, a brass foot warmer, and the like. After all, these were the things his grandparents and parents had told him about, things pictured in the time-yellowed family albums in which he now buried his solitude. And his collection contributed to the legend of the mansion.

In recent years, Xie had started to teach painting at home. He was said to have an unwritten rule for his students: he would only accept young, pretty, talented girls. According to some people who had known him for years, the sixty-plus-year-old Xie might be fashioning himself after Jia Baoyu in the *Dream of the Red Chamber*.

Jiao went to Xie's painting classes despite the fact that Xie had hardly received any formal training as a painter, and she went to the parties despite the fact that most of the partygoers were old or old-fashioned or both.

To explain all this, Internal Security had come up with a scenario. Xie must have functioned as a middleman, introducing Jiao to the people interested in the Mao materials in her possession. Foreign publishers would be willing to pay a huge advance for a book about Mao's private life, just as they had for the memoir by Mao's doctor. The parties would have provided opportunities for her to meet with those potential buyers.

The course of action proposed by Internal Security was to raid the house on grounds such as obscene or indecent behaviors, or whatever excuse would get Xie into trouble. In their opinion, he would not be a hard nut to crack. Once he spilled, they could take care of Jiao.

But the Beijing authorities didn't like the proposed "tough measure," nor were they convinced that such a measure would work. Which was why they had called Chen in.

In the file, Chen didn't find a copy of the book written by Mao's personal doctor. It was banned. Nor was there a copy of the bestseller *Cloud and Rain in Shanghai*.

He was intrigued by the title of that book. "Cloud and rain" was a stock simile for sexual love in classic Chinese literature, evocative of the lovers' being carried away in a floating soft cloud and of the coming warm rain. It had originated in an ode describing the King of Chu's rendezvous with the Goddess of Wu Mountain, who declared that she would come to him again in cloud and rain. But "cloud and rain" was also part of a Chinese proverb: *With a turning of the hand, the cloud, and with another turning of the hand, the rain*, which referred to the continuous, unpredictable changes in politics.

Could the title have a double meaning?

He looked at the clock on the nightstand. Ten fifteen. He decided to go out to buy a copy of *Cloud and Rain in Shanghai* at a neighborhood bookstore, which stayed open late, sometimes until midnight.

THREE

IT WAS A PRIVATELY run bookstore, no more than five minutes' walk from his home. From across the street, enveloped in the dark, Chen could see that the light was still on.

The bookstore owner, Big-Beard Fei, had started his business in the hopes of making money selling serious books while writing his own postmodernist novel. When his hopes were eventually smashed like eggs against a concrete wall, he turned into a practical bookseller, running a store full of sensational bestsellers and not-so-sensational junk. On one miniature shelf, however, customers might still be able to find some good books—his way of being nostalgic. And he kept the store open late, he declared, because of the insomnia caused by the postmodernist novel he had never finished.

For Chen, the store's late hours were a blessing. Besides, there was a nice dumpling restaurant just around the corner. Sometimes, after buying a couple of books, he would walk to the restaurant and read over a portion of dumplings, steamed or fried, and a cup of beer. The waitress wore a bodice like a *dudou*, moving briskly in high-heeled wooden slippers, as if emerging out of Wei Zhang's lines: "*Shining brighter than the moon, / she serves by the wine urn, / her wrists dazzlingly white, / like frost, like snow.*" She was nice to him, and to her other customers as well.

"Welcome," Fei greeted him with his habitual smile from behind his beer-bottle-bottom-thick glasses, combing his thinning hair with a plastic comb.

They had never talked at length, but that might be just as well. Fei wouldn't have talked as freely had he known Chen was a chief inspector. Unlike in the *shikumen* houses in the old quarters, people in the new apartment complexes here did not really know each other.

Instead of just asking for the book in question, Chen decided to browse around a little first, as he usually did. There was no point rousing any unnecessary speculation.

To his surprise, he came upon several books on modern revolutionary Beijing operas—the only operas available during the Cultural Revolution.

"Why the sudden interest in them?" he asked Fei.

"Well, those who enjoyed them then are middle-aged now. They are nostalgic for the past—for their idealistic youth. Whatever the reality was, they don't want to write off their own youthful years. So these 'red antique books' sell quite well. Can you guess which the most popular one is?" Fei paused for a dramatic effect. "*Little Red Book of Mao.*"

"What?" Chen exclaimed. "Billions of copies were printed back then. How can it be a rare or antique book?"

"Do you still have one at home?"

"Oh no."

"So you see. People got rid of them soon after the Cultural Revolution, but now they are coming back with a vengeance."

"Why?"

"Well, for those left out of the materialistic reforms, Mao is becoming a mythic figure again. The past is now seen as a sort of golden Mao period where there was no gap between the rich and poor, no

22

rampant Party corruption, no organized crime and prostitution, but instead there were free medical insurance, stable pensions, and state-controlled housing."

"That's true. Housing prices have rocketed. But there are also so many new buildings in Shanghai now."

"Can you afford them?" Fei said with a sardonic smile. "Perhaps you can, but I can't. 'While wine and meat go bad untouched in the red-painted mansion, / people die from cold and starvation in the street.' Haven't you heard the latest popular saying—'You've worked hard for socialism and communism for decades, but overnight, it's back to capitalism'?"

"That's a witty one." Chen then asked casually, "By the way, do you have a book called *Cloud and Rain in Shanghai*? It's a book about those years under Mao, I think."

Fei eyed him up and down. "That's not the kind of book you usually choose, sir."

"I'm on vacation this week. Someone recommended it to me."

"It sold out a while ago, but I have one copy I kept for myself. For an old customer like you, you may have it."

"Thank you so much, Mr. Fei. Was it such a bestseller?"

"You've never heard of it?"

"No," Chen said. The minister had asked the same question. "Isn't it about the tragic fate of a young girl?"

"It is. But there's something else about the book. You have to read between the lines."

"Something else?" he said, offering a cigarette to Fei.

"You must have heard of Shang."

"The movie star?"

"Yes. She was the mother of Qian, the nominal heroine of the book. There's a famous maxim in *Taodejin:* 'In misfortune comes the fortune, and in fortune comes the misfortune.' It's so dialectical." Fei took a deliberate puff at the cigarette. "By the early fifties, Shang's career had started going downhill, but then it took off again. Why? Because she danced with Chairman Mao, whispering in his ears and leaning against his broad shoulder . . . God alone knows how many times Mao came to Shanghai just for that, later into the night, and then into the morning. Dancing, her body surging softly against his, like cloud, like rain—"

"Does the book mention all that?"

"No, or it wouldn't have been published. The author wrote it very carefully. Still, her life story in itself was more than suggestive. Mao could have picked any dancing partner, anytime, anywhere. What imperial favor! Everyone envied her. Eventually, she paid the price when, at the beginning of the Cultural Revolution, a special team came from Beijing, interrogating her in isolation, which then led to her suicide."

"Why—I mean, why the isolation interrogation?"

"According to the book, the special team was trying to coerce her into confessing to 'plotting against and slandering our great leader Mao.' However, there was nothing out of line mentioned in the book except that after her first dance with Mao, she told a friend, 'Chairman Mao is big—in everything.'"

"Come on, 'big' may simply mean 'great.' People always called Mao a great leader," Chen said, stroking his chin again. "So then why the persecution?"

"You still don't see? Madam Mao was a fury. Shang was younger, prettier, and more in Mao's favor—at least for a while. As soon as Madam Mao gained power on through the Cultural Revolution, she retaliated by dispatching that special investigation team to Shanghai. That's the real story behind the story of Qian in the book."

That was a story that the average reader could easily imagine, but it didn't account for the Beijing authorities' sudden interest in Jiao. Chen decided to push his luck a little further.

"Speaking of Mao, do you carry a book written by his personal doctor?"

"If that book were ever found here, my store would be closed overnight. You're not a cop, are you?"

"Oh, I was just curious, since we were already on the subject."

"No, don't carry it and haven't read it, but a friend of mine has. It is filled with stories about Mao's private life with sordid and vivid details you'd never find in any official publications."

"I see."

"Let me dig out *Cloud and Rain in Shanghai* for you," Fei said, disappearing behind a shelf, into the back.

Chen chose a book on the history of the Shanghai movie industry and another about intellectuals and artists during the Cultural Revolution. Along with *Cloud and Rain in Shanghai*, he might be able to patch together Shang's life story. He also put into his basket a new volume of Tang-dynasty poetry. There was no point making Fei suspect he was researching Shang.

Fei came back with a book in his hand. There was a picture of Qian on the cover, in a corner of which was another picture, that of Shang, faded, nearly lost in the background.

As Chen was taking out his wallet at the counter, Fei seemed to think of something else. "Look at her," he said, pointing at Shang's image. "What a tragedy! I sometimes wonder if she was murdered."

"Murdered!"

"Many celebrities committed suicide during those years, but many of them were practically beaten or persecuted to death. Suicide, however, was nobody's fault but the dead—a convenient conclusion for the Party government."

"Ah," Chen said, more or less relieved. Again, Fei's comment was no more than common knowledge about what happened during those years.

"As for the special team from Beijing, there's another interpretation," Fei went on. Chen was the only customer in the store, and Fei appeared unwilling to let him go. "Shang might have known some deadly secret. So they silenced her once and for all. Remember the trial of the Gang of Four? Madam Mao was accused of persecuting movie stars associated with her in the thirties."

That was true. The stars had suffered persecution because they knew Madam Mao as a notorious third-rate actress. But Shang would have been too young then.

Chen thanked Fei and left with his books for the dumpling restaurant.

When he arrived at the corner, he was disappointed to see a boutique mandarin dress store where the restaurant had been. The store was closed and there was only a mannequin posing coquettishly in an unbuttoned red dress in the window.

There was another eatery open late at night and not too far away, but he had lost the mood. Instead, he plodded home, carrying the books.

Back home, he started reading on an empty stomach. In the distance, a siren pierced the night air. Absurd, he thought, turning a page. There's no guaranteeing a rational account of human existence. Soon, he lost himself in the story—and the story between the lines.

About two hours later, he finished skimming through *Cloud and Rain in Shanghai*. Stretching his sore neck, he slumped on the sofa like the crushed fish in Shang's death scene in the book.

The story was pretty much as he had anticipated. It was a tale of a beautiful woman's suffering, which echoed an archetypal motif about a beauty's "thin fate." The writer was clever, focusing the narrative mainly on Qian, keeping Shang in the background. Like a traditional Chinese landscape painting, the book invited readers to see more in its blank spaces.

There was little about Jiao, though. When Qian passed way, Jiao was only two years old, and the structure of the book made her omission understandable.

Chen rose to pace about in the room. Lighting a cigarette, he thought he had a rough idea about Shang's relationship with Mao, but no idea what Mao could have given Shang.

Another question presented itself. Could Mao have known about the special team from Beijing? After all, Shang wasn't merely one of the "black artists." Things could have been more complicated than Minister Huang had said.

So what was Chief Inspector Chen going to do?

It was an investigation he couldn't refuse to do. Even so, he might try to conduct the investigation in a "rebellious" way, in his way—meaningful to himself, if not to others.

Like most people of his generation, Chen had not taken the Mao issue too seriously. As a child, he had worshipped Mao, but the Cultural Revolution shook his belief in the Chairman, particularly after the early death of Chen's father. After that, things changed dramatically for Chen. Now, as one of the "successful elite" in present-day society, he tried to convince himself that he anchored himself with his faith in the Party. So he was in no position to think too much about Mao and he used his heavy workload as a chief inspector as an excuse not to do so. While the Party newspapers still paid lip service to Mao, a lot of things were different today in practice. So why bother?

Chen had heard stories about Mao's private life. After the Cultural Revolution, Mao's bodyguards and nurses had produced memoirs that turned Mao back into a human being somewhat by highlighting, for instance, his idiosyncratic passion for fatty pork or his unwholesome aversion to brushing his teeth. The books sold well, though possibly because of people's interest in things behind those stories. But there were also other stories, not published but nonetheless circulated among the people. Since Mao's archive was still locked up and considered top secret, Chen did not really believe or disbelieve those "other" stories.

Besides, Chen considered Mao too complex a historical figure for him to judge. After all, he wasn't a historian, he was a cop, having to investigate one case after another. In recent years, however, he'd found it more and more difficult, even as a cop, to steer clear of the nation's history under Mao. In China, a lot of things and a lot of cases had to be seen in a historical perspective, and Mao's shadow still lingered there.

So it was the time for him to take on a case concerning Mao—the Mao case. If nothing else, the chief inspector might be able to gain a better historical perspective through the investigation.

And it could also keep him busy—preferably too busy to think about his personal crisis.

He sat back at the table, pulled up a piece of blank paper, jotted down the ideas that came to mind, and worked on combining them into a feasible plan. In the end, he decided to break his investigation into two parts. For the Jiao part, he would cooperate with Internal Security, but for the Mao part, he would go ahead on his own.

He was going to find out, first of all, what material or information could be used against Mao, and he would do this by going to the root—the relationship between Mao and Shang. Like the story behind the story in *Cloud and Rain in Shanghai*, it would be an investigation behind the investigation.

To begin with, he needed a comprehensive grasp of that period of history. An ideal scenario would be to contact the then special team from Beijing, but that was practically impossible. It had happened so long ago. And the people concerned would be put on alert as soon as he made the request.

Alternatively, he would contact the author of *Cloud and Rain in Shanghai*, who might not have included in the book all the information available regarding Shang's death. In the meantime, he would also try to obtain a copy of the memoir by Mao's personal doctor. In addition, he would try to secretly interview the people who were close to Qian and Shang.

Now, how could he possibly accomplish all this by himself? The clock ticked, almost imperceptibly. Chief Inspector Chen, unlike the character in a ridiculous fairy tale he had read, did not have three heads and six arms.

A glance at the clock told him that it was almost two in the morning. He would not be able to fall asleep, not anytime soon. So he took a couple of sleeping pills and swallowed them with cold water.

Lying in bed, he reopened *Cloud and Rain in Shanghai*, turning to the part about the first meeting between Mao and Shang at the China and Russia Palace of Friendship, where the melody rippled in the splendid ballroom, Shang's steps soft as a cloud, light as the rain . . .

In about fifteen minutes he felt the pills gradually taking effect. As if surfacing from under waves of drowsiness, a fragment of a poem by

Li Shangyin came to mind. Li happened to be Mao's favorite Tang dynasty poet too.

Oh, last night's star, last night's wind, / west of the painted chamber, east of the cassia hall./ Lacking the soaring wings of a colorful phoenix, /our hearts speak through the magic rhinoceros horn . . .

FOUR

CHEN WOKE UP WITH a fast-fading dream scene: a young woman in a red mandarin dress emerging out of nowhere, her footstep light as a summer rain of grateful tears, a fallen leaf caressing her bangled bare feet, a song coming on like a white cloud, like a light rain, but disappearing into a mural in the subway station . . .

Disoriented, he slowly managed to bring himself back to the first morning of the Mao Case—a case name he had made up the previous night.

However, his thoughts kept circling around the dream image.

Possibly because of Ling, who had worn a similar dress in a different color, he recalled, rubbing his temples; or possibly because of Shang, who was wearing one in a black and white picture in the book, or possibly because of a serial murder case he had investigated not too long ago—

But dreams images are irrational, he thought, when another idea came to him, unexpectedly, like the lady in the red mandarin dress in the dream.

Swinging out of bed like a sleepwalker, he dialed a number from his address book.

"Sorry to call you so early in the morning, Mr. Shen."

"Oh, Chief Inspector Chen. An old man wakes up early. I've been up for a couple of hours. What can I do for you?"

"Do you happen to know Xie, the owner of Xie Mansion on Shaoxing Road? You used to live quite close to that neighborhood, I remember."

"Yes, I know him. Nowadays he's an authority on the thirties, on the fashion of those years too. He talked to me about it two or three weeks ago."

"Have you been to his parties?"

"No, I'm too old for those fashionable parties of his, but I went to his father's. So he calls me uncle. That was before 1949, of course. What do you want with him, Chief Inspector Chen?"

"So you're like an uncle to him! That's great. I've been thinking of a book project about old Shanghai. It would be fantastic if you would be so kind as to introduce me to him."

"Well, the golden and glittering thirties could serve as another myth of the city for the upstarts today. They have to invent a tradition to justify their extravagance. But I'll introduce you to him. No problem."

"Thank you so much, Mr. Shen. Oh, by the way, you may tell him that I'm a writer—and an ex-businessman too—with an interest in the thirties. Don't mention that I'm a cop."

"What Xie's really up to, I don't know," the old man said hesitantly, "but I think he is harmless."

"I'm not going to get him into trouble, Mr. Shen. I give you my word. It's only because he might not talk freely to a cop."

"I trust you, Chief Inspector Chen. I'm giving him a call and write you a letter of introduction too—about the talented writer and a good man that I know. Don't worry. I'll have the letter sent to you by special delivery."

"I don't know how to thank you enough."

31

"There's no need." Shen added with a chuckle, "Just give me a copy of your book when it's published."

As he put the phone back, Chen saw a word on the back of a matchbox on the nightstand—*Poetry*—scribbled in his own sloppy handwriting.

What could that possibly mean?

He had gotten sentimental over Li Shangyin's poem before falling asleep last night, but that was not something worth writing down.

There was a knock on the door. Another special delivery package for the case, he suspected. It was a package, but to his surprise, it was postmarked as from abroad—from London. It was from Ling—he guessed she must have mailed it during her honeymoon trip. That the couple went abroad was no surprise. The newlyweds were both successful entrepreneurs with HCC background and could easily afford the trip.

He tore open the package to find a large book inside: *The Waste Land: A Facsimile and Transcript of the Original Draft Including the Annotations of Ezra Pound.* There was no note enclosed.

It was a book about the writing of T. S. Eliot's "The Waste Land," containing the manuscripts with the changes made by Eliot and by Pound and the marginal notes made at different stages. The book would shed light on the connection between Eliot's personal life and his "impersonal" work, Chen contemplated, as he leafed through a few pages.

But it was not the time for him to sit down and read it. Nor was he in the mood. There's nothing more accidental than the world of words. And ironical too. Had he gotten the book shortly after his college years, he would have used it in his translation of Eliot—possibly making it a better translation, which might have changed his career's course. At the moment, however, in the midst of the Mao Case, it was irrelevant, and at best, it was only a consolation prize for having lost Ling—perhaps even less than that. She hadn't totally forgotten about him, but it was like a footnote on a closed chapter.

He was pondering the wording for a thank-you card when there was another knock on the door. This time, it was a stranger standing there, reaching out his hand formally. He was a tall man with a serious-looking square face and broad shoulders, probably in his early forties. He produced a badge to show to Chen.

"I'm Lieutenant Song Keqiang of Internal Security. Minister Huang called about your joining us in our investigation."

"Oh Lieutenant Song, I was going to contact you. Please come in," Chen said. "I've just read the file. We need to talk about it."

"Well, all the basic information is in the file," Song said, sitting on the chair Chen pulled out for him. "Do you have any questions, Chief Inspector Chen?"

"About the Mao material—about whatever Shang left behind, I mean—have you any idea what it might be?"

"Pictures, diaries, letters, anything is possible."

"I see. Is there anything new—anything that's happened since the file was compiled?" Chen said, pouring a cup of water for the visitor. "Sorry, there is no tea left at home."

"Do you know about Xie's ex-wife?"

"I know he has an ex-wife. What about her?"

"She has just come back. Last week, she met with Xie and then was seen sobbing in the garden."

"I know they are divorced, but was there anything suspicious about their meeting, Lieutenant Song?"

"She cut all ties when she left China. There were no letters or phone calls for years. So why meet now?"

"Well, with things between a husband and wife, who can tell? Xie's worth something now, with his mansion and his collection, and they have no children. You know what I mean."

"It's more than that. A couple of days ago, she brought a foreigner to the mansion. What for? We've also found out that she has booked a return ticket for two weeks from today."

"What does that mean?"

"That means we have to conclude the investigation before she goes back to the States."

"So I only have two weeks?"

"Less than two weeks, Chief Inspector Chen. If your approach does not work, we'll need time to wrap it up our way."

Chen didn't like Internal Security's way. It was too easy for them to apply "tough measures" to Xie or Jiao using any available excuse. As a cop rather than Internal Security, Chen was disturbed, and not only about the possible consequences. But he didn't want to confront Song during their first meeting. Internal Security might have every reason to be upset with Chen, since his assignment to the case was a challenge to their competence.

"According to Minister Huang, you have suggested a point of entry for me—through Xie's parties."

"Yes, with your English and poetry, you'll be like a fish swimming in the water."

"You don't have to say that, Lieutenant Song." Aware of the sarcasm in Song's comment, Chen retorted, "You must go to a lot of his parties too, like a dragon stranded in a shallow pool."

"We have someone who goes to them. If you want, you may go with him to the next party."

"Thank you, but I've already made a couple of phone calls about the party. I think I may go there by myself and meet your man there. What's his name?"

"So you are going by yourself? That's great." Song added without answering his question, "You're moving fast."

"It's a special case, isn't it?"

"Well, since you're going, you'll see everything for yourself," Song said, standing up abruptly. "Let's talk again after your visit."

Chen also rose, accompanying him to the door.

Why had Song come? Chen pondered, listening to the sound of the lieutenant's steps fading away in the concreted staircase. It could have been a sort of formal gesture made for the sake of Minister Huang and other "leading comrades in Beijing," but Chen doubted it.

He wondered whether Detective Yu had heard anything about it in the bureau. But as close as the two had been, he would not enlist Yu's help for this case. A case concerning Mao could have unpredictable consequences, possibly serious ones for the cops involved.

Instead, he thought of Old Hunter, Yu's father, a retired cop whom Chen knew and trusted. As a retiree, Old Hunter might also know more about things that happened during the Cultural Revolution, when Chen was still in elementary school. For this case, Chen thought he'd better sound out the old man first. People had very different opinions of Mao. In these days of increasingly rampant corruption and an ever-enlarging gap between the rich and poor, some were beginning to miss Mao, imagining that they had had better days under him. The utopian society of egalitarianism as advocated by Mao remained attractive to a lot of people. If Old Hunter was so inclined, Chen would not even broach the subject. They would meet simply for a pot of tea.

Back at the table, the blank thank-you card struck him as an equally difficult job. He didn't know what to say, but he had another idea. He might send a present to Ling rather than a card, just as she had. A message in the absence of a message.

Yet another knock came at the door. This time it was only Shen's introduction letter with his signature plus a red seal at the bottom. Shen recommended Chen warmly, raving about his business career and literary interests. As represented in the letter, Chen was ready to settle down to work on a literary project about Shanghai in the thirties.

His cover story was another weird coincidence. Chen recalled Ouyang, a friend he had met in Guangzhou, saying something similar except that Ouyang was a real businessman, who never made enough money to work on a literary project.

FIVE

IN THE EARLY AFTERNOON, Chen arrived at Shaoxing Road, a quiet street lined with old magnificent buildings behind high walls.

It was an area he was relatively familiar with because of a publishing house located nearby. Still, behind the high walls, behind the shuttered windows, the houses seemed to be hinting at mysterious, inexplicable stories within.

Instead of heading directly to Xie Mansion, he went across the street, into a miniature café. It must have been converted from a residential room and had only three or four tables inside. A narrow bar sporting several coffee makers and wine racks took up one third of the space. He cast a curious look toward the partition at the back of the room. The proprietor apparently lived in the space behind the partition wall.

He chose a table by the window. For the party in the late afternoon, Chen had put on a pair of rimless glasses, changed his hairstyle, and donned an expensive suit of light material. The people there probably wouldn't recognize him except for the one from Internal Security.

While Chen was known in his own circle, he thought those at the party would be a different lot, and he looked at his window reflection with a touch of ironical amusement. Clothing makes, if not a man, at least the role for a man.

A young girl emerged from behind a door in the partition wall, through which Chen caught a glimpse of a back door that led into a lane. She looked like a middle school student, helping the family business, serving coffee to his table with a sweet smile. The coffee was expensive, but it tasted fresh and strong.

Sipping at the coffee, he dialed the Shanghai Writers' Association. A young secretary answered the phone. She was quite cooperative but knew little about Diao, the author of *Cloud and Rain in Shanghai*. Diao was not a member of the association and had become known to the association only after the book's publication. She checked through files and said that Diao might have been invited to a literary meeting somewhere, but she didn't exactly know where. Diao wasn't in Shanghai, of that much she was sure.

Chen followed up by making a long-distance call to Wang, the chairman of the Chinese Writers' Association in Beijing, asking him to find out the whereabouts of Diao. Wang promised to call back as soon as he learned anything.

Placing the phone by the coffee cup, Chen took out the file on Xie, turning to the part about the history of the mansion.

A lot had happened to the prestigious buildings in this area. In the early fifties, high-ranking Party officials had moved in, driving out most of the former residents, only a few of whom remained. Things got much worse at the beginning of the Cultural Revolution. At the time, a large house could be forcefully seized by dozens of working-class families, each of them occupying one room—a "revolutionary activity" that abolished the remaining privileges of the pre-1949 society. In the early nineties, a number of those old buildings were pulled down to make way for new construction. It was a miracle that Xie kept his house intact for all these years, and according to the legend told and retold in that social circle, it was achieved through a sacrifice made by Xie's ex-wife. It was said that she had an affair with a powerful Red Guard commander, who consequently let the family remain in the house undisturbed. Then she and her husband divorced and she went to the United States before the value of the mansion was rediscovered.

Whatever the truth behind the stories, the mansion across the street looked magnificent in the afternoon sun. Looking up from the file, Chen didn't see anyone approaching the building yet. He decided to measure out his time, alone, with the coffee spoon.

A group of young people came in, clamoring for coffee, Coca Cola, and a variety of snacks in a boisterous chorus. They took no notice of him.

About twenty-five minutes later, he saw a black car pulling up in front of the mansion. Two girls emerged, waving their hands to the driver. There was no taxi sign on top of the car. They went up to the front door and pushed the bell. From where he was sitting, Chen couldn't see who opened the door for them. Soon another man arrived in a taxi and headed toward the door.

Chen rose, paid for his coffee, and walked out.

On close examination, Xie Mansion struck him as slightly shabby and dilapidated. The paint on the door had faded badly. There was no intercom. Pressing the discolored doorbell, he had to wait minutes before a lanky man in his early fifties came out, examining the Italian leather briefcase in Chen's hand like a business card.

"Mr. Xie?" Chen said.

"He is inside. Please come in. You are a bit early for the party."

Chen didn't know the exact time the party would start, but newcomers seemed to be arriving from time to time. People who might not necessarily know one another.

He walked into a spacious living room, which was oblong, with large French windows on one side looking out into a garden. There were several people standing by the windows, holding drinks in their hands. The party hadn't started yet and no one bothered to greet or acknowledge him. He noticed a middle-aged woman in the group, slightly plump, incessantly fanning herself with a round silk fan. The air conditioning was barely on. Opposite the French window, there were several chairs along the wall, unoccupied.

At the other end of the living room, there was another room with frosted-glass sliding doors. Through the slightly opened door, Chen caught a glimpse of a red skirt. That had to be where the female students had their painting lessons. It seemed that there were two events this afternoon, the painting class, and the dancing party.

He moved over to the group by the French window. These people were sometimes called Old Dicks in the Shanghai dialect—from the phrase *Old Sticks* in Colloquial British English. In Shanghai the phrase carried association of high-class gentlemen in the thirties, brandishing brass-topped walking sticks, hence the embodiment of the values of that time. Now in the nineties they had staged a comeback, their knowledge of the thirties marketable and fashionable.

"My name is Chen," he introduced himself to a silver-haired man with gold-rimmed glasses and a gold watch chain dangling from his vest pocket. "I'm a writer."

The silver-haired man nodded, adjusting the gold-rimmed glasses along the ridge of his aquiline nose, saying not a single word in response. He continued talking to a chubby old man in the group.

Chen was not one of them, apparently. None of them seemed interested in him. Still, he managed to introduce himself around, trying to fit in. The Old Dicks were invariably nostalgic, looking backward at the past as if it were the only real life. They kept exchanging anecdotes of the "good families," out of which they came, as a means of criticizing the present-day upstarts who possessed neither history nor taste. They remained indifferent to the presence of a stranger with apparently neither an illustrious family background nor knowledge of those glittering years.

It was not until fifteen minutes later that a man came striding out of the other room, extending his hand even at a distance. An ordinary-looking man in his early sixties, fairly short, slightly overweight, with thinning hair and an angular face, he wore a gray jacket and black dress pants. He spoke with a strong Shanghai accent.

"I'm Xie. I didn't know you had arrived, Mr. Chen. So sorry about that. I'm holding a class inside."

Xie led Chen to the other room—possibly a large dining room originally, now it was a studio being used for his painting class. There were six or seven girls there, including the two he had seen arrive earlier from window of the café, all of them busy working on their in-class assignments. They were each dressed quite differently. One girl was in a paint-covered overall, another was in a summer dress with something like a turban tied around her hair, and still another was in an extra-large T-shirt and frayed jean shorts. Possibly it was a common scene for a painting class, but Chen hadn't been to one before.

He then recognized Jiao, a tall girl in a white blouse and a jean skirt by the window. She had large eyes and a straight nose, her melon-seed-shaped face bearing a faint resemblance to Shang. She appeared younger than in the picture from the file and, working on a sketch, was vivacious and animated with a glowing radiance.

Xie didn't introduce him to the girls, who appeared to be absorbed in their work. Gesturing him to a corner sofa, Xie pulled a chair over for himself.

"It's quieter here," Xie said in a low voice. "Mr. Shen speaks highly of you."

"I talked to him about my book project and he recommended you to me," Chen said. "I know how busy you are, but it would greatly benefit the writing project for me to come over from time to time."

"Come anytime you like, Chen. Shen's a good old friend of my father's, he's like an uncle to me. He has also given me a lot of information about the clothes in the thirties. Whoever he introduces is a welcome guest here. You also speak good English, I'm told, and we occasionally have foreign guests."

"I hope I won't be any inconvenience to either your class or your party."

"I teach students two or three times a week. If you're interested in painting, you can sit in. It is not a formal class. As for the parties, the more people, the more fun."

The young girl in the overalls came over with a large watercolor in her hands. Xie took it from her and studied it for a minute before he pointed to a corner of it and said, "There is too much light here, Yang."

"Thanks," she said, patting his shoulder with a familiarity not usually shown to a teacher.

Xie appeared to mix well with his students. Nodding, he said to Chen, "Girls are really made of water."

It sounded like an echo from the *Dream of the Red Chamber*. Xie might really fancy himself as Baoyu, the charming, irresistible protagonist of the classic novel, except that Baoyu was young, born with a piece of precious jade in his mouth.

A stout, middle-aged man pulled open the door and burst in, leading a willowy model-like girl to Xie.

"Oh, let me introduce you," Xie said to Chen. "This is Mr. Gong Luhao. His grandfather was the white fox king."

"White fox king?" Chen's voice rose in puzzlement.

"Oh, my grandfather was in the fur business before 1949, especially known for his unrivaled supply of white fox," Mr. Gong said, turning to the girl. "Her grandfather was connected to the Weng family. She wants to study with you."

"She may submit her sample work to me," Xie said. "This is Mr. Chen. A successful entrepreneur, and now a writer as well. Mr. Shen, of the Industry Bank in the thirties, introduced him to me."

"Oh Mr. Shen, my father knew him well."

Apparently, Chen was nobody here, welcome only because of Shen's introduction.

In the living room, somebody started ringing a bell, declaring in a loud voice, "Time for the ball, Mr. Xie."

"Class time is over," Xie said to his students. "If you want to continue your work here, you may stay, or you may join the party."

Xie led Chen out to the party in the living room, putting a hand on Chen's shoulder like an old friend, most likely for the benefit of the others.

The scene at the party looked as if time had really rolled backward.

The lights were confusing and the melodies played were popular in the thirties, one of which Chen recognized from an old Hollywood movie. There were quite a number of people there, many of whom must have arrived while Chen was with the host in the other room.

Xie was busy greeting and making introduction, saying only a few words to each guest. Still, he managed to take good care of Chen, emphasizing whenever possible that he was introduced by Mr. Shen. While none seemed to be interested in the would-be writer, none were suspicious of him, either. Thanks to his association with businessmen, Chen could talk like one. Curiously, no one at this party turned out to be a real businessman.

Then dancing started. Most of the people here knew one another. Some of them had to be well-practiced partners, coming here for the purpose alone. Chen thought about inviting someone to dance, but then he thought better of it. Though he had studied ballroom dancing, he had hardly had any opportunity to practice. So instead he found himself sitting alone on one of the chairs against the wall. It wasn't a bad idea for him to take a break and look around. He thought of an English expression: a wallflower, which usually refers to a woman, he thought with a touch of self-irony.

Xie was now busy, constantly changing the records. Instead of a CD player, he kept an old gramophone and a stack of old records. He would wipe each record carefully with a white silk handkerchief, as if it were the most meaningful thing in the world.

The party didn't strike Chen as that remarkable. The people there overindulged in a world of nostalgic imagination, slow-dancing, giving themselves to the languorous tide of the music, relishing anecdotes of old glories, caring little about what was happening in the outside world. What was the point? he wondered.

But what else could they do? Their "better" days gone, they were merely trying to hold on to the illusion of some meaning or value in their lives. As Zhaungzi mused long, long ago, *You are no fish, and how can you know the fish does not enjoy it?* It was not a cop's business to worry about it.

He caught sight of Jiao again. She had perched herself on the arm of the sofa Xie was seated in. They talked for a couple of minutes, almost whispering. She appeared to be rather nice to Xie, but most of the girls were nice to him.

The girl named Yang came over to Chen, still in her overalls, smiling at him. He smiled back, shaking his head apologetically. She understood, moving across to another man. The living room was getting warm.

After a while, he slipped back into the studio. With the sliding door slightly open, he could look out. One of the dancers could be from Internal Security, but he wasn't particularly concerned. He went over to the sketch Jiao had been working on. He was impressed by it, a picture of hyacinth blossoming out of a young girl's arm, into a neon night ceaselessly changing in the background. Chen noticed that, on a corner table beside the couch, there was a pile of magazines, most of them published in the thirties. Sitting down on the same sofa, he picked up a painting album.

To his surprise, Jiao then walked into the studio, wearing high-heeled slippers, holding a long-stemmed glass in her hand.

"Hi, you're new here."

"Hi. My name is Chen. It's the first time for me."

"My name is Jiao. You are a novelist, I've heard."

She could have overheard his earlier conversation with Xie or heard this from Xie a couple of minutes ago.

"No, I have just started writing," he said.

"That's interesting."

That seemed to be a stock response to his new identity. Instead of leaving, however, she perched herself on the chair Xie had occupied earlier, drawing one leg under her. Twirling the glass in her hand, she appeared content with his company in the studio.

"It's a lousy crowd out there. It's not a bad idea to take a short break here," she said, waves of smile rippling in her large eyes. "According to Mr. Xie, you are a successful businessman. Why do you want to change your career?"

It was a question he'd prepared for, but it was the first time that anyone had asked.

"Well, I've been asking myself another question. People are busy making money—true, they live on money, but can they live in money?"

"People make money, but money makes people too."

"An excellent point, Jiao. By the way, I forgot to ask about your line of business—or your illustrious family, as the people here have made such a point of bringing up their family background."

"I'm glad you didn't. And please don't start now. You want to write about the past, not live in the past," she said, lifting the glass to her lips. Her teeth were white, slightly uneven. "But what a coincidence! I've made some money working at a company, like you, so I'm doing what I want to do—recharging myself for a short period."

He wasn't too surprised at the response. She must have given the same answer many times. Only it didn't sound convincing, given what he knew of her work history. The character he was playing had a company of his own and could have saved enough to "be a writer." She had been a receptionist, however, working at a company for low pay.

"In today's society, it's not easy for a young pretty girl like you to retreat courageously from the swift waves," Chen said, paraphrasing a proverb like a would-be writer. "Mr. Xie must be a wonderful teacher."

"Most of his works are of the old mansions in the city. He has a passion for his subject matter, so he projects a sort of value in what he sees through his passionate touches. Each of the buildings in his paintings seems to have a story shimmering through its windows. It's really fascinating. Of course, he has his skill as well as his perspective."

"That's very interesting," Chen said, his turn to resort to a stock response. "How long have you been taking lessons here?"

"About half a year. He's quite well-known in this circle." Sipping at her wine, she changed the subject. "Tell me about what you're writing, Mr. Chen."

"It's about old Shanghai, in the thirties. That's why people recommended Xie to me."

"Yes, there's no better man for that purpose. No better place, either," she said, rising. "Now that we've taken a break, let's go out and dance. It'll be good for your book."

"I can hardly dance, Jiao."

"You'll learn so quickly. I didn't even know the difference between a two-step and a three-step a year ago."

That was probably true. At that time, she still worked at a low-end job, alone, with no social life at all.

They went back to the party and onto the "dance floor." She was a capable and patient partner. It was not long before he found himself being guided around by her, not that smoothly, but not precariously, either. Turning in her high-heeled slippers, she danced in an effortless way, her black hair flashing against the white walls.

It was a summer evening. Holding her supple waist, he noticed she left the top button of her white blouse unbuttoned, revealing an alluring cleavage, as a dreamy ballad swelled into the soft fantasies of the mansion. She looked up at him, wisps of her hair brushing against his face, the lambent light burnishing her cheek with a painter's brush. He suddenly thought of what he had read about Mao and Shang, in another magnificent mansion like this one, in the same city . . .

In the celestial palace, which year is this year? A fragment of a Song-dynasty poem came swirling across his mind, her hand clasping his.

"You're not bad at all," she said, her soft lips close to his ear, in a mock-serious assessment of his qualities as a dancing partner.

"Perfect," Xie said, gliding by them in the arms of the middle-aged woman.

"She's leading me well," Chen said.

"Oh, some people are playing Monopoly over there, a fascinating game." Xie added, "All in English, if you care to join."

A popular Western game—Chen had heard of it. Little wonder that it was being played here, but it reminded him of the lines by Li Shangyin about a different game, at a different party.

Here, the game of the palm-hidden hook / between the seats, the spring wine warm, / the candlelight red, and the game / of the napkin-cover surprise in groups.

When the Tang-dynasty poet felt like a total outsider in spite of being around others enjoying a happy night, he composed those lines, lamenting about "lacking the soaring wings of a colorful phoenix" to fly to his love far away, and comparing himself to "a tumbleweed turning and turning around" for no purpose. At least he had written some wonderful lines out of the experience. What about Chen himself?

The night went on, one dance after another, one cup after another, one melody after another . . .

Chen did not dance much. He talked to some others, including the silver-haired man with the gold spectacles and the gold pocket watch— Mr. Zhou, from the illustrious Zhou family that had monopolized the importation of red wine in the thirties. Zhou proved to be friendly after learning of Chen's connection to Mr. Shen.

"Xie is an embroidered pillow stuffed with straw," Zhou commented. "What a joke! But Mr. Shen is of the real old class, from a prominent banker family and himself a man of great learning too."

Chen was surprised at the harsh criticism of the host. He murmured something vague in response. There were Old Dicks and Old Dicks.

Alternating between talking and dancing, Chen managed to stay to the end of the party. With the melody of "Auld Lang Syne" falling in the half-deserted room and Xie rubbing his sleepy eyes, Chen left along with Jiao and several other girls.

They parted outside the mansion. He saw a luxurious car waiting for one of the girls. Jiao and another girl nicknamed Golden Oriole shared a taxi, for they lived not far from each other. Jiao since waved out at him under the starry night. Chen waited for a second taxi.

Standing on the curb, alone, he thought he heard a piano from an open window somewhere along the quiet street. He decided to walk along Ruijin Road to the subway station. It hadn't been too bad a start, he reflected, strolling along.

There was no judging Jiao from just one meeting. He couldn't rule out the possibility of her being a kept girl, but at least there was no car waiting for her at the end of the party. A Big Buck would have arranged for her to be picked up. Nor did she get any phone call during the party, either. A clever, vivacious girl, she didn't strike him as being involved in some "little concubine" arrangement.

As for Xie, Chen did not see him as a straw-stuffed pillow. Rather, he seemed to be playing a role, one designed to create some meaning missing in his life. Perhaps having played the role for so many years, Xie found the role had taken him over.

Chen caught himself humming a snippet from "When Can You Come Again?" one of the nostalgic pieces Xie had played at the party.

The chief inspector, too, was playing a role, though for two weeks only, as a would-be romantic writer. Which Internal Security would probably already have reported, having witnessed him dancing with Jiao.

SIX

OLD HUNTER WAS GREATLY intrigued by Chen's invitation to a teahouse on Hengshan Road.

The chief inspector knew about his passion for tea but didn't know much about tea itself, Old Hunter contemplated as he caught sight of the magnificent teahouse Tang Flavor. Such a fashionable place would charge for service, for atmosphere, for so-called culture, but not for tea itself.

A slender waitress in a florid mandarin dress with high slits hurried over in her high heels, leading him to an antique-looking private room where a mahogany table was already set up with an array of delicate tea cups, as small and exquisite as peeled lychee.

Chen hadn't arrived yet, so Old Hunter had a cup for himself. The tea tasted watery, disappointingly ordinary.

As the old saying goes, one does not come to the Three-Treasure Temple without praying for something. So what was Chen going to talk to him about? A special case, presumably. If so, Chen shouldn't discuss it with him but with his son, Detective Yu, who had been Chen's partner for years. The two were good friends.

Old Hunter had also been in close contact with Chen, of whom he had a high opinion. A capable and honest cop, Chen was a rarity in an age of wide-spread corruption. Yu was really lucky to work with a boss and partner like him.

Still, there was something elusive about Chen—he was stubborn, scrupulous, and smart, yet shrewd and occasionally sly in his way. His promotion to chief inspector when only in his thirties spoke for itself. A hard-working cop himself all his life, Old Hunter was only a sergeant when he retired.

Old Hunter still had connections in the bureau, so he also knew Chen had received a phone call during the political studies meeting, a message from Beijing regarding his HCC girlfriend. Chen had supposedly looked devastated. The next day, he took a sudden leave of absence. The gossip about that spread through the bureau fast.

As Old Hunter was about to sip at his second cup of tea, the waitress returned, leading Chen into the room.

"Sorry, I must have kept you waiting," Chen said, taking a cup of tea from Old Hunter. "Thank you."

"No, that's my job," the waitress said, taking over the teapot in haste. She added hot water to the purple sand teapot before pouring the tea in a graceful arc into the tiny teacups. Instead of serving them the tea, however, she poured it out into the pottery basin beside her. "That was to warm up your teacups," she explained, her fingers dazzlingly white against the cup. "It's the beginning of our tea ceremony. Tea has to be enjoyed in a leisurely way."

Old Hunter had heard of the so-called Japanese tea ceremony, but he made a point of having nothing to do with anything coming from Japan. His uncle had been killed in the Anti-Japanese War, and the memory still rankled. When the tea was finally served in a tiny cup, he drained it in one gulp—in his way. She hastened to serve the second cup.

He noticed Chen was drumming his fingertips on the table, absent-mindedly. Possibly a sign of acknowledgement, but also one of impatience. The way the tea was served, with the waitress standing and waiting, they wouldn't be able to talk.

"In Japan, tea drinking is advocated as a sort of cultivated art. That's bull. You enjoy the tea, not all the fuss about it," Old Hunter said. "It's like in an old proverb: an idiot returns the invaluable pearl but keeps the gaudy box."

"You're quite right, especially with a collection of old sayings to back you up." Chen nodded, turning to the waitress with a smile. "We will enjoy the tea for ourselves. You don't have to stay with us and serve."

"That's the way it is done in our teahouse," she said, blushing in embarrassment. "It is very fashionable nowadays."

"We're old-fashioned. You cannot carve anything fashionable out of a piece of rotten wood," he concluded. "Thank you."

"Sorry," Chen said after the waitress left. "This is the only teahouse I could think of—with a private room where we could talk, I mean."

"I see," Old Hunter said. "What's new under the sun, Chief?"

"Oh, we haven't talked for a long time."

That was an excuse, Old Hunter knew, so he asked casually, "So you're enjoying your vacation?"

"Well, not exactly."

"In this world of ours, eight or nine times out of ten, things will not work out in accordance to your life's plan, but as the ancient proverb tells us, who knows if it's fortune or misfortune when the old man of Sai loses his horse? A vacation will do you good, Chief. You've worked too hard."

"I wish I could tell you more about fortune or misfortune," Chen responded elusively, "but I'm not taking vacation for personal reasons."

"I understand. You know what? For the last few months, I've been enjoying the Suzhou opera version of the *Romance of Three Kingdoms*. The lines at the end are simply fantastic. 'So many things, past and present, are told by others like stories over a cup of tea.'"

"You do have a passion for Suzhou opera," Chen said. "Time really flies. When I first read *Romance of Three Kingdoms*, I was still an elementary school student. There was a lot I didn't understand in the novel. For example, the episode about Cao Cao building his tombs in secrecy."

"Yes, I remember—he built several tombs and killed all the workers afterward. So no one knew the location of the real tomb. And Cao Cao was not the only one. There was also the First Emperor of Qing, who had human beings as well as terracotta soldiers buried with him in different tombs."

"Indeed, knowledge of the emperor's secret could be deadly."

Old Hunter put down the teacup, detecting a strange note in the younger cop, who wouldn't have invited him out simply for a leisurely talk about the emperors and their tombs.

"So is that what worries you, Chief?"

Chen nodded without responding to the question and raised a teacup. "Look at the phrase on the cup. 'A long, eternal life!' Originally, that was a chant for the emperors. During the Cultural Revolution, the first English sentence I learned was 'A long, eternal life to Chairman Mao!' Exactly the same phrase as was used with regard to the emperors for thousands of years. Mao surely knew that, but did he object to it?"

Old Hunter began to suspect that there was a secret investigation concerning Mao. He had worked with Chen, though not as his partner, and they trusted each other. Chen would usually have come to the point directly. But anything involving Mao would make the situation different. Chen had to be cautious—and not just for himself. Whatever the situation, Old Hunter had to assure Chen of his support.

"You hit the nail on the head, Chief. Mao was a modern emperor, for all his talk about Marxism and communism. During the Cultural Revolution, whatever he said—a sentence, a phrase—was called 'the supreme decree,' and we had to celebrate by beating drums and marching under the scorching sun through the streets. And you couldn't complain about the heat. Once I even suffered sunstroke. In ancient times, an emperor was compared to the sun, but Mao simply was the sun. One politburo member was thrown in jail for the crime of slander against Mao, because he wrote an article about the black spots on the sun."

"You know a lot about those years, but it may not be fair to judge Mao on something like that, considering the long feudalistic history in China," Chen said.

"I don't know about the so-called feudalistic history—not a familiar term to me. An emperor is an emperor, that's all I know." Old Hunter took a slow sip at his tea, the tea leaves unfurling unexpectedly, like tadpoles in the white cup. "Now, let me tell you about a case I had toward the end of the Cultural Revolution.

"In Suzhou opera, a story has to be told from the very beginning. To understand the things that happened during the Cultural Revolution, you have to learn about it from the beginning."

"You certainly talk like a Suzhou opera singer," Chen said, "using tricks like enriching your speech with proverbs and tantalizing the audience with digressions before coming to a crucial point. Yes, please, start at the very beginning. The tea is just beginning to be tasty, and I'm all ears."

"I was about your age at the time, Chief. Li Guohua, then the associate Party secretary, gave me an assignment—the first 'major political case' in my career. In those days, everyone believed wholeheartedly in Mao and the communist propaganda. A low-level cop, I was so proud of working for the proletarian dictatorship. I swore to fight for Mao just like those young Red Guards. So I secretly called that case a Mao case."

"A Mao case?"

"Oh, it gave such a tremendous boost to my ego. It was just like pulling a large flag over my body as if it were a 'tiger skin.' The suspect in the case was named Teng, a middle school teacher accused of slandering Mao in his class. Born in a worker's family and a member of the Communist Youth League, Teng was dating a girl with a good political family background, so he appeared to be an unlikely culprit. He had no motive whatsoever. So I went over to the school, where Teng had already been in isolation interrogation for days."

"How did Teng commit this crime?"

"I'm coming to it, Chen. You cannot enjoy the steaming hot tofu if you are so impatient," Old Hunter said, holding his cup high in the air. "In those years, Mao's poems made up a large part of the middle school textbook. In class, Teng was said to have given a viciously slanderous interpretation of one of Mao's poems. However, Teng insisted that what he presented to the class was based on official publications, that he had done a lot of research and preparation beforehand—"

"Hold on, which poem are you talking about?"

"Mao's poem to his wife Yang Kaihui."

"Ah, that one—'I lost my proud Yang, and you lost your Liu—'" Chen said, murmuring the first line of the poem. "In my middle school years, that poem was held up as a perfect example of revolutionary romanticism. In a flight of imagination, Mao described Kaihui's loyal soul flying up to the moon, where the Moon Goddess danced and served of osmanthus-fermented wine to her, and she shed tears in a pouring rain upon learning of the victory of the Communist Party. Mao missed his first wife very much—"

"No, his second wife," Old Hunter cut him short. "Mao actually had a first wife, Luo, at his old home in Hunan. According to Mao's official biography, Luo and Mao got hitched through an arranged marriage. So he didn't acknowledge Luo as his wife, though he had lived with her for no less than two or three years. Of course, no detail of their married life ever appeared in official publications. Then he fell in love with Kaihui and married her. This time, the marriage was seen as a revolutionary act, under the circumstances."

"Old Hunter, you are a Mao authority. I should have known that earlier." Chen raised his cup. "I'm sorry that it's only tea, but cheers to your expertise."

"Damn my expertise!" Old Hunter said, waving his hand. "Getting back to the case in question. According to Teng, he was trying to show his students what great sacrifices Mao had made for the revolution. His younger brother, his wife Kaihui, their children, and then the children by his next wife, Zizhen, all of them either died or were lost to their parents for the sake of revolution—"

"There's nothing wrong with that," Chen cut in again.

"That's what I thought too. So I had a hard time straightening things out. Teng had been in isolation interrogation for days and was already a broken man only capable of repeating his statement over and over like a robot, 'I just put together information from several books. The books must have it wrong.'

"So I interviewed his colleagues. They all declared that Teng did a conscientious job—at least on the surface. There was no copy machine in schools in the seventies. He had to work his butt off cutting stencils, copying passages from a number of books, proofreading all of it by himself, and paying for it out of his own pocket. I gathered together the information he had collected, including that concerning Mao's second wife, Kaihui, and third wife, Zizhen. The material Teng distributed to his students was from official publications—and all written in an effort to eulogize Mao's revolutionary spirit, no question about it.

"But here was the problem. One of the students read through the material and said in the class, 'Teacher Teng, there's a mistake. Chairman Mao couldn't have married Zizhen that year.' Now Teng was a very bookish and stubborn man. He happened to have the original book in his bag, so he took it out and double-checked the date in front of the class. 'That's correct. Study hard and don't bother me.' The student, being exasperated by Teng's response and overly influenced by Mao's theory of class struggle, reported him to the Mao Thought Propaganda Team in school, saying that Teng represented Mao as having married Zizhen when Kaihui was still alive.

"Now, in most official publications, there was no mention of the date of Mao's marriage to Zizhen. It was taken for granted that he married her after the death of Kaihui. But in the sources Teng assembled, one text had a paragraph mentioning the date of Mao's marriage to Zizhen, and another had a sentence containing the date of Kaihui's death. The overlap of dates was unmistakable."?

Old Hunter paused for dramatic effect, picking up the teapot, but to his dismay, no water was left. He decided to go on without asking for more hot water. It was a crucial juncture in his story.

"It became evident that Mao was guilty of bigamy. And that meant a disaster for Teng. If he hadn't been so devoted to accurate scholarship, he could have claimed that it was a typo. But confronted with the Mao Thought Propaganda Team, he insisted that he had carefully proofread all the material. What's more, he produced the very book that gave the date of Mao's marriage to Zizhen."

"Who wrote the book?"

"Someone who had worked under Mao—Mao's personal orderly. So the Mao Thought Propaganda Team had to put Teng in isolation interrogation, lest he keep blabbing. They sent a report to the police bureau, passing the problem on like a burning hot potato. And then the case came to me.

"After researching everything, I proposed to Li that we write to the author, asking for his cooperation. Li gave me a dressing down, declaring that I didn't understand the complexity of the class struggle and that there was no possibility of contacting the author. Teng had to confess he slandered Mao, Li insisted, or at least to admit that it was a gross typo on his part. So I had no choice but to go on 'investigating,' turning myself into a mouthpiece for Mao's famous quotation: 'Leniency to those who confess their crime, and severity to those who resist.' I tried to give advice to Teng by citing what proverbs I could think of, such as 'A hero cuts his losses, for the moment' and 'You have to hang your head low under other's eaves,' but he wouldn't listen. A couple of days later, he committed suicide, leaving a will written in blood, with only one sentence: 'A long, eternal life to Chairman Mao!' "

He paused again to take a sip from the empty cup, feeling his throat suddenly dry.

"Now, that was as an acceptable conclusion according to Li. 'The criminal committed suicide, aware of the punishment for his crime.' So that was the end of the Mao case. About two or three months later, Mao himself passed away."

"What a case!"

"It was a case I could never get out of my mind. *It was just an assignment*, I've told myself Old Heaven alone knows how many times.

After all, millions and millions of people died like ants, like weeds, during the Cultural Revolution. Apart from shouting that Mao quotation to Teng, I didn't put any extra pressure on him. I was a cop, simply doing what I was supposed to. But I still wonder: could I have tried to do something more? To help him, I mean. It's a question that is like a fly, inevitably buzzing back to the same spot, continuously bugging me.

"After the Cultural Revolution, there was a short period of 'rectifying the wrong cases.' Without talking to Party Secretary Li about it, I dropped in at Teng's school one day. To my consternation, there was no 'rectifying the wrong case' with regard to Teng, because there was no case. Nothing in official record at all. He committed suicide during an unofficial investigation. That's all there was about it. Disaster comes in and out of the mouth, as an old saying goes. With Mao in the background, no one was willing to talk about it.

"I kept a notebook on the case, so I got hold of the books mentioned in Teng's class notes, as well as some new publications about Mao. I had hoped to prove that it was Teng's typo, so he, too, was at least partially responsible. Alternatively, that one of the authors had made a typo. Either way, I wouldn't have to hold myself responsible. A deceiving and self-deceiving trick, you may say, like silencing a ringing bell by stuffing up one's own ears. But the more I read, the lower my heart sank—"

"Wait a minute, Old Hunter," Chen interrupted at the sight of the returning waitress. "Bring more hot water."

"Two thermos bottles of hot water," Old Hunter said.

"We don't serve hot water like that," she protested weakly.

"We paid for a private room. At least we should be able to have the tea our way."

After she brought the hot water as requested, Old Hunter waved the waitress out of the room, poured a cup for himself, and resumed.

"About Mao's marriages, here's a summary of what I've gathered from various sources. After their marriage, Kaihui gave birth to three sons. In 1927, Mao went to the Jingjiang Mountains as a guerrilla fighter, leaving Kaihui and their young children behind in the suburbs of Changsha. Less than a year later, however, Mao married Zizhen, who was then only seventeen, nicknamed 'the flower of Yongxing County' and a guerrilla fighter in the mountains. What proved this beyond any doubt was an article in defense of Mao's marriage to Zizhen. It was written by a senior Party official and published in *History Magazine*. According to the author, it was simply another sacrifice for the revolution: Zizhen was the younger sister of a guerrilla leader who had arrived in the mountains earlier, so Mao had to marry her so as to consolidate the revolutionary forces there. 'Any criticism of Mao's marriage with Zizhen was irresponsible, made without proper historical perspective.' "

"That's unbelievable! Such a brazen excuse."

"Whatever the excuse, Mao married Zizhen—an act of undeniable bigamy. In the mountains, he lost himself in the cloud and rain of her youthful, supple body, which bore a daughter for him that same year."

"But Mao could have been lonely in the mountains, or lost in a moment of passion," Chen said. "It might not be fair to judge him on one episode in his personal life."

"Whatever he did as the supreme Party leader is not for me to judge. I was simply looking into what he did as a man to his women."

"Perhaps Mao believed Kaihui had already died."

"No, that's not true. Kaihui knew nothing about his betrayal, and had someone carry handmade cloth shoes to him. She also asked several times to join him in the mountains, but he always said no. Like in a Suzhou opera line, he heard only the new one's laughter, not the old one's weeping. And there's something else," he said, sipping at his tea, deliberately, like wine. "Something you will not believe."

"Oh, the climax of the Suzhou opera is finally coming," Chen said nodding, like a loyal audience.

"At first, the nationalists in Changsha didn't bother Kaihui and her children. In 1930 though, when Mao led a siege of the city of Changsha, the situation changed drastically. Kaihui and her children were in danger. Mao should have moved them out of the city, but no rescue effort whatsoever was made. The siege lasted about twenty days, and Mao and his troops were close to where she was, but he did nothing. He didn't even try to contact her.

"After the siege failed, the nationalists retaliated and arrested her. They wanted her to sign a statement cutting all ties with Mao, but she refused. She was executed in 1930. It was said that she was dragged barefoot to the execution grounds—according to a local superstition, her ghost would therefore be unable to find her way back to home, to Mao."

"What a horrible story!" Chen exclaimed, picking up the teacup but putting it back down right away. "And what an old hunter you really are to have dug up all that information!"

"I am not saying that Mao had her killed on purpose. But it's not too much to say that he was responsible for her death. He should have thought about the consequences."

"Now I understand something Mao said years later," Chen said, "'For the death of Kaihui, I could not atone by dying hundreds of times.' He must have written that poem to her out of guilt."

"I've discussed the poem with an old friend, a senior history teacher, who has done extensive research on Mao, and not just about his personal life. He called Mao a man of snake and spider heart, and he believed that Mao got rid of Kaihui that way because he couldn't afford to let the two women confront each other in the mountains. There is no ruling that out as a possibility, and he actually did similar things to his comrades in the Party."

"Well, people have opinions and opinions."

"I don't want to dwell on it, but the memory of the Mao case has haunted me all these years. When Yu came back to Shanghai as an 'ex-educated youth,' I took early retirement so that he could start working at the bureau in my place. That was the main reason, of course, but there was another. The Mao case. Because of it, I am not a worthy cop. We've known each other for many years, Chief, but I have never told you about this case. Nor anybody else, not even Yu. It's a rock on my heart."

"You did all you could. It was the Cultural Revolution. Why be so hard on yourself?" Chen said with emotion in his voice. "I really appreciate your telling me about the case. It is not only a lesson about how to be a conscientious policeman, but also an enormous help on the assignment I'm going to discuss with you."

"An assignment concerning Mao, I suppose. What can I do to help?"

"You're so perceptive. Now you have talked to me about your case, I don't think I should have any hesitation in talking to you about mine. You've helped more than you can imagine."

"What do you mean, Chief Inspector Chen?"

"I've been assigned to my own Mao case, to use the name you called yours. It doesn't concern him directly, and I'm full of doubts and reservations. For one thing, I used to like his poems, like the one for Kaihui, without knowing anything about the real background. So I could hardly bring myself to believe some aspects of this case. But if Mao did that to Kaihui, he could have easily treated other women similarly." After a pause, Chen resumed earnestly, "At this stage, I can tell you little about it, because that's about all I know."

"I understand," Old Hunter said. "As for what Mao was capable of doing to his women, you may have heard about what happened to Zizhen. According to the official version, she had to be treated at a Moscow mental hospital, leaving Mao alone in Yan'an, so they sort of 'naturally separated.' Then Jiang Qing sneaked in and became Madam Mao. But mind you—Mao was separated, not divorced. Mao made Zizhen stay at the Moscow hospital for years, all alone, speaking no Russian, having no Chinese rice, while he wallowed in his imperial lust for Madam Mao—a sexy B-movie actress."

"If he acted like that to his wives, first to Yang, then to Zizhen, I have no doubt that he could have done the same to Shang."

"Shang—do you mean the movie star?"

It was Chen's turn to summarize his Mao case, which the chief inspector did briefly. Old Hunter listened, understanding now why Chen had come to him instead of his son, Detective Yu. Chen's summary might have skipped over the details, but there was no point to pushing for them.

"You definitely need help, Chief Inspector Chen. There is no way you could you manage to cover it all on your own. I'm a retired busybody, as everybody knows. If I ask a question or two about things from those years, no one will take it seriously. As an advisor to the Traffic Control Office—thanks to you for this honorary position—I may choose to patrol any particular area, pretending it is a sort of a field study. Indeed, you couldn't find a better assistant."

"You're really experienced. You must have heard the old saying, 'People think of a capable general at the sound of the battle drums,' so I want to discuss the case with you. I don't exactly know how to proceed, but you could help, I think, by paying attention to the area where Jiao lives. You have to be careful. There may be somebody else walking behind you."

"They may take the broad way, but I'll cross the single-plank bridge. Don't worry about me. People don't call me Old Hunter for nothing."

"Also, there are a couple of men for you to check out. Tan, Qian's first lover, who died years ago, and then Peng, her second one, who is still alive." Chen wrote down their names on a scrap of paper. "Whatever single-plank bridge you choose to cross, never go as a cop, either active or retired. Internal Security is involved."

"Internal Security indeed! So the last battle may be the best. The Mao Case. Thank you, Chief Inspector Chen," he said, rising slowly. "Now I've finally got a chance to redeem myself."

SEVEN

IT WAS HIS FOURTH visit to Xie Mansion in the last few days. Chen rang the doorbell with one hand, carrying in his other a large box of chocolate, Lindt's, the expensive German brand just recently available in Shanghai for the newly rich.

That afternoon, it took longer than usual for the host to answer the door.

Chen thought that he was fairly well accepted by the others, who took him as simply party-chaser, one who used a book project as a pretense. Which might be just as well. One's identity might always be in conjunction with or a construction of others.

There were two or three parties there every week. As it turned out, the role of an ex-businessman interested in the old Shanghai was not too difficult for him to play. He was able to mix with the Old Dicks, throwing in English phrases, using business jargons, and showing off literary anecdotes as well as lines from old movies, all of which successfully made him out to be someone other than a cop.

With a different identity, Chen found himself thinking about them.

He had come to accept these people, who were pathetic yet harmless, simply trying to hold on to an illusion, in whatever way possible. These old-fashioned parties happened to be one of their ways. They might be aware of their own absurdities, but what else could they do? If they couldn't be Old Dicks, they were nothing.

So it was for Chief Inspector Chen—he was aware of the absurdity of his own behavior, but if he wasn't an investigator, what was he?

There was another advantage in his calculated guise: it enabled Chen to approach Jiao with a seemingly natural interest in the old movies. Jiao did not talk about her family background, but it was no secret there that her grandmother was Shang. Chen had been cautious, exhibiting only a reasonable curiosity. Jiao was nice to him, as she was to a lot of people.

Chen got along well with several of the others. He had a long talk with Mr. Zhou about Zhang Ailing, a writer first discovered in the thirties and rediscovered in the nineties. Chen's knowledge of her novels impressed Zhou.

"I danced with her at the Joy Gate," Zhou declared with a light glinting behind his gold-rimmed spectacles. "What a woman! She danced like a poem, and those beautiful words of hers seemed to dance for page after page. Alas, she should have stayed in the city of Shanghai. A Shanghai flower could not survive the wind and storm in Los Angeles."

Chen murmured an indistinct response, wondering whether Zhou's story was true, especially the part about dancing with Zhang Ailing.

Yang, the girl he became acquainted with during his first visit, also appeared to be taking to him, and she was intent on taking him to another sort of party.

"You shouldn't immerse yourself only in the old-fashioned parties of the thirties, Mr. Chen. You have to experience the nineties. An international vote recently named Shanghai the most desirable city for young people. There's a pajama party this weekend—"

"You are right, Yang," he cut her short, "but let me indulge in the thirties a little longer—for my book project."

"Your book project again. I can't figure you out, Mr. Chen."

As for Chen, he couldn't really figure out those girls in the painting classes. For some, it might be fashionable to come here, or necessary for their self-conscious social status—taking private lessons at the celebrated mansion. Quite a few of them were like Jiao, with no regular job or any known income. If there was anything different about Jiao, it was that she was hardworking, not only staying after, but occasionally arriving before the session as well. She painted in the studio, in the living room, and in the garden. She sometimes attended the parties too, though she didn't seem so interested in the elderly dance partners.

Having unsuccessfully pressed the bell several times, Chen started knocking with his fist. Finally, Xie came to the door.

"Sorry, something's wrong with the old doorbell, Mr. Chen," Xie said apologetically.

As usual, Xie led Chen straight into the studio, where Xie was giving the class. Chen saw Jiao painting by the window, wearing a pair of beige overalls, practically barebacked, her hands and feet covered in paint, her hair tied up simply with a light blue handkerchief. She was absorbed in her watercolor, oblivious to his entrance. So were the other students, all busy with their sketches or oil paintings. The afternoon light came streaming in through the large window, painting the people in the room too.

There was something informal, almost intimate, about the class. Xie gave no formal lectures. There were no models from the outside, either, though some of the students themselves might have posed. Sitting on the same worn-out sofa in the corner, Chen thought he recognized a girl student in a couple of nude sketches that were stacked against the corner.

He knew little about painting so he couldn't judge. His knowledge of poetry, however, enabled him to make occasional comments about image and symbol without giving himself away. At least, no one objected to his presence in the painting class.

Xie moved from one student to another, but he seemed moody that afternoon, saying very little. The students were all painting in silence.

After a few minutes, Xie sat himself in a plastic chair by the long table, his right cheek pressed against his fist.

Yang worked on a sketchpad next to Jiao, attacking the white paper with a stick of charcoal, ripping off one sheet of paper, striking out at the new one. Abruptly, she threw away her charcoal stick in frustration and stamped her sandaled feet on the hardwood floor.

"I'd better not disturb the class," Chen whispered to Xie. "Let me sit outside."

"I'll go out with you," Xie said.

So they moved out into the garden. It was huge, considering its location in the center of the city, but far from well-kept. The grass was uncut, the meadow showed brown and bare patches here and there, and the bushes were untrimmed, withered, black in color as if burnt. To their left, a winding trail overrun with rank weeds led to an open pergola, which was dust-covered, seemingly deserted for a long time. Apparently, Xie couldn't afford professional help, and as a rather feeble man in his sixties, Xie himself could do little about gardening.

Lieutenant Song had a point, Chen reflected. Without any regular income all these years, Xie had to be in dire need of money. What he got from his paintings was barely enough to keep up the appearance of the building—just enough for utilities and basic maintenance. The air conditioning alone, though never on very high, had to run up a huge electricity bill. Not to mention all the drinks and snacks at the parties. Those Old Dicks, more often than not, arrived empty-handed. In fact, all the other rooms in the building, according to Mr. Zhou, were barely furnished, and except the bedroom upstairs, not used at all. So people never got to see beyond the living room. As for the fees from his students, they were symbolic at best.

There was one thing that Chen was pretty sure of. Xie's ex-wife had left him because of the financial strains, what with his refusal to find a regular job or to sell off the old house or anything in it. The Old Dicks lost no time telling Chen that account. So the scenario suggested by Internal Security about Xie's need to act as an agent for Jiao was not totally without basis.

"Let's sit here under the pear tree," Xie said. "It used to be my grandfather's favorite spot."

They seated themselves on two plastic deck chairs. Half reclining, Chen thought of what Huan Daoji, an Eastern Jing-dynasty general, said at the sight of a large tree: "The tree has grown like this, how about the man?"

Chen was surprised to see a squirrel scurrying across the lawn, something he had never seen elsewhere in the city. There was an air of melancholy, and the two men did not start talking for two or three minutes. Then, Xie sighed, crossing and uncrossing his legs.

"You have something on your mind, Mr. Xie?"

"Well, East Wind Property Company has come again, making an offer on the house. They want to pull it down and build a high-end apartment complex here."

"You don't have to sell it to them," Chen said, moving his chair closer. "In today's market, it's worth a huge fortune."

"Their offer is ridiculous—and a capped offer too, but that's irrelevant. I won't sell. I'm nothing without the house. But the buyer has connections—in both black and white ways."

It might not have been the first time that Xie had received an offer for his house, but the combination of the "black," in reference to the Triad gangsters, and the "white," to the government officials, was proving more than he could handle. Chen had heard of stories about these powerful developers.

"Such a buyer is capable of anything," Xie concluded.

"Your house is of historical significance," Chen said contemplatively, "and should be preserved as such. Officially, I mean. That way no one could snatch it from you so easily, no matter what their black or white connections. I happen to know someone in the city government. If you think it's okay, I can make a couple of phone calls on your behalf."

"What a resourceful man you are!" Xie said, his face lighting up. "As I said to you when we first met, Mr. Shen has never recommended someone so highly. I happened to call him yesterday, and he said that you are not just well-connected, you are simply a modern Menshang— generous in your help to people. You must have helped him too, I bet."

"Modern Menshang—come on. Don't take his words too seriously. Shen's an impossible poet."

"I am not a man of the world, you know what I mean, Mr. Chen. I don't know how I can ever thank you enough. If there's anything I can do, for your book project, please tell me."

"There is no need for that. It is such a pleasure for me to come to your party and class, or to sit in the garden like today. There is no place like it in the city, and coming here helps my book project greatly. Let's just chat a little more here," Chen said, smiling. "I'm from an ordinary family. My father was a schoolteacher. It's quite an experience for me to mix with people from good old families. Jiao in particular. The first day I came here, someone told me that she's from a most well-known family, but she herself does not talk about it."

"A well-known family background indeed. Her grandmother was Shang, as you know, but Jiao may not know any more than that."

"That's fascinating. How did she come to study painting with you?"

"People are interested in my work because of the subject matter— the old mansions. Most of them have already disappeared except in the memory of a has-been like me, but they are suddenly fashionable again," Xie said, with a self-deprecating smile. "Some students may come here to be trendy, but I believe Jiao is earnest."

"I'm no art critic, you know. Still, I think there's something in her paintings, something she can call her own. Unique, though I don't know how to define it," Chen said, choosing his words carefully. "She's still so young, and she has a long way to go. She's almost a full-time student here, isn't she? She must have a comfortable nest egg."

"I wonder about that too, but I've never asked her about it."

"Do you think her parents have left her a huge fortune?" Chen added. "I'm just curious."

"No, I don't think so," Xie said, looking up at him. "Considering the circumstances of her mother's death, she couldn't have left anything to her. Besides, any valuables at her family's home were taken away by the Red Guards."

"Such a tragedy for her family—her grandmother and mother."

"It's depressing even to think about those years."

Xie was obviously not comfortable with the direction of their conversation. Chen switched topics. "People talk about the thirties and about the nineties, as if the history between the two periods had been wiped out like a coffee stain."

"You're absolutely right," Xie said, glancing at his watch. "Oh, it's the time for the class to end. I have to move back in."

"Go ahead, Mr. Xie. I'll stay in the garden for a while."

From where he was sitting, Chen shifted slightly, looking toward the living room window. Soon he saw the silhouette of Xie moving from one student to another, talking, pointing, gesturing. He could not hear anything across the lawn.

He pulled out his phone and dialed Old Hunter. The call didn't go through. But he noticed there was a missed call—from Yong in Beijing. He decided not to call her back. He knew it was about Ling.

You said you would come—only in a dream, and gone without a trace, the moon slanting against the window at the fifth-night watch.

Again, he found himself thinking of lines from Li Shangyin, his favorite Tang-dynasty poet. After translating a collection of classical Chinese love poetry, Chen was contemplating a selection from Li Shangyin, having already translated more than twenty of his poems. Chen imagined that someday he might be able to collect them. He had made a special study of Li's poems in relation to Li's love for and marriage with the daughter of the Tang prime minister. It was not an impersonal way of reading poetry, not the poetics that T. S. Eliot would have approved of.

Then Chen saw a few students in the living room gathering their things. They were beginning to leave.

Jiao seemed to be staying on, however, still adding touches to her work. There might also have been another student there, of whom Chen caught only a fleeting glimpse.

Shortly afterward, Xie also left the room.

Chen remained sitting, like a writer lost in reveries, when Jiao came out into the garden. She was still in her overalls, high-stepping barefoot among the tall grass, her legs long and elegant, moving like a dancer. Her face bore a radiant smile.

"Hi. You are enjoying yourself in the garden, Mr. Chen?" she asked. "Xie has a headache. Let me keep you company."

"Oh, I wanted to absorb the atmosphere—for my book project, you know."

"Mr. Xie told me about your generous offer to help. We appreciate it," she said, perching on the edge of the chair Xie had recently occupied.

He wasn't surprised that Xie had told her, but he was surprised that she had said "we."

"Oh, it's nothing."

"Nothing to you, but everything to him."

Their talk was interrupted by the arrival of another girl, Yang.

"Come with me tomorrow evening, Jiao. How can a young girl like you spend so much time in one ancient place? The world outside is young, exciting. They have a home theater, and a better karaoke machine than in the Money Cabinet."

"Money Cabinet" was the name of the top karaoke club in Shanghai. So it was probably a party at an upstart's place, more luxuriously equipped than the club.

"But I'm not that keen on the fashionable parties," Jiao said.

"There's no party here tomorrow night. If you really don't like it there, you can leave anytime you like. So why not?"

"I'll think about it, Yang."

"What about you, Mr. Chen?" Yang said, pouting her lips provocatively.

"I'm no dancer. Last time, Jiao had to teach me step by step."

"Then you're not only responsible for yourself, Jiao. You have to bring Mr. Chen along with you," Yang said, turning to scamper away. "Bye, Jiao, bye Mr. Chen."

It was an interesting interruption, as it raised a question he himself had about Jiao. For the Old Dicks, the mansion was symbolic of their youthful dreams, so their frequent visits made sense. They didn't have anywhere else to go. That wasn't so with Jiao, surely.

"Yang always talks like that," Jiao said, her knees drawn up on the chair, her arms wrapped around her legs. "She's a butterfly, flitting from one party to another. Those parties can be exhausting, you know."

Perhaps those parties were full of fashionable people and were wilder, longer, like in the TV movies. He didn't know.

There was another question he refrained from asking. What was Yang's background? Moving from one party to another, always in stylish clothes, she was surely an "expensive girl." A couple of times, he had seen a limousine waiting for her outside.

But it wasn't his business to be concerned about any other girl here.

"Moving from one party to the next," he repeated. "What's the point?"

"Well, it depends on your perspective. What is it from the perspective of a butterfly?" she said, a pensive smile playing on her lips. For instance, "you may have noticed the brass foot warmer by the fireplace in the living room. Granny Zhong used it as a trash bin in the old neighborhood. But here, it became a valuable antique, symbolic of old Shanghai when well-to-do ladies put their feet above the warmer in the winter."

Granny Zhong was someone Jiao had not mentioned before. And where was the old neighborhood? Jiao grew up in an orphanage. Possibly some relatives. Someone of Shang's generation. He failed to recall anyone with that name from *Cloud and Rain in Shanghai*. He might have to check it again.

"You have a good point, Jiao. So is painting going to be your career?"

"I don't know if I have the talent. I'd like to find out, so I've been studying with Mr. Xie."

"Now, I'm just curious: Xie may be well-known in this circle, but he hasn't had any formal training in painting. So how did you come to study with him?"

"You went to college, but not everyone is as lucky, Mr. Chen. I started working quite young. For me, it was a stroke of unbelievable luck to find a teacher like Xie."

"That's an unusual decision for a girl like you."

"I am learning more than painting here. Mr. Xie is no upstart, and his work captures the spirit of the time."

He was not clear about what she meant by "the spirit of the time," but he waited, instead of pressing her for a definition.

"He really captures it all," she went on wistfully, "in that distinctive frame of his. A frame that puts the picture in perspective."

It reminded Chen, surprisingly, of a remark made by his late father, who saw Confucianism as a frame that provided an acceptable shape for the working ethical system. Perhaps the same could be said of Maoism, except that it wasn't really a working frame. Not even for Mao himself, whose own double life might have resulted from its failure.

"You are insightful," he said, pulling himself back from his wandering thoughts.

"It's just my way of looking at his paintings—so informed by his aspirations and afflictions through these years."

He was amazed by her response. Perhaps Jiao was nice to Xie not because of his help as a middleman for the "Mao material," as Internal Security suspected, but because of her sincere appreciation of Xie's work.

"According to T. S. Eliot, you have to separate the artist from the art. A poem doesn't necessarily say anything about a poet, nor does a painting—"

His phone rang, interrupting him before he could bring the conversation around to a question he wanted to ask. She stood up quietly, waving a finger at him as she headed for a shaded corner of the garden.

It was Wang, chairman of the Writers' Association in Beijing. Wang told Chen that Diao, the author of *Rain and Cloud in Shanghai,* had attended a literary conference in Qinghai, but at the end of the meeting, Diao had gone somewhere else instead of returning to Shanghai. At

Chen's request, Wang promised to continue his efforts to find out the exact whereabouts of Diao.

Closing the phone, Chen looked around to see Jiao squatting in the corner, plucking weeds and twigs with her bare hands, her overalls daubed with paint and her bare feet dotted with soil, like a hardworking gardener. Or like someone living in the mansion, taking care of her own garden.

It was a poignant image: a blossoming girl silhouetted against the ruins of an old garden, her bare shoulders dazzlingly white in the afternoon sunlight, the sky dappled with drifting clouds like sails, the smell of the grass rising in a fresh breeze.

She was vivacious, and smart too, in spite of her lack of good education. He wished he could come to know her better, watching the curve of her slender bottom as she leaned over her work. But it was a Mao case, he told himself again, and he had only about one week left—the deadline set by Internal Security. He had to "approach" her more effectively.

He got up and moved over, squatting beside her, joining in the work. There was a bunch of uprooted weeds by her feet.

"Sorry about the phone call. I was enjoying our talk."

"So was I."

"There's no party here this evening, Jiao?"

"No."

"I would love to stay longer," he said, glancing at his watch, "but I have some urgent business to take care of. But it won't take long. If you don't have anything this evening, how about continuing our talk over dinner?"

"Well, that would be nice, but—"

"Then let's do it," he said, his eyes holding hers momentarily. "There is a restaurant not far from here. It used to be Madam Chiang's residence."

"You're so into the past. The food is not that great, I've heard, and the restaurant is expensive. Still, many people want to go there."

"They want to imagine themselves as President Chiang Kai-shek or

71

Madam Chiang—for an hour or so—over a cup of sparkling wine. Illusion cannot be too expensive."

"Oh horror!"

"What do you mean, Jiao?"

"Why can't people be themselves?"

"In Buddhist scripture, everything is appearance, including one's self," Chen said, rising. "The restaurant is very close. You can walk there. So I'll see you this evening."

Striding out of the premises, he saw a middle-aged man loitering outside the small café, looking stealthily across the street. Possibly an Internal Security man, Chen thought, though he hadn't seen him before. If so, Internal Security would soon witness him and Jiao sitting together at a candlelight dinner and report back that the romantic chief inspector was making his "approach."

After all, it was like a couplet in the *Dream of the Red Chamber*, "When the true is false, the false is true. Where there is nothing, there is everything."

Jiao saw in Xie's painting something not only invisible to others but also closely connected to Xie's life. Chen thought of the book Ling had sent him; in it, critics claimed to have discovered evidence of Eliot's personal crisis in the manuscript of *The Waste Land*—his future as a poet uncertain, his marriage on rocks, and his wife a neurotic drag. According to them, the water in the poem could signify what the poet didn't have in his life, metaphysically as well as physically—

He was struck by an idea—not exactly new, since it had actually crossed his mind the night that he was assigned the Mao Case. That night, in the midst of a confusion of ideas, he had thought of the connection between Li Shangyin's life and his poetry. That was why he scribbled the word *poetry* on the matchbox before falling asleep. Only he had forgotten its relevance to the Mao Case by the next morning.

It was the possibility of learning something through Mao's poetry.

Not just as a critic, but as a detective. In spite of all the revolutionary messages in Mao's poems, some of the lines must have come from his personal experience and impulses, consciously or subconsciously, untold and previously unknown to the public. If Old Hunter could manage to dig out the personal stuff behind Mao's poem to Kaihui, Chen should be able to do a better job, given his training in literary criticism.

So he really did have some urgent business to take care of, as he had told Jiao, before joining her for dinner. He turned onto a side street, taking a short cut to the subway station, where, in a medium-sized bookstore in the underground mall, he would start searching for all the books about Mao's poems, like a devoted Maoist.

EIGHT

DETECTIVE YU WOKE EARLY Sunday morning and reached for his wife Peiqin, but she wasn't in bed beside him. Probably shopping, he guessed. She would usually go to the market early on Sunday morning.

He thought he heard a muffled sound outside the door. The building was old and housed many families—it was likely some residents were already up and moving. He didn't get up. Reaching for a cigarette, he went over in his mind what he had done for the last few days.

With the Party's emphasis on "a harmonious society," the bureau suddenly had a new focus. Several cases were assigned to the special case squad, temporarily under Yu during Chen's leave. Those cases didn't seem that special to Yu, but Party Secretary Li saw them in a different light. For instance, the squad was told to keep an eye on a "trouble-making" journalist who tried to expose the officials involved, directly or even indirectly, in a corruption case. Li's lecture for the job was delivered in the name of "political stability" as a precondition for the "harmonious society," condemning the journalist's efforts, which could cause people to lose their faith in the Party. Yu didn't have his heart in those assignments. Keeping an eye on someone didn't necessarily mean seeing something, or doing something, as he told himself again, taking a long pull at his cigarette.

His mind wandered off to the unannounced "vacation" for Chief Inspector Chen. It wasn't the first time Chen had taken such a vacation, but it was the first time he had done so without saying anything about it to Yu. On the contrary, Chen had contacted Yu's father, Old Hunter, instead.

According to the retired officer, Chen's decision was utterly understandable. Too much risk was involved. "Some knowledge can really kill, son."

But Yu felt terribly let down. He should have been told about what kind of an assignment it was. He had worked with Chen on many cases, weathering storms in the same boat. What was more frustrating was that even Old Hunter begrudged him the necessary information, hemming and hawing while trying to enlist him to help. And even that was only because of Yu's personal connection to Hong, the neighborhood committee cop in charge of the Jiling district. Old Hunter had likely already approached Hong without success. So it was up to Yu to do a background check on someone named Tan who had once lived in the district. In addition, Yu was told to be alert to anything seen or heard at the bureau regarding Internal Security.

Hong had also been an "educated youth" in Yunnan Province and had joined the Shanghai police force around the same time as Yu. They had known each other for more than twenty years. Hong cooperated without asking a single question, but the information he provided only mystified Yu.

In the mid-seventies, Tan, the only son of a capitalist family, tried to sneak across the border to Hong Kong in the company of his girl-friend Qian, also of black family background. They were caught making the attempt. Tan was so badly beaten that he killed himself, leaving a note in which he shouldered all the responsibility, trying to shelter his girlfriend from the consequences of their act. It was an unquestioned suicide, and an understandable one too. For such a "crime," Tan could have spent his next twenty or thirty years rotting in prison.

Tan's parents died shortly thereafter. Qian died a couple of years later. A sad story, but how someone who had died twenty years ago could have any bearing on Chen's assignment today, Yu failed to understand.

He didn't stop there, though. He went on to look into the background of Peng, another lover of Qian's. The initial check yielded little. In those years, it was a crime for people to have sex without a marriage license, and Peng was sentenced to five years for his affair with Qian, a woman then ten years his senior. He never recovered. Nor had he had a regular job since his release. If there were anything remarkable at all about Peng, it would be his ability to muddle along all these years.

Yu had no idea how any of this could be helpful to Chen, who could have easily gotten the same information with a couple of phone calls.

In the meantime, Yu had heard nothing concerning the movements of Internal Security, at least not within the bureau. There was something unusual about the quiet. Party Secretary Li's reticence about Chen's leave spoke volumes about it. Yu ground out his cigarette, more confused than before, and lonely too.

Then, in spite of himself, he dozed off before putting the ashtray out of sight.

When he opened his eyes again, Peiqin was in the room, half sitting, half squatting on a wooden stool, plucking the feathers from a chicken in a plastic basin full of hot water. A bamboo-covered thermos bottle stood beside. There was also a basket full of vegetables and soybean product on the floor.

"The common kitchen area is too crowded," she said, glancing up at him, then at the ashtray on the nightstand.

So the sound he had heard earlier outside the door could have been the chicken struggling in Peiqin's hand. It was too late, now for him to hide the ashtray.

"Where is Qinqin?" he asked.

"Group study with his schoolmates. He left early and won't be back until late in the evening."

Lifting his towel blanket, Yu sat up. "Let me help, Peiqin."

"You have said that since our 'educated youth' days in Yunnan, but have you ever helped with a chicken?"

"But I did in Yunnan, at least once—I 'acquired' a chicken in the middle of the night, remember?" He was pleased that she didn't bring up the issue of his smoking first thing in the morning.

"Shame on you! For a cop to talk about that."

"I wasn't a cop then." He smiled in spite of himself. During their "educated youth" years in Yunnan Province when they were poor and starved, Yu once stole a chicken from a Dai farmer during the night, and Peiqin cooked it in stealth.

Today, in the morning light, her bare arms were specked with the chicken blood, just like so many years ago. He fought down the temptation to light another cigarette.

"It's almost over," she said. "We're going to have home-grown hen soup today. You and Qinqin have been working so hard."

As a rule, Peiqin didn't put something special on the dinner table unless their son Qinqin was at home. It was an unwritten rule Yu understood well. Nothing was spared in support of Qinqin's effort to get into a good college, which would be crucial to his future in the new China.

"A chicken soup, plus carp filet fried with tomato and shepherd purse blossom mixed with tofu," Peiqin said with a happy smile. "Because it is Sunday, you may have a cup of Shaoxing yellow wine too."

"But you don't have to get a live chicken. It's too troublesome."

"You haven't learned anything from your gourmet boss. He would tell you that there is world of difference between a live home-grown chicken and a frozen one from the so-called chicken farm."

"How could you be wrong, Peiqin, with even Chief Inspector Chen supporting your chicken choice?"

"Now you can help me by lying on the bed, and not smoking. It's Sunday morning. You have hardly had the time to talk to me lately."

"But you've been busy too."

"Don't worry about me. Soon Qinqin will be in college, and I won't be busy anymore. Well, anything new about Chen's leave?"

He knew she would get around to that topic, and he reached for the ashtray absentmindedly. He told her what he had learned, mainly from Old Hunter.

"Perhaps Chen chose Old Hunter," she said finally, "because your father isn't a cop anymore, and no one will pay close attention to him."

"But Old Hunter also withheld information from me."

"He either doesn't know, or he must have his reasons. Now, what has the old man been up to?"

"He has been busy patrolling somewhere—shadowing somebody, I believe. But if not for my connection to Hong, Old Hunter might not have let me do anything."

"What did you find out?"

"I just did a background check on two men linked to a woman named Qian, who died about twenty years ago in a traffic accident. Of the two men, the older one, Tan, died two years before she did—suicide. There was nothing suspicious about the circumstances of his death. As for the second, Peng, he's a nobody, one of those jobless loafers you see everywhere nowadays."

"Then, why all the fuss?" She put the pair of stainless-steel tweezers in the plastic basin. "Who is Old Hunter shadowing?"

"A young girl named Jiao, Qian's daughter. Possibly a kept girl—a little concubine."

"Who keeps her?"

"No one knows. That's what Old Hunter has been trying to find out, I think, but he has forbidden me to do anything concerning her."

"That's strange. A Big Buck will show off his mistress like a five-karat diamond ring—a symbol of his success. Unless he belongs to a different circle . . ."

"What do you mean?"

"Instead of being a Big Buck, he might be a high-ranking Party official, so he is trying to keep their relationship a secret. But he can't keep it secret for too long if cops are looking into it."

"Not just the cops, but Internal Security too."

"And Chief Inspector Chen as well. That's not good," she said broodingly. "Did you learn anything else from your father?"

"He apparently had a long talk with Chen, mentioning a story about how the tomb builders of Cao Cao were killed because of what they knew, but that happened more than a thousand years ago."

"That sounds ominous! Some knowledge can be really deadly. Did you notice anything unusual about him?"

"He had a book with him—with a strange title, like a weather book about Shanghai . . ."

"Do you think the book has something to do with Chen's investigation?" She added, "The old man is not a great reader."

"Yes, that's what I think."

"Hold on, Yu—can you recall the name of the book?"

"*Cloud and Rain* . . . something."

"*Cloud and Rain*—oh I see, now I see—"

"What do you see?" he said, noting an anxious and eager look in her eyes, a sort of scared opacity, as if she were staring at something strange, monstrous.

"*Cloud and Rain*—" She jumped up from the stool, wiping her hands on her apron while bending to pull a cardboard box out from under the bed. "I've got a copy of it. *Cloud and Rain in Shanghai.*"

"That's it. That's the name of the book," he said, his eyes following her. In the room, the makeshift bookshelf belonged to Qinqin. Peiqin had her own books, like her favorite novel, *Dream of the Red Chamber*, but he didn't know where she kept them. The cardboard box was an old one, originally used for Meiling brand, canned lunch meat, possibly from her restaurant.

She had found the book in question and started leafing through it in great excitement.

"What are you looking for?"

"Yes, that's it—Qian. And Tan too, sure enough," she said, holding the book up in her hand. "Have you heard of a movie star named Shang?"

"Shang? I've never seen her movies. She was popular in the fifties, I think, and she died during the Cultural Revolution."

"She committed suicide."

"Yes?"

"Yes," she said, taking another look at the page, "Qian was Shang's daughter."

"Is that book about Shang?"

"No, it's about her daughter, Qian, but it was popular because of Shang, or rather because of the man she slept with."

"Who are you talking about?"

"Mao!" she said in the shifting morning light that dappled her face like in a painting. "That's why Chen doesn't want to get you involved. That's also why Party Secretary Li is keeping his mouth shut. It's all because of Mao."

"I'm lost, Peiqin."

"You haven't heard about Mao's affair with Shang?"

"No, not really."

"There's a book titled *Mao and His Women*. Have you never heard of it?"

"No, but you cannot take those stories seriously. Have you read it?"

"No, but I read some excerpts in a Hong Kong magazine that a customer left in the restaurant. The book is banned here, of course, but they are true stories. Mao liked dancing with beautiful young women. It's acknowledged in the official newspapers, which say that Mao was under a lot of stress, so the Party Central Committee wanted him to relax through dancing. Shang was a regular partner of his and they danced together many times."

"You never talked to me about this."

"I don't want to talk about Mao. Not in our home. Hasn't he brought enough disaster for all of us?"

Yu was taken aback by her vehement response. Considering what her family had suffered during the Cultural Revolution, however, her reaction was understandable.

"Mao lived in Beijing, and Shang, in Shanghai," he said. "How was that possible?"

"Well, Mao came to Shanghai from time to time. Whenever he was here, the local officials would arrange parties for him at a grand mansion that had belonged to a Jewish businessman before 1949. Shang was waiting for him there."

"He might have danced with her, but that did not necessarily mean he slept with her."

"Come on, Yu. Mao could have danced with anyone in Beijing. Why come all the way to Shanghai?"

"But Mao traveled a lot. There's a song about his traveling for the welfare of the country, I remember."

"You've never heard these stories about Mao? I can't believe you, Yu. Shang wasn't the only one. Mao had so many personal secretaries, nurses, orderlies. Remember Jade Phoenix, the pretty secretary who took care of him day and night at his imperial residence? Now mind you, she was a young woman with only elementary school education who actually worked as the confidential secretary for Mao. Again, it was written up in the Party newspapers that even Madam Mao had to suck up to Jade Phoenix. Why? Everybody knows the answer."

"Yes, Jade Phoenix was in a documentary movie in Yunnan, that I do remember. It was just a glimpse of a knockout helping Mao walk out of his room. You know what? In that moment, I, too, couldn't help speculating about their relationship, and I felt so guilty about it afterward, as if I had committed a most unforgivable crime."

"You didn't have to feel guilty at all. Jade Phoenix is now an honorable manager of a Mao restaurant in Beijing and she sits there occasionally. The business is booming and reservations have to be made days beforehand. All the customers go there for a chance to see Jade Phoenix."

"But it all happened so many years ago. Why this assignment for Chen, all of a sudden?"

"That I don't know," she said, shaking her head. "Some power struggle at the top?"

"No, I don't think they are going to remove Mao's portrait from the Gate of Tiananmen Square, not anytime soon."

"Chen's not working on some cover-up for him, I hope."

"But what can I do to help?"

"He'll come to you when he's in need. Don't worry about it, but—I do understand Old Hunter's concern," she said, rising abruptly. "Oh, I have to put the chicken in the pot. I'll be right back."

She hurried back in a minute, picking up the copy of *Cloud and Rain in Shanghai* again. "I'm going to reread it closely. Perhaps I can find some clue for your boss."

"You, too, have a soft spot for our irresistible chief inspector," he said with mock jealousy. "He also has a personal problem at the moment."

"What problem?"

"Ling, his HCC girlfriend in Beijing, has married somebody else—people have been gossiping about it at the bureau."

"Oh that," she said.

"He got a call from Beijing during the bureau political studies meeting a couple of days ago. Somebody overheard the conversation—a few words of it. Chen looked devastated afterward."

"It might not be that bad for him. He's a successful cop—and not because of her. In fact, I wondered what he would become if they stayed together. You know what I mean."

"He's become a chief inspector on his own merits, no question about it," Yu readily agreed. "Which is easy for others to see, but not for him."

"Then now he can turn over a new page. With his HCC girlfriend constantly at the back of his mind, it was impossible for him to see other girls. White Cloud, for instance."

It was another of her favorite topics. Peiqin appeared to think that the breakup had come as a shock to Chen, but Chen's relationship with his HCC girlfriend had long been on the rocks. Last year, Chen

82

had passed on an opportunity to go to Beijing, but Yu decided not to mention that to Peiqin at the moment.

"No, not White Cloud," he said instead. "I don't think she's a good one for him, either."

"You know what I found in a bookstore the other day?" she said, delving into the book box again to pick up a magazine. "A poem written by your chief inspector. For his HCC girlfriend, though it isn't that explicit. Even then and there, they were already lost in their different interpretations. It's entitled 'Li Shangyin's English Version.'" She took off her apron and started reading aloud.

> The fragrance of jasmine in your hair / and then in my teacup, that evening,/ when you thought me drunk, an orange /pinwheel turning at the rice-paper window./ The present is, when you think/ of it, already the past. I am / trying to quote a line / from Li Shangyin to say what / cannot be said, but the English version /at hand fails to do justice / to him (the translator, divorced / from his American wife, drunk, found English / beating him like a blind horse), any / more than the micaceous mist / issuing from a Lantian blue jade / to your reflection. // Last night's star, / last night's wind—the memory / of trimming a candle, the minute / of a spring silkworm wrapping itself / in a cocoon, when the rain / becomes the mountain, and the mountain / becomes the rain . . . // It is like a painting /of Li Shangyin going to open / the door, and of the door / opening him to the painting, / that Tang scroll you showed me / in the rare book section / of the Beijing Library, while you / read my ecstasy as empathy / with the silverfish escaping / the sleepy eyes of the full stops, / and I felt a violent wonder / at your bare feet beating / a bolero on the filmy dust / of the ancient floor. Even then / and there, lost in each / other's interpretations, we agreed.

"I can make neither heads nor tails of it," Yu said with a puzzled smile. "How can you be so sure it's a poem written for her?"

"She worked at the Beijing Library. But more importantly, why Li Shangyin? A Tang-dynasty poet, Li was seen as a social climber because he married the daughter of the then prime minister. Unfortunately, the prime minister soon lost his position, which cast a shadow on Li's official career. He wrote his best lyrical poems in frustration."

"So that turned out to be good for his poetry, right?"

"You could say so. Chen's too proud to be seen as a climber."

"If he had really cared for her, why should it have mattered so much?"

"No one lives in a vacuum, not to mention all of the politics at your bureau."

She was passionate in Chen's defense, waving the magazine dramatically, her face flushing like a flower.

"Oh, the chicken soup," she said, dropping the magazine. "It's time to turn the fire down low."

He watched her hurrying out with a touch of amusement. After all, the chicken soup proved to be just as important as Chen to her. But then he started worrying about Chen again. It was an investigation fraught with danger, involving knowledge which could kill, as Old Hunter had warned.

Detective Yu had to do something, whether Chief Inspector Chen included him or not.

NINE

CHEN WOKE UP, BLINKING in the glaring sunlight streaming in through the half-drawn curtain. Still lying in bed, he reviewed his unsuccessful "approach" to Jiao in the restaurant the previous night.

In spite of the "romantic" dinner in the well-preserved attic room under the time-sobered beams allegedly from Madam Chiang's days, with a couple of tiny red paper lanterns dangling overhead, he had learned little that was new. Sitting opposite, in a pink tank top and white pants, her shoulders dazzling against the candlelight, Jiao appeared preoccupied, "the autumn waves" in her eyes reflecting something far away. Tossing a wisp of hair back from her forehead, she brushed off his efforts to bring the talk around to her family background. "No, let's not talk about it," she said. A silver knife lay beside her plate, like a footnote, the waiters and waitress coming and going, all dressed in the fashion of the thirties.

Perhaps she had met people like him—more interested in her grandmother than in her. He knew better than to pressure her further. Besides, their conversation was disturbed by a loud Manila band and other louder diners, bantering tales about Madam Chiang, popping off the corks on expensive champagne like in the old days.

At the end of the meal, Jiao let him pay the bill like the ex-businessman he claimed to be. He didn't really worry about the expense since the staggering bill might function, for once, as proof of his conscientious work. She told the waiter to box the leftovers—"For Mr. Xie, who doesn't know how to cook."

It was yet another confirmation of her being considerate of Xie.

Parting outside the restaurant, they shook hands, and he had a feeling that her hand lingered in his for a moment. He saw a wistful smile flick across her face, as if touching a string, a peg in a half-forgotten poem.

But that wasn't enough for Chief Inspector Chen, far from the breakthrough he needed, as he concluded as he got up from the bed.

He checked the cell phone first. No message. The information from Old Hunter so far, including the little indirectly from Detective Yu, didn't appear promising.

So he decided to sally out onto his second front, a move first contemplated after his talk with Jiao in the garden, supported in his thoughts about Eliot's poetry, and necessitated by his unsuccessful approach at the restaurant.

For the first attempt along that new front, Chen had actually done his homework. Before and after the dinner the previous day, he'd come up with a list of scholars' works on Mao's poetry. Though it could be said he had done some of the homework long before: He had read a number of books on the subject as early as his middle school years, when *Quotations of Chairman Mao* and *Poems of Chairman Mao* were his textbooks. Upon graduation, he had copied several lines in his diary as self-encouragement: *The mountain pass may be made of iron, / but we are crossing it all over again, / all over again, / the hills stretching in waves, / the sun sinking in blood.* After the Cultural Revolution, Chen, like many others, chose not to think too much about Mao or his poems. It was a page finally turned. Besides, Mao wrote in the traditional verse form, different from Chen's free verse. Now, those poems

86

of Mao's came crowding back, fragmented more or less in the mind of the worn-out cop.

Most of Mao's were "revolutionary," at least in the official interpretations, including the poem composed for his second wife, Kaihui, and another poem written about a picture taken by his fourth wife, Madam Mao. The two poems were the only ones he could remember that had any relation to Mao's personal life.

Some critics thought otherwise, perhaps. In traditional Chinese literary criticism, there was a time-honored tradition of *suoying*, i.e., an effort to find the true meaning of a work in the author's life. Such an approach to Mao's work might not have been practicable, for there was only the official version of his life. Still, a scholar in the field might know something inaccessible to Chen.

On the list of Mao poetry scholars Chen had made, some were so established that it was beyond Chen to attempt a quick contact, let alone a quick breakthrough; some of them were high in their Party positions, having worked with Mao, which also excluded the possibility of Chen's learning anything from them; some had passed away; and some were too far away from Shanghai. So the only one approachable at the moment was Long Wenjiang, a "scholar" quite different from all others, but in Shanghai, and a member of the Writers' Association too.

As a Mao poetry critic, Long had come to the fore during the Cultural Revolution. Not because of his academic studies but because of his class status as a worker. Having spent years collecting various annotations and interpretations of Mao poetry, he put them together into a single volume. The publication of the annotated edition immediately established him as a Mao scholar in the years when workers and peasants were encouraged to be the masters of the socialist society. He became a member of the Writers' Association, as well as a "professional writer."

But Long's luck dipped after Mao's death in 1976. For several years, few were interested in anything related to Mao. Mao scholars started working on different projects, like Tang or Song poetry, but Mao was the only subject Long knew anything about. Instead of giving up, he plodded on, betting on a revival of interest in Mao. The revival finally came with Mao's becoming a brand name in the materialistic age, with Mao restaurants and Mao antiques and people collecting Mao badges and stamps for their potential value in the market. Plastic Mao images had even become potent charms for taxi drivers, dangling in front of windshields, supposedly effective against traffic accidents. Chen, too, had a lighter made in the shape of the *Little Red Book*—click it and a spark would shoot up, like Mao's prediction about the red revolutionary flame sweeping over the world.

But there was no market value for Mao poetry in the collective revival. No publishing house showed any interest in Long's revised edition, despite his passionate speeches and protests, both in and out of the Writers' Association.

That was not the only trouble for Long. In the last few years, the Writers' Association had suffered several cuts in their government funding. People began to talk about reforming the system of "professional writers." In the past, those acknowledged as professional writers could get their monthly pay from the association until retirement, regardless of their publications. Now a contract period was suggested, with each member's qualifications being examined and determined by a committee. Long was desperate, beginning to write something like short anecdotes—totally unrelated to Mao—in his effort to remain in the contract.

Chen happened to remember Long because of such a short piece published in *Shanghai Evening*. It was a vivid anecdote about river crabs, but "politically incorrect" in the judgment of the committee of the Writers' Association, of which Chen was a member. So he dug the newspaper out and began rereading it. For a change, he added half a lemon and a spoonful of sugar into his tea.

Several years before the economic reform started in the eighties, my old neighbor, Aiguo, a Confucianist middle school teacher disappointed with the political banishment of Confucius from the classroom, began to develop a crab complex. He made a point of enjoying the Yangchen river crabs at least three or four times during crab season. His wife having passed away, his son having just started working in a state-run steel plant and dating a girl, Aiguo justified his one and only passion by making reference to well-known writers like Su Dongpo, a Song-dynasty poet, who declared a crab feast the most blissful moment of his life, "Oh that I could have crabs with a wine supervisor sitting beside me," or like Li Yu, a Ming-dynasty scholar, who confessed that he wrote for the purpose of making the crab-money—his life-saving money. As an intellectual immersed in what "Confucius says," Aiguo had to restrain himself from lecturing about the sage in public, but he followed Confucius's ritualistic rules for crab-eating at home.

"Do not eat when the food is rotten; do not eat when it looks off-color; do not eat when it smells bad; do not eat when it is not properly cooked; do not eat when it is off season; do no eat when it is not cut right; do not eat when it is not served with the appropriate sauce . . . Do not throw away the ginger . . . Be serious and solemn when offering a sacrifice meal to one's ancestors . . ." Aiguo would quote from the Analects by Confucius at the dinner table, adding, "It's about the live Yangcheng crabs—all the necessary requirements for them, including a piece of ginger."

"All are excuses for his crab craziness. Confucius says," his son commented with a resigned shrug to the neighbors, "don't believe him."

Indeed, Aiguo had such a weakness, suffering a peculiar syndrome with the western wind rising in November, as if his heart were being pinched and scratched by the crab claws. He had to conquer the craving with "a couple of the Yangcheng river crabs, a cup of yellow wine," and only then would he be able to work hard for the year, full of energy to throw himself into whatever "Confucius says," until the next crab season.

Aiguo retired at the beginning of the economic reform. The price of crabs had rocketed and a pound of large crabs cost three hundred yuan. For an ordinary retiree like him, a pound of crab cost more than half of his monthly pension. Crabs became a luxury affordable only for the newly rich of the city. For the majority of the Shanghai crab eaters, like Aiguo, the crab season became almost a season of torture.

In the same shikumen house lived Gengbao, a former student of Aiguo's. Gengbao hardly acknowledged Aiguo as his teacher, for he had flunked out of school, having received a number of Ds and Fs from Aiguo himself. As it is said in Taodejing, "In misfortune comes fortune": because of his failure at school, Gengbao started his cricket business in the early days of the reform and became rich. In Shanghai, people gamble on cricket fights, so a ferocious cricket could sell for thousands of yuan. Gengbao was allegedly catching his most fierce crickets in a "secret cemetery," where the crickets, having absorbed all the infernal spirits, fought like devils. Anyway, it proved to be a fabulous niche market for him. Despite all the money he made, however, he chose not to move away from this feng shui attic room of his, which he believed had brought his fortune, though he bought a new apartment somewhere else. In the old building, he still shared the common kitchen as well as a common passion with Aiguo: the crab. Unlike Aiguo, Gengbao could afford to enjoy crabs to his heart's content, of which he made an ostensible show, parading crabs through the kitchen, nailing crab shells like monster masks on the wall above the coal briquette stove. Aiguo suffered all this, sighing and quoting from a Confucian classic, "It's the teacher's fault to have not taught a student properly."

"What do you mean?" Aiguo's daughter-in-law responded. "Gengbao is a Big Buck nowadays. Your ancestors must have burned tall incense for you to have such a successful student."

If there was any cold comfort for Aiguo, it would be that he could talk about Confucius openly again. However, retired, he could give his lecture only to his grandson, Xiaoguo, a third-year elementary school student.

The array of the mysterious crab shells on the kitchen wall seemed to be more appealing than Confucius to Xiaoguo, who had never tasted a crab before.

"What does a crab taste like, Grandpa?"

It was an impossible mission for the retired teacher. There's no tasting a crab without putting it into your mouth. Aiguo adored his grandson, and as Confucius says, "You have to do what you should do, even though it's impossible to do so." Finally, Aiguo managed to demonstrate how delicious a crab could be by concocting a special crab sauce of black vinegar, sugar, ginger slice, and soy sauce.

"It's somewhat like that," Aiguo said, letting Xiaoguo dip a chopstick into the sauce and suck on the tip, "but much better."

Unexpectedly, that experiment developed for Aiguo into an ongoing pursuit of a way to satisfy the crab-craving. All the crab-rich memories had come back to him the moment that the chopstick tip touched his own tongue. He pushed the experiment further by stir-frying the egg yolk and white separately in a wok and mixing them with the special sauce. It resulted in a special dish richly redolent of the celebrated Fried Crab Meat at Wangbaoh restaurant. And to his surprise, small shrimp or dried tofu dipped in the special sauce could occasionally produce a similar effect too. On those days when he could not find anything in the refrigerator, which was under the strict surveillance of his daughter-in-law, he would simply dip the chopsticks in and out of the special sauce, sipping at his yellow wine, and chewing the ginger slices.

Needless to say, all the experiments added to the curiosity of the close-observing Xiaoguo.

"Living in a poor lane, and dipping in nothing but the crab sauce, one still enjoys life," Aiguo said, seemingly absorbed in Confucius again, to his bewildered grandson. "Confucius says something very close to that about one of his best students."

One day, on the way to school, Xiaoguo passed by a new house with the door open and caught sight of people busy making huge banquets of sacrifice to their ancestors. It had to be a rich family, with so many luxurious cars parked in front, and with scripture-chanting monks engaged from a Buddhist temple too. He could not help taking a closer look. To his surprise, he saw a crab scurrying out *of the door to the sidewalk. It must have escaped from the kitchen in the midst of the hustle-bustle. No one paid attention to it. So Xiaoguo took off his hat and, like a streak of lightning, picked up the vicious-looking crab. Instead of going to school, he ran back home, prepared the special sauce after a fashion, and boiled the crab. After devouring it without really tasting it, he painted a multicolored face on the crab shell with a Chinese character beneath it—swear. He hung the shell like a primitive mask on the wall. When Aiguo came back, seeing the mask, and learning the story from Xiaoguo, who was still washing his hat in the sink, he snapped and slapped his grandson in fury.*

"How can you skip school for a crab? Shame on you! And a stray crab from others' offering to their ancestor too! That's totally against the Confucian rites. What's more, you put the crab in your hat. Not one of Confucius's students had to straighten his hat before dying." Aiguo softened as the kid sobbed in a heartbreaking way. "Study hard. When you get into college, I'll buy crabs for you."

"What's the point?" Xiaoguo said, sobbing and smacking his lips, "Both you and Father studied at college, but what good was it?"

"Then what are you going to do?"

"I'll be a Big Buck, so I'll buy crabs for you then. Tons of crabs, I swear. That's why I pledged on the crab shell."

"Confucius says—"

"Crap!"

It was a realistic piece. Chen looked in the *Analects* for the many "do not eats" about crabs, and he found all of them in the chapter "Old Home," though Confucius talked about meat and fish in general, not about crab. At least not about crab exclusively, despite what Aiguo told his grandson. Long had clearly read other books beside Mao. The committee at the Writers' Association didn't like the narrative because it "joined the complaining crowd without representing the immense progress the reform has achieved in China." Nor did it read like a story with any plot or craftsmanship, to be strict about it. Still, Chen liked the mouth-watering anecdote, suspecting that those vivid details had come from Long's own passion for crabs. Chen, too, liked crabs, and though he was not a successful entrepreneur like Gengbao, he was far luckier than Aiguo. As a chief inspector, he was acquainted with Big Bucks who would occasionally treat him to crabs and other delicacies.

As if through mysterious correspondence in the wireless space, his cell phone vibrated with a call from Gu. Gu was a prosperous entrepreneur who owned several companies, restaurants, and clubs. Chen couldn't help mentioning the story of crabs during the course of the conversation, wondering whether people could still purchase crabs at the state price nowadays.

Afterward, he dialed the Shanghai Writers' Association. He had a long talk with the executive secretary, and got the information he needed about Long.

Chen started preparing a list of questions for his visit. Halfway through it, he heard a knock on the door. To his surprise, a bamboo basket of live river crabs was waiting there—at least ten pounds of live crabs. Attached was a short note from Gu.

You're too busy to come to my restaurant, I know. Another basket was sent to your mother's place.

Chen regretted mentioning the crab story to Gu. The cost of such a basket could be exceedingly high, though it came without a price tag—at least not yet. But for now Chen chose to tell himself a cliché: the end justifies the means. After all, it was a Mao case, and the basket might come in handy for the important visit to Long.

Chen dialed Long's number and proposed coming over for a visit. The two had met at the association before, but his call must have come as a surprise to Long, especially when Chen added at the end, "I'll bring along something to eat, so we'll talk over a cup."

TEN

ABOUT AN HOUR LATER, Chen arrived at a small street in the Old City area and saw Long waiting in front of his apartment building. In spite of Chen's tip on the phone, Long was flabbergasted at the sight of the basket of river crabs.

"My humble abode is brightened by your visit," Long said. "Now you are overwhelming me with all the crabs."

"I was impressed by your crab story, Long. And I happen to know someone at a restaurant. After I was able to get some at the state price, I decided to come over."

"I'm not surprised by your connections, Comrade Chief Inspector Chen, but the 'state price' more than surprises me."

Chen smiled without giving any explanation, but Long was right about the nonexistence of "state price."

Long welcomed Chen into his efficiency apartment—the bedroom, the living room, the dining room, and the kitchen were all in one room. A red-painted table was already set out in the middle of the room. On the side closest to the door, there was a sink and a coal briquette stove. On one of the white walls, Chen saw a couple of scarlet crab claws as decoration.

"My wife has to babysit at her sister's place today," Long said. "We'll talk to our hearts' content over a crab feast. Let me prepare them first. It'll take just a few minutes."

Long put the crabs in the sink underneath the window and started washing them with a short bamboo broom. With the water still running and the crabs crawling, he took out a large pot, filled it half full with water, and put it on the propane gas tank.

"Steaming is the simplest and best way."

"Can I help, Long?"

"Slice the ginger," Long said, taking out a piece of the root, "for the sauce."

Long bent down over the sink to clean the crabs with an old toothbrush. As Chen finished slicing the ginger, Long started binding the crabs, one by one, with white cloth strings.

"This way, the crabs won't lose their legs in the steamers," Long commented, putting them into the pot.

By now Chen was convinced that Aiguo in the story was none other than Long himself. The way he prepared the crabs was impressive.

"I'll tell you what, Chief Inspector Chen. I, too, used to have crabs every month back in the early seventies."

That was during the Cultural Revolution, Chen thought, when Long was a "revolutionary worker scholar," capable of enjoying privileges not easily available to others.

"That's what I guessed. Your story must have been more or less drawn from your own experience."

The special sauce of vinegar and sugar and ginger was prepared. Long dipped his chopsticks into the sauce, tasted it, and smacked his lips. He opened a bottle of Shaoxing yellow rice wine, poured out a cup for Chen, and poured a cup for himself.

"Let's have a cup first."

"To a crab evening!"

"Now let's wash our hands," Long said. "The crabs will soon be ready."

As Chen seated himself at the table, Long took off the cover of the steamer, picked up the contents, and placed on the table a large platter of steamed crabs, dazzlingly red and white under the light. "Crabs have to be served hot. I will leave some of them unsteamed for the moment."

So saying, Long fell to eating a fat crab without further ado, and Chen followed suit. Spooning the sauce into the crab shell, Chen dipped a piece of crab into the amber-colored liquid. It was delicious.

Only after having finished the digestive glands of the second crab did Long look up with a satisfied sigh and nod. Turning the crab's entrails inside out, he had something that looked like a tiny monk sitting in meditation on his palm.

"In the story of the White Snake, a meddlesome monk has to hide somewhere after he has ruined the happiness of a young couple. Finally he pulls himself into a crab shell. It's useless. Look, there's no escape."

"A marvelous story. You are truly a crab expert, Long."

"Don't laugh at my exuberance. It is the first crab-treat for me this year. I can't help it," Long mumbled with an embarrassed grin, a crab leg still between his teeth. "You're an important man. You may want to talk to me about something, but you don't have to bring all those crabs."

"Well, you are an authority on Mao's poetry. In ancient times, a student came to his teacher with a ham, so it's proper and right for me to come here with crabs. They are far from enough to show my respect for you."

Poking the meat out of the crab leg with a chopstick, Long said, "I really appreciate it."

"I've been reading his poems. Whatever people may say about Mao nowadays, his poems are not bad at all."

"The most magnificent poems," Long said, raising his cup. "It's not easy for a young intellectual like you to say so. You, too, are a poet."

"But I write free verse. I don't know much about regular verse. So you have to enlighten me on that."

"In terms of poetic tradition, Mao wrote *ci* poems, which have elaborate requirements for the number of characters in a line, and for the tone and rhyme patterns too. But you don't have to worry about the versification to appreciate his poems. Like 'Snow,' which is full of original and bold images. What a sublime vision!"

"A sublime vision indeed," Chen echoed. It might be well to start with a poem not directly related to the investigation. "What an infinite expanse of imagination!"

"That's true," Long agreed. His tongue loosened with the wine, he quoted the last line with a flourish. "*To look for the really heroic, you have to count on today!*"

"But the poem was also controversial, I have read. Mao made that particular statement after listing well-known emperors in history and pronouncing himself a greater one."

"You cannot take a poem too literally. 'The really heroic' here can be singular or plural. It doesn't have to refer to Mao alone. Also, we have to take into consideration that Mao and the Communist Party were then regarded as 'uneducated bandits.' So the poem showed Mao's learning and won applause from the intellectuals."

"Yes, your interpretation throws much light on it," Chen said, though not at all convinced. "That's why I am coming to an expert like you."

"There are interpretations and interpretations. Some people may have a personal grudge against Mao—quite possibly because of their suffering during the Cultural Revolution, but we have to see Mao from a historical perspective."

"Exactly, but people cannot help seeing him from their own perspective."

"Now, from my perspective, the sauce is a must. Simple yet essential, it brings out the best of the crabs," Long said, changing the topic as he poured the sauce into another crab shell. "Once I even dipped pebbles into the sauce, and with my eyes closed, I still enjoyed all the memories of the crabs."

"That's something, Long," Chen said. "I'm learning a lot today—apart from Mao's poetry."

"Few publishing houses are interested in poetry today," Long said, looking him in the eye. "Are you trying to write something about his poems?"

"No, I'm no scholar, not like you. I majored in English, so I'm interested in translation."

"Translation?"

"Yes, there was an official translation of Mao poetry in the seventies—by celebrated scholars and translators. One of them was a professor at Beijing Foreign Language University, where I studied. But the 'politically correct' interpretation could have been taken too far during those years. For instance, some of his poems could be personal, not just about revolution, but translators at the time had to translate them into revolutionary poems."

"That's true. Everything could be political in those days."

"Poetry translation doesn't simply mean word-to-word rendition. They should read like poems in the target language." Chen opened his briefcase and took out his translation of classical Chinese love poems. "That's a collection translated by Professor Yang and me. An American edition of it has just come out. We didn't make much money, but we got a lot of publicity."

"In today's market, perhaps you could have a poetry collection of your own published here, and abroad too. You went to a conference in the United States not long ago, I remember. You know a lot of people there."

"Some," Chen said, thinking Long must have heard stories about him as the head of the delegation attending the literature conference— if not about his police work there. "That is why I'm coming to you today. A publishing house is interested in a translation of Mao's poetry."

"I'm not surprised. People know what a poet-translator you are," Long said, crushing a crab claw with a small hammer—not a special crab hammer, but more likely a fine carpentry hammer, which served the purpose just as well. "I appreciate your thinking of me for the project. My annotated edition was published years ago, but I've recently finished an index of the new publications on his poetry. You surely can have both of them."

"I have a copy of your annotated edition at home, but your new index may be very important. Since most of the books on the subject were published during the Cultural Revolution, the sourcing of their information was limited. You alone have continued your research, so you would have a lot of the latest information."

"I've been working on a manuscript about his work, but it is not finished yet. As for new information, there may not be such a lot, I'm afraid."

"I can't wait to read it," Chen said. In a manuscript meant for publication in China, however, the "new" material would be understandably limited. Nor would it provide what he was looking for. "Now with translation, the first step is interpretation. The poem Mao wrote for Madam Mao's picture, for instance, could be a personal one."

" 'Inscription on a Picture of the Celestial Cave in the Lu Mountains Taken by Comrade Li Jin.' " Long began reciting the poem from memory, holding a crab claw like a stick of chalk. "*Against the gathering dusk stands a pine, sturdy, erect / in composure with riotous clouds sweeping past. / What a fairy cave it is, born out of the nature! / Ineffable beauty comes at the perilous peak.*"

"In the sixties, the poem was read as a revolutionary stance against imperialism and revisionism—riotous clouds could be symbolic of the reactionary force, and also as an example of the closeness between Mao and Madam Mao," Chen said, taking up a crab leg and, like Long, holding it like a piece of chalk. "After the downfall of the Gang of Four, Madam Mao became dog shit, and the poem was said to be simply the expression of Mao's revolutionary spirit—nothing to do with Madam Mao. However, there's a recent interpretation by Wang Guangmei." Long would not need to be told who Wang Guangmei was—everyone was familiar with the wife of Liu Shaoqi, the late chairman of the People's Republic of China. "According to Wang, Mao invited her to swim. Afterward they had lunch together without waiting for Madam Mao, who was pissed off. To appease her, Mao wrote a poem for her picture."

"Yes, I heard about that," Long said, nodding over the dazzling white meat and the shining scarlet ovary of a female crab he had just broken open, "but I doubt it's reliable. Mao wouldn't have told others about the occasion. Nor would Madam Mao. It is quite possibly merely a guess by Wang, who may still bear a grudge against Mao. And it's understandable. After all, her husband was persecuted to death during the Cultural Revolution."

"True. But even so, and even though Madam Mao was a shallow bitch, Mao could also have written it as man to woman, in a moment of passion. There is need to insist on a political interpretation, right?"

"That's right, but what can I do for you, Chief Inspector Chen?"

"Help me understand the background of these poems, so we'll have a reliable interpretation. I'll acknowledge your help as a consultant for the project. And I'll put it in my foreword that my translation is based on your studies."

"You don't have to do that—"

"Furthermore, I'll pay you ten percent of the royalty, both here and abroad."

"That's way too much, Chief Inspector Chen. You have to tell me more specifically what you need."

"Let's continue on with that poem for Madam Mao. I've heard of another interpretation—an erotic one. In classical Chinese literature, a 'fairy cave' can be a metaphor for—well, what you know. The journey to the perilous peak is even more loaded with sexual suggestions. The fact that it was a poem between husband and wife lends itself to such an interpretation, though Madam Mao later used it for her own political gain."

"No, that's not the way to interpret a poem."

"But you can't miss some images. The sturdy and erect pine. And that against the dusk too. As if all those weren't enough, there is the image of flying clouds. You know what cloud and rain mean in classical Chinese literature. Finally there is the perilous peak at the end of poem. Mao wasn't young at the time. It might not have been so easy for him to reach the peak, you know what I mean."

"But that's almost absurd!"

"For a romantic poet, after a night of cloud and rain, in the fantastic view of the Lu Mountains—is it so hard to believe?"

"The poem was written in 1961. Mao and Madam Mao had separate room arrangements long before that. They didn't live together in the Central South Sea. Why, all of a sudden, should Mao have written such a poem for her?"

"Well, after an unexpected reunion or reconciliation up in the mountains. Mao knew better than to write about such a night in an explicit way—"

"It's in our poetic tradition to write about a painting or a picture—as a compliment or a comment. People shouldn't read too much into it. That's really all I can say, I think."

"That's fine, Long. Let's set this poem aside for the moment and take a look at another one. 'On the Photograph of a Militia Woman.' Not a difficult poem. Also in the poetic tradition of writing about a picture. During my school years, the poem was even made into a song."

"Yes, I can still sing it." Long rose, eager for a change in their discussion. "*Valiant and handsome, she shoulders a five-foot rifle, / in the parade grounds first lit by the sunlight. / A Chinese girl with an extraordinary aspiration, / she loves her military attire, not the extravagant fashion.*"

"You are singing it so well," Chen said, waving a crab leg meditatively like a conductor's wand.

"Mao said that the Chinese people, every one of them, should be soldiers. The picture embodied such a heroic spirit. The poem was a great inspiration to people in the sixties."

"But have you heard about the background of it—about the identity of the militia woman in the poem?"

"Well, some stories shouldn't be taken too seriously."

"From what I've heard, Long, Mao wrote the poem to please that militia woman."

"No, that's nothing but hearsay. Give me a poem—any poem you choose—and I could claim that it was written for someone and come up with a far-fetched story."

"But it was in an official newspaper—the identity of the militia woman, I mean."

"I'm sorry that I cannot help you," Long said with hesitation, visibly troubled, looking over his shoulder. "Oh, the crabs are getting cold. Let's steam more fresh ones."

"Good idea."

While Long was busy putting more crabs into the steamer, Chen sized up the situation. His approach had proved to be too abrupt. In spite of his offer of the crabs and the book project, Long remained unwilling to reveal details of Mao's private life to a cop.

So Chief Inspector Chen had no choice but to play his trump card. For the Mao Case, such means were justified.

When Long returned to the table with another platter of steaming hot crabs, Chen resumed speaking in a more serious tone, "Now, I have to tell you something from the Writers' Association."

"Oh yes, you're an executive member."

"People want to carry out reforms to the system of professional writers. Because of the government funding cuts, you know, some changes may be inevitable."

That change was barely relevant to Chen, who had his regular income from the police department, but for a number of professional writers like Long, it would be crucial. And it would be hard for them to find another job in the current, highly competitive market.

"What have you heard?"

"To be fair to the professional writer system," Chen said, unraveling the thread around a crab, "the change has its merits. We have to take into consideration the special circumstances of each writer. For some, with their bestsellers, they don't need any money from the association. But for some, whose work requires a lot of research, the 'professional writer pay' is still necessary, even more so in today's society. I made a point of it at the meeting."

"What did others say?"

"They made a point about publication. After all, people may say a lot about their own works, but there has to be a criterion. So it will come to vote in a special committee."

"And you're on the committee?"

"Yes, I am, but I think the odds are against me. Now," Chen paused to crack the crab claw with his fist, repeatedly, on the table, "with this new English translation, and with you being the Chinese advisor for the book, I can definitely say something on your behalf. And on mine, too."

"Yours?" Long cut in. "You're not even a professional writer, are you?"

"Some people have been saying that I'm interested only in Western modernism. That's untrue. I have translated a number of classical Chinese poems. And a collection of Mao's poetry may speak volumes for me."

That sounded like a convincing motive to Long, who nodded, having heard comments about Chen's controversial work.

"With your publication both here and abroad," Chen went on, "I don't think anyone could vote against you."

"Chief Inspector Chen, I appreciate your support, and I admire your passion for Mao's work," Long said, raising the cup slowly. "Your insistence on a reliable and objective translation speaks for your integrity."

Chen waited for Long to continue. What made the difference was the threat to his "professional writer" status. Without Chen's support, his case was hopeless.

A short silence ensued, broken only by the noise made by the crabs still crowding and crawling at the bottom of the plastic basin, blowing bubbles.

"Back to your questions, Chief Inspector Chen," Long resumed. "I've gathered some information that didn't come from proper research. It is more or less hearsay, you know. But as a responsible translator, you surely know how to select and judge."

"Of course I'll have to do that," Chen said, seeing this as a necessary step for Long to distance himself from the information. "I will take full responsibility for the translation."

"Now, about the identity of the militia woman, where did you read this?"

"In a Beijing newspaper. According to the article, Mao wrote the poem for a phone operator in the Central South Sea. She took a picture of herself in a militia woman's costume and showed the photograph to Mao. But how could that have happened? An ordinary phone operator wouldn't have been able to get close to Mao."

"Exactly," Long said, crunching a crab leg forcibly. "There are actually several different versions of the story behind the poem. It's no secret that Mao had a number of dancing partners. In addition to those ensemble girls, his partners also included those working for him, like the waitresses in the special train, the special nurses, and the phone operators. In one version, a special nurse instead of the phone operator showed the picture to Mao, who wrote the poem to show his appreciation."

"So what are some of the other versions?"

"Well, have you heard of a movie actress named Shang?"

"Yes, what about her?" Chen said, immediately alert.

"She, too, danced with Mao. The poem was said to be for the actress who played a militia woman in a movie. I saw the movie for that very reason and Shang won an award for her performance. But how reliable is the story about her being the inspiration? I don't know. Stories about Mao are often blown out of proportion. Anyway, there's no 'final word' about the identity of the militia woman."

"Can you go into more details here? About Shang, I mean."

"She's quite well-known, called 'the phoenix of the movie industry.' There's a Beijing opera called *Dragon Flirting with Phoenix*. Have you seen it?"

"Yes, it's about a Ming emperor's romantic affair with Sister Phoenix."

"In traditional Chinese culture, the dragon symbolizes the emperor, and the phoenix, its female partner."

"I see." Whether Mao believed in such an interpretation, consequently falling for Shang, Chen didn't know, but he understood the roundabout way in which Long responded to his inquiry.

"That also could be related to the poem for Madam Mao too," Long went on, finishing the cup in one gulp. "In another, more elaborate version, Madam Mao knew the origin of the militia-woman poem, so she asked Mao to write one for her picture as well—for balance of imperial favor, or like in the old saying, 'to share the favor of the divine rain and dew.' Mao came to Shanghai so many times . . . By the way, have you read the book *Cloud and Rain in Shanghai*?"

"Yes, I have."

"So you know the story. With the background research I've done, I'm more inclined toward the supposition that Shang was the militia woman in the poem."

"Why?"

"Mao actually copied poems for Shang. I interviewed a colleague of hers and, according to him, when he visited Shang's place before the outbreak of the Cultural Revolution, he saw a scroll in Mao's calligraphy in her bedroom."

"The 'Militia Woman'?"

"Not that one, but 'Ode to the Plum Blossom.'"

"Really!" Chen had never thought about that poem in connection with the investigation. He took out a copy of Mao's poems from his briefcase and turned to the ode.

After wind and rain seeing off the spring, / flying snow comes as a harbinger of the spring. / On the ice covered cliff, / the plum blossom still shines. / Pretty, she does not claim the spring for herself, / content to be a herald of spring. / When hills are ablaze with wildflowers , / in their midst she smiles.

"It was written in December 1961, after a poem by Lu You, a Song-dynasty poet," Long said. "It's also a poetic convention, you know, to write in response or correspondence to another poem. In both poems, the plum blossom symbolizes an unyielding spirit, but in each, from a different perspective."

"Yes, I think you're right." Chen turned a page and read Lu's poem as an appendix.

Outside the posthouse, beside the broken bridge / a lone plum blossom stands deserted, / against the worries of the solitary dusk, / against the wind and rain. / Not anxious to claim spring for herself, / she endures the envy of other flowers. / Her petals fallen, in dust, in mud, / in spite of a remaining fragrance.

"Like other poems, 'Ode to the Plum Blossom' was commonly read as one full of Mao's revolutionary spirits," Long said, stirring the sauce in the crab shell with a toothpick. "That interpretation is taken for granted. According to an article I read, someone who had worked with Mao wrote him a letter, quoting Lu's poem to express admiration, and Mao wrote his ode in response. But mind you, Lu's poem has nothing to do with admiration. If anything, it is full of complaint and self-pity. A patriotic poet, Lu wanted to serve his country by fighting against the Jin army, but he wasn't able to, serving instead as merely a petty official. Again, it's conventional in our traditional poetics to compare someone disappointed to a deserted beauty or neglected blossom, so the meaning of the poem is unmistakable."

"I think you are brilliantly perceptive here," Chen said, poking the meat out of a crab leg with a chopstick.

"So who could have sent that poem to Mao? A reasonable guess would be a woman with an unusual relationship with Mao. Only in that circumstance would such a gesture have made sense. She knew that Mao had other women, but she knew better than to complain to his face. So Mao's poem in response was one of approval of her stance. From his perspective, it's nothing but natural that an emperor should have three hundred and sixty imperial concubines. In spite of knowing about the other flowers competing for spring's attention, she should be content as one favored by him earlier, smiling in the midst of all the flowers over the mountains."

"Why did those official critics cover up the real occasion of the poem? I think the answer is self-evident," Chen said, hardly able to conceal the excitement in his voice. "Yes, Shang's perhaps the only one with enough education to quote a poem like that to Mao. Those working around him were mostly young, little-educated, working-class girls."

Long bent over the crab shell, draining the sauce in it in silence.

"Also, about that scroll of the poem in Mao's calligraphy," Chen said. "Did Shang's colleague tell you anything else? For instance, when Mao wrote a poem to someone else, he would usually add a short line as a dedication, and a red chop seal as an indication of its authenticity. Did her colleague see anything like that on the scroll?"

"No, he didn't see clearly—just a glimpse of it. It was in her bedroom, you know. But he was sure it wasn't a photocopy, which wasn't available at the time."

"If possible, I would like to meet with that colleague of Shang's. It could be crucial to establish the identity of the person Mao wrote the poem for. Of course, we don't have to get into explicit details in our book."

"I'm not sure if he's still in town. I contacted him several years ago, But I'll try."

"That would be fantastic. Let's toast to our collaboration—"

The door opened unexpectedly, however, before either of them heard the turning of the key in the lock.

Long's wife returned, a short woman with gray hair and black-rimmed glasses, who frowned at the sight of the litter on the table.

"Oh, this is Chief Inspector Chen of the Shanghai Police Bureau, also a leading member of the Shanghai Writers' Association." Long introduced him in a sudden stutter suggestive of a henpecked husband. "He brought a whole bamboo basket of crabs. I have kept some for you."

It was out of the question for them to continue talking about Mao in her presence.

"Oh, you shouldn't have drunk so much," she said to Long, pointing at the empty Shaoxing yellow rice wine bottle standing like an inverted exclamation mark on the table. "You are forgetting about your high blood pressure."

"Chief Inspector Chen and I are working together on a new translation of Mao's poetry to be published here as well as abroad. So I won't have to worry about my 'professional writer' status anymore."

"Really!" she said incredulously.

"This calls for a celebration. Oh, we will have crabs just like before."

"I'm sorry, Mrs. Long. I didn't know about his high blood pressure, but he is giving me so much help on this book project," Chen said, rising. "I have to leave now. Next time, I promise we will have nothing but crabs, not a single drop."

"It's not your fault, Chief Inspector Chen. I'm glad you have not forgotten him." She turned to her husband and said in a low voice, "Go and look at your face in the mirror. It's as red as Mao's *Little Red Book*."

"Look at the table," Long said a little blurredly, accompanying Chen to the door, "It looks like a battle field deserted by the nationalist troops in 1949. Remember the poem about the liberation of Nanjing?"

Looking back, Chen found the littered table looked somewhat like a deserted battlefield, with broken legs, crushed shells, scarlet and golden ovaries scattered here and there, but he failed to recall the image from that particular poem by Mao.

ELEVEN

DETECTIVE YU DECIDED TO interview Peng, Qian's second lover.

Yu didn't know the neighborhood officer in charge of Peng's area that well, so he had to approach Peng by himself, without telling anybody or revealing that he was a cop. It was a necessary move after an encounter Old Hunter had unexpectedly witnessed between Jiao and Peng—a suspicious meeting in a grocery store, where Jiao gave money to Peng.

What was going on between the two?

Peng's affair with Qian had lasted no more than half a year before he was thrown into jail. When released, he could hardly take care of himself, let alone Jiao. They didn't have any contact for all those years. She wasn't his daughter, or even a stepdaughter.

As Old Hunter considered himself more experienced at shadowing a person, he wanted to focus on Jiao. So it was up to Yu to tackle Peng.

Early in the morning, Yu arrived at the market where Peng worked as a pork porter but was told that he had been fired.

"A good-for-nothing guy, capable of soft-rice-eating only," an ex-coworker of Peng's said, hacking at a frozen pig head on a stump, spitting on the ground littered with rotten cabbage leaves. "You'll probably find him eating white rice at home."

It was a harsh comment, particularly the "soft-rice-eating," a phrase that usually referred to a parasitic man dependent on a woman. But, if in reference to Peng's affair with Qian, it was not true. It had happened many years ago, when Qian had little money. As in a saying Old Hunter would quote, it's easy to throw rocks at one already fallen to the bottom of a well. Yu thanked the ex-coworker, from whom he got Peng's home address.

Following the directions, Yu changed buses twice before he found himself at a shabby lane near Santou Road.

He saw a heavily built man squatting at the lane's entrance like a stone lion, half burying his face in a large bowl of noodles, holding a clove of garlic on the edge of the bowl. The noodle-eater wore a faded T-shirt, which was way too small on him, making him look like an overstuffed bag. Yu couldn't help taking another look at the man, who stared back at Yu, still gobbling loudly.

"So are you Mr. Peng?" Yu said, recognizing him from the picture. He offered the man a cigarette.

"I'm Peng, but without *Mr.* attached to my name for twenty years. *Mr.* gives me goose bumps," Peng said, taking the cigarette. "Oh, China. A smoke costs more than a bowl of noodles. What can I do for you, man?"

"Well," Yu said. He was going to play a role—just like his boss, who sometimes claimed to be a writer or a journalist when canvassing on a case. "I'm a journalist. I would like to talk with you. Let's find a place. A nearby restaurant, perhaps?"

"The restaurant across the street will do," Peng said, holding the noodles bowl in his hand. "You should have come five minutes earlier."

It was a mom-and-pop place, simple and shabby. At the moment, between breakfast and lunch, there were no customers inside.

The old proprietor looked curiously at the two, who made a sharp contrast. Peng, a down-and-out bum, and Yu, in a light-material blazer Peiqin had prepared for the occasion. She had even ironed it for him.

"You're familiar with the place, Peng. Go ahead and order."

Peng ordered four dishes and six bottles of beer, which came close to a banquet at this place. Luckily, nothing on the menu proved to be expensive. Peng shouted out his order loud enough that people outside the restaurant could have heard it too. Possibly it was a message to the neighborhood as well: that he was still somebody, with well-to-do people buying a big meal for him.

"Now," Peng gave a loud burp after swigging down the first cup of beer, "fire away."

"I just have a couple of questions about your experience during the Cultural Revolution."

"I know what you're driving at." Peng started gulping down the second cup. "About my damned affair with Qian, right? Let me tell you something, Mr. Journalist. I was only fifteen when I first met her. More than ten years older, she seduced me. If a white voluptuous body, like a bottle of iced beer in the summer, was put in front of you, for free, what would you do?"

"Drink it?" Yu responded sardonically, astonished by the callousness with which Peng spoke about Qian.

"In those years, a young boy like me didn't know anything. I was a substitute, there to satisfy her lust. She didn't care for me at all—only for my pathetic resemblance to her dead lover. And after I got out of prison, my best years and opportunities all gone, I couldn't find a decent job. A wreck with no skills or experience. No future."

Staring at this middle-aged man, sloppy and sluggish, swigging down beer as if there were no tomorrow, Yu wondered what Qian could have seen in him.

"Things have not been easy for you, Peng, but it's such a long time ago. You can never know what she really thought at the time, and she

111

paid a terrible price for her actions too. So please, go ahead and tell me the story from the beginning."

"You mean the story of me and Qian?"

"Yes, the whole story."

"Come on, I'm not that dumb, Mr. Journalist. The story is worth tons of money. You aren't going to buy it for a couple of beers."

"What do you mean?"

"Someone came to me long before you. A writer, at least he introduced himself as one." Peng put a large piece of pot-stewed beef into his mouth. "I was naïve enough to tell him everything, and he didn't even buy me a bottle of beer. Only a couple of cigarettes—Red Pagoda Mountains. Such a cheap brand. He wrote the book, sold millions of copies, and I got nothing."

"Have you read the book?"

"I'm just a rascal in the book, I've heard."

The writer, presumably the author of *Cloud and Rain in Shanghai*, might have portrayed Peng in a negative light in contrast to Qian, a romanticized and glamorized heroine.

"Listen, Peng, I don't really have to listen to your story. I can read the book. So how about a hundred yuan for a couple of questions?" Yu said, producing his wallet, imagining Chen's move under the circumstances. Chen, however, had funds available to him as a chief inspector, which Yu did not.

"Five hundred yuan." Peng helped himself to a large spoonful of the Guizhou hot fish soup, slurping, smacking his lips.

"Let me tell you something." Yu banged the table with the bottom of the beer bottle. "You were following Jiao, and taking money from her the other day. It was a tip from a cop friend of mine, and I stopped him from taking action against you. After all, you're a victim of the Cultural Revolution."

It was a long shot. Peng might have blackmailed her. But even if he hadn't, his history was such that it wouldn't be too difficult for the police to get him in trouble.

"Those damned cops. They came to me about a month ago, treating me like shit. Naturally, they got nothing," Peng said in a dramatic way, stretching out his arms, snatching the hundred-yuan bill from Yu. "Jiao's my step-daughter, isn't she? She has so much it's only fair for me to share a little bit of it."

"So Qian must have left something behind?"

"A treasure trove—that's a matter of course. What was her mother? A queen in the movie world. How many rich and powerful men had she slept with?"

"But the Red Guards must have ransacked her home and taken the valuables away."

"No, I don't think so. I've done some serious thinking—I'm not a brainless rice pot. At that time, the local Red Guards didn't rush to her house like with some other families. She could have hidden her riches away."

The idea of treasure must have been mind-boggling for Peng, given the little he made at those odd jobs. The scenario was possible, but would it have taken Internal Security, and Chief Inspector Chen too, to launch such an investigation?

"I called the writer," Peng went on. "He gave me no money, and no money to her either, he said. So she must have Shang's hoard."

"Jiao was as poor as you until about a year ago. If Shang had left something behind, Jiao would have sold it much earlier."

"Shang must have left something, I know."

"How?"

"You're a clever man," Peng said with a mysterious air, poking out the steamed carp's eye and rolling it on his tongue. "Shang danced with Mao, who came from the Forbidden City, with the treasury of the ancient dynasties at his disposal."

"That's just your imagination, Peng."

"No. I've done my research. Only recently has the antique market become so hot. Two or three years ago, there was no way to find a buyer for the stuff from the Forbidden City. Not at a good price anyway. This explains why she suddenly became rich about a year ago. Besides, I can tell you something that will prove it," Peng added, trying to pick up a soy-sauce-stewed pig tail with his chopsticks. "But you have asked your question, and I have given my answer."

"Really?" Yu produced his wallet again, in which there was about two hundred yuan left. "That's all I have here. One hundred more. And I have to pay for the meal. Tell me how you can prove it."

"You'll have your money's worth, Mr. Journalist," Peng said, pocketing the bill while taking another big draught of beer. "I've been shadowing Jiao for quite a while. As I suspected, she has been selling the antiques—piece by piece. No one could have afforded the whole set. So one day I followed her to the Joy Gate."

"Joy Gate?" It was a dance hall where Shang had once shone like the moon, as Peiqin had told him. Then he remembered another case with a sudden ache in his heart. Not too long ago, one of his colleagues had been murdered there while he was stationed outside. "That's nothing too suspicious, I think."

"But the way she went there was. She kept looking over her shoulder, like she was worried that she was being followed. Then she slipped into a hair salon and, instead of having her hair done, she left through the back door, putting on a pair of sunglasses before she emerged out of a side lane. I happened to be buying a pack of cigarettes nearby, so I didn't lose sight of her. To follow her into the Joy Gate, I spent all the money in my pocket for an entrance ticket. Sure enough, she was there, dancing with a tall, robust man who had a round face like a full moon."

"Do you mean that she's a 'dancing girl'?"

"No, I don't think so. Those dancing girls don't make a lot of money. And that was the only time I saw her go there. Most of the time, she goes to Xie Mansion. There are dancing parties there every week."

"So the man is someone she knows from Xie Mansion?"

"That I don't know. I will never be admitted there and I know better than to try. But that same evening, I think I saw him at her place."

"You tailed her from the dance hall back to her home?"

"No, not exactly. She danced only a couple of dances and then she left. I was curious, so I followed her out. She hailed a taxi and I squeezed into a bus. It took me much longer to get to her apartment complex.

There's no way I could get in, of course, so I walked around, hoping to confront her if she came out. Then looking up, I saw someone standing by the window of her room—the man from the dance hall. For a short moment, she was leaning against him, in a most intimate manner."

"When was this?"

"About a couple of months ago."

That was before Chen's investigation started, possibly before Internal Security's too, Yu reflected. Apparently, no one had been seen at her place since.

"Anything after that?"

"The light went out and I saw nothing more."

"That could have been a neighbor of hers."

"It was the man she had danced with, I'm positive. That round-moon-like face of his was unmistakable. I followed her for several more days, but without ever seeing him again. I wasn't able to watch her all the time. I had to work, carrying frozen pigs on my back at the food market. Then I was fired and yesterday I confronted her."

"What did you say to her?"

"When I told her that I'd seen the man in her room, all the blood went out of her face. She kept saying it was none of my business. I told her I'd been fired and that she could help me a little. So she took the money from her purse, about two hundred and fifty. She said she'd call the police if I ever tried to approach her again."

"Are you going to contact her again?"

"I haven't made up my mind yet, but there must be something going on between Jiao and the man. He must have given the money to her."

"Hold on, Peng. How did she get her money—from the man as a lover or as a buyer?"

"Perhaps both, but who cares? It's just like the old saying: If she weren't a thief, she wouldn't feel guilty or nervous. She wouldn't have given me the money for nothing."

"But that's blackmail. If she reported it to the police, you could get into big trouble."

"I'm a dead pig. What difference would it make throwing me into a cauldron of boiling water?" Peng said, crunching the last sweet and sour rib and wiping his fingers on the paper napkin. "What I did in those years is nothing today. Go to any high school, and you can see so many students billing and cooing on campus, behind the trees and in the bushes. But I went to jail for many years for that."

"Many people suffered in those years."

"I tried to start over but people avoided me like a piece of stinking meat. And after all these years, they are still telling their horrible stories about me and Qian. Do you think I really care about anything now?"

Peng was lost in self-pity, half drunk, his face red like a cockscomb. Yu didn't think he could get any more out of him, not with six bottles of beer empty on the table.

"You have suffered a lot, but don't try things like blackmail. It won't do you any good."

"Thank you, Mr. Journalist. I won't if I have any other choice."

"If you happen to think of anything else, you may contact me," Yu said, putting down his cell phone number on a scrap of paper.

"I will," Peng said, draining the last cup.

"Don't tell anybody about our talk. Some people may try to get you into trouble," Yu said, rising. "Take your time here."

"Don't worry about that. I'm going to finish the noodles too."

Walking out of the restaurant, Yu turned back to see Peng burying his face in that bowl of noodles again, the same scene he had witnessed earlier. Perhaps there was a reason Peng's coworker had commented on his rice-eating capability.

TWELVE

CHEN ARRIVED AT THE teahouse on Henshan Road, in the company of Old Hunter. The waitress recognized them, led them into the private room, and left them alone.

As soon as he seated himself at the table, Old Hunter started briefing Chen about what he had done and what Yu had found out from Peng. For once, he wasn't like a teasing Suzhou opera singer but instead talked fast, not digressing at all. Chen listened without interruption. Old Hunter then drained his cup and stood up. "I have to leave, Chief."

"Why such a hurry?" Chen said. "The second cup of tea is the best."

"I have to get back to the hot-water house opposite her apartment complex. An old security guard named Bei has a habit of fetching hot water in a stainless-steel cup and scurrying back to his cubicle around noon. I bet he buy a penny's worth of hot water to warm up his cold rice. The owner of the hot-water house will try to introduce me to him today."

"Be careful. Internal Security is watching."

"Don't worry. I'll be sitting there, it will be simply a chance meeting between two old customers at the hot-water house. Who'll bother? So you see, I'm going to have a second pot of tea in an hour. Bei's retired too. Two retirees may have plenty to talk about."

"Really, like in one of your favorite proverbs, a piece of older ginger is spicier indeed."

"Spicier indeed," the retired cop echoed with a wry smile. "But I'll tell you what! It's another Mao case, and my left eyelid has been twitching all morning. That may not be a good omen."

"Rub your left eye three times and say, 'It's a good omen,'" Chen said, smiling. "It works, according to my mother."

Chen rose to accompany the old man to the door of the teahouse, watching him until he was out of sight. Then Chen came back to the table, to the suddenly solitary teacup. The waitress must have removed the other one.

He was disturbed at the thought of Yu's involvement, though it might not be something that could be helped. For such a Mao case, Old Hunter alone could do only so much, and Detective Yu had to chip in, a reinforcement which was already making a difference. There was no stopping a loyal partner like Detective Yu from throwing in his lot with Chief Inspector Chen.

What Yu had discovered was a possibility not to be ignored, Chen contemplated, sipping at the tea without tasting it.

If Peng had seen the mysterious round-faced man only once and Internal Security hadn't seen him at all, either before or after, it practically excluded the possibility of his being a secret lover. More likely, he was a one-time buyer who negotiated with Jiao at Joy Gate. It would have been out of the question for her to bring the valuable antique to the dance hall. So they then chose to close the deal at her apartment. As for Peng's glimpse of the "intimate scene" at her window, it might not mean that much. After all, Peng might not be a reliable narrator.

Such a scenario threw light, however, on several aspects of the mystery: the source of Jiao's money and the timing of it too. In today's market, those antiques could be worth millions—so long as she could find a buyer. That also explained her frequent visits to Xie's place—potential buyers. Furthermore, selling the hoard piece by piece accounted for the fact that Jiao didn't have a large bank account but yet was capable of living in affluence.

At least it appeared to be more solid than the scenario about a book advance. A publisher could hardly have paid the money if they didn't get the Mao material, whatever it might be.

There was something that didn't add up, however, in the treasure scenario. True, Mao could have easily carried anything out of the Forbidden City. Kang Sheng, one of Mao's closest allies in the Party, smuggled out quite a lot from the palace. Since Kang was tied up with the Gang of Four during the Cultural Revolution, his stealing was exposed. But Mao didn't have to smuggle out artifacts. Mao was more than an emperor—he was a communist god. Women ran to him, not the other way round.

Such a scenario could be a scandal, but the Beijing authorities didn't have to acknowledge it. After all, nobody could prove it. So why would they have launched an investigation?

The solitary teacup on the table stared back at him.

Finally, as he was about to leave, his cell phone vibrated violently, as if rippling out of the half-empty cup.

"A girl's body was found in Xie's garden," Lieutenant Song said shortly.

"What?" Chen stood up. "When?"

"Early this morning. I called your home, but you weren't in. So I got your cell phone number from Party Secretary Li."

Chen thought he had given Song his number, but it wasn't the time to worry about that. He glanced at his watch. It was probably already two or three hours after Internal Security had arrived at the crime scene.

When Chen made it to the mansion, to his surprise, he didn't see any police outside.

Nor a curious crowd lingering on the street.

There was no one in the living room, either, as he stepped in.

At the end of the living room, however, he glimpsed a plainclothes cop stationed at the foot of the staircase. Xie must be in his bedroom upstairs.

Chen walked out into the garden. The body had been removed. Internal Security hadn't waited for him. There were two cops still checking around the area cordoned off with yellow plastic tape. It was close to the spot where Chen sat with Xie the other day, under the blossoming pear tree.

Song strode over, and Chen gestured for the lieutenant to follow him to the back of the garden. He didn't want others to overhear anything.

Song showed Chen pictures of the crime scene in silence. The girl was in a yellow summer dress, with the straps fallen off her shoulders, her skirt pulled high over her thighs, and one white sandal missing from a bare foot. She appeared to have suffered some sort of sexual attack. There wasn't much indication, however, of any struggle in the pictures—nor in the garden, as Chen shifted his gaze to the cordoned-off spot.

It was Yang, the girl who had tried to take Jiao and him to another party just a couple of days earlier. Like Jiao, she was also said to come from a "good family," though Chen had no idea what hers really was.

"Considering the circumstances, we have blocked the news for the time being," Song said. "She was killed in a struggle against a sexual attack."

Chen nodded, holding up a picture for close examination. "Any clues?"

"The identity of the deceased has been established. Yang Ning. One of Xie's students. The time of death is estimated to be between ten p.m. and midnight last night."

"But there was no class yesterday, as I remember."

"No class. No party in the evening either."

"Then how did she come to be here?"

"The question is," Song said deliberately, "how did she get *in* here?"

"What do you mean, Song?"

"She couldn't have flown into the garden like a butterfly. Someone must have opened the door to let her in. Who else was here at the time? Nobody but Xie."

"What did he say?"

"He didn't know anything, of course. What else would he say?"

Chen didn't have an immediate answer.

"Xie says he alone has the key," Song went on. "With the place frequently mentioned in the media, he makes a point of keeping the door locked all the time. People have to ring the bell and be let in. Yesterday evening he went to bed early."

"Well . . ." Chen knew what Song was driving at.

"We've put a man outside his room."

Could the body's appearing in the garden be a set up? It would serve as an excuse for "tough measures" by Internal Security, but Chen decided to put such a possibility aside for the moment.

"Tell me more about the discovery of the body, Song."

Song provided a rather scanty summary. Around seven, Xie took his usual morning walk in the garden, where he was shocked by the sight of the body, lying face down under the tree. He called the police. It took about twenty minutes for the first officers to arrive at the scene. And it wasn't until the cop turned over the body that Xie recognized it as Yang, a student in his painting class. He had no idea how she had come into the garden.

"Yang could have sneaked in by herself," Chen commented, "with a key she had obtained."

"Technically possible, but for what, Chief Inspector Chen?" Song countered. "To be attacked and killed by someone who had sneaked into the garden earlier?"

"She could have chosen the garden as a romantic place for her rendezvous. Quiet and secluded, especially when there's no party at the house. Xie usually goes to bed early, which she knew."

"Do you think that she would have gone to the trouble of obtaining a key for that purpose?"

"For some, it is a romantic place. These students come here not just for the painting class, you know," Chen said. "Did Xie have any visitors yesterday?"

"He hemmed and hawed, saying only that he fell asleep early."

That was a problem for Xie. No alibi. It might not be uncommon for a man of his age to go to bed early, but that wasn't good enough for Song, in spite of the fact that Xie himself had called the police.

"What are you going to do, Song?"

"We're going to conduct a thorough search of the house," Song said. "As for Xie, we'll take him into custody first."

So the Mao Case was back to ground zero: the "tough measure" that Internal Security had opted for—to break Xie, and then Jiao, for the sake of the Mao material.

"A body in his own garden, and no alibi—Xie whould have known better," Chen resumed. "No one would be that stupid. Besides, what could be his motive?"

"Xie's different. What's his motive for his classes and parties? You never know."

"He's different, but if we lock him in as the suspect, it could mean the real criminal will walk away."

"We have waited for your approach to work, patiently, for a week, but what? A young life was wasted. Had we acted earlier . . ."

Song was upset. So was Chen.

But for the case—the Mao Case—such a move could prove disastrous, even more so in the light of the latest information from Detective Yu. Chen was debating whether he should share it with Song when the latter's cell phone shrilled out. Presumably it was something new about Yang. Song listened, furrowing his forehead, while cupping the phone in his hand.

Chen made a vague sign to Song and headed back to the living room.

He was surprised at the sight of Jiao standing behind the French window, her eyes slightly squinting in the sunlight. She wore a white T-shirt and jeans with a leather label near the waistline. She could have seen them talking in the garden.

That morning, she was the only visitor there—apart from Chen.

"Oh you're here," he said.

"No one else will come today, I'm afraid," she responded. "How did you get in?"

"I didn't know anything, so I came over, as usual."

"You had a long talk with the cop out in the garden. It must have been about the death of Yang. Does he have any clues?"

"No. Nothing so far. According to Officer Song, she couldn't have gotten in by herself. Someone must have opened the door for her—that is, unless she had her own key."

"Her own key?" Jiao repeated, a frown creasing her brows. "No, I don't think so. Yang came only for the class."

"At her estimated time of death, Mr. Xie was alone in the house, but he knew nothing about it."

"Oh my god! So is Xie a suspect?"

"Well—" he said, struck by the concern on her face. "I'm no cop. It's not for me to say."

"But do you know the policeman? He showed you something."

"No. I've read a lot of mysteries so Officer Song thought he could discuss the case with me a little, and he showed me a picture. He asked me a considerable number of questions too."

"Xie couldn't have done anything like that."

"Does he have any enemies—or people who hate him?"

"I don't think he has any enemies—except some distant relatives of his, who also lay claim to the house. If he got into trouble, it might be their chance."

That made him think of another possibility—the real estate company with connections in both black and white ways—but he asked instead, "Do you think Yang could have sneaked into the garden?"

"No, not without a key. Xie always keeps the keys with him—on his key ring." She then added hesitantly, as if in afterthought, "About three months ago, Xie was sick. We helped him to the hospital, taking care of him there in turns. So Yang could have gotten hold of his key."

"That's a possibility, but it won't help much. Anybody could say that his key was stolen and duplicated."

"He didn't do it, that I know. You have to help him. You are so resourceful, Mr. Chen."

"I don't think he did it either, but cops think only of evidence or alibis—"

"Alibis?"

"An alibi proves," he said, looking her in the eyes, "someone was incapable of committing the crime because he was somewhere else, or with somebody else, at the time of the murder."

"Xie's incapable of telling a lie!" she exclaimed.

"But you have to prove it."

"Oh—what's the exact time the murder took place?"

"Her time of death was estimated as roughly the period from ten o'clock to midnight, according to Officer Song."

"Alibi—let me think—now I remember, I do remember," she said. "He was with me at the time. I was posing for him in this room."

"What! You were posing for him then? Then why didn't he say so?"

"I posed for him—yes—nude," she said with an inexplicable glimmer in her eyes. "He couldn't afford professional models, so I did it for free. He didn't tell people about it because he was concerned about my reputation. That's why."

That was a stunning revelation. Chen had heard stories about Xie's students posing in the studio, but even if that might not be uncommon for a painting class, he had to wonder: was she posing for "romantic" reasons? Chen suspected that, what with the mansion, the collection, the painting, and the parties, not to mention what Xie had gone through during the Cultural Revolution, the older man had no money or energy left to do more than pose as a Baoyu or Don Juan, but one never knew.

Still, Jiao's statement made some sense. Even in the nineties, in Shanghai, a nude model was seen as someone shameless. Jiao wasn't even professional, and stories about it could easily lead to speculation.

Jiao was already running toward the staircase, raising her arms, calling out loud upstairs:

"Xie, you should have told the cops that I was posing for you here last night."

It was a dramatic development. The officer stationed at the foot of the staircase looked flabbergasted. Chen wondered whether she was shouting for Xie's benefit upstairs.

But Xie could have told Song about his painting session with her; he didn't have to say that she was posing nude. There was no need for him to be that overprotective—at such a cost to himself.

If what she said wasn't true, however, why did she take the risk of making up an alibi for him? That confirmed, if anything, his earlier impression that there might be something between Jiao and Xie.

Chen was lighting a cigarette for himself when Song hurried back into the living room.

"What, Chen?"

"Jiao was with Xie last night."

Song stared at Chen, who said nothing else. It was a surprise move by Jiao, for which Chen didn't hold himself responsible, though it served his purpose.

He decided to leave. There was no point staying with Song, who appeared increasingly infuriated with the unexpected development. With Xie and Jiao providing alibis for each other, it would be out of the question for Internal Security to revert to their original plan.

Besides, Chief Inspector Chen was going to make a phone call to Beijing, like a capable and conscientious cop, as the minister had commended.

THIRTEEN

AGAIN, CHEN WAS LOST in a recurring dream scene—of an ancient gray gargoyle murmuring in the twilight-covered Forbidden City, in the midst of black bats flapping around the somber grottos—when he was awakened.

For several seconds, he lay with his face burrowed in the white pillow, trying to tell whether it could possibly be the sound of water dripping in the palace. It was the phone shrilling through the first gray of the morning. Picking it up, he heard Yong's voice coming from Beijing.

"She has come back. You know what? He has a little secretary, that heartless bastard. She just found out. So she's staying with her parents for now." Yong's voice was crisp and clear, not at all like the blurred murmuring in the dream. He listened, rubbing his eyes, still disoriented.

"What?" he said. "Who has a little secretary?"

"Who else? The damned bastard she married."

"Oh." He reached for a cigarette when the anger in Yong's voice finally dawned on him. He propped himself up on an elbow.

"Now don't keep saying *oh*. Say something else. Do something, Chen."

But what could he do?

It wasn't for the police to catch somebody's "little secretary," which had become part of the "socialism with Chinese characteristics." An upstart invariably had a little secretary—his young mistress—as a symbol of his wealth and success. In some cases, even a "little concubine" as well. For Ling's husband, a businessman and official of an HCC family background, it would actually be surprising for him not to have one.

"Things might not be beyond hope between you two. Come to Beijing, Chen. She isn't happy. You and Ling should talk. I have a lot of suggestions for you."

"I'm in the middle of an investigation, Yong," he said, his mouth inexplicably dry. "An important investigation."

"You've always been busy—thinking of nothing but your police work. That's really your problem, Chen. She told me she thought of you even on her honeymoon. You may be an exceptional cop, but I'm so disappointed in you."

Yong hung up in frustration—an echo of his neighbor's door slamming shut across the corridor.

Chen dug out the ashtray full of cigarette butts and burnt matches from the last couple of days. What he had told Yong was true. This was a Mao Case, he couldn't explain even to her.

It wasn't the time for a trip to Beijing, even for all the suggestions Yong would offer him Ling's honeymoon was barely over—whatever problem she might have at the moment, it wasn't up to him to interfere.

He finished his cigarette before getting up. Still groggy from the shattered dream, he went to the sink and brushed his teeth vigorously, the image of the gray gargoyle fading, yet a bitter taste lingering in the mouth.

There wasn't much left in the small refrigerator. A leftover box of roast duck from about a week earlier and half a leftover box of barbeque pork from god-knows-when—both from meals with business associates—and a bowl of cold rice as hard as a rock. He was in no mood to have his breakfast out. In the last two weeks, he had already spent his monthly salary and had to dig into his savings again. He could have some of the recent expense reimbursed in the name of his special assignment, but he wasn't sure how the Mao Case would end up, and he didn't want to submit a staggering bill for nothing. He decided to make himself a chop suey with all the leftovers boiled in a pot of hot water, along with the remaining scallion and ginger and dried pepper from the refrigerator. On an impulse, he took out the small bottle of fermented tofu and threw in the last piece along with the multicolored liquid.

As the pot was boiling on the gas head, Song called.

"I've talked to Gao Dongdi, a lawyer for whom Yang had once worked, as well as some other people close to Yang . . ."

To be fair, Chen admitted to himself that Song, though pushing for the "tough measure," had lost no time checking into other aspects of the murder.

Chen listened, lighting another cigarette. If Xie was not the criminal, there was a murderer at large, responsible for Yang's death and for planting her body in the garden. It might not necessarily be part of the Mao Case, but it was nonetheless a case for him.

"People go to Xie Mansion for their own reasons," Song went on. "Some may go for a sense of elite social status, but others, for something real or practical. For instance, in the case of Yang, who had something of her own business network, it was for connections. She was also in the business of making herself irresistible to Big Bucks, and possibly she had something more substantial in mind—the mansion itself. Xie is in his sixties. Divorced. No heir."

"So that's a possible motive for murder—" Chen said, "at least for those young rivals who're close to Xie."

"But in that scenario," Song said, contradicting himself, "Yang's body would have appeared anywhere but in Xie's garden."

Besides, Yang hadn't been close to Xie, as Chen had noticed. She wasn't a likely threat to a rival.

As for someone really close to Xie, it would have to be Jiao. Her consideration for Xie had gone further than Chen had expected, not to mention the alibi she had provided for him. Still, Chen couldn't bring himself to conceive of Jiao as a materialistic girl with such a motive. It didn't fit what he knew of her.

But for once, Song and Chen seemed to be converging on the same point the possible relation between Xie and Jiao.

After finishing the phone conversation, Chen lost himself in thought for several minutes before he found the chop suey badly burnt on the gas head. He moved to stand by the window, lighting a third cigarette that morning, staring out at the new high-rises that had been popping up around the city like bamboo shoots after a spring rain. His left eyelid started twitching. An ominous sign, according to the folk superstition Old Hunter believed in. Chen frowned, trying to find a strong tea that might suit his mood.

Searching the drawer again, he saw only a tiny bottle of gin. Possibly a souvenir from an airplane trip. How it could show up this morning, like the gargoyle in the dream, he was confounded. The bottle was tiny, smaller than the "small firecracker" he had seen in Gang's hand the day when he first got the assignment.

A plan for the morning came to mind, abruptly.

He was going to the eatery near his mother's place. Gang had said that he would be sitting there, from morning until evening. It was a long shot, but Chen wanted to give it a try. A breakfast there wouldn't be expensive at all. And he might drop in at his mother's place for a short visit afterward.

At the eatery entrance, Auntie Yao was selling warm rice balls stuffed with fresh fried dough stick to the customers that stood waiting in line, yawning or eye-rubbing. She appeared astonished at Chen's arrival that morning, looking over her shoulder while wrapping the sticky balls in her hands. Chen saw Gang sitting at a table inside by himself.

"Oh, Little Chen. You're quite early today," Gang said.

"This morning I found this bottle of gin by chance, so I thought of you."

"When you hear the battle drums and gongs, you think of a general. You are something of a gentleman from ancient times."

Gang had only a cup of cold water on the wine-stained table. No rice ball or fried dough stick. No liquor, either. He was sitting there perhaps because it was like a home to him.

"It's too early for me," Gang said, taking the tiny bottle.

"Two bowls of spicy beef noodles, Auntie Yao," Chen gave his order.

"The foreign stuff may be too much for breakfast." Gang studied the bottle of gin closely, turning it over in his hand.

"You're right." Chen said loudly to Auntie Yao again, "And a bottle of Shaoxing rice wine too."

"You have not come here for noodles, I believe," Gang said, a sharp light flashing in his eyes. "Let me know if there's anything I can do for you."

"All right, let's get to the heart of the matter, Gang. You were a Red Guard leader at the beginning of the Cultural Revolution. I have some questions about the campaign of Sweeping Away the Four Olds. I was young then, you know. There was a lot I didn't understand. So you may start by giving me a general background introduction on the campaign."

"Well, Mao wanted to snatch back power from his rivals in the Party, so he mobilized young students into Red Guards as a grassroot force fighting for him. As the first campaign of the Cultural Revolution, Red Guards were called on to sweep away the Four Olds—old ideas, old culture, old customs, and old habits. So the class enemies like capitalists, landlords, well-known artists and intellectuals, all of them became easy targets. They suffered mass criticisms, and their homes were searched for 'old stuffs,' which were either smashed or swept away."

"Yes, my father's books were all burned. And my mother's necklace was snatched off her neck."

"I'm sorry to hear about your family's suffering. Mao declared 'Sweeping Away the Four Olds' to be revolutionary activities, and the

Red Guards believed in whatever he said. We beat people, but later we ourselves were beaten too." Gang bent to pull up the bottom of his pants. "Look, I was beaten into a cripple. Karma."

"It was the Cultural Revolution, and you paid a price for it too. You don't have to be too hard on yourself, Gang. But there were so many black class enemies at the time, and so many Red Guard organizations, how was the campaign conducted?"

"For each factory or school or work unit, there was a Red Guard organization or something like it, but there were also larger organizations, like mine, which consisted of Red Guards from various schools. A Sweeping Away action against a particular family usually didn't take a large organization like ours to carry out. For instance, your father was a professor, so it should have been the Red Guard organizations of the university that raided and ransacked your house."

With the arrival of the noodles and the rice wine, Gang stopped talking. Auntie Yao had the beef slices placed in a separate small dish instead of atop the noodles. She also gave them a dish of boiled peanuts for free.

"The across-bridge noodles," Gang said excitedly, opening the rice wine bottle by knocking it against the table corner, raising his chopsticks for an invitation gesture as if he were the host. "So we can have the beef for wine. Auntie Yao is really considerate."

"But some special teams were also sent over from Beijing, I've heard, from the Cultural Revolution Group of the Central Party Committee."

"Why are you interested in that?" Gang said, looking up.

"I'm a writer," Chen said, producing a business card provided by the Writers' Association. "I'm going to write a book about those years."

"Well, that's something worth doing, Little Chen. Young people nowadays have no idea about the Cultural Revolution, or if anything at all, only about Red Guards being evil monsters. There should be some objective, realistic books about those years," Gang said, putting down his chopsticks again. "Back to your question. Who headed the Cultural Revolution Group of CCPC in Beijing then? Madam Mao. Who's behind her? Mao. When those teams were sent to Shanghai, they were very powerful, capable of doing anything—beating, torturing, and killing people without reporting to the police bureau or worrying about consequences. In short, they were like the emperor's special envoy brandishing the imperial sword."

"But did they contact your organization? After all, they were like dragons from somewhere far away, and you were the biggest local snakes."

"It was usually a small team with a secret mission. Occasionally, they could require our cooperation. For instance, if they wanted to crack down on someone, we would provide all the help, and if need be, keep other organizations away from the target."

"Do you remember Shang?"

"Shang—just that she was an actress. That's all I remember."

"A special team came for her during the campaign of Sweeping Away the Four Olds. She committed suicide."

"So that's what you want to find out." Gang drained his cup in one gulp. "You can't find a better one to help you, Little Chen. I happened to have learned something about those special teams. Some actors knew about Madam Mao in the thirties—about her notorious private life as a third-rate actress. That's why she wanted to silence those people, persecuting them to death and destroying any incriminating evidence—like old newspapers or old pictures—old stuff, no question about that. What Madam Mao did during the campaign was mentioned as part of her crimes at the trial of the Gang of Four."

"That's a possibility." Though not much of a possibility in Shang's case, Chen reflected, raising the cup to his lips without tasting it. Shang was much younger, incapable of possessing information or material about Madam Mao's years as an actress.

"But I'm not sure about Shang. It's not a name I remember about those days," Gang went on, pouring himself another cup. "Perhaps I was too busy. But I can try to contact my then assistant about it. I haven't seen him in years."

"It would be great if he could remember something."

"You treat me like a man of the state, and as such, I should naturally do something in return."

"I really appreciate it," Chen said, adding his cell phone number to the business card. "Don't call the office number. I'm not usually there."

"Oh, you're a city representative too." Gang examined the business card closely. "The other day when you condescended to sit with me, I knew you were different. You're somebody, Little Chen. Now, you're always welcome to drop in here, but you don't have to drink with me. Otherwise Auntie Yao would kill me."

"What are you two talking about?" Auntie Yao said, moving over to the table on full alert.

"About what a gold-hearted woman you are, having tolerated a good-for-nothing drunkard like me for so many years."

"Anything else?" she said to Chen without responding to Gang.

"No, I'm leaving. Thank you," he said rising. "Don't worry, Auntie Yao. Gang told me not to drink with him. I'll have nothing but noodles next time."

FOURTEEN

IT WAS A WARM and bright morning outside the eatery. Glancing at his watch, Chen changed his mind about the visit to his mother. Next time, he told himself. After the Mao Case, perhaps. He should have asked Auntie Yao to deliver some food to her. It was quite close, Chen thought belatedly, hurrying to the subway station at the intersection of He'nan and Nanjin Roads.

Squeezing into the train, he failed to find a seat. He had a hard time even trying to stand firm without being elbowed around. During rush hour in the city, taxis crawled like ants, while the subway was at least guaranteed to move. He thought of Gang again, a disabled man who would never be able to get in a train like this one. In his college years, the ex-Red Guard must have studied the classics, the way he filled his conversation with quotes. People should be responsible for their own actions, but Gang had been so young and hot-blooded then, choosing to follow Mao. And a high price Gang had paid for it.

It was getting hotter in the train. Chen wiped the sweat from his forehead and neck. The train increased its speed with a sudden lurch, and he staggered, stepping on the foot of a young girl, who was seated reading a morning newspaper. He murmured his apology. She smiled and went on beating her sandaled feet on the train floor. Wearing a yellow summer dress like a butterfly, she reminded Chen of Yang.

Tapping Gang could be a hopeless long shot, but the chief inspector couldn't leave any stone unturned. He had a heavy heart, holding himself responsible for two cases, rather than one—the two possibly interrelated, though the connection was still beyond his grasp.

Half an hour later, he arrived at Xie Mansion, his shirt sweat-soaked. He felt obliged to comb his damp hair with his fingers before pressing the bell.

As a result of the murder case, the weekend party and class were cancelled. People didn't believe Xie was involved, but no one wanted to be there when the cops were dropping in and out, asking questions and occasionally requesting statements.

Jiao walked out to open the door for him.

"Oh welcome, Chen. You are the only visitor today. Mr. Xie doesn't feel well this morning. After the shock, you know. But he'll come down shortly."

She was wearing a pink and white mandarin dress, sleeveless and almost backless. A fashionable variation of the elegant high-class dress, but with a white apron tied over it, her feet in pink satin slippers.

"I am too early," he said, wondering what she was doing there, with no class or party scheduled that day.

"Don't worry about that." Aware of his curious glance at her apron, she added, "I've come to help a little."

"That is so considerate of you."

"I'm no cook, but he doesn't know anything about the kitchen. Please be seated," she said, producing a cut-glass bowl containing assorted dried fruit. "What would you like to drink?"

"Coffee."

"Good. I've just made a fresh pot for myself."

She behaved as though she were the hostess there. After serving him a mug of coffee, she glided back to the sofa close to the French window. There was a cup of coffee beside an antique typewriter on a mahogany corner table. She must have been sitting there, by herself.

There was a small sketch against the wall. It could be hers, just finished. He didn't start speaking at once. He sat quietly sipping at his coffee, seemingly at ease.

Looking at him, she might be wondering at the purpose for his visit. The high slits of the mandarin dress revealed her shapely legs.

"I'm concerned about Mr. Xie," he said. "I know a couple of good attorneys. If necessary, I could contact them for him."

"Thank you, Chen. Song didn't bring too much pressure to bear on Mr. Xie, not after he provided his alibi. Song asked me some questions too, but not too many. We've already talked to an attorney Mr. Xie has known for years—just to be on the safe side."

"Yes, it is better to be on the safe side," he said. "By the way, did you know Yang well?"

"No, not that well. She was a fashionable girl, flitting around like a butterfly. She seemed to know a lot of people."

"I see," he said, taking "a butterfly" to be a negative metaphor. "She attempted to drag you to another party the other day, I remember."

"You're very observant, Mr. Chen."

"I couldn't help noticing you," he said, smiling. "You're so different, like an immaculate crane standing out among the chickens."

Now it sounded like flirting with an attractive girl—the "approach" Minister Huang had implied. He didn't push, though, and took another sip of the coffee, which tasted strong and bitter. Nor did she respond, sitting there demurely, her eyes downcast.

The short spell of silence was punctured by the ringing of a cell phone in her dainty purse.

"Excuse me," she said, jumping up and hastening out through the French window, leaving her slippers behind. The phone against her cheek, she stood framed against the window as if in an oil painting, merging into the verdant background. In her pink and white mandarin dress, she looked like a plum blossom, which vaguely reminded him of a poem. Slightly pensive in the morning light, she seemed to be nodding to that invisible speaker on the phone. She raised her right foot up backward against the window frame, scratching at her ankle, her red-painted toes shining like petals.

Years earlier, Mao could easily have been fascinated by someone like her . . .

Chen stood up, walked over to the antique typewriter on the corner table. *Underwood*. There was no paper in it. He struck two or three keys at random, all of which were rusted, stuck together. Worthless junk somewhere else, yet a valuable decoration here.

"Sorry about the phone call, Mr. Chen," she said, sliding back into the room. "By the way, you have a maid at home, don't you?"

"A maid?" He wondered why she was asking him about a maid. And it came out more like a statement than a question. Perhaps it was something taken for granted given his assumed identity. He responded vaguely. "You must have one too."

"I used to, but she quit abruptly, without explanation or notice. Now things are a mess here and I have to come over to help. I need someone at home."

He didn't have a maid at home. There was no need for one. His mother had talked about the necessity of having someone to take care of things for him, but he knew what she was driving at. It meant anything but a maid.

Was Jiao really in need of a maid? Only a year ago, she was working as a receptionist, a position that paid little more than a maid. She was young, living alone, probably not much housework in her apartment.

But it presented an opportunity he couldn't afford to miss. She hadn't invited him to her home. Nor was that a possibility in the near future. Having a maid there, keeping her eyes open for him, could make the difference.

"Yes, you definitely need one."

"Those people recommended by agencies are not dependable. It takes weeks to find a good one."

"Mine is quite reliable," Chen said, improvising. "I trust her. She has been working in her field for years. She must know some good people."

"That would be fantastic. Could you find one for me? I trust you."

"I'll talk to her about it today."

She appeared genuinely relieved. Picking up her coffee cup, she shifted her position on the sofa, resting her feet on the sofa arm. It was a pose not becoming for one in a mandarin dress, but she wasn't exactly a lady like Shang. Actually, she struck him as uniquely lively, sitting like that, with a blade of grass from the garden stuck on her sole, a tiny detail that actually made her real, close—not an insubstantial echo from the faraway legend of Mao and Shang.

After what help he had offered, first with the real estate company and then with the Yang murder case, though indirectly, both Xie and Jiao had become quite friendly to him. The candlelight dinner with Jiao might have made a subtle difference too. There was something in the way she spoke to him. At least she had come to trust him, as she had just said. He wished that he could prove to be truly trustworthy.

She got up again, aware of the wistful expression on his face. "I'll take a look upstairs and tell him you're here. You may have something to say to him."

"No, don't worry about it. I have to leave now," he said, rising too, "for a lunch appointment."

He was going to find a maid for her. That could be a move crucial to the investigation. The maid had to be someone he himself was able to trust, making it out of the question to approach the bureau for help.

Hardly had he stepped out, however, when he realized that he didn't have her phone number. So he turned back in haste.

Jiao was speaking on her cell phone again. She said something hurriedly at the sight of him.

"Oh, I forgot to ask for your phone number, Jiao."

"Sorry, I forgot about that too," she said, covering the phone with her palm. "I have yours. I'll call you in a few minutes, so you'll have mine too."

Leaving again, closing the door after him, Chen decided to walk for a while. In the late summer morning, he heard cicadas screeching, sporadically, in the green foliage of French poplars that lined along the street. The area had belonged to the French Concession in the early years of the century.

He took out his phone and started dialing White Cloud, but he halted after pressing only the first three numbers. It wasn't only too much of a risk for her. She was too young and too fashionable. No matter how she tried, she wouldn't pass as a maid. After a minute's hesitation, he dialed Old Hunter, explaining the situation.

"So I need to find a maid for Jiao. A reliable one. Not really for her, but for us. Someone who can work inside while you patrol outside."

"I'll talk to my old wife about it. She knows quite a lot of people," Old Hunter said. "I'll call you back as soon I have any news."

Putting the phone back into his pants pocket, Chen looked ahead to see a stinking tofu peddler bending over a portable stove and wok on a shaded side street. Chen realized he must have smelled it first, the familiar tang strong in a breeze. A typical Shanghai snack with a special pungent flavor, which he liked—an unlikely moment for temptation, which he tried to resist.

Still, he found himself turning down the side street, at the end of which he could take a shortcut to the subway station. He had walked this route before. It was also quieter here, better for his thinking.

If there was anything interesting to the visit this morning, it was the extraordinary concern Jiao had, once again, exhibited for Xie. It was perhaps more than what was usual between a student and his teacher, but he couldn't identify the ulterior motive that Song—and Chen himself—had suspected.

He passed by a wrought-iron gate across the entrance to a lane. In front of it squatted a man wearing a black Chinese-styled short-sleeved shirt, smoking, who looked up at the passing Chen from under a white canvas hat pulled low, shading most of his face. It was not an uncommon sight in the city, with so many people laid off in the recent years. The smell of the stinking tofu floated nearer, more pleasantly pungent . . .

But then Chen became aware of footsteps hurrying up from behind. Glancing over his shoulder, he glimpsed the white-hatted man rushing over to him, wielding an iron bar in one hand, cursing between clenched teeth, "You busybody bastard!"

Chen hadn't been trained at the police academy, but his reflexes were sharp. He ducked his head to the side and swirled around. The assailant, having put the weight of his body behind his blow, missed, lurched forward. The two were now in a typical kongfu hand-push position. Chen swung his arm over, bearing it down hard on the back of the attacker, who staggered, his blue-dragon-tattooed forearm flailing out for support. Before Chen could deliver a second blow, however, he caught sight of another black-attired man dashing across from Shaoxing Road, brandishing an identical iron bar. The two gangsters could have been sitting in ambush, waiting for him at the intersection.

"You must have taken me for another, brothers," Chen said, trying to think of Triad jargon as the first gangster was regaining his balance. "The flood is surging into the Dragon King Temple."

"Who are your brothers? An ugly toad let its mouth water at a beautiful swan! You should pee and take a look at your own reflection," the second man said, charging toward him in a lightning-fast movement.

Dodging, Chen counterattacked with his right fist. He felt the iron bar brushing against his left shoulder. Reeling, Chen fell backward, his head bumping against the umber brick wall of a two-story house at the street corner. But he managed to kick out simultaneously, his feet hitting the abdomen of the second thug, who then doubled over in pain. Chen moved a step to the left, blocking instinctively with his numbed left arm another blow from the first one. Panting, swaying, he sized up the situation with a sinking heart. He could cope with one, but against two, both wielding iron bars, he had no chance.

His only way out would be to cut back to Ruijing Road. With more people moving around and a cop standing there—possibly a plainclothes Internal Security as well—the gangsters might not be able to chase him all the way, especially if he raised hue and cry in the broad daylight.

Pivoting, he hurtled back toward the main street, with the two gangsters running after him.

Neither a cop nor an Internal Security man was in sight as he sprinted onto Ruijing Road.

Only a couple of pedestrians were visible in the intersection, neither of them choosing to do anything, watching like the spellbound audience at an absurd scene in a martial arts movie.

The door of Xie Mansion was closed, as usual. It was then that his glance swept across the street, to the small café he had visited. On the front door flashed a neon sign saying "open." And there was a back door behind the partition wall, he recalled.

He spun round and dashed across the street, nearly colliding with a bike. A couple was emerging from the café, chatting and holding hands. He ran through them, sending the woman sprawling against the window and the man flinging his arm in rage. Bursting into the café, to the consternation of both the customers and waitress, he closed the door and locked it behind him, before slipping out through the back door and darting into a small lane.

It was only a matter of a minute or less before the gangsters started to bang on the front door, but it was enough time for him to escape the lane without the two barking at his heels. Turning onto Shaoxing Road, he thought he heard terrible shouts and crashes somewhere in the lane.

A taxi sped along. Waving his hand frantically, Chen rushed toward it and hurried in, gasping for breath.

"Drive."

"Where?"

"Anywhere. Drive."

It wasn't until after the taxi swung into Fuxing Road that Chen was capable of reconstructing the encounter in clear sequence.

Ambush. No question about it. The gangsters could have been

following him for days. A couple of times, he had walked along Shao-xing Road and turned down the side street as a shortcut to the subway station. The attackers had stationed themselves at the intersection, waiting for him whichever way Chen might have turned.

Judging by their clothing, the iron bars, the tattoo on one's arm, and their jargon, the two were undoubtedly Triad members. They didn't try to disguise it.

But he couldn't remember having ruffled the feathers of any particular organization. Of late, there had been a special squad formed at the bureau for the purpose of coping with organized crime in the city. His Special Case Squad's main responsibility was dealing with politically special or sensitive cases. Thanks to his connection to Triad-related people like Gu, Chen had been able to keep himself out of troubled water.

There was no ruling out the possibility of mistaken identity, but he couldn't count on it.

And as for an ambush, what would be the purpose? In the Triad tradition, as far as he was able to figure out, an ambush was either a warning or a punishment. The iron bars, characteristic of the Triad culture, could have been intended for a nonfatal beating, as in a Triad movie he had seen, in which the victim writhed on the ground, beaten and crushed, while the gangsters hissed out the message: "If you don't mend your ways, it will be worse next time."

What the thugs said to him, however, pointed to different possibilities.

"Busybody" probably referred to his getting involved in something the Triad thought he shouldn't have. Chen had no idea what it was. After all, a lot of things the chief inspector had done could have been interpreted that way.

As for the "toad and swan" metaphor, it had originally been about a man going after an unapproachable woman—usually an ugly man or one in inferior position going after a beautiful woman or one in a superior position. So it could have come as a warning to him about an impossible relationship.

There was no woman in Chen's life, not at the moment. Ironically, Ling could have qualified as a "swan" with her HCC family background, but she had just married somebody else.

As for White Cloud, a young pretty college student who had once worked as his "little secretary," there had never been anything serious between them—at least not on the part of Chen. It made some sense, however, if a jealous lover saw Chen as an insurmountable obstacle. It was a remote possibility, but Chen thought he should talk to Gu about it.

Alternatively, the warning could have come from his mixing with the girls at Xie's place. Most of them had wealthy and powerful men behind them, and one of those men could have become insanely jealous. But he was a newcomer to the circle, a bookish if not clownish would-be writer who hadn't made advances on any of them, not even Jiao. In the mansion, most people could be a little flirtatious with one another, dancing and drinking under the somber light, in the lambent music. No one took it seriously—

"So where are you going, sir?" the driver asked again.

"Oh, Fuxing Road," Chen said, his shoulder hurting terribly. He'd better see a doctor. Dr. Xia, having retired from the bureau, was working at a private clinic on Fuxing Road.

"Then we have to make a detour."

"Why?" he asked absentmindedly.

"New construction. An expensive apartment complex is going up along Tiantong Road."

Another possibility flashed across his mind. The real estate company with connections in the black and white ways. He might have been seen as a busybody by them. Those companies had long ears and arms, could have learned of him from their contacts in the city government. But what about the "toad and swan" metaphor? That seemed totally unrelated.

At last, the taxi pulled up in front of the clinic. It was a new white building. Through the door, Chen saw a velvet tapestry bearing Mao's quotation in bold characters: *To serve the people.*

He was taking out his money to pay the taxi driver when another idea struck him. Could it have been an attempt to stop him from looking further into the case? In that scenario, possibly on the order from another section. Or from Internal Security, who had their own reasons to be furious at him. Or even from the Forbidden City. He was actually conducting the investigation as a Mao case, at least partially, a move that could affect the legitimacy of the Party. But it was a move known only to Old Hunter and Detective Yu, known only partially—

"Oh, your receipt," the taxi driver said with evident concern in his voice. "Are you all right, sir?"

"I'm fine," he said, taking the receipt, which showed a large amount. The taxi driver must have been driving him around for quite a while before asking him for his destination.

He moved out of the car groggily, his head aching like the Monkey in *Journey to the West*, wearing a cursed hoop around his forehead.

FIFTEEN

TWO HOURS LATER, DR. XIA was writing out a prescription in his office, his silver brows knitted in a frown, after having taken both a CT scan and X-rays of Chen.

Dr. Xia had been on the forensic staff of the police bureau. After retirement, he started working part-time as an "expert" at a clinic close to his home. He and Chen had known each other well in the bureau.

"Really touch and go," Dr. Xia said seriously, examining the X-rays one more time. "Your shoulder injury isn't too bad. No bone was broken. But I'm worried about the impact on your head. You have to rest for a week. Keep away from work and take good care of yourself. Don't forget your breakdown not too long ago."

"You know the work at the bureau—"

His cell phone rang before he could finish the sentence. It was Gang. Chen had to speak under the glare of Dr. Xia.

"I have already contacted Feng, my assistant during the Cultural Revolution. A Big Buck now, he still calls me Commander in Chief."

"That's good," Chen said. "Did he recall anything about the special team from Beijing?"

"They came to get something Shang might have had, but were unsuccessful. She committed suicide."

"Did Feng know what they were looking for?"

"No, he didn't. The special team probably didn't either, but they wanted to prevent any local Red Guards from coming near her, so that was why they contacted Feng for cooperation. It could have been top secret. Also, it seemed to be a different group from those sent by Madam Mao from Beijing. Feng had met with some of those other teams."

"What was the difference?"

"Those other teams knew what they were looking for. Newspaper clippings and pictures concerning Madam Mao in the thirties. They were not that secretive or stealthy, either. In fact, Feng went in with them, helping to turn everything upside down in the houses of those target families. But the special team for Shang didn't request any help like that, nor were they interested in those things from the thirties."

"That is surely different. Did Feng recall any team member's name or keep in touch?"

"One of them was surnamed Sima. A rare surname, that's why Feng remembered it. Probably from a cadre family, that Sima, and he spoke with an authentic Beijing accent." Gang added, "Among other things, Sima mentioned Shang's dresses and shoes, two closets full of them, and the cameras and film-developing equipment at her home, which were rare in those years. So he was impressed. That's about all Feng could remember."

After so many years, that was probably about all anyone could have remembered. Still, it was a sort of random harvest to Chen, particularly the part about the special team looking for something at the request of someone other than Madam Mao. That explained the urgency after so many years. Madam Mao had long turned into "dog shit," and some additional "shit" on her head wouldn't have mattered to the Beijing authorities. So it had to be, as they had said, something directly concerning Mao.

"Thank you so much, Gang. That's very important to my book. And I'll come back to the eatery soon."

But how could he get in touch with Sima, or any other member of the special team? It would be futile to contact the minister or anybody in Beijing for help. On the contrary, the moment his investigation into "the Mao Case" was revealed, the chief inspector would be suspended.

Dr. Xia had been shaking his head the whole time.

"Sorry about the interruption, Dr. Xia. Police work, you know—"

"Tell your 'police work' to others, Chief Inspector, not to me. Now, listen to me carefully. If you suffer continuing giddiness or sickness, you have to come back to me. You must stay completely off work for one week."

"For a week," Chen echoed, wondering if he would be lucky enough to take off one day. Still, given the outcome of his skirmish with the gangsters, he should consider himself lucky—only his luck might not hold the next time. "Not a single word about my visit here to the bureau people, Dr. Xia," he said, rising to leave, when his cell phone shrilled out again.

The number indicated it was a long distance call from Beijing. It was Wang, the head of the Writers' Association there, whom Chen had touched for information about Diao, the author of *Cloud and Rain in Shanghai.*

"Diao has just come to Beijing, staying with his daughter."

"Is he coming back to Shanghai soon?"

"I don't know. He's taking care of his grandson at her place, I've heard."

"Well," Chen said, realizing that could be a job taking weeks or months. "Thank you so much, Chairman Wang. That's what I need to know. I appreciate it."

"Can't you forget about your work for one minute, Chief Inspector Chen?" Dr. Xia said in mounting exasperation. "Take a vacation somewhere where no one can find you. I insist. Get rid of your cell phone too."

"A vacation—where no one knows me. And no cell phone. Thank

you for your suggestion. I'll think about it, Dr. Xia. I give you my word."

Indeed, he could use a vacation. In Beijing. To do something about the Mao Case while there under the disguise of a vacation. He left the clinic.

At this stage, Diao could be crucial to the investigation, capable of providing information not only about Shang's death but also about the special team from Beijing. More importantly, about what they had been looking for at the time. Diao must have done a lot of research for his book, not all of which might have been included in *Cloud and Rain in Shanghai*.

But the "vacation" meant the chief inspector had to leave the situation here unattended for days. In the face of the new developments, however, Chen considered the trip a worthy gamble.

He had a feeling that Mao was at the center of all the confusion and complications. Instead of focusing on his encounter with the gangsters, or on Yang's murder case, he would cope, as in a proverb, by taking the firewood out from under the cauldron.

If his attackers took his vacation as being the result of their warning, so be it. They would come to know Chief Inspector Chen better, sooner or later.

Last but not least, there was something else for him in Beijing, he contemplated with a twinge of conscience.

So he turned onto Chengdu Road, from which he might be able to hail a taxi.

On the street corner, an elderly man was dozing in his wheelchair parked on the sidewalk, wearing a pair of sunglasses, with his feet placed high on the handle bar. Not a comfortable position. Chen couldn't make out why he wanted to take a break like that in his wheelchair. But then a lot of things made sense to one person, but not at all to others—like his vacation plan.

Chen pulled out his cell phone.

The first call went to Gu. Chen told him about his clash with the gangsters.

"What?" Gu exclaimed in a voice of combined shock and indignation. "Some bastards beat you up in broad daylight? Where are you? I'm coming over this minute."

"Don't worry. No broken bones. I've seen a doctor. He wants me to take a couple of days off. So I'm thinking of a short vacation," Chen said. "I'm not sure if the attack is Triad-related, but their weapons and jargon were suspicious."

"That's outrageous. I will find out for you. You have my word for it."

"Have you seen White Cloud lately?"

"Yes. Why, Chief Inspector Chen?"

"One of the gangsters said something about an ugly toad watering its mouth at the sight of a beautiful swan, so it could involve a romantic relationship. But there's nothing going on between us, you know."

"Absolutely nothing, I know, though she adores you like anything. You haven't given her any chance. No, I don't think she has anything to do with it, but I'll talk to her about it. At my request, she has made a point of not mentioning you to other people."

Chen wasn't so sure about that. She was a young, fashionable girl. And Gu could be so proud of his connections.

"Of late, I've helped someone preserve his old house as a historical site. A real estate company concerned may not be pleased with it. The company is called East Wind, supposedly connected to both the black and white ways."

"East Wind, I think I've heard of it. I know some people in the circle. I'll tell you what. I'll dig three feet into the ground."

"You don't have to go out of your way, Gu."

"How can you say that, Chief Inspector Chen? Anyone who attacks you attacks me. It's a slap in my face too," Gu went on seriously. "In today's society, there are not too many honest and capable cops like you left. If I do anything, it's not just for you."

"But don't do anything rash. Don't reveal my identity, either, when you make your inquiries."

"Don't worry. Enjoy your vacation. Call me if there is anything else." Gu added, "Oh, I'll visit your mother over the weekend. White Cloud will do so too."

In Confucian classics, the concept of "expediency" is much discussed, his father had once taught him. For the moment, the Mao Case was the overriding priority, justifying whatever means. Gu had helped before, as he would again this time, full of *yiqi*, like in a martial arts novel. The chief inspector might have to pay him back, eventually, but he didn't want to worry about it now.

His next call was to Old Hunter.

"I've just seen Dr. Xia. He said I have suffered a concussion."

"Did you have an accident?"

"No, I don't think it was an accident. A couple of gangsters attacked me on the street," Chen said simply. "To ensure a quiet recovery period, Dr. Xia insists on my taking a vacation—away from the work and worry. Somewhere that no one knows about. No phone calls. I have to take his advice, I'm afraid."

"But the situation here may develop unexpectedly—"

"I'll contact you from time to time."

"Fine—oh, I got hold of someone, someone very reliable, to serve as Jiao's temporary maid. She may be able to find out something for us."

"Great. That will really help. Tell her to go to Jiao's place at her earliest convenience. I'll let Jiao know about it before I leave. In any emergency situation, you may contact a friend of mine. This is her number. She should know my whereabouts for the next few days."

It was Ling's number. For the moment, there was nobody else he could think of. According to Yong, Ling had moved back to her parents' home.

"Will it be safe to call her?"

"It's a special 'red line' for her high cadre family. You don't have to worry about its being tapped. But don't give it to anybody."

"I understand."

Old Hunter might have guessed. What would he be thinking about

Chen's sudden vacation? That the romantic chief inspector was impossible, rushing to his ex-girlfriend . . .

Chen decided not to worry about that, either.

He had to make another phone call, recommending "someone reliable" to Jiao, who had left a message on her cell number while on his way to the Shanghai Railway Station.

SIXTEEN

FOLLOWING THE DIRECTIONS PROVIDED by Old Hunter, Peiqin arrived at the high-end apartment complex on Wuyuan Road.

She was the "someone reliable" Chen had recommended to Jiao, though he had no idea that it was none other than Peiqin.

Peiqin had volunteered to serve as a temporary maid, to the surprise of both Yu and Old Hunter, who had asked her to help look for one. She made a convincing argument for her candidacy. It was practically impossible to find a reliable maid on short notice, let alone one capable of reporting to the police in secret. What's more, whatever the reason for Chen's vacation, he must be in danger. They had to help. Finally, Yu agreed on the condition that she do nothing there except what was expected of a temporary maid.

Wuyuan Road and the neighborhood around it was an area Peiqin hadn't visited before. Like many Shanghainese who rarely ventured outside of their own circles, she saw no point in exploring areas that were like another city to her. Before and after 1949, Wuyuan was regarded as one of the "upper corners," way above ordinary people like Peiqin and Yu.

In the fast-changing city, the gap between the rich and the poor was once again expanding. The newspapers and magazines had started talking about building a harmonious society, all of a sudden and all at once, like never-tiring cicadas in the trees. She wondered how it could be managed. She showed her ID to the green-uniformed security guard at the complex entrance and declared herself to be a new maid.

Moving through the entrance, she felt momentarily lost, like Granny Liu in the *Dream of the Red Chamber*. The ultraluxurious apartments in front stood like tall magnificent dreams far, far away. Before pressing the intercom at the apartment building, she took another look at her reflection in a pocket mirror. A middle-aged woman in a faded black T-shirt, khaki pants, and rubber-heeled shoes, carrying a white canvas bag. It was the image of a housemaid as commonly seen on TV, a role not too difficult for her to play, after all the housework she had done at home over the years.

"Who is it?" A voice came down from the fifth floor.

"I'm Pei. Mr. Chen told me to come today."

"Oh yes, come up. Room 502."

The lock on the front door clicked. Peiqin pulled the door open and walked over to the elevator.

When she stepped out onto the fifth floor, she saw a young woman standing in the doorway of an apartment on the left.

"So you are the new maid?"

"Yes," Peiqin said, nodding.

"I'm Jiao." She was in a light blue mandarin dress embroidered with a colorful phoenix, her feet encased in matching high-heeled satin slippers, as if she had stepped out of a movie from the thirties. The mandarin dress, apparently custom-tailored, brought out all her curves, with a subtle suggestion of voluptuousness. She was holding a pair of stockings in her hand.

Jiao should have been able to take care of the apartment herself, but Peiqin knew it could be simply a sign of one's social status to have a maid. Peiqin had heard that some upstarts had a cubicle in their apartments called a maid's room, with its own bathroom, so that the live-in-servant wouldn't mix with the master. She had grown up during the age of communist egalitarian propaganda, and she couldn't help feeling a little uncomfortable with her identity in this situation, even though she was merely playing a role, a temporary one.

"Come on in," Jiao said.

"My name is Pei. Mr. Chen wanted me to come here," Peiqin repeated what she had said downstairs.

"Mr. Chen called me, saying that he would send over someone capable and reliable."

"I've known Mr. Chen for years. He's a good man."

"How is he? I tried to call him this morning, but he didn't pick up."

"He is out of town on business, I guess," Peiqin said vaguely, not sure whether Jiao was aware of the latest development.

"Business people are like that." Jiao added, "I'm going out this morning, so let's talk about your work now. You don't have to come every day. Three times a week. Four hours each time. Primarily your duties will be room cleaning and laundry. Occasionally, I'll need you to prepare dinner, like today, but the moment you finish, you may leave. For your help, eight hundred a month, and I'll pay for anything additional. Is that okay?"

"It's fine with me."

"Let me make a list of what you need to buy and prepare for tonight." Jiao scribbled quickly on a piece of paper. "Oh, you don't have to cook, just prepare them."

"I understand," Peiqin said, glancing over the list, which appeared to be quite specific, not only about the items, but about the specific culinary flavors too. "When are you coming back?"

"Six."

"And your dinnertime?"

"Around seven."

"In that case, I'd better start cooking the pork around four, I think, for the pork braised in red sauce takes hours. As for the fish, I'll have it prepared with scallion and ginger in a steamer, so you will just need to steam it for five or six minutes, more or less, as you prefer."

"Right," Jiao said, nodding. "You're quite experienced."

"Anything specific about the pork or the fish?"

"Yes, well-cooked fat pork," Jiao said. "Oh, don't use soy sauce."

"But what about the sauce—" Peiqin began, then had a thought. "I see. I think I can wok-fry sugar until it turns brown and use it for color."

"You're a pro," Jiao said with a smile.

It was a recipe Peiqin had learned at the restaurant. Jiao must have cooked it herself, as she showed no surprise on her face.

"I'll time it so the pork will be well done but not overdone when you come back. You can also add in whatever spice you like."

"Indeed, Mr. Chen has made an excellent recommendation. Do it in whatever way you like. Here's money for your shopping."

Jiao appeared to be in a hurry to leave, talking and pulling on her stockings while leaning against a mahogany chair. She slid her feet into a pair of high heels.

"If it takes more than four hours for a particular day, let me know. I'll pay extra, okay?" Jiao added, heading toward the door.

It was more than okay for a maid, Peiqin thought, listening to Jiao's footsteps fading along the corridor and disappearing into the elevator. She then closed the door.

She didn't know what Chen had said about her to Jiao, but it appeared that her "maid career" had started more smoothly than she expected. Jiao had accepted her without a single question. The work arrangements suited Peiqin too, since she wouldn't even have to ask for a leave from the restaurant. As an accountant with flexible work hours, she could come over at her convenience. Some days she might be able to work her hours here during the lunch break.

Taking an apron out of the canvas bag, she started moving around like a maid, while observing like a cop's wife, looking out for anything out of the ordinary and for objects associated with Mao.

It was a luxurious apartment. The layout appeared to be unusual, but she was not sure. The oblong-shaped living room was huge, with

155

paintings scattered here and there, finished and unfinished. Jiao might use it more like a studio. On one wall hung a long silk-decked scroll of Chinese calligraphy. It was difficult for Peiqin to read the flying-dragon-and-dancing-phoenix-like writing. It took her several minutes to recognize five or six characters in the scroll, and then it dawned on her that the scroll was of a poem by Mao entitled "Ode to the Plum Blossom," which she had read in her middle school textbook.

In classical Chinese poetry, beauties and flowers sometimes served as metaphors for each other. So the calligrapher could have copied the poem for Jiao as a compliment, but as far as Peiqin remembered, the plum blossom was not commonly symbolic of a young, fashionable girl.

Perhaps she was reading too much into it. In today's market, a scroll by a celebrated calligrapher could be invaluable regardless of its contents. It also served to show the refined taste of the owner, young or not. She took another look at the poem. There was a date in the Chinese lunar calendar, which she failed to decipher. She would have to check it in a reference book from the library.

She moved into the bedroom, which, too, was exceptionally large, with a couple of walk-in closets and a master bathroom. The furniture, however, was a stark contrast to that of the living room. Simple, practically plain. What struck her as peculiar was the large wooden bed. It was larger than a king-size, and possibly custom-made. Now, why a young single girl needed such a bed, Peiqin couldn't guess. There was also a custom-made bookshelf built into the plain wooden headboard. In fact, about a third of the bed was littered with books. Leaning to straighten the pillows, she touched the bed. No mattress, only a solid hard board—a wooden-board mattress under the sheets.

Above the headboard hung a large picture of Mao, gazing down from above. It was an unusual bedroom decoration. The picture frame looked like it was solid gold, which it couldn't be, but it was very heavy nonetheless. The picture faced a large mirror on the opposite wall, which was not that lucky in terms of feng shui, for the people in bed.

Standing beside the bed was a cabinetlike bookshelf, with pictures of Jiao on the top, almost level with the picture of Mao.

There were two closets, one large, one small, facing the bed. She opened the doors. There were clothing and painting supplies in them. But Peiqin didn't see anything surprising.

She proceeded into the adjoining room, which looked like a study. On the large mahogany desk there was an album lying beside a miniature bronze statue of Mao. For a study, it was impressive: custom-made mahogany bookshelves stood tall and majestic against three walls. On the shelves were a considerable number of books about Mao, some of which Peiqin had never seen in bookstores. Jiao had done an incredible job collecting so many of them. There was also a section of history books, some of them thread-bound, cloth-covered editions, presumably meant to look impressive. At the bottom of one bookshelf there was a pile of fashion magazines, incongruous with the history books above.

The kitchen, full of modern stainless appliances, was the only place Peiqin didn't find anything associated with Mao. She stood on her tiptoes and looked into the cabinet. There was nothing there but a couple of recipe books, one of which she had at home too.

She decided to go and do the shopping, so she took off the apron and folded it neatly on the kitchen table. On the first day, a maid's responsibility came first. Later on, if she had time, she could check around again.

So she set out with the shopping list. It was an intriguing one. Fat pork, Wuchang fish, bitter melon, green and red pepper, and some seasonal vegetables. The security guard recognized her this time and smiled.

The neighborhood food market turned out to be quite different from what she was accustomed to: granite-floored, white-tile-covered counters displaying vegetables in plastic wrappers and meat in plastic packaging. She walked around for a while before locating several huge glass cages with live fish swimming inside. As with other counters there, there was a sign declaring "No bargaining."

"A large Wuchang fish," she said to a ruddy-complexioned sales-woman in a white uniform and purple rubber shoes.

Peiqin didn't have to bargain, not with the sum given by Jiao, but she asked for a receipt. In response to her non-bargaining attitude, the saleswoman ladled out the swimming fish and handed it to her with a handful of green onion for free.

Peiqin bought everything on the list, choosing some other special sauce and seasonings for the night. According to Yu and Old Hunter, Jiao seldom if ever invited people home. Yet, for a slender girl like her, it appeared to be a huge dinner with a lot of calories and fat. The fat pork braised in red sauce, in particular, once popular in the early sixties for the starved, ill-nourished Chinese people, was practically unimagin-able for fashionable diet-conscious girls.

Back in the kitchen, she started preparing. The live fish kept strug-gling and jumping while she scaled it on the board. As she put it into the steamer, the fish twitched one more time, its tail cutting her finger. The cut wasn't deep, but it tingled. She arranged the fish on a willow-patterned platter along with ginger and scallion and set it in a steamer on the kitchen table. Jiao needed only to turn on the fire upon her re-turn. Peiqin rinsed the rice and put it into an electric rice pot. She fi-nally started working on the pork. It was easy, but took time. She was no restaurant chef but she was a capable cook, and wanted to impress on her first day.

Taking off her apron again, she made a cup of tea for herself, choos-ing a European tea bag she hadn't seen before. She sat on a folding chair close to the table. Breathing into the hot tea, she found the taste not nearly as good as the Dragon Well tea at home. Perhaps the tea bag caused the difference. She like watching leisurely the unfolding of the tea leaves in the cup, green, tender, musing.

She had helped with police work before, because of her husband or Chief Inspector Chen, or because of the people involved.

But this time, it was different.

She felt drawn to the case because of something personal, yet far more than personal.

158

Peiqin had been a straight-A student in elementary school, wearing the Red Scarf of a proud Young Pioneer, dreaming of a rosy future in the golden sunlight of socialist China. Everything changed overnight, however, with the outbreak of the Cultural Revolution. Her father's "historical problem" cast a shadow over the whole family. Youthful dreams shattered, she came to terms with the realities—toiling and moiling as an educated youth in Yunnan, plowing barefoot in the rice paddy, plodding through the muddy trails, day in and day out . . . and ten years later, coming back to the city, working at a *tingzijian* restaurant office with wok fumes and kitchen noises erupting from downstairs, and squeezing into a single room without a kitchen or bathroom, with Yu and Qinqin eking out whatever was available . . . She had been too busy, sometimes working two jobs, to be maudlin about her life. And she had kept telling herself that she was a lucky one—a good husband and a wonderful son, what else could she really expect? At a recent class reunion, Yu and she were actually voted the luckiest couple—both had stable jobs, a room they called their own, and a son studying hard for college. After all, the Cultural Revolution had been a national disaster, not just for her family but for millions and millions of Chinese people.

Occasionally, she still couldn't help wondering what life would have been like without the Cultural Revolution.

The cut on her finger stung again.

Who was responsible for it?

Mao.

The government didn't want people to talk about it, tried to avoid the topic or to shift the blame to the Gang of Four. As for Mao, it was said that he had made a well-meant mistake, which was nothing compared to the great contributions he'd made to China.

Perhaps she was in no position to judge Mao, not historically, but what about personally, from the perspective of one whose life had been so affected by those political movements under Mao?

Her personal factors aside, there was no forgiving Mao for what she had just learned from Old Hunter—for what Mao had done to Kaihui.

As a young girl, she had read Mao's poem to Kaihui, cherishing it as a moving revolutionary love poem. She had also read an earlier one on parting with Kaihui, even more sentimental and touching in her imagination.

Now, what a shock when she learned the truth behind the poems! It wasn't simply a brazen betrayal by Mao; it was practically cold-blooded murder. Mao must have seen Kaihui as an obstacle to his affair with Zizhen, so he had let Kaihui stay where she was, to fall prey to the nationalists' retaliation. Did Kaihui know it in her last days? Peiqin's eyes watered at the thought of Kaihui being dragged to the execution ground, her bare feet bleeding all the way—following the local superstition that the executed couldn't find her way back home without her shoes.

And Peiqin had no doubt about Mao's desertion of Shang. After rereading *Cloud and Rain in Shanghai*, Peiqin lay awake for the night. It was nothing, historically, for someone like Mao to have used and discarded a woman like a worn-out mop. But what about Shang, an equal human being?

Standing up, Peiqin went into the bedroom again. Gazing at Mao's picture above the bed, she realized that it was a portrait not so commonly seen, not now, not since the days of the Cultural Revolution. Mao was sitting in a rattan chair, wearing a blue-and-white-striped terrycloth robe, smoking a cigarette, and smiling toward the distant horizon, the immediate background of the picture suggestive of a riverboat. Presumably it was a picture taken after a swim in the Yangtze River.

Was it possible that Jiao, after the fashion of recent years, had "rediscovered" Mao? Chinese people had always been interested in emperors—for thousands of years. There was a "royal revival" going on in movies and on TV, and the Qing emperors and empresses abounded in current bestsellers.

But how could Jiao, of all people, have entertained any fond fantasies of Mao—since Mao was responsible for the tragedies of her family?

And the Mao mystery aside, how could a young girl like Jiao afford to live like this without a job?

It was possible that Jiao was a kept woman, or "little concubine"— *ernai*, a new term that was gaining currency quickly in the contemporary Chinese vocabulary.

But Internal Security hadn't found a "keeper" in the background, though somebody had been seen in her company, at least once, in the apartment here. For a young woman like Jiao, there was nothing surprising about an occasional visitor or two.

Peiqin pulled out of her thoughts. She hardly knew anything about Jiao, a girl from a different generation and of a different family background. There was no point in speculating too much.

Nor did she have any idea what Chen was really after. As a cop's wife, she had no objection to snooping around for her husband's sake, or that of his boss, but she would have liked more clues about what she was looking for.

Again, she glanced at her watch. Jiao wouldn't come back this early. Peiqin decided to start her "search proper."

She proceeded cautiously, pulling out the drawers, looking under the bed, examining the closet, rummaging through the boxes . . . From a mystery she had read, she learned that people could purposely hide things in the most obvious places, to which she also paid close attention. After spending nearly an hour going through every nook and cranny, she found little except things that further reinforced her earlier impression of Jiao's being obsessed with Mao.

In a drawer, Peiqin found several tapes of documentaries showing Mao receiving foreign visitors in the Forbidden City. Some of them she might have seen in Yunnan in the early seventies; it was during a time when hardly any movies were shown except the eight modern revolutionary model plays and documentaries of Mao. Peiqin and Yu would joke that Mao was the biggest movie star.

How could Jiao have gotten hold of these? Peiqin was tempted to put a tape into the player, but she decided against it. Jiao might notice it had been played.

Instead, Peiqin started to make a list of what seemed unusual, puzzling, incomprehensible, at Jiao's apartment. A list for Yu and Old Hunter. If she couldn't make much out of it, they might. Or possibly Chief Inspector Chen.

First, the large bed, so old-fashioned, with a wooden-board mattress. For the majority of the Shanghainese, it was common to have a *zongbeng* mattress—something woven netlike with crisscrossed coir ropes. Peiqin insisted on having such an airy, resilient *zongbeng* at home. For younger people, a spring mattress was more popular and Qinqin had one. Only some really old and old-fashioned people would think of a wooden-board mattress as a possible choice; they would believe it to be good for their back.

And then there was the miniature bookshelf set into the headboard. Was Jiao such an avid reader? She hadn't even finished middle school. Not to mention the custom-made mahogany bookshelves with those Mao and history books.

Peiqin wasn't sure about the silk scroll of Mao's poem in the living room and the portrait of Mao in the bedroom, but to her, they also seemed unusual.

As for the dinner with all the unusual dishes, Peiqin was inclined to suppose it was a meal for two. The guest could be an old-fashioned one, at least so in his taste, though Jiao hadn't said a word about any visitor coming that night. Peiqin thought that she'd better tip Old Hunter to it, making sure that he would keep lookout this evening.

She was about to dial when a knock sounded on the door. She put the list into her bag and looked out through the peephole. It was a man in a dark blue uniform with something like a long-handled sprayer in his hand.

"What do you want?" she asked uncertainly.

"Insect spray service."

"Insect spray service?" She sprayed at home, by herself, but it was not her business to question it. Rich people might have all kinds of things done by professionals.

"I scheduled it with Jiao," he said, producing a slip of paper. "Look."

Jiao must have forgotten to tell her about it, which wasn't that important.

"So you're the new maid here?"

"Yes, it's my first day."

"I came last month," he said, "and there was another one."

He must have come here before, so she opened the door. He moved in, nodding and putting on a gauze mask before she could get a close look at his face. He appeared quite professional, his glance instantly sweeping round to the kitchen table. "Better cover the dishes, though the spray is practically harmless."

Extending the spray head, he started spraying around, poking and reaching into the corners behind the cabinet.

After four or five minutes, he headed for the bedroom. She followed, though not closely.

"So you're not a provincial girl."

"No, I'm not."

"Then how did you end up here?"

"My factory went bankrupt," she improvised. "Where else could I go?"

After he checked into the corners as well as hard-to-reach areas, he squatted down, reaching into the space under the bed. Perhaps that was the professional way.

When he finally started to pull in the spray head, she said, "How much does Jiao owe you?"

"Oh, she has already paid."

It was almost four when he left the apartment. Peiqin moved back to the kitchen where she tore the steamed eggplant into slices and added salt, sesame oil, and a pinch of MSG. Simple yet good. She also sliced a piece of jellyfish for another cold dish and prepared a small saucer of special sauce.

She finally poked a chopstick into the pork. The chopstick pierced it easily. She turned the fire down to the lowest setting. The pork looked nicely done, rich in color.

That was about all she could do for the day. The clock on the kitchen wall said four forty-five. She surveyed the dishes prepared and half prepared on the kitchen table, nodding with approval.

Taking off her apron, she thought she should let Jiao know about all that she had done that afternoon. So she left a note, mentioning the visit of the insect spray man as well.

SEVENTEEN

MUCH TO HIS CONFUSION, Chen found himself sitting beside Yong in a black limousine, which was rolling down the once familiar Chang'an Avenue in the growing dusk.

He hadn't expected such a grand ride upon his arrival in Beijing.

On the Shanghai-Beijing express train he had decided that, rather than go through a travel agency and have his name registered, it would be better to call Yong, ask her to book a hotel for him, and have her purchase a prepaid cell phone for him to use while in Beijing. He was acquainted with some people in the Beijing Police Bureau, but he decided not to contact any of them.

Nor would he let them know he was taking his "vacation" in Beijing.

With Yong, there was one disadvantage—her unbridled imagination regarding the purpose of his trip. On the other hand, she could tell him about Ling. There were questions he might not be able to ask Ling herself.

It didn't take long for Yong to call back, saying that she had taken care of everything and that she would pick him up at the station.

What surprised him, however, was the sight of Yong waiting for him with a luxurious limousine at the exit of the Beijing train station.

As far as he knew, Yong was an ordinary librarian, riding an old bike to work, rain or shine.

More to his surprise, Yong didn't immediately start talking about Ling, as he had anticipated. A slender-built woman in her late thirties with short hair, a slightly swarthy complexion, and clear features, Yong usually spoke fast and loud. There was something mysterious about her reticence.

After the car swerved around Dongdan and passed Lantern City Crossing, it made several more turns in quick succession before edging its way into a narrow, winding lane, which appeared to be in the Eastern City area. He couldn't see clearly through the amber-colored windows.

The entrance of the lane looked familiar, yet strange, lined with indescribable stuffs stacked along both sides.

"The hotel is in a *hutong*?" he asked. In Beijing, a lane was called *hutong*, usually narrow and uneven. The limousine was literally crawling along.

"You've forgotten all about it, haven't you?" Yong said with a knowing smile. "A distinguished man can't help forgetting things. We are going to my place."

"Oh. But why?"

"To receive the wind, like in our old tradition. Isn't it proper and right for me to first welcome you at home? The hotel is really close, at the end of the lane. It's easy, you can walk there in only three or four minutes."

She could have told him on the phone. But why the limousine? Yong was of ordinary family background, not like Ling.

He had been here before years earlier—for a date with Ling, he recalled, as the car pulled up in front of a *sihe* quadrangle house. It was an architectural style popular in the old city of Beijing, and characterized by residential rooms on four sides and an inner courtyard in the center.

Stepping out, he saw an isolated house standing in a disappearing lane—most of the houses there were already gone or half gone, the ground littered with debris and ruins.

"The local government has a new housing project planned to be built here, but we aren't moving. Not until we are properly compensated. It's our property."

"Are you still living here?"

"No, we have another apartment near New Street."

So they were another "nail family," hanging in until pulled out by force. There were stories about this type of problem in the development of the city.

In the courtyard, he noticed that all the rooms were dark except Yong's.

As she led him into the room, he wasn't too surprised to see Ling sitting there, leaning against the paper window. He looked over her with an overwhelming feeling of déjà vu.

In the limousine, he had suspected some sort of arrangement by Yong. Ling, however, appeared to be genuinely surprised, and she stood up. She could have come over from some business activity, wearing a purple satin mandarin dress, with a purse of the same color and material, apparently custom-made, like in a page torn from a high-class fashion magazine.

There was no "wind-receiving" banquet on the table, not as Yong had promised. There was only a cup of tea for Ling. Yong hastened to pour a cup for Chen and gestured both of them to sit down.

"My humble abode is brightened by two distinguished guests tonight," Yong said. "Ling, CEO of several large companies in Beijing, and Chen, chief inspector of the Shanghai Police Bureau. So my 'nail family' has existed for a good reason."

"You should have told me," Ling said to her.

That was what he also wanted to say, but he said instead to Ling, "I'm so pleased to see you, Ling."

"Now, I have to hurry back to my new place," Yong said. "My man works the night shift and I have to take care of my little daughter."

It was too obvious an excuse. Yong had played a similar trick once before. The memories of a similar occasion were all coming back to him.

Yong left promptly, as years earlier, closing the door after her, leaving the two of them alone in the room.

But things were not as before, not anymore for the two of them.

He found himself at a loss for words. The silence seemed to wrap them up in a silk cocoon.

"Yong is a busybody," Ling said finally. "She dragged me over without telling me why, and insisted on my waiting here."

"A well-meant busybody," he said, his glance sweeping over the room, which appeared little changed. There was still a basin of water in the steel-wire basin holder near the door. The large bed at the other side of the room was covered with a dragon-and-phoenix-embroidered sheet, identical to the one in his memory. And they were sitting at the same red-painted wooden table by the paper windows, against which the old lamp cast a lambent light.

That might be the very effect Yong had intended. The past in the present. Like the last time they were here—Ling, a librarian, and he, a college student. In those days, she still lived with her parents, and he, in a crowded dorm room with five other students. It was difficult for them to find a quiet place to themselves. So Yong invited them to her place, and as soon as they were here, she left them alone with an excuse.

That evening was like this evening. But tonight, as in a couplet by Li Shangyin, *"Oh the feeling, to be collected later / in memories, was already confused."*

"I received the book you sent from London," he said. "Thank you so much, Ling."

"Oh, I happened to see it in a bookstore there."

"So you are back from the trip." It was idiotic to say that, he knew. She thought of him on her honeymoon trip, but what else could he say to her? "When?"

"Last week."

"You could have told me earlier."

"Why?"

"I would have been able—" He left the sentence unfinished—*to buy a wedding present for you.*

There ensued another short spell of silence, like in a scroll of traditional Chinese painting, in which the blank space contains more than what was painted. *There is always a loss of meaning / in what we say or do not say, / but also a meaning / in the loss of the meaning.*

"Oh, did you visit the Sherlock Holmes Museum?" he said, trying to change the topic.

"Now you are really a chief inspector," she said, eyeing the cold tea. "A cop above everything."

That was another blunder on his part. She had a point. He was tongue-tied, as a cop or not, thinking that her response might have also referred to his role in another case, one that had exasperated her father because of its political repercussions. A case Chen didn't have to take, yet he did. The outcome of it had strained their relationship.

"You must have done well on the force," she went on. "My father, too, mentioned you the other day."

"As a monk, you have to strike the bell in the temple, day after day." He was deeply perturbed by the comment about her father, a powerful politburo member in the Forbidden City.

"So it has become your lifelong career?"

"Perhaps it's too late for me to try anything new," he said, not wanting to continue like this, but not knowing how to shift the topic.

"I tried to write you," she said, taking the initiative, her head slightly tilted in the faltering lamplight, "but there's not much to be said. After all, the tide does not wait."

He wondered at her choice of the words—"the tide does not wait." Did it mean she couldn't wait any longer? He wondered whether it was about her marriage choice or career choice. To start a business was nowadays described as "to jump into the sea"—tides of money-making opportunities. She was a successful businesswoman, and her husband, for that matter, was another tide-riding businessman.

Or were they a reference to the *Spring Tide*? That was the title of a Russian novel that they had read together in North Sea Park.

But he was supposed to say something more relevant to the occasion. It was an opportunity not to be missed, as Yong would have urged, a chance for the "salvation mission." Ling was staying with her parents at the moment.

He took a sip of his tea. Jasmine flower tea. Another surprising strike of déjà vu. That evening, so many years ago, she brewed a pot of hot tea for him, putting the jasmine petal from her hair into his teacup—"*The transparently white unfolding in the black.*"

"So are you here in Beijing on another case?" she said.

"No, not exactly. It's more of a vacation. I haven't been to Beijing for a long time."

"Our chief inspector is enjoying a vacation!"

He was upset by the sarcasm in her voice. It was she who had married somebody else, not the other way round.

"Any sight of specific interest on your vacation?" she went on without looking up at him.

Actually, there was one, he suddenly realized. Mao's former residence in the Central South Sea, the Forbidden City. He had just read about it on the train. The residence was closed, and it didn't have a direct bearing on the investigation, but he had taken to visiting the people involved in an investigation or, failing that, their residence, as a way of closing the distance between cop and criminal. For this case, Chen didn't set out to judge Mao. Still, a visit to his residence might help the chief inspector, if only psychologically, gain insight into the personal side of Mao.

Ling should be able to get him into the Central South Sea through her connections in Beijing. "Mao's old home in the Central South Sea," he blurted out, "but it is closed."

"Mao's old home!" she echoed in surprise. "Since when have you become a Maoist?"

"No, I'm not that fashionable."

"Then why?" She gave him an alert look.

He didn't respond at once, trying to recall whether he had ever talked to her about Mao.

"You remember that evening in Jingshan Park? With the evening spread out against the tilted eaves of the ancient, splendid palace, we sat together, and you murmured a poem to me."

And it came back, the memories of her sitting on a gray slab of rock, holding his hand, and of his catching sight of a tree hung with a white board saying, "The tree on which Emperor Chongzhen of the Ming dynasty hung himself," and of his shivering with the memory of the blackboard hung around his father's neck during the Cultural Revolution . . .

"I still have that poem," she said, producing from her purse something like a cell phone but larger, palmlike, which he had never seen before. She pressed several keys on the gadget.

"Here it is," she said, beginning to read aloud from the LCD screen.

It was on a hillside, Jingshan Park, Forbidden City / where the Qing Emperor had succeeded / the Ming Emperor, we sat / on a slab of rock there, watching / the evening spreading out against the tilted eaves / of the ancient, splendid palace. / Below us, waves of buses flowed / along Huangchen Road—a moat, hundreds of years ago. We murmured / words in Chinese, then in English / we were learning. The bronze stork / which had once escorted the Qing Dowager / stared at us. You dream of us becoming / two gargoyles, you told me / at Yangxing imperial hall, gurgling/ all night long, in a language comprehensible / only to ourselves. A mist / enveloped the hill. We saw a tree / hung with a white board saying / "It's on this tree that Emperor Chongzhen / committed suicide." The board reminded me / of the blackboard hung my father's neck / during the Cultural Revolution. The evening / struck me as suddenly cold. / We left the park.

"Yes, the poem. I really appreciate it that you kept it for me—"

"I did it on the airplane. Nothing to do during those business flights."

But he was vexed, almost irrationally, imagining her traveling with

171

her businessman husband, sitting side by side, and reading his poems to *him*. Chen had given her a number of his poems. He started wondering whether she had kept them, and where.

"Oh, about the poems I wrote—I meant the poems for you, Ling. I haven't kept the manuscripts properly, only some pieces here, some pieces there. If you still have them, can you give them back to me?"

"You want them back?"

He regretted the way he had made the request. So impulsive and abrupt. How was she going to interpret it?

But she changed the subject. "I have a friend working in the Central South Sea. A visit to his old home can be arranged, I guess."

Since they were back to talking about Mao, he decided to push his luck further. "Oh, there's a book written by Mao's personal doctor, do you know anything about it?"

"This is about an investigation concerning Mao, isn't it?" she said, looking him in the eye. "You have to tell me more about your work."

So he told her what information he was looking for, though without going into detail. He knew that honesty would be the best way to enlist her help.

"You're somebody in your field, Chief Inspector Chen—"

But her cell phone rang. She snatched it up in frustration. In spite of her initial reluctance, she began speaking in earnest. Possibly an important business call.

"Quota is no problem . . ."

He stood up, pulled out a packet of cigarettes, and made a gesture with it. Pushing open the door, he headed into the courtyard.

The courtyard was even more deserted than he had first thought. The quadrangle house was holding out in desperation against the development. He watched her profile silhouetted against the window paper, the phone pressed to her cheek. Almost like an ancient shadow play. At that instant, she seemed to have moved far away.

She was capable. No question about it. There was no forgetting, however, that she had succeeded in the business world not because of her capability, but because of her family connections. It was part of the system—the way of the system. The quota she was talking about, presumably for export business, was an example: she could get the quota easily with a phone call to her "uncle" or "aunt," yet it was way beyond ordinary people.

He wasn't able to identify with the system, not yet, not totally, in spite of his "success" in the system. In his heart of hearts, he still yearned for something different, something with a sort of independence, albeit a limited one, from the system.

He saw she was finishing the call, putting the phone down on the table. Grinding out the cigarette, he hastened back into the room.

"You're a busy CEO," he said in spite of himself.

"You don't have to say that. As a chief inspector, you're busier."

"It's a job you have to put more and more of yourself into. Then it becomes part of you, whether you like it or not," he said wistfully. "I'm talking about myself, of course. So I may redeem myself, ironically, only by being a conscientious cop."

"Will the visit to Mao's residence make such a difference to your police work?"

She was right to ask the question. The visit alone would make no difference. In fact, the very trip to Beijing could be a pathetic attempt to treat a dead horse as if it were still alive. "A special team was sent to Shang's home," he said, taking her question as a subtle hint. "After so many years, no one could know anything about what they did. The archive may still be listed as confidential—"

But her phone rang again. She took a look at the number and turned it off. "Those businesspeople will never let you alone," she said, her fingers brushing against the paper window, like against the long-ago memories. "That night, I remember, there was an orange pinwheel spinning in the window. You were drunk, saying it was like an image in your poem. Have you totally given up your poetry?"

"Can I support myself as a poet?" He had a hard time following her as she jumped to the topic of poetry. She might be as self-conscious as he was at the unexpected reunion. "I published a collection of poems, but I found out that it was actually funded by a business associate of mine without my knowledge."

"When I first started my business, I, too, had the naïve idea, that among other things, you might be able to write your poems without worrying about anything else."

He was touched by a faraway look in her eyes, but she was intensely present too. She had never given up on the poet in him. Was it possible, however, for him to let her support him like that?

"When I first met you, I never imagined I would be a cop." *And I never thought you would be a businesswoman—* "In those days, we still had dreams, but we have to live in the present moment."

"I don't know when Yong will come back," she said, glancing up at the clock on the wall.

"It's late," he responded, almost mechanically. "It may be difficult for you to find a taxi."

"I'll leave a note for her. She will understand."

So it ended in a whimper, this evening of theirs, but whether Yong would understand it, he didn't know.

As they walked out of the courtyard, he was surprised to see the limousine still waiting there, like a modern monster crouching against the ruins of the old Beijing lane. A wooden pillar still stood out, like an angry finger pointing to the summer night sky.

"Is it your father's car?"

"No, it's mine." She added, "For business."

HCC were no longer something simply because of their parents. With their family connections, they themselves had turned into high cadres, or into successful entrepreneurs like her, or into both, like her husband.

He followed her over to the limousine, her high heels clicking on the stone-covered lane, a sliver of the moonlight illuminating her fine profile.

Holding the door for her, the chauffeur bowed obsequiously, white-haired like an owl in the night.

"Let me take you to your hotel," she said.

"No, thanks. It's just across the lane. I'll walk there."

"Then good night."

Watching the car roll out of sight, he recalled that her earlier reference to the "tide" could have come out of a Tang-dynasty poem. *The tide always keeps its word / to come. Had I known that, / I would have married a young tide-rider.*

He was no longer a young tide-rider on the materialistic waves today.

EIGHTEEN

CHIEF INSPECTOR CHEN STARTED his second day in Beijing by making a phone call to Diao. It was quite early in the morning.

"My name is Chen," he introduced himself. "I used to be a businessman, but I'm trying my hand at writing. I talked with Chairman Wang of the Chinese Writers' Association. He recommended you to me. So I would like very much to invite you to lunch today."

"What a surprise, Mr. Chen! Thank you so much for your kind invitation, I have to say that first. But we've never met before, have we? Nor have I met Wang before. How can I let you buy lunch for me?"

"I haven't read much, Mr. Diao, but I know the story of Cao Xueqin's friends treating him to Beijing roast duck in exchange for a chapter of the *Dream of the Red Chamber*. That's how I got the idea."

"I don't have any exciting stories for you, I'm afraid, but if you really insist, we may meet for a late lunch today."

"Great. One o'clock then. See you at Fangshan Restaurant."

Putting down the phone, Chen realized that he had the morning to himself. So he started making plans.

As he walked out of the hotel, he hailed a taxi, telling the driver to go to the Memorial Hall of Chairman Mao in Tiananmen Square. Afterward, he thought, he could take a short cut through the Forbidden City Museum, to the Fangshan Restaurant in North Sea Park.

"You're lucky. The memorial hall is open this week," the taxi driver said without looking back. "I took someone there just yesterday."

"Thanks."

"It's at the center of the Tiananmen Square," the driver said, taking him for a first-time visitor to Beijing. "The feng shui of the memorial hall is absolutely rotten."

"What do you mean?"

"Rotten for the dead, wasn't it? Hardly a month after Mao's death, his body not even properly placed in the crystal coffin yet, Madam Mao was thrown into jail as the head of the Gang of Four. And inauspicious for the square too. You know what happened in the square in 1989. There was bloodshed all over it. Sooner or later his body will have to be removed, or it will cause trouble again."

"You really believe that?"

"Believe it or not, there's no escaping retribution! Not even for Mao. He died sonless. One of his sons was killed in the Korean War, another suffers from schizophrenia, and still another went missing during the Civil War. It was Mao himself who said that, while he was in the Lu Mountains." The driver added with a sardonic chuckle, "But you never know how many bastards he might have left behind."

Chen made no comment, trying to look out at the much-changed Chang'an Avenue. They had already passed the Beijing Hotel near Dongdan.

When the taxi came to a stop close to the memorial hall, Chen handed some bills to the driver and said, "Keep the change. But tell your feng shui theory to every customer. One of them may turn out to be a cop."

"Oh, if that happens, I'll have a question for that cop. My father—labeled a Rightist simply so his school could meet the quota demand—died during the Cultural Revolution, leaving me an orphan without an education or skills. That's why I am a taxi driver. So what compensation does the government owe me?"

In the anti-Rightist movement launched by Mao in mid-fifties, there was a sort of quota—each work unit had to report a given number of rightists to the authorities. The driver's father must have been labeled a Rightist because of that. Whatever the personal grudge against Mao, however, people shouldn't talk that way about the dead.

"The times have changed," the taxi driver said, poking his head out of the window, as he drove off. "A cop can't lock me up for talking about a feng shui theory."

And whatever its feng shui, the front of the splendid mausoleum, surrounded by tall green trees, had drawn a large group of visitors, standing in a line longer than he had expected. People seemed to be quite patient, some taking pictures, some reading guidebooks, some cracking watermelon seeds.

He joined the end of the line, moving up with others. Looking at a body sometimes helps, if only psychologically, he told himself again. He had to zero in, so to speak, to get a better understanding of someone who was possibly involved.

Peddlers swarmed, hawking watches, lighters, and all sorts of small decorations and gadgets bearing the name of Mao. Chen picked up a watch with an ingeniously designed dial—it showed Mao in a green army uniform with the armband of the Red Guard. The pendulum consisted of Mao's hand waving majestically on top of Tiananmen Gate, endless like time itself.

A security guard hurried over, shooing away the peddlers like insistent flies. Raising a green-painted loudspeaker, he urged the visitors to purchase flowers in homage to the great leader. Several people paid for the yellow chrysanthemums wrapped in plastic as the line swerved into the large courtyard. Chen did as well. There was also a mandatory booklet on all the great contributions Mao made to China, and he bought a copy, but didn't open it.

Scarcely had the line of people turned into the north hall, however, when they were ordered to lay the flowers beneath a white marble statue of Mao standing in relief against an immense tapestry of China's mountains and rivers in the brilliantly lit background.

"Shameless," a square-faced man in the line cursed. "Only a minute after you've paid for the chrysanthemums. They cash in on the dead by reselling the flowers."

"But at least they are not charging an entrance fee," a long-faced man said. "At all the other parks in Beijing, you now have to buy tickets."

"Do you think I would come here if I had to buy a ticket?" the square-faced man retorted. "They just want to keep up the long lines by promising no charge."

Chen wasn't so sure about that, but it took no less than half an hour for the line to edge into the Hall of Last Respects, and then to move up, finally, to the crystal coffin, in which Mao lay in a gray Mao suit, draped with a large red flag of the Chinese Communist Party, with honor gaurds solemnly standing around, motionless like toy soldiers.

In spite of his anticipation, Chen was stunned at the sight of Mao. So majestic on the screen of Chen's memory, Mao now appeared shrunken, shriveled out of proportion, his cheeks hollow like dried oranges, his lips waxy, heavily painted. The little hair he had left looked somehow pasted or painted.

Chen had stood close to Mao in the crystal coffin for less than a minute before he was compelled to move on. Visitors behind him were edging up and pushing.

Instead of turning into the Memorial Chamber with pictures and documents about Mao on display, Chen headed straight to the exit.

Once out of the Memorial Hall, he inhaled a deep breath of fresh air. Peddlers again came rushing over. It was close to twelve, so he decided to start moving in the direction of his appointment.

Passing under the arch of the towering Tiananmen Gate, he purchased a ticket to the Forbidden City Museum, mainly for the short cut. With the traffic snarl along Chang'an Avenue, it could take much longer for him to get to the park by taxi.

The Forbidden City, strictly speaking, referred to the palace compound, including the court, various imperial halls, offices, and living quarters, but just beyond the palace, there were royal gardens and other imperial complexes no less forbidden to the ordinary people. After the overthrow of the Qing dynasty, the palace proper was turned into a museum, with various exhibition halls displaying the splendors of the imperial dynasties.

The palace was apparently too huge for a museum. So booths appeared in the courtyards, along the trails, and at the corners. Absentmindedly, he bought a stick of sugar-glazed hawthorn, a Beijing street food specially. It tasted surprisingly sour.

He began to be aware of a subtle effect the imperial surroundings were having on him. A self-contained world of divine sublimity, where an emperor couldn't have helped seeing himself as the son of the heaven, high above the people, a godly ruler endowed with the sacred mandate and mission for him alone. Consequently, no ethics or rules whatsoever could possibly apply to him.

So for Mao, the anti-Rightist movement, the Three Red Banners, and the Cultural Revolution—all those political movements that had cost millions and millions of Chinese people's lives—might have been nothing more than what was necessary for an emperor to consolidate his power, at least in his imagination within the high walls of the Forbidden City . . .

Instead of stepping into any of the imperial exhibition rooms, Chen kept walking straight ahead. That morning, he was the only such determined passerby there.

Soon, he walked through the museum's back gate, from which he then glimpsed the tip of the White Pagoda in the North Sea Park.

NINETEEN

FANGSHAN RESTAURANT, WHICH CHEN had chosen for the lunch meeting with Diao, was in the North Sea Park, originally an outside imperial garden attached to the Forbidden City, celebrated for its imperial history.

The restaurant choice was also made for a personal reason. During his college years, Chen had talked to Ling about having lunch there. They had never done so, as it had been far beyond his means.

There was still about half an hour before the appointment time. So he took a leisurely walk along the lake. In spite of the park's name, there was no sea, only a man-made lake, which was exaggerated for the sake of the emperor. Still, it was a fantastic park in the center of the city, adjacent to the Beijing Library, where Ling had once worked, and with the silhouette of the White Pagoda shimmering behind.

He made his way toward a small bridge that he remembered from years before. Cutting across a corner, he saw an arts-and-crafts boutique store embosomed in the summer foliage. He stepped in, but things were too expensive inside. In the evening, he might have some time for a visit to Xidan Department Store to choose a present.

Then the bridge came into view. There, a young girl stood leaning against the railing, gazing out to the verdant mountains in the distance, a pigeon whistle buzzing in the air. He was overwhelmed with a sense of déjà vu. *The heart-breaking spring ripple / still so green under the bridge, / the ripples that reflected her arrival / light-footed, in such beauty / as would shame a wild goose into fleeing.*

One afternoon, in his last years of college, Ling had arranged to meet him here with some books he had requested. He was delayed at school, and she must have been waiting for a long time. Hurrying over, he saw her standing on the muddy planks of a little bridge, resting one foot lightly on the railing, scratching her ankle, her face framed by wind-tangled hair. The scene was inexplicably touching: it was as if she was merging into a backdrop of willow catkins, which symbolized ill-fated beauty in Tang-dynasty poetry.

Whether the scene of the willow catkins had foreshadowed their relationship, no one could tell. But it wasn't time for nostalgia, he told himself, heading back in the direction of the restaurant.

Fangshan presented an ancient-looking front. In a quiet flagstone courtyard, a waitress dressed like a Qing palace lady came up and led him to a private room. What struck him first was the ubiquitous yellow color—the color exclusively for the royal family. Against the yellow-painted walls, the table was set up with an apricot-colored tablecloth and gilt chopsticks, and behind him, an old cabinet elaborately embossed with golden dragons. Sitting by the window, he opened the briefcase and took out the information he had about Diao.

Diao was a newcomer on the literary scene—a middle school teacher up until his retirement, with no publications whatsoever to his credit until he suddenly produced his bestseller, *Cloud and Rain in Shanghai*. That practically ruled out the possibility that Diao would recognize Chen. The former wasn't a member of the Writers' Association, and they couldn't have met before. The chief inspector should be able to play a role similar to the one he had at Xie Mansion.

People attributed the success of *Cloud and Rain in Shanghai* to its subject matter, but nonetheless it bespoke of the author's ingenuity. Chen had read the book, impressed by the subtle balance between the stated and the unstated in the text.

At two or three minutes before one, the waitress led in a gray-haired man of medium build, with a deeply furrowed forehead and beady eyes, wearing a black T-shirt, white pants, and shiny dress shoes.

"You must be Mr. Diao," Chen said, rising from the table.

"Yes, I'm Diao."

"Oh, it's a great honor to meet you. I'm Chen. Your book, *Cloud and Rain in Shanghai,* is such a big bestseller."

"Thank you for your invitation to lunch. This is an imperial restaurant, really expensive, and I've only heard about it before."

"I was a student in Beijing years ago, and I would dream of coming here. So it's for the sake of nostalgia as well."

"That's not a bad reason," Diao said with a grin, showing cigarette-stained teeth. "Don't you remember a line by our great leader Chairman Mao? 'Six hundred million people are all Sun and Yao, great emperors.' Poetic hyperbole, to be sure, but Mao's right about one thing. People are interested in being emperors, or being like emperors."

"You are absolutely right."

"It explains the popularity of the restaurant. People come not only for the food, but for the imperial association too. For a short moment, they can imagine themselves being an emperor."

That might have also been true for Shang—she might have enjoyed imagining herself as an emperor's woman. Chen raised his cup, making no comment.

The waitress approached and offered them a small platter of dainty, golden *ououtou*, steamed buns usually made of maize. The ones Chen remembered from his college years had been somber in color, hard to swallow. These looked very different.

"It's made from a special green bean," the waitress said, reading his surprise. "Super delicious. The Empress Dowager's favorite."

"Great, we'll try that," Chen said. "Recommend some other specials to us."

"For the private room, there is a minimum charge of one thousand yuan. You have to spend at least that amount anyway. So let me recommend an exquisite meal of light delicacies. All small dishes, about twenty of them—the Empress Dowager's way. That was the minimum for one meal for her too. To begin with, the live fish from the Central South Sea steamed with tender ginger and green onion."

"That's good," Chen said. No one would miss the association between the Forbidden City and Central South Sea.

"What else?" Diao asked for the first time.

"The roast Beijing duck, of course."

"Duck from the palace?"

"Genuine Beijing ducks. Specially fed, six to eight months old. Most restaurants now cook with an electric oven. We stick to the traditional wood-burning oven, and we use not just any firewood, but a special pine wood so the flavor penetrates deep into the texture of the meat. It was unique practice used only for the emperors," she said with pride in her voice. "Oh, our chefs follow the tradition of blowing up the duck with their mouths and sewing up its ass before placing it into the oven."

"Wow, so much to learn about a duck," Diao exclaimed.

"We offer the celebrated five ways of eating a duck: crisp duck skin slices wrapped in pancake, duck meat slices fried with green garlic, duck feet immersed in wine, duck gizzard stir-fried with green vegetables, and duck soup, but the soup takes about two hours before it turns creamy white."

"That's fine. I mean the soup," Chen said. "Take your time with the soup. Bring up whatever specials you think are the restaurant's best. Today, it is for a great writer."

"You overwhelm me with your generosity," Diao said.

"As a businessman, I've made a bunch of money, but so what? In a hundred years, will the money still be mine? Indeed, as our grand master Old Du said, literature alone lasts for thousands of autumns. It's proper and right for a novice like me to buy a meal for a master like you."

Chen's speech echoed one by Ouyang, a friend Chen had met in Guangzhou. An amateur poet yet a successful businessman, Ouyang had made a similar statement over a dim sum meal.

As far as nonfiction was concerned, however, Chen was legitimately a novice, so he could in fact learn something from Diao.

"Your book was a huge success," Chen went on. "Please tell me how you came to write it?"

"I was a middle school teacher all my life. As a rule, I would start my class by quoting proverbs. Now, for a proverb to be passed on from generation to generation, there must be something in it—something in our culture. One day, I quoted a proverb—*hongyan baoming*—a beauty's fate is so thin. When my students pressed me for an example, I thought about the tragic fate of Shang. Eventually, I started contemplating a book project, but I hesitated to focus on Shang, for the reasons you might guess. In the process of researching it, I learned about the equally tragic fate of her daughter, Qian. Something clicked in my mind. That's how I came to write it."

"That's fantastic," Chen said. "You must have done a lot of research on Shang."

"Some, but not a lot."

"It's like a book behind a book. In the lines about the daughter, people may read the story of the mother."

"Readers read from their own perspectives, but it's a book about Qian."

"So tell me more about the story behind the story. I'm fascinated by the real details."

"What cannot be said must pass over in silence," Diao responded guardedly. "What's true and what's not? You like the *Dream of the Red Chamber*, so you must remember the famous couplet on the arch gate of the Grand Illusion—'When the true is false, the false is true. / Where there is nothing, there is everything.'"

As Chen anticipated, Diao wasn't willing to speak freely to a stranger, not even to just admit that it was a true story, despite the lunch at Fangshan.

"People of my generation have heard all sorts of stories from those years," Diao went on, taking a sip at the tea. "As long as the official archive remains sealed to the public, we may never be able to tell whether a story is true or not."

"But you must have gathered more information than you used in the book."

"I put in only what I considered reliable."

"Still, you must have interviewed a lot of people."

Diao didn't respond. A speaker outside started playing a song from the popular TV series *Romance of Three Kingdoms*. "*How many times, the sinking sun red, / a white-haired man angles, alone, in the river / rippling with stories from time immemorial . . .*" The TV series was based on the historic novel about the vicissitudes of the emperors and would-be-emperors in the third century, and the author ended the novel with a poem from the perspective of an old fisherman.

"Remember the poem titled 'Snow' by Mao?" Diao asked instead.

"Yes, particularly the second stanza. '*The rivers and mountains so enchanting / made countless heroes bow in homage. / Alas, the First Emperor of the Qin and the Emperor Wu of the Han / were lacking in literary grace; / Emperor Tai of the Tang, and the Emperor Tai of the Song / had not enough poetry at heart; / Genghis Khan, / the proud son of Heaven for his generation, / knew only shooting eagle, bow outstretched. / All are past and gone! / To look for the really heroic, / you have to count on today.*'"

The return of the waitress interrupted their talk. She placed a large platter on the table. "The live fish from the Central South Sea."

"I had to distinguish between what would be publishable, and what wouldn't," Diao resumed after helping himself to a large fish filet.

"Tell me about your background research then."

"What's the point? It's nothing but knocking upon one door after another. Let's enjoy our meal. To be honest with you, I'm a budget gourmet."

"Come on. The meal is nothing for a bestselling author like you. That's why I decided to quit my business."

"You keep talking about my book as a bestseller. A lot were sold, that's true, but I got very little for myself."

"That's unbelievable, Mr. Diao."

"Don't dream of making money by writing books. For that, you'd better stick to your business. If it would help, I might as well tell you how much I've made. Less than five thousand yuan. According to the editor, he took a great risk with an initial printing of five thousand copies."

"But what about the second and third printing? There must have been more than ten printings for your book."

"There is never even a second printing. As soon as there is buzz on a book, pirated copies come into the market, and you don't get a single penny."

"What a shame! Only five thousand yuan," Chen said. Some of his more lucrative translation projects had paid him as much, for only ten pages or so, though he knew he had gotten the project because he was chief inspector. He glanced at his leather briefcase. It contained a sum of at least five thousand yuan—which he brought to buy a wedding present for Ling. But he had been having second thoughts about it after watching her leave in that luxurious limousine last night. It might be a large sum for him, but it was nothing to her.

He picked up the briefcase, snapped it open, and took out an envelope. "A small 'red envelope' of about five thousand yuan, Mr. Diao. Far from enough to show my respect, it is only a token of my admiration."

It was a bulging envelope, unsealed, with a hundred-yuan bill peeping, which bore a portrait of Mao, declaring as the supreme Party leader to China, "The poorer, the more revolutionary."

"What do you mean, Mr. Chen?"

"To tell the truth, I'm interested in writing something about Shang, publishable or not. So the envelope is in compensation for your invaluable information. For a businessman like me, it's an investment, but it also shows my respect for you."

"An old man like me, Mr. Chen, doesn't have anything to brag about, but I think I can size up a man well. Whatever you are up to, you aren't after money."

"Whatever you tell me is not black or white. Nor will anyone be able to prove it's from you, Mr. Diao. Outside of this room, you may say you have never met me."

"Not that I was so unwilling to tell you the story about Shang, Mr. Chen," Diao said, draining the cup, "but what I gathered could be just hearsay. You can't take it literally."

"I understand. I'm not a cop, so I don't have to base every sentence on hard facts."

"I didn't write the book about Shang, but that doesn't mean that it shouldn't be written. In ten or fifteen years, aspects of the Cultural Revolution may be totally forgotten. Oh, you're not recording our talk, are you?"

"No, I'm not." Chen opened the briefcase again, showing the contents.

"I trust you. So where shall I begin?" Diao went on, barely waiting for an answer. "Well, I won't beat about the bush. About Shang: believe it or not, I happened to know a peddler, whose fish booth was crushed by her body falling out of a fifth-story window—"

The roast Beijing duck arrived with the waitress as well as a white-clad and -capped duck chef, who peeled the crisp duck skin in front of their table with a flourish.

"The slices of crispy duck skin, wrapped in the paper-thin pancake with the special sauce and green onion was the Empress Dowager's favorite," the waitress said. "As for this one special dish of fried duck tongues mantled with red peppers like maple-covered hills, can you guess how many ducks?"

"Can I ask you a favor?" Chen said to her. "All of these are fantastic, but can you serve the rest of them together? We are just beginning an important talk."

"I'll let our chef know," she said, bowing low like a Manchurian girl before she headed to the door. "You go ahead."

TWENTY

"NOW, BACK TO THE story," Chen said. "You were just talking about the end of Shang's life, about the fishmonger."

"Oh yes, he was indeed a talkative monger, giving a vivid description of her death scene, though I wonder how he could remember those details after so many years."

"Did Shang die instantly?"

"No, she didn't. She said a few words before she lost consciousness."

"What did she say?"

"She said she lived on the fifth floor."

"What could that mean?"

"He had no clue," Diao said reflectively, picking a tiny fishbone out from between his teeth. "Did she want to draw attention to her room on the fifth floor? She could have been tortured or pushed out of the window. Did she want people to call for an ambulance, using the phone in the room? In those days, there was only one public phone station in the neighborhood. What went through her mind in her last moments, no one can say."

"What then?"

"Well, she was so 'black,' people avoided her like the plague while she lay there. No one did anything except for watching and finger-pointing. A couple of red-armbanded men then rushed out of the building, speaking in a Beijing accent—"

"Hold on, Mr. Diao. In your book, you mention a special team from Beijing. So those men were from that team?"

"The fishmonger had no idea who they were, but they stood around her, keeping others away from the scene. When an ambulance finally arrived, she was long dead."

"Did the police come?"

"It took hours for a police car to arrive. What did they do? They tried to wash away the bloodstains on the curb. For that matter, they didn't do it thoroughly. Flies swirled around the dark red spots for days."

"What a tragic fate!"

"A fate full of twists and turns," Diao said, finishing a duck-stuffed pancake and wiping the sauce stain on his fingers with the napkin, as though wiping away memories. "As you know, she first became well-known in the forties. She must have attracted a lot of men—rich and powerful ones—and that shadowed her after 1949. Things were different in the early fifties. Young lovers kissing in Bund Park then could have been detained for pursuing a 'bourgeois lifestyle.' But Shang continued to lead a 'notorious bourgeois life.' What's worse, her husband got into political trouble, which spelled the end of her career.

"It was then that a *guiren* appeared in her life. *Guiren*—you know, an important man who brings about a change of luck into one's life. One day, she got a handwritten note from the mayor of Shanghai, 'Please come, Comrade Shang.' So she hurried to the China-Russia Friendship Hall, where she was received by Mao. There was a grand dance party that evening. Swirling in Mao's arms, she told him about her troubles. Shortly afterward, she was assigned new movie roles, one after another. In the fifties, the movie industry was state controlled and planned. Only a few movies were made each year. A lot of talented actors and actresses couldn't get parts—whether or not they had political problems. Against all odds, in one movie she played a militia woman, for which she even won a major award. She visited several foreign countries as a member of a Chinese artists delegation. And at a convention, the Party leaders would receive the delegation members before or after those visits abroad. So she appeared in newspaper pictures together with Mao."

"You have done a thorough study, Mr. Diao."

"Let me say one thing about my research. Even in the official publications, Mao's passion for dancing has been acknowledged. After 1949, social dancing was condemned and banned as part and parcel of the bourgeois lifestyle, but within the high walls of the Forbidden City, Mao still danced to his heart's content. According to the interpretation given in the *People's Daily*, Mao worked so hard for China that these parties were necessary to provide relaxation for our great leader. But that's nonsense. As for what happened after he danced with Shang, I don't think I have to go into graphic details."

"No, you don't," Chen said. "But I have a question. During those years, perhaps there weren't too many gifted partners in the Forbidden City. As a celebrated actress before 1949, Shang must have danced well. Could it be that Mao came to her for that reason?"

"It takes a couple of hours for a young girl to learn how to dance like a pro. Mao was no dancing master. There was no need for him to go to the trouble to look for a partner in another city. Mao wasn't without rivals at the top, in those days. Even his special train was bugged. What would people say about his relationship with such a notorious actress?" Diao went on, putting a crispy duck tongue into his mouth. "But he couldn't help it. When he first met her, she was in her mid-thirties, in the full bloom of a woman's beauty, elegant, highly educated, and from a good family too. Her dancing was like waves rippling in the breeze, like clouds wafting in the sky. And he could have watched her movies as early as in Yan'an. Madam Mao was also an actress, we shouldn't forget that."

"Mao had an actress fetish, you mean?"

"Whatever you want to call it, Shang's fate changed dramatically."

"But could it be some local officials contributed to the change in her life? Seeing her as Mao's favorite partner, they tried to curry favor. Mao might not have been aware of it."

"They wouldn't have gone out of their way for one of his partners," Diao said. "He had so many. They knew that. And the poems Mao wrote for her were unmistakable."

"Poems—'The Militia Woman,' right?"

"So you've also heard about that poem? Actually, there's another one, 'Ode to the Plum Blossom.'"

"Really!" Chen said, remembering what he had discussed with Long about the poems. "Are you sure? Did you see a scroll of that poem that Mao wrote for her?"

"No, I didn't, but the meaning of the poem is obvious. '*Pretty, she does not claim the spring for herself, / content to be a herald of spring. / When hills are ablaze with wildflowers, / in their midst she smiles.*' It's really in the tradition of the *Book of Poems*. In the first poem of that collection, an emperor's virtuous wife rejoices at his finding a new love. Shang would have known better than to exhibit such a scroll at home, I would think," Diao said thoughtfully. "I interviewed some of her neighbors, and according to one, there was a scroll on the wall of the bedroom. But it was a poem by Wang Cangling, a Tang-dynasty poet, entitled 'Deserted Imperial Concubine at Changxing Chamber.'"

"Yes, I know it. '*At dawn, having swept the courtyard / with the broom, she has nothing else / to do, except to twirl, / and twirl the round silk fan / in her fingers. Exquisite as jade, / she cannot compete with the autumn crow flying / overhead, which still carries the warmth / from the Imperial Sun Palace.*'"

"The meaning of the poem is unmistakable," Daio said, nodding in approval. "Her complaining about the emperor's neglect, feeling worse than an autumn crow that still carries the warmth, as it were, from the Imperial Sun Palace."

"But Shang was no imperial concubine."

"He might have made some promise to her. Then the choice of the poem in her bedroom would make perfect sense."

"You have a point," Chen said. "Was there anything else unusual about her that you found out but didn't mention in your writing?"

"Let me think. There were some details, but I didn't pay much attention to them," Diao said, picking up a piece of pickled garlic. "Oh, she had a passion for photography, among other things."

"You mean she liked taking pictures?"

"Yes. I tried to find some of those pictures for the book. According to her neighbors, she took a lot of pictures of Qian, but the special group from Beijing must have taken them all away. That's another thing she and Madam Mao have in common. They both loved photography. A weird coincidence. Not many Chinese in the sixties could afford cameras. Shang even did her own developing, having converted a storage room into an occasional darkroom."

"That's unusual," Chen said.

The waitress reappeared with a golden cart, on which she brought to their table an impressive array of special dishes.

"Shark fin stewed in the shape of Buddha's fingers, camel paw braised with scallion, Mandarin-duck-like prawns, abalone in white sauce—"

"Why like Buddha's fingers?" Diao asked again.

"The Empress Dowager had long, long fingernails, like Buddha's," the waitress explained glibly. "In her day, people at the palace called her Old Buddha—"

"Thank you. We'll enjoy them at our leisure," Chen cut her short before she could start an elaborate introduction. "If we need anything else, we'll let you know."

"A different question, Mr. Diao," Chen said as the cart wheeled out of the room. "In her last days, did Shang say anything concerning Mao to the Red Guards or to the special team from Beijing?"

"I talked to the Red Guards from her movie studio. According to them, she said something to the effect that Chairman Mao knew how much she loved him. No one took it seriously. At least not in the sense that she might have been suggesting. Every one could have said those words at the time. But I know nothing about what she might have said to the special team."

"Now, why a special team from Beijing?"

"A common interpretation is that it was because of Madam Mao. Her persecution of her ex-fellow artists was brought up in the charges against her after the Cultural Revolution. For her, those who knew of her notorious past, especially those with old newspapers and letters in their possession, had to be silenced. Another guess was that it was because of Madam Mao's jealousy. Once she became the head of the CPC Cultural Revolution Group, she ran amuck for her revenge. Several people who were supposedly 'intimate and close' to Mao were persecuted to death. Weishi, a young and beautiful Russian interpreter for Mao, was thrown into jail at the beginning of the Cultural Revolution and found dead in a stinking cell there, stark naked, her body bruised all over."

"Madam Mao worshipped Empress Lu of the Han dynasty, lauding her to the skies during the Cultural Revolution. I'm no scholar, but I remember one story about Empress Lu," Chen commented, chopsticking up a piece of shark fin shaped like a Buddha's finger. "After the emperor died, Empress Lu threw his favorite concubine into jail. Cutting off her ex-rival's arms and legs, severing her tongue, and gouging out her eyes. The empress kept the mutilated woman moaning and writhing in a sordid cell that was a stinking sty, her body naked and soiled. Empress Lu chose to show the woman to her own son like that, saying that it was a human pig."

"Yes, her son never recovered from the shock, fell sick and died. That's another story, of course."

"So I have a question, Mr. Diao. Empress Lu did that after the death of the emperor. Madam Mao attacked her rivals when Mao was still alive. Wasn't she afraid of him?"

"That was a question for me too. She described herself as a dog loyal to Mao, biting and attacking whomever he wanted her to. He

194

might have needed her badly during the Cultural Revolution. Besides, Mao cared little for women no longer in his favor," Diao said, taking a careful bite at the abalone. "This is the first abalone I've ever had."

It was not the first for Chen, but it was the first time he was paying for it. He waited for Diao to continue.

"He dumped his wife Kaihui, without so much as divorcing her or notifying her, when he married Zizhen in the Jinggang Mountains," Diao went on. "In fact, Kaihui's death resulted from his siege of Changsha, a consequence he should have anticipated. After the Long March, he dumped Zizhen like another worn-out mop, letting her suffer alone in a Moscow mental institution, while he wallowed in the clouding and raining on the *Kang* bed with Madam Mao. So he dumped Shang, just one of the women he had slept with. It's no surprise he didn't do anything to help her."

"That's unbelievable," Chen said, the slice of the stewed camel paw slipping from his chopsticks, splashing gravy out of the platter. He had no idea how the emperors could have enjoyed the fatty greasy taste.

"Think about what happened to Liu Shaoqi. Once the chairman of the People's Republic of China, he, too, died naked in prison without any medical treatment, and his body was instantly cremated under a false name. Mao was so cold-blooded."

"Leaving Mao aside, you mentioned in the book that the special team put a lot of pressure on Shang, to try and make her cooperate, but what could they have been trying to obtain from her?"

"From what I learned, it was something like 'her evil plan to harm Mao.' No one believed it."

"Then what do you think it could be?"

"For one thing, an unpublished poem to her in his calligraphy."

"That's intriguing. A poem knocked off during a moment of amorous passion?" Chen said. But would that have triggered a special team from Beijing? After all, a poem could be open to many interpretations, unless it was downright erotic or obscene. He doubted it. "Whatever it might be, did they find it?"

"I don't know, but I don't think so."

"So could Shang have left it to her daughter Qian?"

"Not likely. Like other kids of black family background, Qian denounced Shang, and she didn't come back home until after Shang's death. No, Shang had no time to do so before jumping out of the window."

"So Qian went through a dramatic change—from one radically cut off from her black family to one hopelessly lost in bourgeois carnival passion?"

"She was a girl traumatized at a young age, plagued by those stories about Shang's 'shameless sex saga,'" Diao said. "I don't want to be too hard on her."

"I couldn't agree more. Qian, too, suffered a lot. But her death too was quite suspicious, I've heard."

"Her death was an accident—almost at the end of the Cultural Revolution. I don't see anything suspicious about it."

"I see," Chen said, picking up a pork-stuffed sesame cake, a surprisingly ordinary snack that tasted more agreeable than the exotic delicacies. "You must have talked to Jiao too."

"She knew little about her mother, let alone her grandmother. An ill-fated girl."

Diao must have contacted Jiao a couple of years earlier and was unaware of the subsequent change in her life.

"She's doing fine now, I think," Chen said. "Now, tell me more about what happened to Qian after Shang's death."

"Qian was driven out of her apartment—"

"Immediately?"

"No, two or three months after Shang's death."

"So, hypothetically, she could have looked around the apartment for something left behind by Shang."

"Well, Shang could have left something behind, but the place had been turned upside down by the special group—"

Once again the waitress entered, serving the celebrated duck soup. The table now appeared overcrowded, several dishes untouched or hardly touched.

"The emperor's way. You have to have a table full of dishes. Symbolically complete," the waitress said, smiling before retracing her light-footed steps, "like the complete banquet of the Manchurian and Han."

"That's why people want to be an emperor, paying for a banquet they cannot finish," Diao said, putting a spoonful of the soup into his mouth. "The soup is hot."

"One can see meaning in anything from the perspective one chooses. For a different question, was there anyone else close to Shang in her last years?"

"No. There's a superstitious belief about an emperor-favored woman being different, almost divine, through the cloud and rain. In ancient China, the imperial concubines or palace ladies had to remain single all their lives, even after the demise of the emperor. Untouchable, forbidden too, like part of the Forbidden City. People could have heard of her relationship with Mao. They may have known better than to get involved with her."

"But I don't necessarily mean in that sense—not necessarily men."

"She didn't have any close friends, not with such a well-guarded secret." Diao added broodingly, "Well, except perhaps for that maid of hers, who had been with Shang before her first marriage and stayed with her until the outbreak of the Cultural Revolution."

"Yes, there are stories about exemplary relationships between master and servants, mistress and maid, in classical Chinese literature. Like in the play *Seeking and Saving the Only Heir of the Zhao*. It even inspired Brecht, as I recall. So do you think Shang could have trusted her?"

"You're no literary novice, Mr. Chen," Diao said, casting him a sharp look.

"I'm a novice beside you," Chen said, regretting that a moment of unrestrained bookishness had given him away.

"If it was something concerning Mao, I don't think Shang would have given it to the maid. The maid, because of her class status, could have easily denounced Shang in those years."

"But did you hear anything about the maid after Shang's death?"

"In my research about Jiao's childhood, I learned that nobody visited the girl in the orphanage except an unidentified old woman who came a couple of times. I'm not sure if it's the maid, who must have been old then," Diao said, visibly more and more uncomfortable with the direction of the talk. He must have started to suspect Chen's purpose. He glanced at his watch. "I'm sorry, I have to go back to babysitting, Mr. Chen. This lunch has taken much longer than I expected. You may call me if you have other questions."

It was almost three. A long, protracted lunch. Chen also rose, shaking hands with Diao, watching him leave.

Afterward, Chen sat alone in the private room for several minutes, facing the littered table, on which a number of dishes remained untouched.

He then picked up his cell phone and dialed Old Hunter in Shanghai, while meeting the glare of a golden dragon embossed on the vermilion-painted pillar.

TWENTY-ONE

IN THE HOT-WATER HOUSE, Old Hunter sat alone, drinking tea in silence, in the afternoon sunlight.

The hot-water house was far less than a teahouse, with the sort of dual function of providing hot water to the neighborhood and tea to occasional customers. There were only a couple of rough wooden tables behind the stove. There were several cheap snack booths nearby. In the past, people sometimes came to the hot-water house with baked cakes and steamed buns, spent a penny or two for a cup of tea, then would talk and enjoy themselves like lords.

But Shanghai was rapidly turning into a city of contrasts and contradictions. Across the street stood expensive new apartment buildings, but here beside the hot-water house, it remained pretty much a slum. In fact, no tea-drinking customers came in for hours.

It suited Old Hunter well, though. He didn't have to play a role. An old, non–Big Buck tea drinker, that's what he was, even bringing in his own tea. All he needed to pay for was the hot water. He could sit there for hours, talking about the tea to the proprietor, or, like that afternoon, drinking tea alone without a single waiter walking around with a long-billed kettle, ready to serve.

The tea was getting cold but was still black as hell. He had put in a large handful of oolong, trying to revive himself with extra-strong tea. It was because of the scene he had caught at Jiao's window last night and had continued watching, sitting there across the street, late into the night. As a result, the next day, he was feeling as groggy as a sick cat.

He was old, he admitted, spitting out the bitter tea leaves, but the case—though not *his* case—was special to him. He thought about his interview yesterday of Bei, the security guard at the Jiao's apartment complex.

The meeting with Bei had yielded little. Like him, Bei was a retiree, working at a post-retirement job to supplement his scant pension. Unlike Old Hunter's, Bei's job paid little, and the security guard had to stand at the complex entrance, rain or shine, six days a week. To their pleasant surprise, the retirees shared a passion for tea. So they went to a better place, the celebrated Lake Pavilion Teahouse at the City God's Temple Market, where Old Hunter tapped Bei for information about Jiao over the exquisite Yixing tea set on the mahogany table. Bei started talking without reservation.

According to Bei, Jiao had few visitors here. It was a well-guarded subdivision, where visitors had to call up from the entrance, so Bei was quite sure about that. Nor could Bei remember having seen her in the company of any man. Then he recalled that about half a year earlier, Jiao had had an unusual visitor, a poor old woman dressed in rags—a rare sight for the complex—who claimed to come from Jiao's old neighborhood. She was not educated, not even that coherent, and Bei questioned her long and carefully. When he finally called up, Jiao hurried out to usher the visitor in. After two or three hours, Jiao accompanied the visitor out, calling her granny and hailing a taxi for her. The old woman never appeared again.

It wasn't too surprising for Jiao to be nice to a visitor from her old neighborhood. If anything, the question was, which neighborhood?

She had grown up in an orphanage. After that, she shared a room with "provincial sisters" until she moved over here.

But Jiao had other visitors, at least another one, who went unnoticed by Bei, and by Internal Security. Old Hunter pondered, taking another drink from the half-empty cup, raising his hand, about to bang the table like a Suzhou opera singer, when he restrained himself. What he had seen last night, after his talk with the security guard, confirmed Peng's suspicions about Jiao's secret life. From across the street, the view of her room wasn't good, but the one glimpse of the two standing close to the window was unmistakable, though it was just one fleeting glimpse.

Now, a security guard like Bei might not have closely watched each resident every minute, but Internal Security's video camera should have. How could the mysterious man have entered the building, and then her apartment, without being noticed even once? Old Hunter chewed the tea leaves he had scooped up from the bottom of the cup. A habit picked up from reading about it in a memoir about Mao.

There was no progress in the investigation of Yang's murder, either, not from what he had heard. No suspect arrested or even targeted. Lieutenant Song was furious with Chen's unexplained vacation.

Like Detective Yu, Old Hunter didn't think the chief inspector was taking the vacation for personal reasons, even though the emergency number given by Chen suggested that during his stay in Beijing, he was in contact with, if not in the company of, his HCC ex-girlfriend.

It was then that Old Hunter's cell phone rang. It was Chen.

Without saying anything about his vacation, Chen went straight to the suspicious involvement of the special team from Beijing at the beginning of the Cultural Revolution. Among other things, Chen mentioned Shang's passion for taking photographs, some of which might still be around, and Shang's maid. It was a hurried call; Chen sounded guarded, as if nervous that the call was being tapped. He didn't divulge the source of the information and hung up before Old Hunter had time to ask any questions.

Still, Old Hunter managed to copy down the number from Beijing.

It was not Chen's usual one. The phone call was clearly a tip on a direction Chen wanted him to follow here in Shanghai.

Regarding the special team, Old Hunter had used up all his connections making inquiries, but got nothing. They came to Shanghai such a long time ago, and in such a secretive way.

As for Shang's pictures, he had also drawn a blank. It was trendy nowadays to collect old photographs—not just of Shang, but of other celebrities as well. Whatever the case, he had no luck in finding pictures of or by Shang.

So the only thing for him to do was to approach the maid. Possibly the same old woman who had visited Jiao in her apartment here.

Consulting the Yellow Pages, he lost no time getting in touch with the orphanage. According to the secretary who answered the phone, there were records that people had visited Jiao years earlier, but there was no name or address of the visitor recorded.

Still, it could have been Shang's maid. In Suzhou opera, there were stories about such loyal, self-sacrificing maids.

After several more phone calls, he managed to acquire some basic information about the maid, who was surnamed Zhong and now in her eighties. Instead of going back to the countryside after leaving Shang's household, Zhong had stayed on in the city, alone, eking out a living on the "minimum allowance" of her registered city residence.

Old Hunter put the small envelope of tea leaves back into his pocket. The owner of the hot-water house still remained behind the partition wall, indulging himself with a popular TV soap opera. For five cents per thermos bottle, the business was just an excuse to keep the place registered as business property—which would mean more generous compensation in the event of its being torn down for a new housing project. Lunch time was over and no one would pop in until dinnertime, when provincial workers might purchase hot water for their cold rice.

Throwing ten cents on the table, Old Hunter left for a visit to Zhong.

He had to take two buses before getting off at a stop close to Sanguantang Bridge, which spanned the darksome water of Suzhou Creek. Zhong lived in Putou District, an area mixed with old slums, new skyscrapers, and ongoing concrete and steel constructions.

Was Zhong going to tell him anything? He wasn't going to approach her as a cop, as someone with authority, who could make her talk. He slowed down, thinking, in the small clearing under the beginning curve of the bridge, perhaps only about a couple of minutes away from the lane she lived in. He lit a cigarette.

In a convenience store by the lane entrance, he bought a plastic bag of dried lychee. The end of the small lane brought him to an ancient two-story building. The black-painted door opened in to a narrow corridor littered with coal briquette stoves and bamboo baskets, and to a dark staircase leading up to an attic room. He fumbled for a while without finding a switch. So he groped up the stairs in the dark, the staircase creaking precariously underfoot, until he reached the top.

The door opened without waiting for his knock. An old woman presented herself in the doorway, probably in her eighties, short and shrunk. In the light streaming down from the attic window, she looked like an ancient peasant woman from a backward village, wearing a gray towel around her hair and a string of Buddhist beads at her neck, and twirling a shorter string of beads in her right hand. Still, she appeared to be quite alert for her age.

"What do you want with me?" she said, showing a frown on her deep-lined forehead.

"Oh, you must be Auntie Zhong. I'm Old Yu," he started with a rehearsed story. "Please forgive me for taking the liberty to visit you. For an old retiree like me, I have only one wish unfulfilled in this mundane world."

"What's that?"

"I'm a loyal fan of Shang, having watched every one of her movies, but I haven't seen a real-life photograph of hers. You were blessed to have been with her for so many years, Auntie Zhong. I wonder if you could show me or sell me some of her pictures."

"She had so many fans. But what difference did it make in her last days?" She stepped back, however, making a vague gesture to let him in the pigeon coop–like attic room. "Now, after so many years, you come out of nowhere, asking for her pictures."

"Now listen to me, Auntie Zhong. I knew nothing about her troubles at the time. Later on, I searched for her pictures everywhere, but without success. It was only yesterday that somebody told me about your relationship to her, and about her passion for photographs. So I thought she might have left some to you as souveniers."

"No, Mr. Yu."

"If you don't have any pictures, would you be able to tell me where I can find them?"

"Why can't you leave an old woman in peace? I already have one foot dangling in the coffin. And have mercy on Shang, leave her in peace too."

"It's more than twenty years since her death, but not a day passes by that I don't have her in mind. A matchless pearl with her beauty radiating from her soul. These new movie stars nowadays are mud-covered hens compared to a graceful phoenix like her." He declared, lifting the plastic bag, "I'm an ordinary retiree. This is just a token of my heartfelt gratitude to you, for all the help you have given her and her family. You're the one sending a cart of charcoal to her in the dreadful winter."

"Oh, I'm only an ignorant, illiterate woman," she said. "I was nothing until Shang took me to Shanghai."

"Please tell me something about her."

"I was with Shang, then with Qian, and finally with Jiao too," she said, appearing to be softening, taking the plastic bag. "Things are gone and past like the drifting smoke, like the passing cloud. What can I really tell you? At the beginning of the Cultural Revolution, I had to leave her. Otherwise, she could have been charged with another crime—the crime of bourgeois life style."

"Yes, that was so considerate of you."

"She was so pitiable. She hung on to a last straw of hope that the *guiren* would come to her rescue."

"Can you be more specific about that *guiren*, Auntie Zhong?" *Guiren*—an unexpected luck-bringer—was another word often heard in Suzhou opera.

"He didn't come," she said, sniffling. "Nobody came. She gave herself over to despair. *Kalpa.*"

In Suzhou opera, *kalpa* meant predestined disasters. He noticed a Buddha statue standing on the only table in the room, with a bronze incense burner in front of the statue.

"*Kalpa* or not!" he said. "People should have helped. Was there not a single one?"

"No, not a single one," she said. "If the *guiren* chose not to do so, who else could?"

He understood the reason why she kept using the term *guiren*. They both knew who they were talking about. "Back to my earlier questions, did she show you her pictures?"

"Some of them."

"Including those with the *guiren*?"

"I don't remember exactly."

"Yes, it's such a long time ago," he said, taking it as not a downright denial. "After her tragic death, did any of those pictures come to light?"

"Not that I know of."

"Do you think she could have left them behind somewhere?"

"No, I don't know that, either."

For her age, she proved to be more than alert. So he decided to push on in a new direction.

"Oh, Buddha is really blind. Such disaster for Shang, and for Qian too. They did nothing to deserve such *kalpa* or karma."

"Don't ever talk like that, Mr. Yu. Buddha is divine. Karma works out in a way far, far beyond us. Whatever might have happened to Shang and Qian, a real *guiren* finally came to Jiao."

"What do you mean?" He added in haste, hardly able to conceal the excitement in his voice, "Didn't Jiao grow up in an orphanage, alone all those years?"

205

"Someone helped her through those years—a *guiren* in the background. Now that Jiao has settled down comfortably, I think I can leave the world in peace. Buddha is so great!"

"Oh? Who helped?"

"A gold-hearted man." She rose to put some tall incense into the burner. "I burn incense for him every day. May Buddha protect him!"

"Hold on, Auntie Zhong. A *guiren* in Jiao's life. How do you know?"

"Like you, some people know about my relationship with the Shang family. So he came to me one day."

"What kind of a man is he?"

"A real gentleman. He said that he knew Jiao's parents. He is about their age, I guess. He gave me money to buy food and clothing for Jiao."

"When did that start?"

"Two or three years after the end of the Cultural Revolution. In the late seventies or early eighties. He did all his good deeds anonymously, insisting that I not say anything to Jiao. What noble benefaction!"

"What Buddhist spirit!" he sort of echoed, trying to come up with more Buddhist improvisations. "A peck, a drink, everything happens with a cause and consequence."

"You, too, kowtow to Buddha, don't you? He might not have been that rich at first, giving me just a little cash each time, but he must have come from a good family, the way he talked and behaved. Good deeds will never go unnoticed. Now he's so incredibly rich. So is Jiao— all through his help."

"Can you give me his name and address, Auntie Zhong? I really want to thank him for what he had done for the Shang family."

"He sows without caring about reaping. In fact, he has never given me his real name." She said shaking her head resolutely, "I wouldn't give it to you even if I knew. It's against his principles."

"I don't know how to thank you enough," he said as he got up, realizing it would be useless to push any further. "Like that noble benefactor, you have done so much for her family. The way of Buddha is truly beyond us. Karma works out in the life of her granddaughter."

"Yes, may Buddha bless her, and him too. Good bye, Mr. Yu." Zhong rose, and opened the door to the dark staircase.

He nearly stumbled again, beginning to grope slowly down, grasping the railing, his stiff legs moving with difficulty. It took him several minutes before he reached the foot of the staircase, the way down being even longer than the way up.

Walking out into the busy and bustling street, he blinked in a burst of afternoon sunshine. It was a random harvest. He lit a cigarette, waving the match. The information from Zhong threw light on some, if not on all, of the mysteries about Jiao's life. Particularly regarding the self-effaced "incredibly rich" benefactor. Zhong seemed convinced that his fortune had brought about the metamorphosis in Jiao's life.

Could the benefactor be the man Old Hunter had glimpsed in the company of Jiao the other night? Not likely. The man seemed to be younger, whereas Zhong described the benefactor as being about the same age as Jiao's parents.

It wasn't until he was passing by the convenience store again, that he thought of something. In spite of Zhong's ambiguous response about what she had told Jiao about her benefactor, if the changes in her life had been related to him, Jiao should know him by now.

Jiao didn't seem to have any friend that age—not from what he had learned from Chen—except Xie. An old-fashioned gentleman, and from a good family too, but Xie was far from rich.

So Old Hunter would get hold of a picture of Xie and with it, go back to Zhong. She might acknowledge the man in the picture even if she didn't know his name.

He started humming some fragments from a Suzhou opera.

"Bursting with anger, I denounce you . . ."

TWENTY-TWO

CHEN GOT A TEXT message on his cell phone early the following morning.

"I've talked to a friend who works at his residence. She'll arrange a visit for you today. Her name is Fang, and her number, 8678856."

The message was unmistakable, even though the sender didn't leave a name.

He hastened out the hotel, got into a taxi, and headed for Tiananmen Square again.

The traffic wasn't too bad along Chang'an Boulevard that morning. The taxi driver, for once, was not a talkative one, looking sullenly ahead, his face in the rearview mirror almost as gray as the sky. Chen rolled down the window. A pigeon whistle could be heard trailing high overhead.

It took him only fifteen minutes to arrive at Xinhua Gate, the magnificent front entrance to the Central South Sea, which was located just west of Tiananmen Gate.

Originally, the Central South Sea had been something of an extension of the Forbidden City, with gardens, lakes, villas, woods, halls, and studies for the imperial household. After the overthrow of the Qing dynasty, Yuan Shikai, the first president of the Republic of China, took the Central South Sea as his government office site. To Yuan, who later failed to become an emperor himself, the choice was symbolically significant, for the Central South Sea was synonymous with the Forbidden City.

After 1949, the Central South Sea was turned into a residential complex for the top Party leaders, enclosed by high walls, providing all the majestic luxury, privacy, and security imaginable for the residents inside.

That morning, the front of the Central South Sea appeared little changed from the Qing dynasty, presenting the vermilion gate, red walls, and glazed yellow tiles as of old. There were two armed soldiers standing at the front entrance. The half-open gate revealed a large screen bearing Mao's gilded inscription: *To serve the people.*

Chen dialed the number sent in the text message.

"Oh it's you, Chen," Fang responded. "Please come to the side entrance."

So he walked over to a shaded side street, and to the alternative entrance also guarded by an armed soldier. Fang was waiting for him in a booth outside. A handsome woman in her early thirties, with almond-shaped eyes and a straight nose, highly spirited in her army uniform, she stepped out, extending her hand, a wisp of hair straying out of her green cap.

"So you must be Chen. The residence hasn't been open to the public since 1989. Today you are a special visitor. Ling tells me you're nostalgic."

"Thank you so much, Fang, for going out of your way for me," Chen said, believing Ling hadn't revealed his real purpose. "It's one of the places I've always wanted to see."

"You don't have to thank me," Fang said in a crisp voice. "Ling called us, speaking to both me and my boss. She's a friend of mine. She's told me of you. She asked me to do whatever possible for you. For one thing, I could serve as your guide—that is, if you'd like."

"I appreciate your offer, but I'd like to take a walk around first. If I need anything, I'll let you know. Oh, but maybe a map?"

"Some other Party leaders still live here. You are supposed to walk around only the area where Mao used to live. Here is a map, and Ling has something else for you," she said, giving him a large envelope with the map on top of it.

The bulging shape of the envelope suggested something like a book inside. He thought he could guess what it was. Once again, Ling had helped him, not only with access to the Central South Sea. He didn't tear open the envelope in the presence of Fang.

So he checked the map and headed for the Harvest Garden, the original name for Mao's residence. In the Qing dynasty, the Harvest Garden had been used as a scenic imperial study. It was in the shape of a large quadrangle house, with five rooms in a row along each side and a courtyard in the middle.

The Harvest Garden looked deserted that morning. Chen walked in, started looking around here and there. Some of the rooms were locked. He pushed open the door of the bedroom.

What first struck him as unusual in the room was the extraordinarily big bed. Larger than a king-size one, apparently custom-made, but apart from its size, it was simple and plain. About a quarter of the bed was practically covered with books. It appeared as if Mao had slept with books.

Chen reached out and picked one up. *Zizhi Tongjian*, sometimes called the "Mirror of the History." It was a history book written by Sima Guang, a renowned Confucian scholar in the Song dynasty, intended to mirror history in such a way that emperors could learn lessons by examining it. Mao was said to have read it seven or eight times. Most of the books on the bed turned out to be similar classics and histories.

According to Mao, history is an ever-continuous process of one dynasty succeeding another. Those at the bottom rise in rebellion to overthrow the one at the top, though the successful rebel inevitably turns into the emperor, as corrupt and oppressive as was the predecessor. Being part of modern Chinese history, having actually shaped that part of history which shaped him as well, Mao declared, "All the theories of Marxism can be summed up in one sentence: it is justified to rebel." As an ambitious and accomplished rebel, marching under the banners of Marxism and communism, Mao put to good use the knowledge he had learned from those history books, some of which Chen was holding in his hands.

And Chen couldn't help imagining Mao alone in the room, reading late into the night. According to the official publications, Madam Mao didn't live with Mao. In his last ten years, Mao lived by himself—except for his personal secretaries, nurses, and orderly. Behind the communist-god mask, Mao must have been a solitary man seeing his dream of the grandest empire slipping away, not prepared to lead the country into the twentieth century, yet anxious to prove himself an emperor greater than all those before. So he wielded such terms as "class struggle" and "proletarian dictatorship," launching one political movement after another, stifling all the opposition voices, until things came to a head during the Cultural Revolution. At night, however, surrounded by the ancient books, paranoid of "capitalist roaders" who would try to usurp his power and "restore capitalism," Mao suffered from insomnia, hardly able to move because of his failing health . . .

Chen leaned down, touching the bed. A wooden-board mattress, as he had read in those memoirs, which claimed that Mao, working for the welfare of the Chinese people, cared little about his personal comfort. Chen wondered whether Mao had ever thought of Shang while on this bed.

Chen turned to look at the bathroom. In addition to the standard toilet, there was another one on the floor, shaped like a porcelain basin, over which one had to squat—specially designed for Mao, who must have carried with him to the Forbidden City his habit acquired as a farmer from a Hunan village.

It was another puzzling detail, but not all details would be relevant to his investigation. He hadn't been able to establish a connection, he thought, between himself as investigator and Mao as a suspect. Instead, he came to find himself in the presence of another man, long dead and mysterious, but not the god Chen remembered from his school years.

Carrying the large envelope in his hand, Chen moved out into the garden. There seemed to be something sacrilegious about reading the book Ling sent him while in Mao's room. But he wanted to read it here instead of back at the hotel, while looking up at the tilted eaves of the palace shimmering in the summer foliage, as if the location made a difference.

He perched himself on a slab of rock, on which Mao might have sat many a time. A stone *kylin* that had once escorted the emperors here stared at him. Lighting a cigarette, he remembered Mao was a smoker too—a heavier one. Chen hadn't the slightest desire to imitate Mao.

Sure enough, as he had guessed, the large envelope contained the book written by Mao's personal doctor. There was another envelope inside, smaller and sealed—probably the love poems written for Ling, long ago. He wasn't going to read them at the moment. So he opened the book, turning to the introduction. The author claimed to have served as Mao's personal physician for over twenty years, to know the intimate details of Mao's life.

Instead of reading from the beginning, Chen moved to the index at the end. To his disappointment, there was no listing for Shang. Leafing through the book, he tried to find anything relevant.

The book didn't focus exclusively on the personal life of Mao. The doctor also wrote about his own life, from an idealistic college student to a sophisticated survivor in those years of power struggle. For common readers, however, the appeal of the book lay in the description of Mao's life—of an emperor both in and out of the Forbidden City. The chapter Chen was reading happened to be about Mao traveling around luxuriously in a special train. In the train, he actually took a young attendant named Jade Phoenix to bed. She was only sixteen or seventeen at the time. Afterward, he brought her back to the Central South Sea as his personal secretary. She eventually became more powerful than the politburo members, for she alone understood what he mumbled after his stroke, being one of few he could really trust. But she was only one of the many "favored" by Mao, who actually picked up women all over the country, in a variety of circumstances, including at those balls arranged for him in Shanghai and in other cities.

Mao seemed to have a preference for young girls with little education, not intelligent or sophisticated—simply young, warm bodies in a cold night. Shang was different from Mao's usual type. But then a celebrated actress would have her attractions. It was nothing for an emperor to have dozens of imperial concubines.

The book confirmed what Chen had learned from other sources. Like an emperor, Mao set no store by his women, taking them as nothing but the means to satisfy his "divine" sexual needs.

A blue jay flew by. Chen thought he caught a flash of the afternoon sunlight on its wings.

Whatever Mao might have done as the supreme Party leader, what he did to Shang was inexcusable, not to be easily written off, not even from a policeman's perspective. Chief Inspector Chen was too depressed to think long along these lines.

He took out the smaller envelope, in which Ling might have left a note for him.

To his surprise, he found, instead of his poems, a manila folder marked, "Records of the Special Team from CCPC Cultural Revolution Group: Shang."

How could Ling have got hold of this crucial information? It must have been at great risk to herself, as in another case years ago.

Only there was no stepping twice into the same river.

He started reading what was in the folder. It consisted of reports submitted by the special group. Most of them were written in the "revolutionary language" of the time, so he had to guess at the meaning couched in the political slogans and jargon.

According to Sima Yun, the head of the group, they were responsible to a "leading comrade" in Beijing, who was working in collaboration with the CCPC Cultural Revolution Group. They were instructed to deal with Shang in whatever way necessary to make her give up something important, possibly related to Mao, which had never been defined or explained to them. So they resorted to beating and torturing her. Shang said that Chairman Mao, had he known, wouldn't have allowed them to do so. Sima told her that Madam Mao knew, and that was as good as from Mao himself. After that, Shang never said anything about Mao until her suicide. The team was summoned back to Beijing, bringing with them whatever they had found, including several albums.

It confirmed a couple of points on the case that Chen had speculated about.

First, the special team hadn't been sent directly by Madam Mao, but by someone else. No name was given, but the "leading comrade" wasn't she, who was only "in collaboration."

Second, the special team itself wasn't clear about what to extort from Shang. Except that the Party's interests were at stake—some Mao material. So they interrogated Shang the hard way.

Rubbing the ridge of his nose, Chen checked another report in the folder, written on a somewhat smaller paper, possibly by another member of the team. To his astonishment, it was written at a much later date—as late as the end of 1974.

Apparently, Beijing remained concerned about the Mao material. In 1974, the year when Tan and Qian were caught in their attempt to flee across the border, some of the original special team members were summoned back to find more information. So the young lovers were brutally interrogated. It was suspected that they intended to smuggle something out, which also was not defined.

According to the statement made by Tan, the pair tried to go to Hong Kong because they saw no future in the mainland. He took all the responsibility. Because of his death, the investigation came to an abrupt end, even though an interview list had been made by the local committee concerning the close contacts of Tan and Qian.

Chen was about to read the last page in the folder when he was startled by an apparition, a grizzled man shuffling over from the far end of the garden, green canvas satchel slung across his shoulder. He checked around, picking up a fallen leaf with his free hand, and putting it into the satchel. He didn't appear to be a gardener, nor did the satchel look like a proper tool. Chen hastened to put the book and the folder back into the large envelope.

"Who are you?" the gray-haired man demanded with an air of authority. "How did you get in here today?"

"I'm Chen. I've always dreamed of coming here—ever since childhood," Chen said. "A friend of mine works here, so she let me in."

"So you've come to pay homage to Mao? That's the spirit, young man. People still worship him today, I know. Oh, I'm Bi. I served as Chairman Mao's bodyguard for twenty years."

"Oh, it's a great honor to meet you, Comrade Bi."

"I'm retired, but I still come here from time to time. Oh, those unforgettable years by the side of our great leader! He built a socialist new China out of a poor, backward country. Without Chairman Mao, without China."

Without Chairman Mao, without China? Chen didn't ask. It sounded like a much-chanted line from a popular song in the sixties, except that it was a statement then, not a question.

"What a great man!" Bi went on in an emotional voice. "During three years of natural disasters, Mao refused to eat any meat."

"Yes, millions of people died of starvation under the Three Red Flags those years," Chen blurted out. The so-called "three years of natural disasters" was but a way to shift the blame for the disaster caused by Mao's political campaign. In a different version of events, Chen had been told that Mao made a public show of eating no meat while still enjoying fish and wild game, some of them live, directly from the Central South Sea. At least Mao never starved in the Forbidden City.

"No, you can't talk about history like that, young man. China was surrounded and sabotaged by imperialists and revisionists then. It was Chairman Mao that led us out of the woods."

That was the official version. Chen knew it would be pointless to argue with Bi, an old man who had spent years by the side of Mao. Chen decided to sing a different tune.

"You're right, Comrade Bi. I've just visited Mao's bedroom. So simple, not even a soft mattress on the bed. It embodies our Party's fine tradition of hard work, simple living. Indeed, few had the privilege of working with Mao. You, too, have made a contribution to China."

"Working under Mao, I should say," Bi said with a toothless grin.

"Now, I'm just curious. In his bedroom, there's such a large bed, covered with books. But almost nothing else. Did Madam Mao live here?"

"No, she didn't."

Chen didn't push. Instead, he produced a cigarette, lit it respectfully for Bi, and waited.

"Madam Mao's a curse," Bi said, exhaling loudly.

Another officially approved statement. In the Party newspapers, the Cultural Revolution had been attributed to the Gang of Four, headed by Madam Mao.

"So Mao lived here all by himself?" Chen probed cautiously.

"You know what? Mao had long been estranged from her. If she wanted to see him, she had to make an appointment, speaking to me first."

"Oh, Mao must have trusted you so much."

"Yes, we stopped her several times. She tried to break in, but Mao gave us instructions that no one could barge in without reporting to us first."

That was unusual between a husband and wife. Bi didn't say why, but it echoed what Chen had just read in the memoir. A guard wouldn't have had the guts to stop Madam Mao, unless specifically instructed by Mao for a reason.

Instead of moving on to an elaboration of the unspoken reason, Bi leaned down, grinding out the cigarette on a slab of rock and putting the butt into the satchel.

"I have to make my rounds. It's not easy for you to be let in. Stay here as long as you want. You'll be able to bathe in the greatness of Chairman Mao."

Bi shuffled away, humming a song to himself. "Red is the east, and rises the sun. China produces Mao Zedong, a great savior who works for happiness of the people."

It was a tune that Chinese people would sing every day during the Cultural Revolution. And that the big clock atop the Custom House on the Bund played every hour. Watching Bi's retreating figure against the deserted garden, Chen thought of a Tang-dynasty poem titled "The Outside Palace."

> In the deserted ancient outside palace,
> the flowers bloom
> into a blaze
> of solitary, scarlet splendor.
>
> Those palace ladies long left behind
> there, white-haired,
> sit and talk in idleness
> about Emperor Xuan.

For a moment, Chen found himself confounded. He was no politician. Nor a historian. Nor a poet any longer, according to Ling, but a cop who did not even know what to do here.

The blue jay flapped by again, its wings still shiny like in a lost dream. The sudden ringing of his cell phone broke into his confusion. It was Detective Yu from Shanghai.

"I had to call you, Chief. Old Hunter gave me your temporary cell number—wherever you are. Song was killed."

"What?" Chen stood up.

"I don't know the details of his death except that he was attacked on a side street."

"Attacked on a side street—by whom?"

"Internal Security will say nothing. But from what I've heard, it is possible he was mugged by gangsters. The fatal blow against his skull was made by something like a heavy metal bar."

"A heavy metal bar—" A tell-tale weapon for Chen. "Now, who's in charge of the investigation?"

"Another person from Internal Security. They called the bureau, demanding to be told your whereabouts. Party Secretary Li came to me, his face pulled as long as that of a horse."

"I'm coming back today, Yu," he said. "Find the name of the Internal Security officer for me. And his phone number too."

"I'll do that. What else, Chief?"

"You have done some asking around about Qian's lovers, both the first and the second, haven't you?"

"Yes, Old Hunter must have told you about Peng, the second one."

"Now about Tan, the first one. A group of people from Beijing conducted a special investigation into him before his death."

"Do you have anything about the investigation?"

"No, I don't. Contact his neighborhood committee again. The neighborhood cop, I mean, since you know him well. At the time, the neighborhood committee provided something like an interview list for the Beijing group. A list of the people close to Tan and Qian."

"I'll go there," Yu said, "and get the list. Anything else?"

"Call me immediately if there's anything new."

Closing the phone, Chen knew he had to leave the Central South Sea.

He was in no mood to go back into Mao's rooms, though he had conveniently called this the Mao Case.

TWENTY-THREE

THE TRAIN WAS RUMBLING along in the dusk.

Chen had obtained the train ticket through a scalper, paying a much higher price for it. He didn't try to bargain. There was no possibility of purchasing an airline ticket without showing official documents, which he didn't have. It was a hard seat in a third-class car, but he considered himself lucky to have gotten on the train at the last minute.

During his college years, he had frequently traveled between Beijing and Shanghai, sitting on the hard seats, reading, dozing through the night. Now he was finding it very uncomfortable—his legs were stiff, and his back strained. He was unable to doze, let alone sleep. He didn't have a book with him except for *Cloud and Rain in Shanghai*, which he was in no mood to take out, and the memoir by Mao's doctor, which he couldn't read openly.

He must have been spoiled by his chief inspector-ship, he mused with a touch of self-irony. In the last several years, his trips had been by airplane or in the soft sleeping cars, and he had forgotten about the discomfort of traveling on the hard seat.

Sitting opposite him, across a small table, was a young couple, possibly on their honeymoon trip. Both were dressed too formally for the overpacked train: the man was wearing a new shirt and well-ironed dress pants, the woman, a pink dress with thin straps. Initially, she sat leaning against the window, but soon she shifted in her seat and was nestled against him. For them, the discomfort was nothing, as long as they had the world in each others' eyes.

Beside Chen was a young girl, apparently a college student, who wore a white blouse, a grass-green skirt imprinted with vines and trails, and light-green plastic slippers. There was a book on her lap—a Chinese translation of *The Lover* by Marguerite Duras. He had read the book, still remembering that the beginning of the novel echoed the lines by W. B. Yeats, "*When you are old and gray and full of sleep . . .*"

He wondered whether he was able to write—or even to say anything like that.

"The train is reaching Tianjin in a couple of minutes. Passengers for the city of Tianjin should get prepared." The train announcer spoke melodiously in the typical Beijing dialect, with the "er" sound more pronounced than in standard Mandarin.

The train was already slowing down. Looking out, he saw on the gray platform several peddlers walking and hawking Dogs Won't Leave. An unbelievable brand name for the steamed pork-stuffed buns, a special snack of Tianjin. Perhaps originally from a compliment: "The buns taste so good that the dogs won't leave." One of the peddlers moving up to the train looked like a thug, pushing a basket of buns up to the windows with an almost fierce expression.

More people came crowding in at Tianjin, rushing and squeezing with luggage on their shoulders and in their hands, jumping at any vacant seat they could find. According to railway regulations, only passengers boarding at the first stop could be guaranteed a seat.

The train started moving again, the green banner waving on the platform in the growing dark.

He leaned against the window, trying to focus on the new development in Shanghai, the wind ruffling his hair as the train gained speed.

Looking over the scant information available so far, Chen soon concluded it was pointless to speculate. But Song's death was not from a random mugging on the street, of that much he was sure.

A train conductor began pushing a dining cart through the aisle, selling snacks, instant noodles, teas, and beer. Squatting at the bottom rack of the cart were long-billed brass kettles. Chen chose fried beef and scallion instant noodles in a plastic bowl, into which the conductor adroitly poured out an arch of hot water. In addition, Chen had a tea-leaf egg soaked in it. It wouldn't be pleasant to squeeze all the way through the train to the dining car and then back.

He waited two or three minutes before taking out the egg, and he put a package of seasoning into the soup. The instant noodles tasted palpable, with the green specks afloat on the soup remotely redolent of chopped scallion. Just like in his college years, except that instant noodles then didn't come in plastic containers.

The couple opposite produced a stainless-steel container of fried steak and smoked fish, along with paper-wrapped chopsticks and spoons. They must have prepared well for the trip. The woman started peeling an orange and feeding her partner, segment by segment.

Chen finished his egg, thinking he might as well have bought a couple of Dogs Won't Leave buns. And he was surprised by the thought. He hadn't lost his appetite even during such a trip. He fished for a cigarette in his pocket but did not take it out. The air was bad enough in the train.

Beside him, the girl started reading her book without eating anything. She must have felt uncomfortable, sitting so long in the one position, so she kicked off her slippers and put a bare foot on the edge of the seat opposite. She highlighted paragraphs with a pen, her fingers tapping on the seat. Young, yet serious, her way with the book might just be like her way with the world. He tried to stretch his legs without disturbing his neighbors, but it was difficult. He nearly tipped over the noodle bowl onto the table. The woman opposite glared at him.

What he had read about Mao's special train came back to mind. The sleeping car was equipped with all the modern conveniences, the special bed with the wooden-board mattress, and those pretty conductors and nurses who waited on Mao hand and foot . . .

Chen was massaging his brows, half closing his eyes, in an effort to ward off an onslaught of headache, when his cell phone rang. It was Detective Yu again.

"Hold on," Chen said into the phone.

He excused himself and squeezed out into the aisle, heading to the door. To his surprise, several people stood leaning against the door. Apparently, they were the seatless passengers. Behind them, he saw a toilet marked "unoccupied." So he hurried in and locked the door behind him.

"Now, tell me what you've found," he said, opening the small window. It was stuffy and smelly in the toilet.

"I went to the neighborhood committee. Hong wasn't a neighborhood cop at the time, but he talked to Huang Dexing, the one before him. There was a group of people who came in from Beijing. The local government called Huang, telling him to cooperate in whatever way requested. It sounded like a highly confidential assignment. The team searched through both Tan's and Qian's places. And they wanted to talk to the people close to them."

"Did they find anything?"

"No. Huang helped make up an interview list, but it wasn't used. Tan died, and Qian almost died, lying delirious in a hospital bed for days. So the group gave up and went back to Beijing."

It was now like an oven in the train toilet, though the sun had long gone down.

"Huang tried to remember the interview list, but with no success," Yu went on. "It happened so many years ago, and there is no record of it anywhere. As far as he could remember, the list included some people from the circle Qian moved in, before the outbreak of the Cultural Revolution, and from the middle school Tan graduated from. One of them seen with him shortly before his attempt to flee to Hong Kong, and another one was also from a black family background. I went one step further and checked into the Great Leap Forward Middle School.

I talked to a retired teacher who had taught Tan. According to him, one of Tan's close friends was Xie—"

"What do you know about Xie, Detective Yu?"

"Well, Old Hunter followed Jiao to Xie Mansion. So he must be connected to the case, I guess."

In spite of his warning, Detective Yu had moved ahead on his own, which Chen should have anticipated. But the information just obtained by his capable partner could prove to be crucial. It put Xie into the perspective, as someone who, to say the least, had been withholding information.

"The information about Xie is important. But remember, you and Old Hunter keep your hands off him. I'm on my way back to Shanghai. We have to discuss Xie before anyone makes a move. Now, have you found anything else out about Song's death?"

The door handle started rattling. Someone waiting outside was impatient.

"Nothing. But I got the name of his replacement, Liu, and Liu's cell number, Chief."

"That's great." Chen put the number into his phone. "I'll call you when I'm back in Shanghai."

Chen decided to make a phone call to Liu, in spite of the raging door handle. A short call.

"Liu, I'm Chen Cao."

"Oh, Chief Inspector Chen! Where have you been?"

"I'm on the train back to Shanghai. Meet me in the train station around eight in the morning," he said without answering Liu's question, and then added, "I was sick."

Hanging up, he finally walked out of the toilet. A giant of a man with a large beard glared at him, hurried in, and slammed the door behind him.

There was a pleasant breath of wind streaming in from the crevice of the door. But he had to squeeze back to his seat. A middle-aged, stout woman was sitting on the floor with her legs stretched out in front, and her small daughter, behind her in a similar position, their backs supporting each other. Chen had to step carefully, high lifting his feet.

Edging near to his seat, he was surprised to see an elderly woman seated there, with her face resting flat on the small table. She had to be in her seventies or eighties, dressed in black homespun, her silver hair shining. Possibly one of the passengers from Tianjin, who had taken the seat during his phone call.

"She didn't understand my words," the young girl murmured apologetically, who might have tried to speak up for Chen, but to no avail.

"Call the conductor over," the man sitting opposite said. "That's against the rules."

The conductor was supposed to drag the black-attired woman away, who mumbled something indistinct in response to him, sitting there without budging, like a rock.

"It would be hard for her to stand throughout the night," a passenger across the aisle said.

"That can't be helped," the conductor said, beginning to push at the old woman. "Rules are rules. There's a sleeping berth available. An upper berth. One can go there by paying the extra."

"A sleeping berth," Chen said. It could have become available when someone got off in Tianjin. "I'll take it."

"Two hundred yuan extra," the conductor said. "Far more comfortable. That will solve the problem for a Big Buck like you. You don't have too much luggage, do you?"

"No, I don't have much luggage, but you may take the old woman there. I'll pay for it. I like the seat here."

The couple opposite eyed him in surprise. Chen took out two one-hundred-yuan bills. The old woman turned out not to be that hard of hearing. She rose without further invitation. The conductor, relieved to get the matter over with, led her away without further ado.

"Not too many people want to learn from Comrade Lei Feng anymore," the man across the aisle commented. "It's not Mao's time."

Chen took his seat against the window without response. With an upper berth in a sleeping car, it would be more difficult for him to climb up and down in case of another phone call. His decision had nothing to do with a model of selflessness like Lei Feng during Mao's time. Even though he was burdened with a Mao case.

"You must be somebody," the girl said, sitting close, "but you ate instant noodles instead of going to the dining car."

"Oh, I like the instant noodles." He smiled a self-deprecating smile. In today's society, an instant-noodles-eater on a hard seat was nobody, incapable of paying an extra two hundred yuan for himself, let alone for someone else. The gap between the rich and the poor was an appalling given, but even more appalling was people's reaction. In Mao's time, it was supposed to be an egalitarian society, at least in theory. Chen was disturbed. "It's nothing but a business expense—I mean, the ticket."

It wasn't exactly true. He might not have the train ticket reimbursed. Still, two hundred yuan wouldn't worry him.

The night lights went on in the train. The couple opposite closed their eyes, leaning against each other. The car gradually became quiet. Chen gazed at his reflection in the window, reflecting on the countryside in darkness.

Beijing was left far, far behind.

Drunk, I whipped an invaluable horse; / I'm worried about burdening a beauty with too much passion. The two lines by Daifu came unexpectedly back to his mind. Years earlier, a friend of his had once copied the couplet for him in a paper fan, which he had lost. And he hadn't even given Ling a call before leaving Beijing, he realized, with a wave of guilt.

But then his thoughts wandered off to another poem Mao had written for Yang in their youth:

Waving my hand, I am leaving. / Unbearable for us to stand / looking at each other, inconsolably. / Our sufferings told over and again, / your eyes brimming with sorrow, / holding back tears with difficulty. / You still misunderstand my letter, / but it will pass / like cloud and mist. / You alone understand me in this world./ Oh my heart aches, / does the heaven know?

Chen didn't like that poem, which was full of clichés. And it was still hard for him to understand how Mao could have been so callous to Yang, and to his other women.

The ringing of his phone broke into his musing. It was Old Hunter. Chen glanced at the girl beside him, who, too, was dozing, with her mouth slightly open.

Chen decided not to get up this time. A couple of fragmented sentences out of context might not be comprehensible to one who overheard them.

"Oh, I'm on the train coming back to Shanghai. A crowded train, a lot of people sitting and standing around," he said, making sure the retired cop would get the hint.

"I went to see her maid." Old Hunter went straight to the point, in sharp contrast to his characteristic Suzhou opera way. "Her name is Zhong."

"Her maid?" It must have been Shang's maid, Chen realized. "Oh I see. That's great. Did you learn anything from her?"

"Xie visited Jiao at her orphanage. According to Zhong, he helped a lot financially."

"That's something."

"Zhong says Xie's behind the change in Jiao's life."

"Really!"

"With the help of Zhong, I'm going to check into it."

"No, don't do anything, Old Hunter. I'll be back early in the morning. Let's discuss this first."

Chen had never thought about the possibility of Xie being the one behind the change in Jiao's life. Financially, it wasn't possible. Xie could hardly make his own ends met.

Still, there was something between Xie and Jiao, something now beyond doubt, given the new information from both Yu and Old Hunter.

Then why all the concealment on the part of Jiao and Xie? Neither of them had said anything about it, keeping it a secret from him—and not just from him. No one at the parties seemed to have known anything. If

Xie had visited Jiao, a small child in her orphanage, he did it out of friendship with Tan. Nothing wrong or improper that would require a cover-up. If anything was surprising at all, it was Internal Security's failure to learn the history between Xie and Qian.

The case seemed to be getting more and more mystifying.

The girl next to him began snoring, though ever so lightly, a thin trace of saliva visible at the corner of her mouth.

Around three, sitting stiff and straight like a bamboo stick, his head bumped against the hard seat, his mind worn out with thinking in the dark, he managed to doze off.

His last thought was about that wooden-board mattress in the Central South Sea. Not a comfortable bed, by any means.

TWENTY-FOUR

FINALLY, THE TRAIN ARRIVED at the Shanghai Railway Station.

The new station was larger and more modern. It was another attempt to upgrade the image of the "most desirable metropolitan city internationally," as advocated in the Shanghai newspapers.

Chen got off after the couple, who hugged and kissed, stepping out onto the ground in Shanghai for possibly the first time, before they merged into the throng, oblivious to the crowd milling around. The young girl came down after him, waving at him before disappearing in another direction.

He remained standing on the platform, next to the train door, waiting for five or six minutes before he spotted a middle-aged man hurrying over, raising his hands in a gesture of recognition. He could have seen Chen before—or his picture. The man was of medium build, yet heavy-jawed and broad-shouldered, inclined toward stoutness.

"Comrade Chief Inspector Chen?"

It was Liu, the officer who succeeded Song as head of the special Internal Security team.

They walked out into the hall swarming with people, where, in the midst of escalators running up and down, Chen saw the young girl again, studying an electronic information display.

"Someone you know?" Liu asked.

"No," he said, moving down the escalator after Liu.

The square outside appeared no less crowded, with people standing in lines for tickets, peddlers showing their products, and scalpers shouting with tickets in their hands. The restaurants and cafés nearby appeared noisy and cramped. It was out of the question for them to find a quiet place to talk.

Liu led Chen across the square, into a parking lot tucked in behind the station tower. Liu pressed a remote control, unlocking the doors to a silver Lexus in the corner. As soon as they got into the car, Liu started the engine and turned on the air conditioning before handing Chen a folder about Song's murder, all without saying a word.

Chen started reading immediately. He understood Liu's accusatory silence. Beyond a shadow of a doubt, Song had been killed because of the investigation he had been pursuing—in the company of Chen, until the chief inspector's unannounced, and so far unexplained vacation.

It was no coincidence that Chen had been attacked in similar circumstances. Only Chen had been luckier.

Lighting a cigarette, waving his hand over the document, Chen couldn't shake the feeling that he was responsible, at least partially, for Song's death. Fragmented memories of their unpleasant collaboration spiraled up with the smoke. Had he let Song have his way, the situation could have developed differently; had he informed Song of the attack on him, Song might have acted with more caution; had he stayed in Shanghai, he himself might have been the target.

In spite of the air conditioning in the car, Chen began to sweat profusely. Liu remained silent, puffing hard at his cigarette—his third one. Chen wiped at his brow with his hand, like a mole smoked in a tunnel.

There wasn't much in the folder. Song had been plodding along in another direction, different from Chen's. There must have been some point of overlap that bundled the two of them together in this investigation, a something known neither to Song, nor to Chen, but to the murderer alone. Chen failed to find anything helpful in the file.

Now, who would have been desperate enough to murder Song as a way to force a stop to the investigation? It had been focused on Jiao and Xie, and after Yang's murder, on Xie in particular.

"We have to shake them up," Liu said at the end of his third cigarette. "We tried to get hold of you, but no one knew your whereabouts."

"You mean—" Chen didn't finish the sentence. What Liu wanted to do, Chen could guess, but he wasn't in any position to argue against it. Nor to give a satisfactory account of his "vacation." Instead, he said slowly, closing the folder, "Can you give me a more detailed account of what Song had been doing for the last few days?"

"I have a mental list," Liu said readily. "While you were away on vacation, Song did a lot of work—visiting Xie's place, talking to him, and to Jiao, interviewing people related to Yang, meeting Hua, the boss of the company where Jiao worked, and Shang's old maid, checking into Jiao's phone record—"

"Yes, he left no stone unturned," Chen said. Some of the stones he had also tried to turn—through the help of Old Hunter and Detective Yu. It wasn't exactly a surprise that Song, too, had approached Shang's maid. "Anything or anybody seem suspicious?"

"No. But our net was closing. Someone struck out in desperation."

"Someone" referred to Xie, Chen had no doubt about it. "Can I have a medical report about Song's death?"

"It'll be delivered to you today, but since the murder happened in broad daylight, I don't think there will be much for you to learn from the medical report."

"Let me go over the material one more time, and I'll make a report to Beijing. We shouldn't wait too long, but I don't think we should rush to action."

"How long shall we wait, Chief Inspector Chen?"

For Internal Security, it had been a harsh slap to the face. While Xie Mansion was under their close surveillance, the dead body of a young girl was discovered in its garden, and then the dead body of Song, the officer in charge of the investigation, was found in a side street nearby. They might consider themselves above the police, but with their comrade fallen in the line of duty, they were beside themselves, just like cops, crying for revenge. They couldn't put it off anymore.

"When you called me from the train," Liu went on without getting a response from Chen, "we were dealing with a target."

"A new target?"

As it turned out, one of Liu's colleagues had seen Jiao meeting with Peng. They lost no time getting hold of Peng, and obtaining from him a full confession, which strengthened their determination to use "tough measures."

"Here is a tape of the interrogation," Liu said, handing Chen a cassette tape. "We had no time for transcription."

Chen put the tape into the car tape player and listened. During the interrogation, Liu and his colleagues more or less fed him the answers, but they were probably also what Peng himself believed.

It was a similar version to what Peng had told Yu, a scenario of Jiao having gotten the valuable antique left by Shang through her affair with Mao, but Peng was careful enough not to mention Mao by name. Nor did he say anything about Yu, which suggested that Peng must have continued blackmailing Jiao.

"It's so unfair," Peng concluded in a wailing tone. "She got it all from Shang—from the Forbidden City. I should have my share . . ."

His testimony was enough however, to get Jiao into trouble. "Selling state treasures" was a serious crime. Internal Security didn't need another excuse.

"With his testimony, we're expecting a search warrant from Beijing," Liu concluded. "We believe that whatever it is is at Xie's place. Yang could have been killed because she saw something there. So could have Song."

231

Chen, too, had come to believe that Jiao had something, though it wasn't likely to be the "palace treasure," as Peng called it. But Chen had nothing with which to prevent Internal Security from taking action.

Xie would crumble under their pressure. But would Jiao cooperate? If not, would what had happened to Shang happen to Jiao today? To obtain their goal, Internal Security would stop at nothing. Chen saw no point, however, in asking for more time from Liu, and said instead, "When do you think you can get the warrant?"

"We're reporting to Beijing this morning."

"Let me know when you get it."

"You don't have to worry, Chief Inspector Chen," Liu said, glancing at his watch. "Now I have to rush back to the office."

So that signified the end of their talk. Internal Security was going on ahead, regardless of Chen's opposition. Liu didn't even offer to give him a lift.

"I have to make some phone calls too." Chen pulled open the door and stepped out. "You know my number."

"I'll call you." Liu started driving out, rolling down the window for the first time, watching Chen head in another direction.

TWENTY-FIVE

ABOUT FORTY-FIVE MINUTES LATER, Chen arrived at Xie Mansion, and he pressed hard on the recently-fixed doorbell. He, too, wanted to shake things up.

It took quite a while for Xie to appear at the door. He must have come from bed, wrapped in a scarlet silk pajama robe tied with a silk sash. For the first time, Xie really looked like an Old Dick.

"I've just come back, Mr. Xie. Sorry to drop in like this. So many things have happened during the last few days. I'm worried about you."

"Yes, I'm worried too. Cops have been coming in and out of my place like a market. Oh, it's terrible."

"I can imagine," Chen said. "Let's go out to the garden."

"Garden?" Xie said, looking up. "Yes, let's talk there. Follow me."

They walked over to the plastic garden chairs, which had been moved from under the flowering pear tree. Chen wondered if Xie had sat in the garden since Yang's death. They probably wouldn't be overheard there.

"I heard about what happened to Officer Song," Chen went straight to the point, seating himself on the dust-covered chair.

"I talked to Officer Song just a couple of hours before his death."

"Song was murdered and they see you as the main suspect. I'm trying to help, but you have to tell me everything. You're an intelligent man, Mr. Xie. I don't see any point in beating about the bush."

"No, of course not, but what do you mean by telling you everything?"

"To begin with, your relationship with Jiao's parents."

"What, Mr. Chen?"

"When Song talked to you about Yang's murder, you made a statement, saying that you did not know Jiao before her visit to you about a year ago. That was a lie. You misled the investigation, especially because it was Jiao that provided your alibi. She didn't tell the truth, either. That's perjury, involving both of you, and obstruction of justice. A felony."

"Perjury! I don't know what you're talking about."

"Song's colleagues are out for revenge," Chen said, picking up a brown twig from its edge of the chair and breaking it. "What they are capable of, you don't need me to tell you."

"Do you think I really care? I'm nothing but a straw man, striving hard to keep up an appearance. And I'm sick and tired of it, Mr. Chen. They may do whatever they want."

"But what about Jiao?"

Xie didn't come up with an instant response.

"What worries me, Mr. Xie, is that there is something ominous about this case. Already two people have been killed. First Yang, and then Song. Both were connected to you and Jiao. As a result, much more will happen, I'm afraid. Not necessarily to you, but to Jiao."

"Oh, my God! But why?"

"Now, this is just my guess, Mr. Xie. People are desperately searching for something. Until they get hold of it, they will never stop. Nor will they stop at anything."

"What can it be? When I came into the world, I brought nothing

234

with me. Nor will I take away anything with me upon leaving. So let them have it. Nothing's worth having so many people dying for it."

"It may not be in your possession."

"How can she—" Xie cut himself short and came up with a question. "I wonder how you know all this—and what you can do to help?"

"What I can do to help, to be frank, I don't know, not at this stage. But I happen to know all of this," he said, taking out his business card and badge, "because I am a police investigator. I'm telling you more than I'm supposed to. That's why I brought you out into the garden. The house may be bugged. They are Internal Security, not the ordinary police."

"I trust you, Mr.—" Xie stammered, examining the business card, "Chief Inspector Chen?"

"You don't have to trust me, but you trust Mr. Shen, don't you?" Chen produced his cell phone. "Give him a call."

"No, I don't have to. Mr. Shen's like an uncle to me," Xie said reflectively, and then, resolutely, "So you want to know about my relationship with Jiao's parents?"

"Yes, please tell me from the beginning."

"It was such a long time ago. In the fifties, my family and Qian's family knew each other, but things were already changing. My parents were urging me to behave with my tail tucked in, and not to mix with Qian."

"Because of the stories about Shang?"

"Do you think anyone would have talked to a young boy about those things?"

It was obvious that Xie had heard the stories but Chen didn't push, further breaking the withered twig in his hands.

"At the beginning of the Cultural Revolution, our two families were plundered by the Red Guards. But it was worse for hers. Shang became a target of relentless mass criticism. One scene is still fresh in my memory—of her standing on something like a stage, half of her hair shaven off in a so-called yin/yang style, and wearing around her neck a string of worn-out shoes as a metaphor for her body being used by so many men. Red Guards threw stones and curses and eggs at her. Needless to say, Qian, too, suffered horrible discrimination. We were called 'black puppies.' She was once marched onto the stage to stand beside Shang—as a companion target of mass criticism. That was too much for Qian. She denounced Shang and moved to the school dorm."

"I can understand all that, Mr. Xie. I was younger then, but my father was also 'black.'"

"If there's any difference between me and Qian, it was that I still had the old house to fall back on. There was nothing for her. Shang died. Qian was driven out of her home, and she sort of disappeared for weeks. When she reappeared, she had changed so much. Like in an old saying, she threw a broken jar like a broken jar, but unfortunately, the broken jar happened to be herself. Then she fell for Tan, a good friend of mine, another black puppy of a capitalist family. He told me about their affair. In those days, it was a crime to have sex without a marriage license, but what else could two doomed young people do? She soon found herself pregnant. I was worried sick about them. One early morning, Tan sneaked into my place and pushed into my hands a large envelope, saying that it was something from Qian. He hurried away before I could ask questions. About a week later, they were caught in their attempt to flee to Hong Kong. He was beaten so badly on the way back to Shanghai, he committed suicide, leaving a note in which he shouldered all the responsibility. That's how she was acquitted."

"That's how she survived, I see. Did you approach her after his death?"

"Qian was under surveillance. I knew better than to look for trouble. Besides, I was disappointed with her. So soon after Tan's death, she found herself another lover—a new body hot in her arms with the old body not yet cold in the grave. And nothing but a lustful stud, almost ten years younger than she. They were caught in the act, with him doing something perverted, so he was jailed as a 'degenerate hooligan.' Of course, I still planned to give the package back to her, but then she died too."

"What happened afterward, Mr. Xie?"

"Well, things started improving, though my wife left me to go to the United States. I must have told her too much about the American dream. Karma."

"That's not your fault, but her loss. Please, come back to our topic."

"In the early eighties, people once again called me Mr. Xie. I no longer had to sulk about like a homeless skunk. My house was described as a symbol of the old Shanghai in the glittering thirties. So I ventured out to look for Jiao. It was a promise I made to Tan's memory. She lived in the orphanage, where Zhong, Shang's old maid, occasionally visited her. I gave some money to Zhong for Jiao's sake—not much, but things were so hard for Jiao."

"Did you meet Jiao there?"

"I tried not to, but one afternoon, she happened to see me in the company of Zhong, who introduced me as her father's friend. Not long afterward, she left the orphanage and started working odd jobs."

"Did you still keep that package with you?"

"Yes, I did. She shared a small room with three or four provincial girls, no privacy at all. I didn't want to give it to her under the circumstances, whatever it could be."

"You did the right thing, Mr. Xie, but a lot of things changed for her, yes?"

"Yes, and suddenly too. She quit her job and moved into a high-end apartment—"

"Hold on. You had nothing to do with the change?"

"No, not at all. I actually learned about it from Zhong, who thought I had helped. But how could I? Look at this garden. I can't even afford a gardener."

"You should have one," Chen said nodding, looking at the wasted garden.

"After a few months, Jiao came to me, first as a visitor, and then as a student."

"Did she inherit a large sum of money?"

"No, not that I know of."

"But she came to you after the publication of the book *Cloud and Rain in Shanghai*, I assume."

"I think so. As a student in my class, she's well-qualified, but why she came to the class, I don't know. Possibly it is her way of paying me back—her tuition is, I mean." Xie said with his brows knit tight, "She's helpful. It's really beyond me why she provided an alibi for me the other day. Repaying me with more than money? I have done so little for her."

"Perhaps it was little from your point of view, but a lot from her point of view. Anyway, have you heard any speculation about the changes in her life?"

"Most people believe that there's someone behind her. An upstart who provides everything for her. But in matters like that, you can't ask a young girl for an explanation if she chooses not to tell you."

"That's true." Chen said, "But back to the package. Did you give it to her after she became a regular visitor here?"

"Not at first. I wasn't sure, what with the unexplained change in her life, and with the possibility that there was someone else behind her. But I eventually did, several months ago. It's hers, isn't it? I had no reason not to give it to her."

"Did you find out what was inside?"

"No. Whatever secret it contained, it wasn't mine. Some day I may have to swear," Xie said, his eyes slightly squinting in the light, "that I have never seen anything."

The afternoon sunlight, sifted through the foliage, illuminated the shrewd lines on his face. A survivor of these tumultuous years, Xie had to be cautious.

"Did she tell you anything about what was inside the package?"

"No, she didn't." Xie changed the subject abruptly, "By the way, have you heard about the burglary at her place about a month ago?"

"No, I haven't," Chen said. But it wasn't difficult for him to understand why Internal Security hadn't said anything about it, and why Liu believed that what they wanted to find was in Xie's place.

"Hers is in a well-guarded complex. Yet a thief managed to sneak in, though he left without taking anything valuable."

"Has she told anyone about the package?"

"I don't know. She should know better, I think."

"She has since been a regular visitor to your place and the two of you have a lot of contact. Apart from the package, have you noticed anything unusual about her?"

"Well, for a young girl living in affluence, she's not really happy, but that may just be my impression. If anything is a little unusual, I think it's her frequent visits. It's understandable for the Old Dicks to come over and over again; they have nothing else to do and nowhere else to go. But for someone like Jiao, it beats me."

"That's a puzzle," Chen said. "Also, a Big Buck would show off his 'little concubine' like he would a Mercedes, but no one seems to have seen Jiao appear in that kind of situation for anybody. Do you know anything about it?"

"No, I have never seen or heard of such a Big Buck in her company."

"Do you think she lives by herself all the time?"

"Yes, I think so. Now that you've raised the question, though, I think there may be something. One afternoon, two or three months ago, she got a phone call in the middle of her painting lesson here and left in a great hurry, saying, 'Somebody's waiting for me at home.' She lives there by herself, doesn't she? How could someone be calling her from there? Also, it was on a red cell phone she has never used before or since."

"You're observant. No wonder you're a painter. But it might have been simply an unexpected visitor at her home," Chen said reflectively. But Xie was observant, perhaps not simply in his capacity as a painter and teacher. "Well, as her tutor, is there anything unusual about her painting?"

"I may not be a good judge. According to some critics, I'm no more than an arm chair impressionist—with nothing to share but impressions of those decadent years."

"We don't live in the opinions of critics, Mr. Xie. Anything you have noticed of late, not necessarily as a judge?"

"Well, not anything remarkable, I would say. Recently, she did a painting of a witch riding a broom, flying over the Forbidden City. Surprisingly surrealistic in terms of the subject matter."

"A witch riding a broom?" Chen said. "Like in an American cartoon?"

"Yes. I don't think she has tried her hand at a cartoon before. Nor have I noticed such a surrealistic streak in her work."

"That may be something, but I'm no art critic. Anything else, Mr. Xie? Anything you can think of that may help me—and help you too?"

"That's really about all I can think of." Xie added in earnest, "Don't worry about an old, useless man like me, Mr. Chen. But Jiao is a good girl. So young, and beautiful. She thinks highly of you. You'll do whatever possible to help, won't you?"

Xie might have taken Chen's offer to help as coming out of a romantic motive. Chen, too, thought well of Jiao, but that was irrelevant.

His cell phone rang before he managed to say anything in response. He pressed the button. It was Gu.

"Thank god. You have finally come back, Chief," Gu said. "I've called you so many times."

"What happened?"

"Can you come to the Moon on the Bund this afternoon? There's a cocktail party there. I've something important to tell you."

"Can't you tell me now, Gu?"

"I'm on my way there. It's urgent, involving both the black way and the white way. I'd better tell you in person. You'll meet some people there too."

Gu could occasionally be overdramatic, but Chen had no doubt about his connections with the black way—the Triad world.

"I'll see you there, Gu." Chen turned to Xie, turning off the phone. "I have to go, Mr. Xie. I'll contact you again. Not a single word to anyone about our talk today, not even to Jiao."

"No, not a single word." Xie rose, grasping his hand, "Please do something for her, Mr.—Chief Inspector Chen."

TWENTY-SIX

CHEN STEPPED OUT OF the elevator and into the corridor that joined the two wings of the Moon on the Bund on the seventh floor, just as the big clock atop the Custom Building near the restaurant started striking out its melody. He was startled, looking up out of a corridor window, as if he had heard a cannonball. Perhaps he was too strung out, he thought, remembering the warning Dr. Xia had given him.

For several years after the Cultural Revolution, the melody played by the big clock had been a nameless one, light, pleasant, but it had been changed back to "The East Is Red," the same tune it played during the Cultural Revolution, as hummed by Comrade Bi in the Central South Sea.

The restaurant was built like the converted top floor of an office building on the corner of Yan'an and Guangdong Roads, with a rooftop garden that commanded a magnificent view of the Bund, the Huang River, and the new skyscrapers east of the river. The business was run by a Canadian entrepreneur, who enlisted her chefs and managers from overseas, adding a suggestion of authenticity to the restaurant's upscale image. The price was high, but the restaurant was a huge success among the newly rich, who came here not just for the food or the view but also for a sense of being among the successful elite of the city.

In the Glamorous Bar, Chen greeted several people, talking to them briefly, before he spotted Gu shaking hands with others, holding a glass of sparkling wine.

"Fancy meeting you here," Gu greeted Chen aloud, striding over with a smile, as though overjoyed at a chance encounter.

"What a pleasant surprise," Chen said, responding in the same fashion.

"I've checked and double-checked," Gu whispered, drawing Chen aside into a recess behind the mahogany coat check. "The thugs that attacked you are professionals, but they don't belong to an organization. So it was difficult to find out. A couple of days ago, however, I heard that someone was looking for professional help again, with an emphasis on competence and reliability—payable after delivery."

"A few days ago—" Chen repeated. "Competence and reliability!"

"Yes, when you were away on vacation. So I followed the lead. From what I learned, it might have something to do with a real estate company. For development opportunities in the city, land in a premium location is as good as gold."

"Well, that's possible." Chen could have ruffled feathers with the real estate company that was trying to take over Xie's house. Was it possible that they had targeted Song as well? The emphasis on competence and reliability made sense in that they hadn't delivered on the job with Chen. But Song had done nothing against the interests of the company, not unless he had done something in the last few days, of which Chen had no knowledge. "But why did you want me to come here?"

"Hua Feng, the major shareholder of the company, is here this afternoon," Gu said, shifting his glance to a tall, stout man at the other end of the room. "Connected with the black way."

It was a clue to follow, but perhaps too much of a long shot at the moment. With Internal Security ready for "tough measures" as early as the next day, Chen might not have the time to start exploring that direction. Still, he followed Gu over to Hua, who had a round face and flabby cheeks and was sporting an extensive grin.

"So you are Gu's friend. My name is Hua," Hua said, extending his hand. "Are you also in the entertainment business?"

"My name is Chen. I'm not a businessman," Chen said guardedly. "A writer, an entertaining one."

"Ah, a writer, I see," Hua said, a light flicking in his eyes. "There are so many fashionable writers moving around the city."

"With the city changing so fast," Chen said, not knowing what Hua was driving at, "and so many new buildings replacing old buildings, writers can't help moving around."

"I admire writers, Mr. Chen. You build houses with your words, but we have to build them with concrete and steel."

Chen sensed a subtle shift in Hua's repartee, to something like hostility, though it was fleeting, only a quick flash. He debated with himself as to how much time he should spend talking here. It probably wasn't leading anywhere—not anytime soon.

A blond waitress approached them light-footedly, carrying a glass tray. Hua picked up a tiny roast duck pancake pierced by a toothpick. An exceedingly slender woman in a white summer dress sidled up to Hua, and Chen excused himself.

He saw that Gu was busy talking to others, so Chen left without talking to anybody else. Outside, it was a glorious afternoon on the Bund. He took a deep breath and walked on, trying to think about the latest developments. It might be too late, he admitted to himself. Too late in spite of his efforts and all the help from Old Hunter, Detective Yu, and Peiqin. What he had earned so far concerning the Mao Case were nothing but scenarios without substance. Nothing to prevent Internal Security from taking action the next day.

He took out his cell phone, yet didn't dial. The sound of a siren came trailing over from the river, reverberating into the imagined signal.

It hadn't been his case to begin with. So why not let them take it

244

off his hands? He would have no responsibility or involvement. No worry about the black or white way.

Nor about Mao.

It would not be realistic for an investigation to expect a breakthrough each and every time. There was no point in him being stuck with one particular case. And an absurd case too, for that matter.

Following a flight of stone steps to the raised waterfront, he looked out over the expanse of the shimmering water. Several gulls glided above, their white wings flashing in the afternoon sunlight, as in a dream.

Chen headed toward Bund Park, with a cruise ship sailing into the view, its colorful banners streaming in the breeze. *"Confucius says on the bank, / 'Like water, time flows on and on.'"* Those were the lines Mao had written after swimming in the Yangtze River before the outbreak of the Cultural Revolution. When Chen had read the lines for the first time, he was still a middle school student, walking along the Bund, before or after school. There weren't many classes at school in those years.

It took him only a few minutes to get to the park. Entering through the vine-wreathed gate, he strolled along the bank, which had been recently expanded with colored bricks along the borders.

To his frustration, he failed to find a seat there. A row of cafés and bars seemed to have sprung up overnight along the embankment, like gigantic matchboxes with shining glass walls. It wasn't a bad idea for the park to have a café with a view to the river, but was it necessary to have so many of them that they left no space for the green benches once so familiar to him? Looking in through the glass, he saw only a couple of Westerners sitting and talking inside. The price marked on a pink menu standing outside was staggering. He could afford it, but what about the people who couldn't?

In his middle school textbook, he had read about the park once having at the entrance a humiliating sign: *No Chinese or dogs allowed.* That was at the beginning of the century, when the park was open only to Westerners. After 1949, the Party authorities used the story as a good example for lessons in patriotism. Chen wasn't so sure about the authenticity of the story in his textbook, but now it was pretty much true: *No poor Chinese allowed.*

Finally, when he reached the back of the park, he succeeded in finding something like a stone stump, which was placed there to connect the links of a chain along a winding trail. For him, it served as a seat. Not far away, a young mother was sitting on another such stump with a baby sleeping in an old, worn-out stroller beside her. She had kicked off her shoes, her bare toes grazing the edge of the green grass. Gazing at the baby with affection, in profile she bore a slight resemblance to Shang.

Had Shang come here with Qian? Perhaps Shang didn't sit on a stone stump, and her baby didn't sleep in a ramshackle stroller but had she been as happy, contented?

After all, meaning and essence for each individual life doesn't depend on something divine or imperial. The unfortunate life of Shang an emperor's woman, was an example.

Chen took out a cigarette, but he didn't light it, casting another glance at the baby. The unlit cigarette between his fingers, he felt as if the park had been exercising a subtle effect on him, felt himself thinking with greater clarity.

Yu had sometimes joked that the park must be a place with auspicious feng shui for the chief inspector. As early as the seventies, Chen had started studying English in the park, an experience that led to many things in his life. He didn't believe in feng shui, but that late afternoon, tapping the cigarette on the back of his hand, he wished he could see some signs of it in the park.

He got up and moved over into the shade of a flowering tree, where he dialed Liu.

"What's up, Comrade Chief Inspector Chen?"

"Among the people Song approached in the last few days, was there someone in the real estate business?"

"No, I don't think so."

"Or someone surnamed Hua?"

"I'm not sure. Song talked to a number of people. How am I supposed to remember all of them offhand?"

"Can you check for me?"

"Well, I'm not in the office . . ."

Wherever Liu might be at the moment, Chen thought he heard music flowing like gurgling water and girls' laughter like drifting boats in the background.

"Please find out for me as soon as possible, Comrade Liu."

"I will, Comrade Chief Inspector Chen," Liu said with an edge in his voice. "But we've discussed our plan, haven't we?"

For Liu, Chen's request must have sounded like another tactic for stalling.

"Yes, we have," Chen said, "but you haven't gotten the search warrant yet, have you?"

Afterward, Chen made his way back to the curved walkway above the water, breathing in the air with its characteristic tang from the river. He had done everything possible. Internal Security would take action the next day. Barring a last-minute miracle, the chief inspector would have no choice but to walk away from the case.

He turned around slowly, facing the sight of the pyramid-shaped tower of the Peace Hotel across Zhongshan Road. A gothic-style hotel built by Sassoon, a legendary Jewish businessman in the twenties, it was a soaring symbol of the then most sumptuous building in Shanghai. In the fashionable nostalgia of the city, stories about the extravagances associated with the hotel were becoming elaborate myths. He wondered whether the notorious jazz band of Shanghai Old Dicks would perform in the hotel bar that night. After nearly two weeks at Xie's place, he had little interest in going there.

Then his cell phone rang, the sound almost lost in the siren coming from near the river. It was Peiqin.

"What's up, Peiqin?"

"I'm at Jiao's place, preparing another dinner—for two, that's my guess."

"Tonight?"

"Yes, tonight. Jiao said she won't be back until after eight."

Chen glanced at his watch, almost mechanically. "You're sure about the time of her return."

"I have to make sure that the rice remains warm until she gets back. She was quite particular about that."

"That's something, Peiqin," he said, thinking of what he had discussed with Old Hunter, who swore that he had seen a man in Jiao's room—though only in a fleeting glimpse—the last time she had "a dinner for two" at home. "Have you told Old Hunter about it?"

"I have. He'll be patrolling the area tonight. He told me that the information could be important to you." She added, "Oh, I've made a list of what's unusual in her place. Do you think it might be useful?"

"Of course. Really useful. Can you fax it to my home?"

"Yes, a copy shop can fax it for me."

"I don't know how to thank you, Peiqin."

"Don't mention it. I don't know anything about your investigation, but working at her place, I've learned a few new recipes. Come to our place this weekend."

"I'll think about it, Peiqin."

"Take good care of yourself, Chief. Bye."

Peiqin was concerned about him. He could guess why. He hadn't been to their place for weeks. But his heart sank at the thought of the weekend, by which time her generous help would have come to nothing. He lit the cigarette he had been holding for a long while, inhaling deeply. He was bothered by a feeling of having missed something in the Mao Case. Something elusive, but essential. Peiqin's phone call had intensified the feeling.

Perhaps the park was really an eventful place for him, whatever the feng shui. He had hardly put the phone back into his pants pocket when it rang again. It was Ling, from Beijing.

"Where are you?" she said, sounding so close, like water lapping at the shore. "I called your hotel, but you had checked out."

"I had to rush back to Shanghai. Sorry, I didn't have time to say goodbye to you, Ling. I took the night train, and it was too late to call when I got on it at the last minute." He went on, grasping the phone, "I'm at Bund Park. The park we visited the last time you came to Shanghai, remember? I really appreciate your help. It made a huge difference to my work."

"I'm glad it made a difference to your police work. You can be exceptional in what you choose to do, Chief Inspector Chen. So be an exceptional policeman," she said, her voice suddenly distant again. "Perhaps it's like the poem you wrote, in imitation of a British poet as I remember, about the urgency of making a choice," she said. "*You have to choose your play / Or time will not pardon—*"

"I'm so sorry, Ling," he said, aware of her resignation, after all they had gone through, to his being a cop first, before anything else.

"Keep in touch when you are not that busy. And take good care of yourself."

"I'll call you—"

A click. She already hung up.

But what choice did he have? Again, a cicada chirped in the verdant summer foliage behind him. *Sad it's no longer sad, / the heart hardened anew, / not expecting pardon, / but grateful, and glad / to have been with you, / the sunlight lost on the garden.*

That was the last stanza of the poem she had just mentioned on the phone. In the end, he had no choice except to redeem himself by being a cop.

It came as an answer, however, and not just to that question. In a dazzling illumination of the instant, a new possibility presented itself to him.

He turned and set out for the park security office in haste, where he showed his badge to a gray-haired man sitting at a long desk.

"I'll need to use your fax machine. Someone will fax something here," he said, starting to copy the number.

"No problem, Comrade Chief Inspector," the gray-haired man said. "We know you."

He called Peiqin on his cell phone, wiping the sweat from his forehead. "Are you still at Jiao's apartment, Peiqin?"

"Yes, I'm leaving."

"Leave the key under the doormat when you go."

"What?"

"Yes, and don't tell anybody about it."

"No, I won't."

"Fax your list to this number in five minutes."

"I will."

The moment he finished with Peiqin, he called Gu.

"I need your car for the night. It's a new Mercedes, right?"

"It's yours, it's a Mercedes, 7 Series. Did you find out anything at the cocktail party, Chen?"

"Have your chauffeur pick me up at Bund Park in ten to fifteen minutes. I'll explain it all to you later, Gu. I appreciate all that you have been doing for me."

"You don't have to explain anything to me, nor to thank me for it. What's a friend for?"

Since their first acquaintance during another a case somewhat related to the park, Gu had declared himself a friend to the chief inspector, and he acted like one too. A shrewd businessman, Gu might have seen Chen as a valuable connection. On several occasions, however, Gu had generously exerted himself.

"Whatever you are going to do," Gu went on, "you aren't doing it for yourself, that much I know."

Chief Inspector Chen was going to do something he had never done before, that was about all he knew. He had to be there himself— in Jiao's room.

It wasn't like the visit to Mao's room, Mao being dead such a long time.

Beside him, the fax machine reeled out a piece of paper.

TWENTY-SEVEN

WHEN CHEN ARRIVED AT Jiao's apartment complex, it was almost five in the afternoon.

He sat in the car backseat without even bothering to roll down the window to speak to the security guard. In his experience, they would browbeat an ordinary-looking person lingering in front of the gate, but at the sight of a brand new Mercedes, they would bow and open the gate wide.

As he anticipated, an elderly security man let the car in without asking any questions.

"Pull up at the end of the subdivision," Chen said to the driver. It was a high-end subdivision, with luxurious cars parked here and there. Security might have taken him for one of the new residents. "You may leave if I don't come back in fifteen minutes."

The driver, who must have been instructed by Gu to follow Chen's orders unconditionally, nodded vigorously like a robot.

He stepped out and started back to the building in which Jiao lived, strolling like a resident.

Walking into the building with its door open, he took the elevator to the sixth floor, one floor above Jiao's. Seeing no one along the corridor, he put on a hat and a pair of sunglasses he had purchased at the park. Then he headed to the stairs. He had no idea where Internal Security had installed their video camera, possibly it was hidden somewhere over the landing, but they wouldn't easily recognize him in this disguise. Nor probably would they be watching the camera twenty-four hours a day. Whatever happened tomorrow, he didn't want to worry about it now.

In front of Jiao's door, he squatted down, pretending to tie his shoelace, his back to the staircase and his body covering the view of the doormat, under which he fumbled until he touched the key.

In his college years, he'd read a story about Sherlock Holmes breaking into a criminal's room with the help of a maid working there. If Holmes could justify the means by the end, so could Chief Inspector Chen.

It was no longer just a matter of damage to Mao's image—whatever the Mao material there might be. He was simply making one more effort, so he wouldn't end up like Old Hunter, forever plagued by the thought of what he should have done.

Inserting the key into the lock, he let himself into a large, luxurious apartment. Thanks to the observations made by Peiqin, the basic layout was already familiar to him.

He didn't start searching the place like a cop, though. There was no point in turning it upside down. Internal Security would already have done a thorough job—he had little doubt about who was behind the mysterious burglary here—and he wouldn't have better luck. Nor did he have the time. So he tried to focus instead on the list of the "unusual" items Peiqin had faxed him.

The studiolike appearance of the living room was no surprise. Jiao was a hard-working girl, and she was free to use the room whatever way she liked. The first object that caught his attention there was a long scroll of poetry on the wall. He recognized the poem as one entitled "An Imperial Concubine Waiting at Night" by the Tang-dynasty poet Li Bai.

> *Waiting, she finds her silk stockings*
> *soaked with the dewdrops*
> *glistening on the marble palace steps.*
> *Finally, she is moving*
> *to let the crystal-woven curtain fall*
> *when she casts one more glance*
> *at the glamorous autumn moon.*

Chen was confused. Diao had told him about a scroll of classical Chinese poetry in Shang's room. Not by Li Bai, but by somebody else, though alike in that they were on the persona of a neglected imperial concubine. What he had discussed with Diao wasn't top secret, and as Shang's granddaughter, Jiao might have heard or read similar versions. Why she should have chosen to hang the scroll here, however, was another mystery. The poem would have made sense for Shang, but not for a young girl like Jiao.

Not far from the scroll, he saw several paintings, finished and unfinished, stacked against the wall. Among them, he picked out a sketch of the flying witch. Possibly a draft containing some details Xie hadn't mentioned. The witch was flying on a short-shafted broom over the Forbidden City. There were also two lines written underneath the picture. *Oh to sweep away all the bugs, / I'm invincible!* Chen recognized them as by Mao. Was the painting meant to be a parody?

Moving into the bedroom, he noticed the large bed with one third of its space covered in books. It reminded him of his visit to Mao's bedroom. Was it an elaborate imitation? He touched the bed. Sure enough, it was a wooden-board mattress.

So he opened the door to the bathroom. The sight of the double toilet seats—a normal toilet seat for one to sit on, and a lower, basin-like seat for one to crouch over—confirmed his suspicion. For Mao, it had been a habit carried over from his days as a farmer in the Hunan Province, but Jiao was a girl born and raised in Shanghai. While the orphanage wasn't a fancy place, there was no way Jiao would have picked up such a habit in the city. Besides, it would have been expensive to have her place designed like that.

And Jiao hadn't traveled to Beijing—not before she moved in here. How could she have gotten the ideas and then incorporated them into the interior design?

Once again he took out Peiqin's list of the "unusual." The next on the list was the nature of the books in the study. But what had baffled Peiqin didn't baffle Chen, thanks again to his visit to Mao's old home. He didn't even have to check all the books. A quick look at a couple of titles convinced him that they were similar to the ones in Mao's study.

He moved back to the bedroom. Standing by the window, he tried to empty his mind of all thoughts, closing his eyes and taking a long deep breath.

When he reopened his eyes, he let his gaze sweep around the room, effortlessly, as if still in meditation. And his eyes fell on the black-lacquered cinerary casket on the nightstand.

It wasn't something marked as "unusual" in Peiqin's list. It wasn't something that was commonly kept in a bedroom, but it wasn't unimaginable for a filial daughter to keep her mother's casket there. But how could Jiao have had the casket? When Qian died, Jiao was hardly two years old.

There was an ancient convention, he remembered, about people putting the deceased's clothes and hats into a coffin when the body was missing. He wondered if Jiao had done that for Qian, but it was out of the question that her clothes or hats would fit into such a small casket.

Was it possible that Jiao had hidden something else inside?

It was considered exceedingly unlucky and sacrilegious to disturb the dead by opening a coffin or a container with the ashes of a cremated person. But he succumbed to the temptation. Taking off the lid, he saw only a time-yellowed picture inside, of Shang wrapped in a white robe that revealed her snowy cleavage, standing barefoot by a French window.

He was shocked. It was imaginable for people to put a picture in a casket, but not such a picture of one's grandmother. Looking up, as if under a spell, he stared at another picture, hanging above the headboard—that of Chairman Mao in his robe, waving his hands.

He shivered with the realization of the eerie correspondence between the two pictures.

Jiao must be so obsessed with Mao. But she should know better. Mao was responsible for Shang's tragedy, and for Qian's too, though not directly. A more justifiable reaction from Jiao would be hatred. Instead, it was a fixation on Mao, particularly on a fantasy of Shang's sexual relationship with Mao.

But the discovery in her apartment hardly helped. If anything, it made Internal Security's interest more justifiable. There must be something suspicious going on in secret with Jiao.

He glanced again at his watch. It was almost six thirty. Still more than an hour before her return. He decided to stay and check the bedroom closets. A large one and a small one. Peiqin had mentioned something about the closets on her list.

He pulled open the door of the larger closet and saw an impressive array of designer clothing. Some of the outfits were still wrapped in plastic. A receipt peeped out of one; it was dated about six months ago. The garment was a costly mandarin dress. Because of a recent case, Chen was able to recognize the dress as being in the style of the thirties or forties. Some other dresses in the closet, though slightly different in detail, were in the style of the same period.

Again, Chen didn't remember seeing such a partiality in Jiao. At Xie Mansion she dressed casually. Jeans, blouse, overalls, T-shirts. Except for the last time he met her there, when she was wearing an apron over her pink and white mandarin dress.

He wondered whether these fancy clothes were in Shang's style and whether Jiao, when at home, turned into a reflection of Shang. But then why should she have bought so many clothes without wearing them?

Possibly, somebody else bought them for her, whether she liked them or not.

He was startled by the blaring of his cell phone, echoing loudly in the closet. The number indicated it was Yong in Beijing. He turned it off, not knowing what to say at the moment. Nor could he afford the time.

He then shifted his attention to the smaller closet, which was used to store her painting supplies. Posted on the back of the door was a small note: "Leave things in the closet alone." For the benefit of the maid, presumably. There were tubes of paint, brushes, canvas stretchers, palettes, easels, dippers, and other painting materials he couldn't exactly name. Also there was a paint-smeared robe that had once been white. Several unfinished pieces were stacked against the wall. Apparently, when Jiao woke up at night, she would sometimes start painting in the bedroom. So the small closet served that purpose.

He had no idea how painters worked at home. As a poet, he occasionally woke at night, feeling excited about the possibilities of a fantastic poem, but usually he was too lazy to get up. So he fell asleep again, letting the nocturnal fantasies fade back into the darkness of night. Only on rare occasions did he try to scribble a few words on a scrap of paper he happened to find nearby. He was hardly able to make out the meaning in the morning.

Inspiration might come to Jiao at night, and being more diligent, she may have attempted to capture the fleeting idea there and then. Painting was different from writing. She had to get out of bed, spread out her material, work for hours, and then clean up. It was "unusual," as Peiqin had put it, but it wasn't his business. An eccentric artist, Jiao could live and work the way she pleased.

He was beginning to have second thoughts about his decision to come here, while remaining and rummaging in the closet.

Then his glance fell on a scroll box, which seemed to have been carelessly thrown in there. It caught his attention because he had never seen Jiao scroll-painting in the traditional Chinese style. She studied oil painting and water colors with Xie. He opened the box and pulled out a piece of paper on top. It turned out to be a valuation certificate that declared the scroll to be authentic—and worth a staggering price of more than two million yuan. The valuation was performed three days ago. How could she have left such a valuable possession in the closet like that after the recent burglary? He pulled out the scroll, which was one of Mao's poems done in his brush calligraphy: "Ode to the Plum Blossom." There was also a dedication on the upper right corner: "For Phoenix, in response to hers."

Chen supposed it was possible Jiao had purchased the scroll because of its association with Shang—to be more exact, because of its association with Shang's affair with Mao: Shang was nicknamed "Phoenix." Alternatively, Jiao might have inherited the scroll, but he wasn't sure how.

Could that be the very Mao material the Beijing government was so concerned about?

The dedication on a scroll didn't necessarily mean anything, however. It was conventional for a calligrapher to copy out his work and add a line of a dedication for someone. As it was, the scroll might lead to unbridled speculation, but not to such a disaster as to throw the Beijing government into a panic. After all, someone's nickname was not a conclusive piece of evidence.

Placing the box back into the corner, he saw a broom lying beside it. The broom had a coir head, soft, suitable for the hardwood floor. After Jiao finished painting, she probably had to clean up the mess with the broom.

As he closed the closet door, his mind was in a turmoil. But it was about the time for him to leave. He headed for the front door. On the way, the sight of the surrealistic painting in the living room reminded him of another possibility. She could have used the broom for the painting—

His train of thought was interrupted by the sound of footsteps in the corridor outside, which came to a stop in front of the door. He froze at the sound of a key ring clinking.

TWENTY-EIGHT

AND AT THE SOUND of a key in the lock, he backed up several steps.

When the front door started creaking open, he retreated in haste into the smaller closet, pulling the door closed behind him.

He heard footsteps in the living room, and then the bedroom.

The situation was desperate. The first thing a young girl like Jiao would probably do now that she was back home was change her clothes. That meant a visit to the big closet. And as an industrious art student, she would then start to work. That meant the small closet.

Behind the closet door, Chen couldn't see into the room, but he seemed to catch a whiff of perfume wafting near. He listened, holding his breath. She was stepping toward the large closet, as he had anticipated.

He prayed that after taking off her clothes, she would go to the shower. If so, he might be able to sneak out.

But then there came another sound, indistinctly, from the living room area—

"Jiao, I'm back."

It was a man's voice, with a strong provincial accent, though which province Chen couldn't immediately tell. He was confounded, not having heard someone come in with Jiao, nor hearing the door reopen later. What's more, the voice seemed to come from the other end of the living room, not close to the door—

Could there be another door—a secret one in the living room?

Though it was hard to imagine, it would explain Internal Security's failure to detect a man coming in and out of her apartment.

If so, the mysterious man behind Jiao must be rich and resourceful, having bought this apartment along with the one adjacent, and having a secret door installed between the two. But why all the elaborate secrecy?

He could hear Jiao hurrying out, saying, "Why did you want me to hurry back?"

"What a nice meal," the man said with a chuckle. "Fatty pork is good for the brain. I've been fighting so many battles. An emperor, too, has to eat."

The two met up in the kitchen area. Chen hadn't paid much attention to the dishes on the table there. The fatty pork, which Peiqin had mentioned as one of Jiao's favorites, turned out to be one of the mystery man's favorites, for an uncommon reason.

"It's hot, it's revolutionary," the man said, clanking his chopsticks on a bowl. "You should learn to eat pepper."

Jiao murmured something in response.

"Having just enjoyed the Yangtze River water," the man went on in high spirits, "I am relishing the Wuchang fish."

Chen finally recognized the man's accent as Hunan, possibly affected, as he spoke slowly, almost deliberately. But there was something else mystifying about his comment. It sounded like a paraphrase of the two lines Mao wrote after swimming in the Yangtze River. *"I've just tasted the Yangtze River water, / and I'm now enjoying the Wuchang fish."* The original carried an allusion to the ambitious King of Wu during the Three Kingdom period. The king had wanted to move the

259

capital from Nanjing to Wuchang, but the people were unwilling, saying that they would rather drink the Yangtze River water than eat the Wuchang fish. Mao dashed off the poem, comparing himself favorably to the Wu emperor, having both the water and the fish to his heart's content.

There might be a fish on the table, presumably a real Wuchang fish too.

"No, the Huangpu River water," Jiao responded debunkingly.

Chen slid the closet door open an inch, trying to peep out. From where he stood, however, he couldn't see into the kitchen area. He fought down the temptation venture out farther.

Jiao and her company continued eating in silence.

But Chen saw a mini recorder on the corner table, which reminded him of the one in his briefcase. He took it out and rewound the tape to the beginning.

"Leave the dishes alone," the man said to Jiao. "Let's go to bed."

The two of them were already moving into the bedroom, his footsteps heavier than hers.

"Haven't you put up the scroll I bought you?" he asked.

"No, not yet."

"I wrote the poem for you years ago. Now I finally got it back. I paid a high price for it."

Chen was totally lost. The man was presumably talking about the scroll in the closet, which had a huge price tag. But Mao had composed the poem for Shang, so how could the man outside claim it as his for Jiao?

And what was the relationship between the two? Obviously, he was the "keeper." Judging from her response, Jiao didn't feel strongly about the scroll. At least, she didn't put it up quickly. Having rewound the tape, Chen pressed the button to start recording. It had become hot, almost suffocating, in the closet. He remained still, worried that the man might insist she hang the scroll up right now.

Instead of pushing her, the man started yawning and slumped

across the bed, which then creaked under his weight. Jiao kicked off her shoes, her heels falling on the floor, one after another.

It was still early, but the two on the bed sounded tired. Before too long, hopefully, they would stop talking and fall asleep. Then Chen would be able to get out.

"You've got something on your mind," Jiao said. "Talk to me."

"Well, I have overcome so much, sweeping away all my enemies like rolling up a mat. How can I have anything on my mind? Let's forget our worries in the cloud and rain."

"No, it's useless. And it's too early."

"A plum blossom can always come out a second time."

The conversation in the bedroom struck Chen as inexplicably stilted. The metaphor of "rolling up a mat" sounded like another line by Mao, though Chen wasn't sure. But he was certain that in erotic literature, a plum flower blossoming a second time could refer to a second climax during sexual intercourse.

Their talk was becoming quiet, indistinct, intelligible only to themselves. Chen had a hard time hearing their murmuring to each other, except for occasional exclamations interspersed with moaning and groaning.

"You are really big, Chairman, big in everything," she said breathlessly.

Chen was thunderstruck. She called her bed partner "Chairman." Nowadays, "Chairman" wasn't exclusively reserved for Mao, but "CEO" or "President" would be far more common for Big Bucks in contemporary China. Chen was able to puzzle out the sentence because it was something he had read in the file about Shang—what she had said about Mao after their first night together: "Chairman Mao is big—in everything." It could mean a lot of things. But in the present context, it meant only one thing.

Was Jiao imitating Shang?

The groaning and moaning intensified, rising to a crescendo. Chen had never imagined he would ever investigate a case like a peeping

261

Tom in a closet, or to be exact, an eavesdropping Tom. The sound kept breaking in, wave upon wave, whether he liked it or not.

If he tried to slip out now, he might succeed in getting away unnoticed. Lost in sexual rapture, the lovers might hardly pay attention to anything else, and there was only a faint night light flickering in the bedroom.

But he decided to stay. The two might soon fall asleep, and it would be less risky to sneak out then. Besides, he was intrigued by their talk in the midst of the grunting and grinding on the wooden-board mattress.

"*Oh, oh, against the gathering dusk stands a pine,*" the man burst out in a loud falsetto, "*sturdy, erect—*"

It befuddled Chen. At the dinner table, the man's comment about the fish might have been a witty joke. In the midst of sexual passion, however, he was quoting Mao again, and that was bizarre—

Chen finally recognized the Hunan-accented voice as an imitation of Mao.

Could he be playing a role—that of "Mao?"

From the moment of his entry into the apartment, the man had been talking and acting like Mao, including his remarks at the dinner table about fatty pork being beneficial for the brain, about hot pepper being revolutionary. Those were details from the memoirs about Mao. Not to mention all the quotes from Mao, and now the very poem he wrote to Madam Mao, "On the Picture of the Fairy Cave in Lu Mountains." "Mao" must have heard the erotic interpretation and was applying it to that very context.

The chief inspector had read about sexual fantasies, but what was being staged in the bedroom was far more than that—it was elaborate, perverted, absurd.

Abruptly, something seemed to be going wrong on the bed in the dark.

"*What a fairy cave it is, born out of the nature! / Ineffable— ineffable—*"

"Mao" failed to complete the last line. Could he have forgotten the remaining words in his climb up to the height of sexual ecstasy?

In the ensuing silence, Chen heard Jiao making a muffled sound which went on for two or three minutes before she burst out in frustration.

"What a great pine! A broken one, sapless, lifeless."

"Come on," "Mao" said, "I've just overworked myself of late. There are so many things on my hands, you know."

"So many things on your mind, I know. You've been acting differently."

"Don't worry. *No matter how winds blow and waves beat, / I'm at leisure, like strolling at a courtyard.*"

"Don't quote him all the time. I'm so sick and tired of it. Tonight, you're not even as good as the old man!"

"What old man are you talking about?"

"Aren't you talking about him, acting like him, and being him all the time?"

It dawned on Chen that a fiasco had been playing out in the bedroom. "Mao" kept reciting the poem as sexual stimulation so that he could come in cloud and rain with Jiao, but he failed.

"Let's take a short break," "Mao" said. "I need to close my eyes for a minute."

"I told you not to hurry," she said.

Another short spell of silence engulfed the room.

"Oh, have you met with Chen of late?" "Mao" said abruptly.

"I heard that he's just come back to Shanghai. Where he's been, I have no idea. Why?"

"This afternoon he sort of approached me at the cocktail party."

"He has business connections. Don't worry about him. I've told you that he's a nice man."

"He's very nice to you, of course."

"He has a book project on the thirties, so he asked me some questions."

"So you had a candlelight dinner with him the other night."

"What? How do you know about that?"

"And you're nice to him too." "Mao" said sarcastically, "He's so

263

different, as you've said, talented, and capable of buying you an expensive dinner too."

"No, that's not true. He's nothing but a would-be writer, I assure you."

"He is anything but what he claims to be. He is one who might have high connections. I just got a tip about him, and his appearance at the cocktail party was no coincidence. I'll find out. The damned monkey won't get away from the palm of Buddha."

The "monkey" he referred to was the one in the *Journey to the West*. In the classic novel, Monkey tried to challenge the power of Buddha, who turned his palm into the five-peaked mountains and crushed the monkey underneath. Chen hadn't "approached" a Hunan-accented man, however, at the cocktail party that afternoon.

"What are you going to do about him?"

"See, you are concerned about him even when lying naked in my arms."

"You're being so unreasonably jealous. If that's what you want, I'll stop seeing him. I accepted his invitation because he was helping Xie. There's nothing going on between us."

"Well, let's not talk about him now."

"Mao" didn't seem to want to pursue the subject too far. Whoever "Mao" could possibly be, he was possessive, taking Chen as a threat.

Again, the old familiar sound surfaced, bubbling up from the stillness of the room. This time, "Mao" didn't recite any lines. Chen heard only his labored breathing and the screeching of the wooden-board mattress.

But "Mao" failed again. "I'm too tired today," he mumbled.

Sliding open the closet door a bit, in the semi-darkness Chen could make out only the silhouettes of two white bodies on the bed, both partially sitting up, propped up against pillows.

"You're beat today," she said, "what with your worries about Chen, what with—"

"What are you talking about?" "Mao" snarled in exasperation. "You think Chen could beat me? Tell you what! He won't get away so easily the next time."

"I have nothing to do with him. Really. I swear by my grandma's soul." Jiao took it seriously, whatever he meant by "the next time." "He goes to Xie's place only for his book project."

"Why the hell can't you stop going there? Neither Chen nor Xie is your damned business."

"I've been studying painting there because of you. You wanted me to be educated and cultured—to be worthy of you."

"I wanted you to dabble a little, like Shang—to be like her in every way."

"But I have been learning a lot of things there. Xie's really knowledgeable."

"So you really care for Xie, I see. . . ."

"Oh, how can you say that?" she exclaimed. Then something fell to the floor, like a glass, breaking and splintering.

She might have knocked a cup from the nightstand with a sudden motion. In the *Romance of Three Kingdoms*, Liu Bei, too, dropped his cup when Cao Cao made an unexpected comment about Liu's secret ambition.

"Don't move," she said, springing up from the bed. "I'll get the broom and clean it up."

In the closet, hiding behind the door, Chen caught a partial glimpse of her naked body padding over. He might be able to break away, he calculated, at the instant she pulled open the door. She would be too shocked to react or recognize him, considering the poor light. "Mao," still sprawling on the bed, wouldn't be able to catch him in time to detain him.

He put his hands on the groove of the door, listening closely to her steps, which approached softly on the floor . . .

TWENTY-NINE

A NIGHT-LIGHT POPPED ON in the closet, as if in response to her bare feet moving closer.

It was a tiny light that shed only a faint ring on the floor. Possibly it was on an automatic timer.

Holding his breath, Chen tensed his muscles, and prepared to spring out.

But the closet door didn't slide open.

To his surprise, the footsteps actually started fading away.

She must be heading toward the kitchen, from what he was able to make out, sweating in shock and relief.

A minute or so later, he heard her coming back, most likely with the broom from the kitchen.

It was nothing short of a miracle that she chose to get the broom from the kitchen instead—

"Mao" turned the lamp on the nightstand on upon her return.

Chen was finally able to catch a glimpse of her dazzling white body—the delicate tension of her curved back and buttocks as she bent over to clean up the mess on the floor, carrying a broom and a dustpan.

It was but a fleeting peek. She cleaned up the splintered glass and walked back to the kitchen with the broom and dustpan.

When she returned, she turned off the light the moment she slid back into bed.

But why should she have taken the trouble to walk, naked, all the way to the kitchen for a broom when there was one in the bedroom closet? Maybe she didn't want to use the soft broom for the spilled tea. In Shanghai, a broom of bamboo slices would be common for a *shikumen* courtyard or concrete-floored kitchen. For a bedroom, however, a broom made of *Luhua* reed, or better quality, made of coir—

"At first you said you went there for the painting lessons," "Mao" resumed his interrupted speech. "It might be good for you, I thought, but you spend more and more time there. Lessons, parties, and sometimes with no excuse at all. Why?"

"What am I supposed to do here? You're always busy. You only come in for your cloud and rain."

"And that's not all. You have been taking such good care of Xie, cooking and cleaning and washing for him, while you have a maid helping at home. When he was sick at the hospital, you stayed by his bedside for hours."

"Xie has suffered a lot. Now he's an old man, living by himself, and I try to do something to help, just like his other students."

"Like his other students? Don't try to pull my leg anymore. You went so far as to provide a false alibi for him. That night you came home quite early as I recall. Why?"

"He is incapable of harming people—incapable of killing a fly. He was being set up. I had to help."

"Help? Help by posing naked for him and risking perjury for him?" "Mao" raised his voice. "You told me you never knew him before going to him as a student. That's another lie. He went out of his way to help you—as early as back in your orphanage days."

"I didn't really know."

"Now he's a legend in Shanghai, with a mansion worth a fortune, and a fabulous collection too."

"What do you take me for?"

"How can you care for such a pathetic guy?"

Was that possible? While Chen had observed something between Xie and Jiao, he had never really contemplated that possibility?

Still, Jiao could have been drawn to Xie. Not necessarily because of anything material, but because of something spiritual in her mind. An imagined continuation of Shang's world, which was shattered by Mao. It might also have lent meaning to the tragic life of the young girl, symbolically, for her world, too, was being shattered by Mao's shadow.

"Do you care for me as a human being? No, I'm nothing but an object of your fantasy—like a vase, a decoration, a Mercedes, a piece of property."

"Are you out of your mind? It's for your sake that I purchased that scroll. It cost enough for five Mercedes."

"No, you bought it for your sake. For your fantasy of being Mao."

"I proposed that buyout to Xie for your sake as well. He would be nothing without that damned house of his."

"You're the one behind the offer made by the real estate company! I should have guessed—you with your connections to both the black and white ways."

"But for Chen's interference, Xie would have been homeless today. Now listen to me. Whoever stands in my way will be punished. Not even your Mr. Chen with all his connections. Next time he won't get away with only a warning from my little brothers."

"So that's why he suddenly left the city? You're capable of anything!"

"Yes, I'm capable of getting rid of anybody that's in my way. And don't dream that anybody will help you get away from me. No one under the sun can ever do that. Not Chen, not Xie, not Yang—"

"Yang? Why are you talking about Yang?"

"That bitch tried to take you to other parties—to other men."

"What?" Jiao jumped up from the bed, which squeaked and squealed. "How could you—"

"Use your fucking brain!" "Mao" snarled. "Who else cares for you?"

"You care only for yourself. You fuck me just because Mao fucked my grandmother."

"Only I'm Mao, the son of the Heaven, and you can be nobody else's—nobody else."

Chen was sure that the man on the bed was insane. He wasn't merely imitating Mao, he believed he was Mao.

"But Yang—" Jiao couldn't finish the sentence, wracked by an outburst of sobbing.

"I would let down all the people in the world rather than have any of them let me down. To make revolution is not to invite people to dinner, you stupid woman."

Chen recognized the first sentence as a quote from Cao Cao, a Han-dynasty statesman Mao admired. And the second was a familiar quote from the *Little Red Book,* a favorite line the Red Guards would quote while beating and smashing people and things at the beginning of the Cultural Revolution.

But the man's comment also implied that he had killed Yang—that he'd done so since, in his logic, she had become a threat. Killing her and leaving her body in the garden could have taken care of Xie, another threat, had Jiao not unexpectedly provided an alibi for the old man.

"You are a crazy monster, killing people like weeds," Jiao shrieked hysterically.

"You ungrateful bitch!" He slapped her face hard.

"You bastard of Mao—"

Her protest was replaced by a muffled sound. "Mao" must be stopping her from shouting. A disturbance in the room of a young single woman at night could draw attention from the neighbors.

Chen sprang up, placing his hand on the door, though not sure what exactly to do. Domestic violence wasn't a priority for him at the moment, and he might be able to learn a lot more from their fight.

He tripped over something in the closet, and nearly stumbled. It was the broom. He was transfixed by the bulging sensation under his foot—something tangibly hard inside the coir fiber of the broom head. He bent over and examined it in the glow from the night-light. A worn-out broom head, but with a relatively new binding thread.

Jiao could have unraveled the coir, inserted something inside, and rebound the fiber.

What could be hidden inside?

He touched the broom head again. Whatever was inside appeared to be square in shape. Something like paper. Not just one or two pieces, but a stack of them. The size was smaller than legal-size paper, possibly a notebook, except that it did not feel like a notebook with a hard cover.

What he had learned from Diao came back to him. About Shang's passion for pictures and her photography equipment. Inside could be the pictures of Shang and Mao—possibly in their most intimate moments, in the midst of the rolling cloud and rain.

The presence of the broom in the bedroom closet now made sense. She didn't want to leave the broom in the kitchen, where a maid could use it just like any broom. But in the closet here it was safe and acceptable to her, psychologically. That would explain her choosing not to use this broom a short while ago.

Also, it provided an insight to that surrealistic painting. Her unconscious might have produced a revenge fantasy, in which broom swept over the Forbidden City. The lines by Mao appeared, ironically, so proper and right in context. The concern of the Beijing government was not unfounded.

He took out his pocketknife, ready to cut open the broom head in the faintly-lit closet.

It was really a Mao case after all.

"Chen, that bastard, strikes from the dark—"

Chen was stunned by the mention of his name, as his knife was poised just inches above the broom head. He hadn't made a move against anyone through his connections in the city government, except for lobbying for Xie Mansion to be given the status of a historical site. But somebody else might be paying attention to "Mao."

"His disappearance wasn't the result of the warning from my little brothers. What he's really up to, I don't know."

"Mao" was Mao, who, paranoid that everybody was plotting against him, killed his hand-picked successor Liu Shaoqi, and then the next one, Ling Biao, not to mention thousands of high ranking Party officials who had been loyal to him.

"And he's connected with that bastard cop who came to my office for information about you. I got rid of him, though."

Song—the lieutenant could have uncovered Jiao's connection to "Mao," approached him, and, to "Mao," posed a threat.

"Yes, you have to say yes to me, say yes!" "Mao" shouted. *Yes* echoed in the bedroom.

Jiao didn't respond.

The silence thundered over Chen. When "Mao" stopped his monologue, the bedroom was shrouded in stillness, except for his labored breathing.

Chen opened the door further to see before him an astonishing tableau. "Mao" sat naked on top of Jiao, straddling her abdomen, his back toward the closet door, his muscles stretched taut, tremulous, his hand rising up from her mouth, as if having just given up the effort to stop her shouting. She lay motionless, her white legs spread wide, her pubic hair darkly visible.

Only a tenth of a second, but long enough for all the details to start etching themselves onto Chen's consciousness.

"You—" "Mao" abruptly dropped his Hunan accent. "I did all that for you. Without you, without—"

Wrenching open the door completely, Chen whirled headlong, flinging himself forward, but stumbled over the broom that was falling out of the closet.

"Mao" jerked up and jumped off Jiao. Swinging, he snatched up something from the nightstand and hurled it at Chen. But for Chen's lurch, it might have hit its target. Instead, it missed and smashed against the window, breaking through the glass with a loud crash.

Chen was shocked at the sight of "Mao"—it was none other than Hua, the real estate tycoon he had seen earlier that afternoon at the cocktail party. There Hua had spoken with a strong Beijing accent.

Struggling to regain his balance, Chen countered by lashing out with the knife in his hand. Hua dodged violently, his body hitting Mao's picture above the headboard.

What happened next came close to an absurd slow-motion scene in a horror movie. It appeared as if the picture of Mao had come to life. It groaned, shivered, and crashed hard on Hua's head, with all the weight of its heavy metal frame.

"Mao—" Hua swayed, stared in disbelief, slumped back on the bed, and lost consciousness.

Chen rushed over in two strides and shoved Hua's body off of Jiao. She lay still on the rumpled sheet, her body spread-eagled, cold, and ghastly against the flickering night-light. He touched her throat. No pulse.

How long it had been, he had no idea, suffering a sudden, over-whelming nausea in his whole being.

He was reaching for the cell phone when Hua's body jolted up in a ferocious motion before rolling off the bed with a thud, again cracking against the fractured Mao portrait on the floor.

His fingers touching the phone seemed to signal the abrupt foot-steps running outside along the corridor, and then conjured up a loud pounding on the door.

"Open the door! Police Patrol."

It was Old Hunter, who was inserting a key into the lock.

THIRTY

"OH—CHIEF INSPECTOR CHEN!" Old Hunter bumped in, panting. "I was patrolling on the street when I heard a crash and saw a black object flying out of the window. Is something wrong—"

He cut himself short at the sight of the naked body on the bed—Jiao, lying stiff, still—and then the other one, a naked man on the floor, sprawling over a splintered portrait of Mao.

The utter disarray of the room was presented in ghastly somberness, with only the tiny night-light flickering in the corner. The clothes of the two bodies were scattered around. There was a chunk of plaster on the bedsheet that had fallen from the wall above the headboard. A pocketknife glittered beside the rumpled pillow. A broom lay not too far away, sticking out of an open closet, pointing to the bed.

How did Chen come to be in the midst of all that?

Chen looked distraught, his eyes bloodshot, his hair disheveled, and his T-shirt and pants crumpled and soiled, as if he had been just released from a prison cell. Old Hunter knew that Chen had just come back that morning on the night train from Beijing.

However, nothing about the eccentric chief inspector would be surprising.

"I'm calling for an ambulance," Chen said, producing his cell phone.

Feeling for a pulse on her ankle, Old Hunter said, shaking his head, "It's too late, Chief. Who's the man?"

"His name is Hua. They had a fight. She started shouting, and he tried to stop her—"

"So he strangled her—" Old Hunter didn't finish the sentence, wondering where Chen had been at the time. He checked to see if the man on the floor was breathing. There was a thin trail of blood congealing along his temple, but he breathed evenly. "He's alive."

"I let myself into the apartment and was looking around. Then they came back unexpectedly—no, Jiao arrived first, and then Hua, possibly through a secret door. So I had to hide in the closet. I couldn't see and I could hardly hear."

Old Hunter turned on the lamp on the nightstand. The light glared on her white body, which had a purplish bruise around her shoulders and neck. Her breasts were flat and appeared unbruised, yet bore something like a bite mark. There were no other outward signs of sex—no semen around the genitals, thighs, or in the black pubic hair. Her large eyes remained open, staring. The corneas were not yet cloudy, a sign of a recent death. Her fingernails had hardly lost their pinkish color.

Chen picked up her crumpled dress and covered her in silence.

Technically, they should wait for the arrival of the detectives from the homicide squad or Internal Security before touching anything, Old Hunter thought, shifting his glance toward the closet.

"I should have come—" Again he left the sentence unfinished. *A couple of minutes earlier?* He was outside on the street, unaware of the situation here. As in an old saying, the water's too far away for the fire close at hand. Still, he didn't want to sound too critical of Chen. It could have been hard for Chen to judge the situation in the room while hiding in the closet. "But you subdued him."

"When I became aware that something was terribly wrong, I jumped out of the closet. He hurled the cinerary casket of Shang at me. It was empty except for a picture of Shang inside. Then, in an effort to dodge my attack, he caused the Mao portrait to fall and hit him on the head with the full weight of the metal frame."

"Mao's spirit worked," Old Hunter murmured, shuddering at the realization. He didn't really believe in the supernatural, but there was something so unbelievable about the case. It was almost like those Suzhou operas. "Hua killed Shang's granddaughter under his portrait, and Mao knocked him out. Mao's not dead."

"Mao's not dead—you can say that again."

"But how did Jiao and Hua get together?"

"Here's what I think," Chen said. "Hua learned about her family history while she was working as a receptionist at his company. He then overwhelmed her with his Big Buck advances, buying her the apartment and everything else, cutting a 'little concubine' deal with her. He did all that, however, not because of her, but because of Shang, her grandmother."

"I'm totally lost, Chen. It's even more mind-boggling than a Suzhou opera ghost story. Shang died so many years ago. Is Hua such a crazy fan of hers?"

"No, he fell for Jiao because of Shang's affair with Mao. I should have made that clear."

"So—Hua fucking Jiao was like a parallel of Mao fucking Shang. Is that what you mean?"

"It's more than that. By sleeping with Jiao—Shang's granddaughter—Hua turns himself into Mao. He started talking like Mao, thinking like Mao, living like Mao, and fucking like Mao too."

"But Hua is a Big Buck. He could have girls like Jiao and live like an emperor—like Mao too. Why all the bother, Chief?"

"Being Mao gave Hua a meaning he had never known before. In terms of the cultural unconscious, it's the emperor archetype—Son of Heaven, with the divine mandate and power, all the emperor's men and women. That's why Hua was so panic-stricken about the possibility of losing Jiao, a woman he didn't really care for. Consciously, she was nothing to him. But in his subconscious, Jiao was everything."

"Leaving your psychological jargon aside, he's devil-possessed. He has fucked his brains out! He must have watched too many movies about Mao and the emperors. He's totally crazy."

"It's sheer craziness, but for such a split personality, it makes sense. Jiao provided the mechanism for him to switch into Mao, so he couldn't afford to let anyone know about their relationship. That led to a hell of secrecy: adjoining apartments, a secret door from his apartment into hers—somewhere in the living room, I believe—and financial transactions too. After she quit her job, he no longer was seen in her company, but he kept seeing her in secret. That's how you caught a glimpse of them by the window the other night."

"I'm still confounded, Chief. That bastard is crazy—why would Jiao have played Shang for him?"

"I don't think Jiao liked the role of Shang, but he must have insisted on it as the condition of their Mao deal."

"Beauty has a thin fate indeed. What a curse to three generations! A curse to her grandmother, to her mother, and to her too. But what's the damned point for him?"

"There's not a point in the world—its not like in a Suzhou opera. There isn't always a transcendental point visible in life, so people have to have their own point, or to make one, at least, in their own imagination," Chen said, his dismal smile getting lost in thought. "Anyway, Hua got increasingly uneasy about Jiao's visits to Xie's place, and about her mixing with other people. For instance, Yang kept trying to drag Jiao to other parties—"

Chen's cell phone rang, cutting short his speech.

"Oh, it's Liu," he said to Old Hunter, pressing a button.

"Comrade Chief Inspector Chen, I've got the information you requested. Among the people Song interviewed during your vacation, there's one named Hua. He owns several large companies, including the one for which Jiao once worked. It was just routine. Nothing suspicious on the record—"

"Nothing suspicious on the record," Chen repeated in irrepressible sarcasm. "Then listen to this, Comrade Liu. Less than an hour ago,

Hua killed Jiao in her apartment. He's in my custody. Hurry over here with your people."

"What?" Liu said, too astonished to absorb what Chen had said. "But you didn't say anything about it this morning, or this afternoon."

"You were so bent on your tough measures, expecting to get the warrant tomorrow. Did you really want to listen?" Chen added after a pause, "Hua also killed Yang, who he saw as a potential threat that could drag Jiao away from him."

"He killed Yang! But—why should he have bothered to leave Yang's body in Xie's garden?"

Old Hunter, too, found it hard to believe. How could Chen have discovered it while on vacation thousands of miles away?

"In Hua's imagination, Xie had became another threat because Jiao was nice to him."

"How could an old pathetic fellow have been a threat?"

"Hua's paranoid, and all he saw was that Jiao was nice to Xie. So by getting rid of Yang and planting her body there, Hua tried to kill two birds with one stone."

"You—you have done an amazing job. We're on the way. Stay there, Chief Inspector Chen."

"Yes, I'll stay here," Chen said, snapping the phone closed in disgust. "An amazing job indeed, Old Hunter. Jiao was murdered in this very room, not even a stone's throw away from the closet I was in."

"But you did your job," Old Hunter said in earnest, aware of the agony in Chen's voice. A cop could close many cases successfully, but a single screwup could haunt him forever. "You were in the closet, unable to see or hear clearly. Nobody could have done any better under the circumstances. But for you, the criminal would have got away. What a case—"

Old Hunter lost his words in angst. What a Mao case—so many years ago for him, and now for Chen . . .

"Shang—"

THIRTY-ONE

"SHANG—" HUA WAS COMING round, his features convulsed with bewildered astonishment. "What the hell happened?"

"That is exactly what happened," Chen said, thinking of the superstitious interpretation of Old Hunter's. "You strangled Shang's granddaughter, Mao knocked you out—at least, Mao's portrait did."

"But how did you get in here?" During their fleeting encounter in the dark, Hua must not have seen Chen break out of the closet—probably hadn't realized that Chen had been hiding in there at all.

"You devil, you deserve a thousands cuts!" Old Hunter interrupted. "You won't get away with it. This is murder in the first degree."

Hua appeared very different, his eyes lusterless, his left cheek twitching uncontrollably, his mouth dropping. There was no trace left of the imperial Mao persona. Nor even of a successful businessman. He was totally crushed.

It was a moment for Chen to seize upon. To shake something more out of the fallen. There were still unanswered questions.

But his cell phone shrilled out again, breaking the spell of the moment. It was Minister Huang from Beijing, and Chen had to take the call.

"Liu's just called me, Chief Inspector Chen."

"Oh, Minister Huang, I was going to call you too," Chen said, not surprised by Liu's fast move. Jiao was killed in her apartment by someone named Hua. A nut who tries to imitate Mao. He is in my custody."

"A nut who tries to imitate Mao! That's unbelievable. But how did you get in there? Internal Security is complaining about your singular methods." The minister added quickly, "It's sour grapes, of course. I understand. You beat them again."

"They were so anxious to use their tough measures, but it wasn't a good idea, not on such a politically sensitive case. As you have said, it wasn't in the best interest of the Party. So I decided that I had to act on my own."

"It was very decisive action, I have to say. Now, did you find anything there?"

"Yes, there was something left behind by Shang."

"Really, Chief Inspector Chen!"

"A scroll of a poem in Mao's brush handwriting with a dedication to Phoenix—which was her nickname, you know. It was 'Ode to the Plum Blossom.' And the scroll was certified as authentic. Shall I turn it over to Internal Security?"

"Oh, that—no. Turn the scroll over to me. You don't have to say anything about it to Internal Security. You're working directly under the Central Party Committee. Is there anything else?"

"Not at this moment," he said. Apparently the minister didn't think that the scroll mattered a great deal to the image of Mao. Chen decided not to mention the broom. He still had to verify what was inside first. Besides, Old Hunter and Hua were listening. "I'm going to search thoroughly. Whatever I find, I'll report to you, Minister Huang."

Old Hunter looked confused. So did Hua, though he had been tipped about Chen's high connections. Little did he imagine that the "would-be writer" was actually a chief inspector who was talking to a government minister in Beijing.

279

"Don't reveal anything to the media," Minister Huang said. "It's in the Party's interest."

"Yes, I understand. It's in the Party's interest."

"You solved the case under a lot of pressure. I'd like to suggest that you take a vacation. How about one in Beijing?"

"Thank you so much, Minister Huang," Chen said, wondering whether the minister was aware of his recent trip to Beijing. "I'll think about it."

"As I said, you're an exceptional police officer. The Party authorities can always depend on you. Greater responsibilities are awaiting you."

The minister didn't forget his promise of promotion to Chen probably as the successor to Party Secretary Li in the Shanghai Police Bureau.

Following the conclusion of the phone call, a wave of silence overwhelmed the room.

Hua looked up from the floor, his smoldering glare shifting and settling on Chen.

"What a bastard you are! You've created all this trouble for me, haven't you? But you're so stupid. *Surrounded and surrounded by the enemy, / I stand firm and invincible.*"

Hua was quoting again. Those were lines composed by Mao while fighting the guerrilla war against the nationalists in the days of the Jinggang Mountains. However, it was ridiculous for Hua to attempt the Hunan accent. It sounded hollow, empty, without any conviction.

"What an idiot!" Old Hunter commented. "Still lost in the days of the Jinggang Mountains. That son of a bitch doesn't even know what day it is today."

But what did Hua know about the Mao material? Chen had to find out. Judging by the renewed defiance of "Mao," it would be impossible to make him talk before Internal Security arrived.

"Today? Look at what the so-called reforms have done to China today. A total restoration of capitalism. New Three Mountains are weighing down on the working class, who are suffering once again in the fire, in the water. Indeed, all this I foresaw long, long ago. *Contemplating over the immensity, / I ask the boundless earth: / Who is the master controlling the rise and fall of it.*"

"What the hell is he talking about?" Old Hunter grunted. "The rise and fall of the devil, I say."

"He's quoting again," Chen said, recognizing the lines from another poem written in Mao's youth, which was perhaps less well known. But Hua's speech was a passionate defense of Mao—and self-justification, as well.

But it was a defense made in the most grotesque way, with him lying stark naked on his back, mouthing those heroic lines, waving his arm in a style, fashioned after Mao's—as in the picture beneath him. It was a weird juxtaposition too, not just of Mao and Hua, but of so many things—past and present, personal and not personal. Chen had a hard time fighting off the impulse to kick the hell out of Hua and all that was behind him. It was then that an idea hit the chief inspector.

He flipped out a cigarette for Old Hunter, lit it, and then another one for himself, flicking away the ashes, as if too contemptuous to cast another look at the prostrate figure on the floor.

"The bastard's utterly lost in the spring and autumn dream of being Mao. But he's not worth a little finger, a little hair, a little fucking peanut of Mao. He should pee hard, and see his own ludicrous reflection in it."

"What do you mean?" Hua snarled.

"You're no match for ordinary cops." Chen turned round, his finger still tapping the cigarette. "How can a pathetic bastard like you ever delude yourself into being Mao?"

"You were just lucky, you devious son of a bitch, but the other cop had no such luck."

"But Song didn't even suspect you," Chen pressed on, taking a shot in the dark. "You barked up at the wrong tree."

"He came to me for information about her; he was nosing around.

How could I let him get away with that? Any leniency toward your en-emy is a crime to your comrade."

Liu had said that Song was only conducting a routine interview, but Hua panicked. To a cold-blooded man like Hua, like Mao, it was logical to prevent scrutiny by killing Song. Chen surmised that Hua, in order to hang on to his illusion of being Mao, didn't hesitate to confirm that, if nothing else, at least he could kill as ruthlessly as Mao.

"*Any leniency toward your enemy is a crime to your comrade*," Old Hunter repeated, imitating Mao's Hunan accent with his brows in a knot. "That's the Mao quotation we used to sing like a morning Prayer at the bureau during the years of the proletarian dictatorship. But I can't make him out, Chief. This bastard keeps talking and quoting as if he had a tape of the *Little Red Book* playing in his head."

"He has played Mao so much, he has become Mao incarnate. When Song's investigation posed a potential threat to him, he simply had him killed. It was the same way that Mao got rid of his rivals us-ing one 'Party Line Struggle' after another."

"I am Mao!" Hua screamed. "Now do you finally understand?"

"You're talking in your dreams," Chen sneered. "How could you even come close to the shadow of Mao? For one thing, Mao had many women devoted to him, heart, body, and soul. 'Chairman Mao is big—in everything!' Think about it. Many years after his death, Madam Mao committed suicide for his 'revolutionary cause.' You may quote Mao, but do you have anyone loyal to you? Wang Anshi put it so well: '*Lord of Xiang is a hero after all, / having a beauty die wholeheartedly for him.*' What about you? You couldn't even win the heart of a *little concubine*."

"You bastard," Hua hissed through his clenched teeth, groaning savagely, his eyes darting back and forth like a trapped animal. "Don't fart."

"Don't fart your Mao fart," Old Hunter butted in.

"Don't fart" was a notorious line in a poem published by Mao in his last days, by which time he believed he could put whatever he liked to say into poetry. People joked about it after his death.

"Jiao might have shared the bed with you, but nothing else," Chen went on. "Like the old saying, she dreamed different dreams on the same bed with you. You didn't know anything about her."

"What the hell do you know?"

"A lot, and you're completely in the dark. Like her passion, her dreams, her future plans, we talked about them for hours in the garden and over a candle light dinner at Madam Chiang's house. Let me just give you a small example; her sketch of a broom-riding witch over the Forbidden City." Chen paused in deliberate derision, attempting to drive Hua past mere fury. What was sustaining Hua was only the alter ego of Mao that he'd created and to which he had to cling at any cost. What Chen wanted to find out was if Jiao had given him any inkling of the real Mao material—hidden in the broom head or anywhere else. Pushed hard enough, he might be tempted to divulge that knowledge, like his adamission that he had Song murdered. "It's so symbolic, surrealistic, with something hidden behind the surface—"

"Shut up, pig! You fell hard for her, really head over heels. You tried so hard to charm her with a candle light dinner, with all your literary mumble and jumble, symbolic or not, but you didn't get her, not a hair of her. To show her loyalty, she swore to me she would stop seeing you altogether. *Oh, to the song of 'Internationale' tragic and high, / a hurricane comes for me from the sky!*"

His reaction was that of a wounded lover-emperor, proving that he knew nothing about the Mao material, about the broom head.

"If I couldn't have her, neither could you or anybody else!" Hua went heatedly, spittle flying from his mouth. "You're too late. She betrayed me and she had to die."

With the pressure from the investigation and with his insane jealousy, fear that she might leave him for another man drove Hua over the edge. He strangled her not so much to stop her shouting as from a subconscious resolve to let no one else have her. Again, that was Mao's logic, an emperor's logic. As in ancient times, the palace ladies had to remain single, "untouched," even after the emperor's death.

"You bastard of Mao!" Old Hunter exclaimed.

"Now," Hua said, raising himself up on one elbow, "let me tell you guys something.

"I succeed, and I'm the emperor," he said, his face lit with enraged dignity as he suddenly jumped up to his feet, balancing himself and pivoting around, all in a lightning flash of movement, "you fail, and you're the murderers."

It was an unexpected move, fast, furious, catching them by surprise. He must have recovered during the phone call and the subsequent talk. Hair flying, he flung himself forward and swung out with his right arm. A tall, stout man, he bulled past them with a momentum that sent Old Hunter reeling backward against the wall. Sprinting to the living room, he swerved in the direction of the long scroll of Li Bai's poem on the wall.

It was a turn Chen hadn't anticipated. He thought he glimpsed something like a door behind the scroll, but in the semi-darkness he wasn't sure. Cursing, he took after Hua, who was dashing like a dart. But then suddenly Hua stumbled and swayed with a blood-chilling yell, having stamped his foot down on the dustpan full of splintered glass Jiao had set down.

Chen took a stride over and clubbed him with the edge of one hand. The blow cracked on Hua's head, reopening the wound inflicted by the portrait of Mao. Bleeding, Hua went down, banging his head against the corner of the dining table. He stared up, shook violently as if having a nightmare, and lost consciousness again, still making a blurred sound in his throat.

"Idiot!" Old Hunter hurried over and bent back Hua's arms, handcuffing the unconscious man. "Now what, Chief Inspector Chen? Internal Security is coming any minute. What are we supposed to say to them?"

"We'll play our roles— You're retired, of course, and happened to be patrolling around the area tonight. When you heard the noise, you rushed up. Naturally, you know nothing about the Mao Case—about the case."

Internal Security might not easily swallow that story, but it was basically true. There wasn't much they could do about a retired cop.

Chen wasn't that concerned about himself. He had been authorized by Beijing to act however he chose. With the tape recording he'd made, and with Old Hunter as a witness, he would be able to nail Hua for the murders of Jiao, Yang, and Song. That should be more than enough.

He didn't have to do anything else, except turn the Mao scroll over to Beijing. Nor would it be difficult for him to tell his story. It might be necessary to omit some parts, of course. But it would be best for him, and for everybody else, to have the case conclude this way.

This way it wasn't a Mao case.

Hua would be put away, conveniently, as a "nut." With Mao in the background, no one would raise any questions, and all would be hushed up. A murder case, simple and pure, perhaps with details selectively revealed, such as Jiao being kept by Hua in secret, as a "little concubine." It might prove a plausible interpretation to some: like grandmother, like daughter.

Such a conclusion would be acceptable to the Party authorities. There was no need for them to worry about any Mao material. If she had had any, she took its whereabouts to the grave with her. It was the end of the Shang saga.

And it would be acceptable to Internal Security too. It avenged Song, and brought closure to their nightmare, though they would still complain to Beijing about Chen.

Chief Inspector Chen had delivered what was expected of him—a satisfactory answer sheet to the Party authorities.

But what about the answer sheet he presented to himself?

Brooding, he cast another look to her body on the bed.

He had striven to do a good job, so that Jiao might avoid a tragedy like Shang's. But was he really so anxious to help her? Being honest with himself, he admitted that his responsibility as a law enforcement officer came first. As a cop who worked within the system, and for the system, he went out to retrieve the Mao material despite all his misgivings.

Consequently, he was preoccupied with the broom, not paying attention to what was happening in the room, resulting in two or three minutes of fatal negligence.

"You are really an exceptional cop," Old Hunter murmured, trying to comfort the obviously distraught Chen.

"An exceptional cop," Chen echoed, reminded of what Ling had said to him in that *siheyuan* room, against the memories of the orange pinwheel spinning out of the paper window, of their reading *Spring Tide* together on a green bench at North Sea, of the phone call fading in the glittering wing of white gulls over Bund Park, and the water still lapping against the bank . . .

For that—for the drive to be an exceptional cop—he had given up, or irrecoverably lost, so much. It was too agonizing for him to think about. His head hung low, he stepped back into the bedroom.

He saw the broom lying on the floor, near the closet.

What was he going to do about it?

He would check it out before turning it over to the Beijing authorities. It was up to them to decide what course of action would best serve the Party's interests. Whatever their decision, it would mean more credit for him, and secure his promotion.

It would also be in line with the principle of not judging Mao on his personal life, though as far as Mao was concerned, the personal might not be that personal after all. With T. S. Eliot, the personal went into a poem, into the manuscript of *The Waste Land*, but with Mao, the personal became a disaster for the whole nation.

And what about Jiao's wants?

He didn't have to ask the question. The answer was loud and clear in that painting of the witch flying on a broom over the Forbidden City—*To sweep away all the bugs!* He felt as if he himself were turning into a bug, drowning in waves of guilt, unable to look her in her still-staring eyes.

His head hung even lower, he saw a fleck of chopped green onion on the elegantly arched sole of her foot, a tiny detail that made her feel intensely real, yet forever lost. She had walked barefoot in the kitchen just a short while ago. Admittedly he didn't know her that well. She might have had her problems, possibly she was vain, coquettish, vulnerable, and materialistic, like other girls her age, but like them, she should have lived.

Instead, like her mother, and grandmother, she had perished in the shadow of Mao.

If the chief inspector hadn't been able to save her, he should at least try to do something for her, after death.

He looked again at the broom lying outside the closet. As it was, it would be carefully examined as part of the crime scene. Whatever was hidden inside could be discovered.

The sound of a siren pierced the night, when Chen was seized by the impulse to do something—something not expected of an exceptional cop.

"When I rushed out, I tripped over this broom and fell out of the closet," he said, stooping to pick up the broom. "Let me put it back."

"Well," Old Hunter said reflectively, "you don't have to explain anything to Internal Security. We came in together. I had the master key from neighborhood security. You know what I mean, Chief."

Chen understood the subtle suggestion. It seemed to Old Hunter that it wouldn't be easy for the chief inspector to explain his presence in the closet, and his subsequent failure to stop Hua from killing Jiao. So he might as well say that he had rushed in alongside the retired cop. Hua might contradict his story, but no one would pay much attention to a deranged man.

It was a fact, however, that Chen had been in the closet, and that, but for his zeal to retrieve the Mao material, he might have been able to save Jiao's life.

But Chen was putting the broom back in the closet for a different reason. He shook his head. "No, the broom isn't really part of the crime scene. It belongs in the closet." Chen picked up the long scroll box. "I'll have to turn it in to Beijing."

Whatever happened to the broom now, it would be beyond his control. And not his concern.

He wasn't taking an action that would be against Jiao's will, not with his own hands. At least, so he could tell himself.

Nor was he involved in any effort to cover up for Mao, regardless of other people's judgments or interpretations.

The broom, like a lot of stuff in the room, would eventually be thrown away. Somebody might pick it up, use it as a broom and nothing but a broom, until dirty and worn-out, it would finally turn into dust . . .

There was a chance that the thing inside would come to light one day. By that time, no one would be able to tell that the Mao material—whatever it was—originally came from Jiao. When he was no longer in charge of the case, he would have no objection to seeing it. He, too, was curious.

But for now, as long as he didn't see it with his own eyes, he wasn't witholding information. That was something he had learned from Xie.

"Don't worry about me, Old Hunter. I am authorized by Beijing to investigate in whatever way I choose. And I'm notorious for my eccentric approach."

Outside the window, he heard police cars coming nearer with their sirens wailing and horns honking. Old Hunter walked over to the window and looked down into the street below, suddenly noisy like boiling water.

Looking up, Chen saw a crimson-colored moon riding high in the night sky, as if covered in blood, but being washed by pale clouds and chilled rain.

He began murmuring, almost to himself.

> *The horses galloping, the horn sobbing.*
> *The mountain pass may be made of iron,*
> *but we are crossing it all over again,*
> *all over again,*
> *the hills stretching in waves,*
> *the sun sinking in blood.*

"What's that?" Old Hunter said, looking over his shoulder at Chen.

"'The Lou Mountain Pass,' a poem by Mao," Chen said, "written during the first Civil War."

"Leave Mao in peace," the retired cop said shivering, as if having swallowed a fly, "in heaven or in hell."

THE FIFTH NOVEL IN THE ACCLAIMED SERIES
FEATURING INSPECTOR CHEN.

RED
MANDARIN
DRESS
Qiu Xiaolong

'A thrilling crime story and also an absorbing look
at modern China' *The Herald*

An early morning jogger found her. Clad in nothing but a red
mandarin dress, she had been dumped on a traffic island. The
death of a 'dancing girl' was unpleasant but only unusual in that
she had been left so openly in the centre of town.

Inspector Chen is an intuitive investigator, a talented poet and an
honourable man on the edge of a nervous breakdown. Desperate
to find a way out of the perilous police career that had been chosen
for him, Chen is on leave. Then another girl is found dead.

With a serial killer on the loose, Chen is pulled back to work
and into his most dangerous assignment yet.

'A fine introduction to a series that might well get you hooked.'
Sunday Telegraph

'Engrossing' *Financial Times*

SCEPTRE

THE FOURTH BOOK IN THE THRILLING INSPECTOR
CHEN SERIES SET IN MODERN SHANGHAI.

A CASE
OF TWO
CITIES

Qiu Xiaolong

'A fresh, fast-paced detective thriller that will keep you turning
those pages' *Sunday Express*

'Compelling . . . this fast-moving crime novel admirably
depicts the intriguing struggles of characters grasping a
foothold in a new and rising China,' *Times Literary Supplement*

'A luminescent synthesis of a thriller and a literary novel'
Independent

'Stupendous' *Washington Post*

Inspector Chen is reunited with his counterpart from the US
Marshal Service, Inspector Catherine Rohn when Chen is
summoned to lead a highly charged corruption investigation.

In a twisting case, Chen must find a measure of justice in a
corrupt, expedient world.

SCEPTRE

THE THIRD NOVEL IN THE THRILLING INSPECTOR
CHEN SERIES SET IN MODERN SHANGHAI.

WHEN RED IS BLACK

Qiu Xiaolong

When Inspector Chen Cao agrees to do a translation job for a Triad-connected businessman he is given a laptop, a 'little secretary' to provide for his every need, medical care for his mother. There are, it seems, no strings attached . . .

Then a murder is reported: Chen is loath to shorten his working holiday, so Sergeant Yu is forced to take charge of the investigation. The victim, a middle-aged teacher, has been found dead in her tiny room in a converted multi-family house. Only a neighbour could have committed the crime, but there is no motive. It is not until Chen returns and starts to investigate the past that he finds answers.

But by then he has troubles of his own.

> 'A vivid portrait of modern Chinese society . . . full of the sights, sounds and smells of Shanghai . . . A work of real distinction.' *Wall Street Journal*

SCEPTRE

THE SECOND NOVEL IN THE THRILLING INSPECTOR
CHEN SERIES SET IN MODERN SHANGHAI.

A LOYAL CHARACTER DANCER

Qiu Xiaolong

DANGER

Former dancer and party loyalist Wen Liping vanishes in rural China
just before she is to leave the country. Her husband, a key witness
against a smuggling ring suspected of importing aliens to the US,
refuses to testify until she is found and brought to join him in America.

REPRISAL

A few days later, a badly mutilated body turns up in Shanghai's
Bund Park. It bears all the hallmarks of a Triad killing.

COVER UP

The US immigration agency, convinced that the Chinese government are hiding something, send US Marshal Catherine Rohn to
Shanghai to join the investigation.

Inspector Chen, an astute young policeman with twin passions for
food and poetry, is under political pressure to find answers fast.
When Catherine Rohn joins him he must decide what is more
dangerous: to hide the truth or to risk unleashing a scandal that
could destroy his career.

'Not to be missed' *Guardian*

'Wonderful' *Washington Post*

SCEPTRE

THE FIRST IN THE THRILLING INSPECTOR CHEN
SERIES SET IN MODERN SHANGHAI.

DEATH
OF A
RED
HEROINE

Qiu Xiaolong

WINNER OF THE ANTHONY AWARD
FOR BEST FIRST CRIME NOVEL

'Chen is a great creation, an honourable man in a world full
of deception and treachery' *Guardian*

Shanghai in 1990. Chief Inspector Chen, a poet with a sound
instinct for self-preservation, knows the city like few others.

The body of a prominent Communist party member is found
and Chen is told to keep the party authorities informed about
every lead. And he must keep the young woman's murder out
of the papers at all costs. When his investigation leads him to
the decadent offspring of high-ranking officials, he finds himself
instantly removed from the case and reassigned to another area.

Chen has a choice: bend to the party's wishes and sacrifice
his morals, or continue his investigation and risk dismissal
from his job and from the party. Or worse . . .

S

SCEPTRE